IMPOSTER 13

13

ROB SINCLAIR

ORION

An Orion paperback

First published in Great Britain in 2020
by Orion Fiction,
This paperback edition published in 2020
by Orion Fiction,
an imprint of The Orion Publishing Group Ltd.,
Carmelite House, 50 Victoria Embankment
London EC4Y 0DZ

An Hachette UK company

1 3 5 7 9 10 8 6 4 2

A CIP catalogue record for this book
is available from the British Library.

ISBN (Paperback) 978 1 4091 9357 9

Typeset by Born Group

Printed and bound in Great Britain by Clays Ltd, Elcograf S.p.A.

MIX
Paper from
responsible sources
FSC® C104740

www.orionbooks.co.uk

IMPOSTER
13

IMPOSTER

13

Rob Sinclair specialised in forensic fraud investigations at a global accounting firm for thirteen years. He began writing in 2009 following a promise to his wife, an avid reader, that he could pen an 'unputdownable' thriller. Since then, Rob has sold over half a million copies of his critically acclaimed thrillers in both the Enemy and James Ryker series. His work has received widespread critical acclaim, with many reviewers and readers likening his work to authors at the very top of the genre, including Lee Child and Vince Flynn.

Originally from the north-east of England, Rob has lived and worked in a number of fast-paced cities, including New York, and is now settled in the West Midlands with his wife and young sons.

CHAPTER 1

Muscat, Oman

The glittering marble columns of the cafe's colonial terrace sparkled in the fierce sunshine. Rachel Cox, sitting in the shaded area at the back of the open-air space with her colleague Salman, took a sip from her coffee as she spied on the apartment building across the square.

'What's taking him so long?' Salman, sitting next to her, said in his Eton-educated accent that to Cox, having known him for more than six months, remained an unexpected contrast to his obvious Middle Eastern origins: dark skin, thick black hair and dense stubble that reached uncommonly high on his face.

She took the last sip of her coffee. Finally, across the way she spotted the man they were looking for. Lanky and dressed in drab clothing, he stepped out of the double doors of the stone building. Cox flicked her eyes down, sank a couple of inches in her chair, trying to be as inconspicuous as she could. The man was jittery as he looked around him, but he didn't pay any attention to Cox or Salman, and after a couple of seconds he turned and walked away in the opposite direction.

'Ready?' Salman asked.

Cox nodded. Salman had already paid the waiter minutes earlier, and he quickly finished his water before they both got up from their chairs. Cox noticed a couple of the local

1

men staring at her and she once again averted her eyes, looked down. Yes she had her hijab on, to reduce offence as far as possible, but she couldn't hide her light skin or her green eyes that clearly marked her out as a Westerner. The fact she was consorting with what looked like a local man only further added to the indignation she regularly garnered whenever out and about.

Still, she wouldn't let the glowers put her off the task at hand, and if anyone were to question her presence here she had all the papers required to explain who she was, including her ID showing her as a visiting professor of international studies at the Sultan Qaboos University. A fake ID, that is, but a necessary backstop for a white, single female in the conservative country.

Particularly one who also just happened to work for the British government.

They headed on across the square, Cox's eyes busy as she surveyed the people around her. None appeared suspicious, and none were taking anything more than a fleeting interest in her and Salman. As they approached the doors to the apartment building, Salman slowed and veered off to the left to look into the window of a shop selling men's formalwear. Cox carried on her path, and reached into her pocket to grab the key for the outer doors, which Salman had pilfered the previous day.

She pushed the key into the lock and turned, then pulled open the door and stepped into the cool but dim interior with only a brief glimpse behind her before she shut the door. She paused. The small and sparse atrium was all quiet. She reached into her pocket again and took out the tiny earbud. She already had the equally tiny microphone attached to a fold in her hijab.

'Can you hear me?' she whispered when the earbud was in place.

'Yes,' came Salman's reply.

He would remain her eyes and ears on the outside. Just in case.

Cox took a deep breath then moved for the wide stone staircase in front of her. The apartment building, in a far from seedy or downtrodden neighbourhood in the nation's capital, had certainly seen better days, though its former glory and original class when it was built during the heavy British influence of the nineteenth century remained evident. The staircase was lined with a beautiful wrought iron banister, though the metal was rusted and its paint blistered in places, and the once perfect corners and edges of the stairs had been worn smooth from decades of footsteps and minimal maintenance.

As she headed up, Cox saw no one, though sounds of life from the apartment doors beyond came and went. On the third floor she moved along the corridor, her eyes still busy, her body primed for the unexpected. There were no CCTV cameras in the building, but she kept her head down as much as she could anyway – habit as much as anything else.

She stopped by the worn door to apartment 8 and knocked lightly. Was she expecting – hoping? – for her knock to be answered? They'd already seen Faiz Al-Busaidi leaving the building, but what of his wife, Thuriyah? Cox hadn't seen or heard from Thuriyah, her key asset in Oman, for nearly two days, despite their hours of surveilling the apartment building.

What had happened to her?

Cox's heart drummed with anticipation as she waited a few seconds with nothing but silence around her. She knocked again, only slightly louder this time.

'Rachel? Are you inside yet?' came Salman's smooth voice in her ear. She jumped at the unexpected noise, her heart rate ramping up another few notches.

'There's no one here.'

'Are you inside?'

'I will be in a moment.'

She took the small toolset from her pocket – a torsion wrench and a series of small picks. She worked away on the lock, her nerves continuing to grow. She heard a creak somewhere towards the stairs and whipped her head round.

No one there.

She cursed under her breath, worked on the pins inside the lock again, her fingers becoming clammy and fumbling. She might have worked for MI6 for the best part of a decade, but she'd never learned to enjoy these James Bond moments one bit.

Finally the last of the pins was pushed out of the way. The lock released and Cox let out a long but quiet exhale. She pushed the door open, stepped inside and closed the door behind her as silently as she could. She stood and listened. The apartment, a simple one-bedroom affair with an open plan living space and single bedroom with an en suite, was all quiet. No lights were on and despite the sunshine outside, with the sheer curtains in the living area drawn, the apartment was strangely dull and lifeless.

'Thuriyah?' Cox said as a shiver ran through her, her voice only slightly more than a whisper.

Nothing in return.

At least no one had leapt out to attack her. But where the hell was Thuriyah?

'Come on, Cox,' Salman's voice echoed in her ear. 'You need to hurry up.'

He sounded more strained now, but if there'd been a problem he would have raised the alarm. He was just getting nervous, even though he had the easy job.

'She's not here,' Cox said. 'But I need to find it.'

4

'If Faiz knows about—'

'If he knows, then Thuriyah is already dead. But we still need to retrieve the information.'

'You don't even know what you're looking for.'

Cox ignored that comment. She moved through into the living area. Basic didn't come close to describing the place. The few items of furniture were old and worn, the TV was a tiny set-top box like the black-and-white one her parents still had in the spare room when she was growing up. There was a similarly old-fashioned wireless radio, and the small kitchen area was falling apart. Cox quickly looked around, inside drawers and cupboards, under furniture, behind furniture, under the items of clothing that lay strewn, and the strangely stock-piled tins and packets of food that were here and there.

Nothing.

She moved into the bedroom. No bed. Just a mattress on the floor, a single pine wardrobe and not quite matching set of drawers. Cox rifled through. Nothing of interest. She looked to the door to the bathroom. Bloody images flashed in her mind of horror movies she'd seen – the dead body in the bathtub, red streaks everywhere. She gulped as she stepped forward.

'Cox?'

She didn't answer. She slowly pushed the door open . . .

The bathroom was empty. A murky-looking shower curtain was pulled back to reveal a grimy bath. No body, no blood.

'Where are you?' Cox said under her breath.

'I'm still here.'

She didn't bother to clarify that she'd been talking to Thuriyah.

'There's nothing here,' Cox said. 'The only thing remotely of interest is a crappy laptop.'

'You can't take it,' Salman said, quite snottily Cox thought. 'That's not what you're there for.'

5

She knew that. She clenched her teeth rather than biting back. They couldn't do anything that would risk tipping off Faiz. Stealing his laptop, whatever goldmine of information could be on there, would certainly do that.

'I think you need to leave.'

Cox, despondently, was quickly coming to that conclusion too. She turned, then paused.

'This isn't right,' she said.

'What?'

'Her clothes are still here. In the wardrobe there's a whole row of abayas. Shoes too. Underwear in the drawers.'

'Come on, Cox. What are you doing? Get out of there.'

'But it's all clean. All the worn clothes on the floor, in the basket in the bedroom, are his. Same with the used things in the kitchen. Only one of everything. She hasn't been here. Not in the last few days at least.'

Salman said nothing now. Cox had worried for Thuriyah's safety for weeks. That was the same any time she found an asset like her, who was prepared to speak out against those closest to her. Cox's angst had naturally ramped up over the last couple of days after she'd been unable to get hold of her Thuriyah, but she'd tried her best to convince herself there was a reasonable explanation for the lack of contact.

But now?

Beyond her concern for Thuriyah's safety, was a potentially even bigger concern. What of the intelligence that Thuriyah had promised to garner for Cox. Where was that now?

'OK, I'm coming out,' Cox said.

Moments later she was descending the stairs, more quickly than she'd gone up, as yet more unwelcome and gory thoughts as to Thuriyah's fate filled her mind.

She pushed open the door at the bottom of the stairs and stepped back out into the heat, immediately spotting Salman

6

a few yards away, back pressed up against the wall of the next building along as he casually played with his phone. He stuffed it in his pocket when he saw her and as she reached him they gave each other a casual and concocted greeting to satisfy any watchful eyes, before setting off on foot for the far end of the square.

'What are you thinking?' Salman asked her after a few moments of awkward silence.

What was she thinking? At that moment? Strangely, the colonial era square she was walking across reminded her of one just like it she'd seen on her first ever visit to nearby Saudi Arabia. There, in glorious sunshine, she'd relaxedly looked about the blindingly bright square, taking in the charm of the well-kept illustrious buildings lining the open space. Only to be told, quite casually, by her male chaperone, that the large stone slabs she was walking across were specifically laid with a slight inward slope to allow blood from public beheadings to drain away.

'Cox? Talk to me.'

'I think—'

The vibrating phone in her pocket halted her explanation. She fished for the phone and shielded the screen from the sun with her other hand.

She stopped in her tracks. Salman did so too, immediately looking nervous at the halt in their forward progress.

'Come on, we need to go,' he said. Cox didn't move. 'What is it?'

'She's alive,' Cox said.

She showed him the message on the screen.

Salman shook his head. 'No,' he said. 'This isn't . . . You can't trust that.'

'She's alive, Salman. That's our code. Only she knows it.'

He scoffed at that. She knew what he was thinking.

7

'If she was under duress she would have included our red word,' Cox said. 'You know how it works.'

He held up his hand. 'I'm not your boss. I'm just saying. That doesn't look good to me.'

'Regardless, she's alive,' Cox said. 'And if she wants to meet, I can't say no to that.'

Salman sighed deeply.

'Then we'd better go get the car.'

CHAPTER 2

Two hours later Salman was driving the Toyota Land Cruiser along a dusty, winding track, Muscat miles behind them and long out of view, nothing but rolling hills of sand and rocky outcrops in sight in every direction.

'Ever wish you'd signed up for accountancy training instead?' Salman asked as he jerked the steering wheel when the back wheels of the Land Cruiser lost traction on the sand.

'Never,' Cox said with absolute seriousness and conviction. She looked over at him and saw the wry smile on his face. She'd missed the fact his question had been an attempt at humour, but her answer remained. Despite the danger, this was where she belonged. What she did was for the greater good. Someone had to.

To her relief, her boss back in England, Henry Flannigan, had agreed with her desire to take Thuriyah's message on trust. Or at least he'd gone along with it. Cox was in Oman for a reason, and just because there was a hint of trouble now, that didn't mean the reason wasn't still present and valid or any less important. In fact, Flannigan had taken barely any time to confirm he wanted Cox to follow the lead, which now, sitting in the Land Cruiser on the way to the remote rendez-vous point, did make her question whether it was really a good thing that her boss was so brazen with her safety.

Too late to turn back.

'I don't know Thuriyah like you do,' Salman said, 'but asking to meet out here—'

'It stacks up,' Cox said. 'Her family don't come from the city. Her father was a cattle farmer. Their village is just a few miles from where we're meeting.'

'You've been before?'

'To the meeting point?'

'No, I meant the village. I know you've been to the meeting point before, you said already.'

'I've been to the village too. What's left of it at least. It's just a cluster of ramshackle huts now. The farming in the region has all been conglomerated so most people from back then moved away.'

'Dragged into capitalism.'

She looked over at Salman again, the same wry smile on his face. She often struggled to figure out what he was thinking, where his head was at. That wasn't a bad thing, she mused. His mystery, when he wasn't being a whiny sod, was actually quite intriguing.

'When her dad died – of natural causes I might add – her mum moved across the other side of Muscat. But Thuriyah still has family in the village. An ageing aunt, a cousin and his family.'

'So you think she's been staying with them?'

'We'll soon find out.' And Cox certainly hoped the explanation for Thuriyah's recent evasiveness was as simple as that.

The drive to the remote destination took only another twenty minutes and they soon came over the crest of a hill to see the narrow valley beyond, the remnants of what looked like old farm buildings down below, a few hundred yards away. It wasn't the first time Cox had met Thuriyah here, though she'd never felt this edgy about it before.

She checked her watch. Forty minutes early. Plenty of time to check the area out. From their approach, there was certainly no signs of anyone else there.

Salman pulled the car to a stop fifty yards from the crumbling remains of the farm and stopped the engine before they both got out. The sun in the desert, with no shade from buildings like in the city, was even fiercer than Cox remembered, and within seconds the skin on her face was stinging from its ferocity.

'You check around the perimeter,' Cox said. 'I'll look at the buildings.'

Salman nodded. They once again had their wireless comms to communicate with each other, and they'd patch in to Flannigan too before Thuriyah arrived. Not that he'd be able to help if anything went wrong. There was no on-hand SAS team here to kill the bad guys and whisk them away, but at least with Flannigan online, if something did happen, he would hear it and be able to take subsequent action. Little comfort to Cox really if she was already dead, but better than MI6 being none the wiser.

What they did have was eyes on Faiz back in Muscat. Or at least on his apartment. He'd returned home before Cox and Salman had left the city, and had remained there since.

The fact he was there, and seemingly just carrying on as normal, had to be a good thing, didn't it?

Cox traipsed over to the pile of rubble that had once passed as a building – perhaps more than one. No single wall was fully intact, though open angles remained in the remnants where doors and windows would once have stood.

There were no signs of life, no signs that anyone had been here recently at all.

Cox turned and scanned the surrounding area. The location was sheltered and almost fully enclosed by the hills around it.

'Talk about fish in a barrel,' Cox said, as much to herself as to Salman.

She immediately regretted saying it. He was already doubting their sense in coming here.

'Come again?' he said.

She looked over and saw him in the distance, at the top of the hill on the eastern side.

'Yeah, I see what you mean,' he said. 'But the good news is, there's no one else here, and the road we came in on is the only one.'

She knew that already from the last time she'd been, but was comforted that Salman had come to the same conclusion.

'Nothing you could get a vehicle across, anyway,' Salman said. 'It's too rocky. If there's an ambush here, they'll be coming in the same way we did. If I'm over that side, I'll get a good view of the track. A mile out at least.'

'Sounds good.' Cox checked her watch. 'May as well take up positions now then.'

Cox retreated to the car but remained standing outside it. There was still more than twenty minutes until the planned meet, but not long after . . .

'A single vehicle coming this way,' Salman said.

Cox's nervousness rose. She looked up at the outline of Salman's figure, partially in view to her, but hopefully obscured from the track by the rocks he was crouched behind. She could see he had binoculars up to his face.

'Can you see who's inside?' she asked.

'Too far away still,' he said. 'It's a big car though. An Outlander I think.'

And Thuriyah definitely had one of those. Though bizarrely hearing Salman's words still made Cox that little bit more hesitant.

'How far?'

12

'Closing. A few hundred yards. Let me . . . OK I can see just one person up front. I mean . . . it looks like a woman. She's wearing an abaya . . . '

'Is it Thuriyah?'

A pause. 'Yeah. I'm pretty sure it is. Coming your way. You should see the vehicle any second.'

Cox could already hear the roar of the car's thick tyres on the sand, and the rumble of its powerful diesel engine, but when the Outlander appeared at the top of the hill the sound carried down into the valley, reverberated around and became freakishly loud, only further adding to Cox's angst.

From where Cox was standing, the bonnet of the Land Cruiser was between her and Thuriyah's Outlander. If she needed to she could dive into the driver's seat and pound the accelerator within seconds.

If . . .

Cox took a step away from the Land Cruiser and waved casually. The Outlander was still fifty yards from her when suddenly it swung round ninety degrees to an abrupt stop. Thuriyah's window faced down the hill to Cox, who could make out her 'friend' clearly for the first time. It was definitely her. Yet that was of little relief to Cox, who could see how rattled the woman was, even at this distance.

'Still nothing else coming this way?' Cox asked Salman as she kept her eyes on Thuriyah.

'Nothing. This is it. What is she doing?'

It was a good question. Thuriyah was looking down at her lap. Her lips were moving as her head slowly bobbed back and forth. Was she praying?

'Cox, this is insane. Get in the car and drive off.'

'Leave you here?'

'Very funny.'

'She's getting out.'

The driver's door to the Outlander opened. Cox braced herself, but didn't move from where she was. Thuriyah took an age to step out into the open. An ankle length black abaya covered her body, a hijab covered her head and shoulders. Her face, and the fearful look on it, remained clear to see.

'Thuriyah, what's happening?' Cox shouted over.

Thuriyah straightened up and looked over to Cox.

'What the fuck is she doing?' Salman said.

'Thuriyah, talk to me,' Cox shouted.

'I have it.'

Cox paused.

'The information?'

'Yes. It's all here.'

Cox took a step closer. 'Show me,' she shouted.

'Cox, come on, don't be stupid,' Salman said.

Thuriyah nodded and edged down the bank towards Cox. She moved gingerly. One of her hands just far enough round her back that Cox couldn't see it.

'What's in your hand?' Cox said.

'The information. I need to give it to you. Then I have to go. For good.'

Cox didn't move now. Thuriyah kept on coming forward. She was only fifteen yards away and Cox could see the sweat droplets glistening on her forehead. Her bottom lip quivered. Cox looked her up and down. Her whole body was shaking in fact.

'Thuriyah, stop there.'

Thuriyah didn't.

'Stop!'

Thuriyah paused.

'What's happened?' Cox said. 'Please. Does Faiz know?'

Mention of her husband knocked Thuriyah's determination, but only for a second. She began moving again.

14

'Cox, she's got something.'

'I know she fucking has!' she blasted, her words to her unseen colleague only adding to Thuriyah's jitters. 'It's OK, I've got a colleague here, but he's for the safety of both of us.'

'I told you to come alone.'

'Thuriyah, show me what's in your hand? A thumb drive? A disc? What is it?'

Thuriyah moved forward with more purpose. Her arm twitched and moved away from her side a couple of inches.

Cox realised for the first time what was wrong with the young woman's appearance. The clothes, they were fine – exactly the type of clothing Thuriyah always wore. But the bulge around her waist...

'Thuriyah, stop there!' Cox shouted. 'Please. I can still help you. Just tell me what's happening.'

Thuriyah didn't stop this time. Tears streamed down her face.

'Show me what's in your hand!'

Thuriyah shook her head. She was only a few steps away and Cox shuffled back.

'Please don't do this,' Cox said.

But by now Thuriyah was in some sort of trance. Her steps quickened. Cox looked to the woman's hand. Saw the metallic flash as the sun hit the object.

Then there was a boom and a thwack as a small hole was pierced in Thuriyah's shoulder. Her face twitched. She stumbled forward.

'No! Salman, for fuck's sake!'

'Cox get the fuck away!'

She wanted to help the woman, but instead she backstepped.

Another gunshot, another thwack as the bullet hit Thuriyah in the back and she dropped to her knees. Her hand came forward to stop herself falling flat on her face. For the first time Cox got a full glimpse of what she was clutching. Not a flash drive or a disc or anything of the sort.

A dead man's switch.

'Cox, move!'

Cox's eyes met Ṭhuriyah's. She was sure she mouthed the word 'sorry'. The next second her palm opened, releasing the pressure from the switch. Cox was mid-air, diving behind the Land Cruiser, as the crude bomb exploded.

CHAPTER 3

'Faiz did this,' Cox stammered as Salman raced the Land Cruiser away from the farm, the vehicle jumping and clanking on its suspension as they went.

She wiped a tear from her eye and felt the streak of dirt and soot that doing so left across her cheek. She looked down at her clothes, covered in mess, soot, grit, dust, darker patches of blood from the lumps of chargrilled flesh that had flown through the air at her when the explosion had obliterated Thuriyah. She had to fight to keep her emotions in check, swallowed down hard and clenched her fists so tight her nails cut into the skin on her palms.

'Faiz did this,' Cox said again. 'We have to get him.'

Again, her statement was met with silence.

'Would you just say something!' she shouted.

She looked over at Salman whose eyes remained on the track ahead.

'I hear you,' Flannigan said, his voice crackling in her ear. 'I'm sorry.'

The last thing she needed now was his pity.

'Please,' Flannigan said, 'talk me through it again. Tell me everything.'

Cox closed her eyes as she thought back to the scene. How Thuriyah had been just yards away when the blast went off.

How the Land Cruiser had saved Cox from a similarly gory fate. How she and Salman had quickly searched Thuriyah's car and the few bits of what was left that resembled a corpse before promptly leaving.

'Cox?'

She talked Flannigan through it. Again. She knew his request wasn't some morbid curiosity. Him getting her to recount the fatal incident was both for analysis and to help focus her mind.

'When she first arrived, she didn't get out of the car immediately,' Cox said.

'She was setting the switch,' Salman said. 'The explosives were already on her, but the switch had to be set. She hadn't driven all that way clutching it.'

'She set it herself?' Flannigan said. 'Why would she do that?'

Cox thought for a moment.

'She wouldn't. Not of her own accord.'

'Someone forced her to?' Flannigan said. 'With what leverage?'

'The intention was to kill her and me.'

'But you're saying she didn't *want* to.'

'No. She was forced to.'

'There was no one else there,' Salman said, his sour tone riling Cox.

'No, there wasn't,' Cox said. 'But that doesn't mean it wasn't someone else's hand that made her do it. Perhaps she was given an ultimatum. Faiz found out about her. From that point on she was a dead woman and she knew it. But they didn't just want her dead. If that was the case they would have already killed her. They wanted me dead too.'

'And she just agreed to take you out at the same time?' Salman said. 'Why?'

18

'No,' Cox said, not hiding that she was becoming riled. 'I imagine they blackmailed her. Perhaps they're holding someone close to her hostage too. If she didn't kill me, they'd kill the hostage.'

Which only made Cox feel all the worse. Had saving herself just signed someone else's death warrant?

'We don't know any of that,' Flannigan said.

'We don't. I'm just thinking this through,' Cox said. 'But there is one way we can find out.'

'What?' Flannigan said.

'You want us to try and capture Faiz?' Salman said, not sounding particularly happy by the prospect of more action.

'He tried to have me killed!'

'And your objective in Oman is not one of personal revenge,' Flannigan said.

'Faiz was sitting at home watching TV,' Salman added. 'He still is. If you're saying Thuriyah was put up to this under duress, it wasn't by him—'

'Then he instructed it,' Cox said.

'Instructed others.'

'What's the fucking difference! The man is an extremist, his wife just tried to kill me, and he needs to be stopped!'

Salman said nothing to that. Cox could tell he was pissed off too. Given Thuriyah's secret must have been blown, he was in danger now too, simply by association with Cox. But she had been a direct target, she firmly believed, and as long as Faiz and whoever he worked for were still out there, she remained a target. She could skulk off back to England or wherever else to escape their ire – and perhaps that's what Salman wanted to do – but she'd much rather stand and fight.

'Did Thuriyah have any information that could directly identify you?' Flannigan asked.

19

'Of course not. She only knew me by aliases. It's possible someone at some point could have got a picture of me with her, but that's it.'

'Understood. But we do still need to know exactly what she's told, and who she's told it to. This is now damage limitation as much as it is finding out intel on whatever cell Faiz is working with.'

'Then Faiz has to be the place to start.'

A sigh from Flannigan. Salman said nothing, just stared straight ahead, though Cox could tell he was clenching his jaw – in anger?

Salman's phone buzzed. He lifted it from his lap and glanced at the screen before extending his hand to Cox. She took the phone without either of them saying a word and stared at the message on the screen.

'Faiz is on the move,' Cox said. 'Seen leaving his apartment with a holdall.'

'He's running?' Flannigan said.

'Running, leaving, changing location. It doesn't make a difference. If we want him, we need to move now before we lose him.'

A momentary pause.

'We just need your word,' Cox said.

'Get him,' Flannigan said. 'But you can't stay in Muscat now. Take him to the safe house in Nizwa. I'll try my best to expedite an extraction somewhere else.'

'Got it,' Cox said before there was a click as Flannigan dropped off the line.

Cox looked over to Salman who she could tell remained pissed off.

'You'd better call Mazin back,' he said. 'Make sure he doesn't let Faiz out of his sight before we catch up.'

'This is the right thing to do,' Cox said.

'Probably,' Salman said. 'But I really hope Flannigan finds us a nice place to take Faiz to. Somewhere with a beach. And a spa. And some cocktails with little umbrellas. Working with you, I really need a fucking holiday.'

Cox said nothing to that, just held back a smile as she put the phone to her ear.

CHAPTER 4

Darkness had descended by the time Cox and Salman reached the outskirts of the port town of Suhar. It had soon become apparent from Mazin – their eyes in Muscat – that the target was leaving the capital. To where, who knew. Mazin had been lucky enough to be able to follow on his motorbike when Faiz was picked up in a car not far from his apartment building, and driven straight out of the city.

Travelling at speed from the hinterland, Cox and Salman were only twenty minutes behind Mazin as they traced a path to the coast and then northward to Suhar. Next to her Salman remained focused on driving and they chatted little, though he at least appeared slightly less sullen and angry as time wore on.

Cox had never been to the northern city of Suhar before, and as they traced around the outskirts in the night, it was difficult to see much of what it was about. She knew from her own research and briefing notes on Oman that the ancient once-capital of the country had more recently had a heavy industrial focus – in particular, ongoing investment in its port facilities, given the town's strategic location on the Gulf of Oman, long an important gateway for trade routes between Asia and Europe. It was no surprise therefore when they heard from Mazin that the port seemed to be where Faiz was headed.

'Wait. They've stopped,' Mazin said, his voice tinny and grating through the speaker of Salman's phone.

'At the port?'

'Not quite. We're on a connector road. Looks like a hotel or something, a mile or so south of the port. The place looks . . . derelict.'

'Give me the name,' Cox said, before going to her own phone and opening the map. 'They're still in the car?'

'No. Faiz and another man are out. Faiz has his bag. They're heading inside.'

'Who's the other man?'

'I can't tell.'

'Can you get a picture?'

'Too late, I'm too far away. And it's too dark anyway.'

Salman's phone beeped. Low battery. After all, he'd been in constant contact with Mazin for hours.

'I need to end the call,' Cox said. 'If he moves, let me know. Otherwise we'll see you there shortly.'

She hit the red button.

They arrived on the road connecting to the docks not long after. It was all quiet at night. Mazin had pulled his motorbike over onto the verge at the side of the road. Salman stopped behind him and switched the engine and the lights off. Mazin came over and jumped into the back seat of the Land Cruiser.

Cox had met Mazin only a few times. He was Salman's man really. A local, barely out of his teens, who worked errands for a not insubstantial amount of cash, no questions asked. This was probably the most excitement he'd ever had, more used to simply sitting and spying. Cox felt nervous about him being there now, this was certainly a big step up from his normal role, given they were planning on confronting

23

and kidnapping Faiz. She only hoped his presence wouldn't come to hurt them.

'They're still inside,' Mazin said.

'Any idea how many others?' Cox asked.

'I haven't seen anyone else coming or going. And there are no other cars that I can see.'

'Have you driven past?'

'No.'

Cox thought for a moment.

'What is he doing in there?' Salman asked, though Cox presumed it was rhetorical.

'We have two options,' Cox said. 'We sit and wait, or we go over and get him.'

Silence.

'Well?'

'Or, option three,' Salman said. 'One of us goes and takes a closer look. Scope the place out properly before we make the next move.'

'I'll do it,' Mazin said, reaching for his door handle. Cox thought about protesting but didn't. If he was happy with the risk . . . 'If anyone sees me, far easier for me to explain who I am than either of you two.'

It was a fair point, and probably why neither Cox nor Salman contested him at all.

'Let's connect first,' Cox said.

She used her phone to call him, before he opened the door and stepped out into the night once more. With the door open the sounds of the night, of nearby ships and cranes clunking shipping containers on board in the distance, carried through the air. When the door was closed again the silence felt thick and eerie.

Salman opened his mouth to say something, but Cox put up her hand to halt him.

24

'I know,' she said. 'Something's not right here. Just like you were trying to tell me earlier in the day. But, despite how it ended, we had to meet Thuriyah. You must see that? Now we're here, and we've still a job to do, regardless of how it might go tits-up again.'

Salman relaxed and smiled. 'Don't worry. I don't actually blame you for all the shit.'

'No. But quite often you make it feel like it's my fault.'

He sighed. 'You're only trying to do the right thing. The truth is, I admire you.'

His comment knocked her for a moment.

'Thank you,' she said.

'For what?'

'For earlier. I was horrified when you shot Thuriyah. You didn't know her really, but she was such an innocent person. She didn't deserve anything that happened to her. But I understand you had to do that. To save me. So thank you, for saving me.'

'If there'd been another way, other than shooting her . . .'

The car fell silent again. Up ahead Mazin, hands in his jacket pockets, strolled casually right past the small building that was surreptitiously plonked on the connector road with nothing else around it. In years gone by, before the port had been transformed into the behemoth it now was, the building probably enjoyed a quiet and prominent position on the coast. Now it was just an oddity. Which perhaps explained why it had fallen into disuse. Officially at least.

Not long after, Mazin disappeared round a bend in the road ahead.

'Anything more from Flannigan?' Salman asked.

'Not since we told him we were headed to Suhar.'

'So we need to get Faiz and transport him all the way back to Nizwa still? Seems like a better spot here to get him out of the country. Shove him on a boat. Probably his plan, isn't it?'

'Shove him on a boat to where exactly? I'm not sure the Saudis or the Iraqis will welcome us with open arms.'

Salman scoffed but didn't otherwise respond.

'But you've got a point,' Cox said. 'Let's get Faiz first, then make that call.'

Salman nodded.

'Are you there?' came Mazin's distant voice. He sounded out of breath. Cox picked the phone up and put it on speaker.

'Yeah.'

'I couldn't see anything. No other cars parked down here. No lights on inside the building. The hotel definitely isn't open any more though.'

'What's round the back?' Cox asked.

'Nothing much. No access that way. They have to be inside still.'

Cox's mind whirred with different thoughts. Was it possible they'd been duped? That Faiz had already scarpered through a secret exit?

'If there's no one else inside, we should just go in,' Salman said. 'Before more of them arrive.'

Cox really didn't know what the best option was. She'd led plenty of raids and extractions in her time, but usually they were well planned and involved specially trained agents, tactical teams, quite often direct from the military, taking up the firing line. She and Salman were intelligence agents, not action heroes. Mazin wasn't even that. None of them had the expertise to launch an armed raid, particularly against an unquantifiable target.

'No,' Cox said. 'We have to wait.'

'Wait for what?' Salman said.

'For Faiz to show his face.'

'We have no idea when that will be.'

'But we'll do it anyway. For now at least. If the field of play changes, we'll adapt, but no point running headfirst into the unknown.'

'But that's what we've been doing all along. You're so good at it.'

That cheeky smile again. At least it was better than when he was being downright sullen.

'Come back to the car,' Cox said to Mazin.

'On my way,' he said.

Moments later he came back into view again.

'Shit,' he said before she saw him drop his hand down, stuffing the phone away.

Then a figure stepped out from the front of the building.

'Faiz?' Salman said.

Cox couldn't be sure.

Mazin kept his head down and his pace up, but Cox could tell the man was giving him a suspicious eye as he made his way to the parked car. His head turned as he followed Mazin, then kept on going until he was facing the Land Cruiser and the motorbike.

The man paused.

'Shit,' Cox said.

'He's seen us.'

Salman twisted the key and the Land Cruiser's engine roared to life. Mazin glanced behind him, then broke into a run.

The man reached down to his side.

'He's got a gun!' Cox screamed.

Salman thumped the accelerator and the Land Cruiser shot forward.

'Get down!' he shouted to Cox.

She did as she was told. Kind of. She hunkered down, but she couldn't not look. Mazin was running for his life towards them. His face caught under a street light and in the orange glow Cox could see his panic. But the man with the gun didn't aim at him. He aimed at the onrushing Land Cruiser.

Cox braced herself then winced when the flash of fire erupted from the barrel, before there was an almost instantaneous clunk as the bullet lodged in the front of the vehicle.

'I said get down!' Salman screamed.

Cox now did so. Not a second later the windscreen shattered when another bullet hit. She didn't dare look again, and however much she was braced, she was still unprepared when moments later Salman let out a determined shout before the Land Cruiser came to a crashing halt. The sudden impact sent Cox shooting forward before her seat belt caught and with her head already bowed in front of her, it cracked off the dashboard at the same moment the airbag exploded, giving her a double whammy of impacts.

Dazed, it took Cox several beats as she waited for the stars to clear.

'Cox, come on,' she heard Salman say, his voice distant at first. 'Cox!'

She snapped herself back into focus. Her head was spinning and pounding, her ears ringing. She reached a shaky hand out to the door and collapsed onto the tarmac outside. Her vision was still blurred and she realised as she rubbed at her eyes it was because one of them was filled with blood coming from her forehead.

With a grunt of determination Cox hauled herself up to her feet. Her eyes fell on the devastation at the front of the vehicle where the Land Cruiser had ploughed head-on into Faiz's car. The crumpled bonnet was wedged into the rear end of the smaller vehicle. Steam hissed. There was broken glass and shards of metal and plastic bent and twisted and protruding all over. And in between the whole mess, draped over what remained of the Land Cruiser's front end, the twisted and crushed torso of the man who'd shot at them moments before.

Cox stepped over, shocked by the ghastly sight, though relieved to see it wasn't Faiz.

'Cox, there he is!'

She looked up to see Faiz on foot, nearly a hundred yards away, pounding across the tarmac away from the hotel.

'Shit, come on.'

She broke into a run, groaning as she did so, only then realising her body was already seriously battered and bruised from the crash. She just hoped adrenaline would see her through.

Salman was five yards ahead of her. Gun in hand. He slowed in his step as he raised the weapon.

'No!' Cox shouted.

He lowered the gun and picked up the pace again.

'I was . . . going for his legs,' he said through heavy breaths.

'Not worth the risk. He's . . . going nowhere.'

Though she wasn't quite sure about that. Did he know this place?

Cox glanced behind her. No one was following from the hotel. So Faiz and his companion really had been alone in there?

She heard a distant rumble behind her. Glanced over her shoulder again to see a single headlight beam. Mazin. On his motorbike. The engine whined as the revs peaked.

What the hell was he doing? If he mowed Faiz down . . .

Seconds later the motorbike blasted past. Faiz, in the distance, seemed to sense the onrushing vehicle too. He looked behind him, increased his pace for a second as though he was going to try and outrun the bike, before he abruptly changed direction, heading right, where he clambered over a chain-link fence into an industrial yard filled with shipping containers.

'Great,' Cox said.

Mazin slammed the brakes and the bike skidded and weaved as it came to a stop. He jumped off the bike and launched himself up and over the fence.

'Keep on him,' Cox shouted. 'But don't get too close.'

Nothing from Mazin in response, who, like Faiz, was soon out of sight among the maze of containers. Salman darted right too and sprang over the fence. Cox followed and made a much less elegant ascent up and over, only just managing to stay on her feet as she scrambled down the other side.

She looked around. There were no lights on in the yard, the only illumination coming from the road behind them. Beyond the shipping containers stacked in front of her, Cox could hear the gentle lapping of the sea. For the first time she took her own handgun from its holster on her side. She hated guns, and as much as she knew she couldn't afford to shoot and kill Faiz, out here in the darkness she needed it for her own sense of comfort as much as anything else.

She jumped when Mazin appeared from behind a container on her left.

'He's gone towards the water,' he said quietly.

'What the hell were you thinking?' Salman blasted in an angry whisper.

Cox gave them both an indication to shut up.

'Mazin, go left, Salman right. If Faiz makes a break in either direction shout. Otherwise keep quiet. We'll corner him.'

Both nodded before they set off. Cox took two deep breaths then slowly moved forward, keeping close to the container on her right. As she approached the end of it her heart rate ramped up in anticipation. She jumped around the corner, gun out. She spun the other way. No one there. She waited a moment. No sounds at all except her own breathing and the gentle ripple of the unseen sea.

She carried on. Cleared two more sets of containers. She wouldn't have classed herself as claustrophobic, but being

30

stuck alone, in the dark, in the middle of the looming metal boxes, stacked several storeys high in places, was unnerving to say the least.

More worrying though, where was Faiz? Had he slipped by them somehow?

And where the hell were Salman and Mazin?

Cox was beginning to regret insisting on their silence.

'Cox!'

It was Mazin.

'He's here!'

His voice was a welcome relief. However panicked he sounded. As she raced towards where the sound had come from, she heard commotion. Groans. Thuds. She raised her gun. Turned the corner round the next container to see Mazin sprawled on the floor. A figure disappeared from view just a few yards in front.

'Crap. Salman, where are you!' Cox shouted.

'Here,' came the nearby reply a second before he blasted past in front of her. Cox set off at pace too. Mazin groggily propped himself up as Cox reached him.

'You OK?'

'Fine. Go.'

She didn't break stride as she raced past in hot pursuit. With a brief glimpse of Salman every now and then she snaked through the yard, until they came to a large clearing, looming cranes in the near distance along the edge of the docks, the blackness of the water beyond. Salman was just in front of her, Faiz further ahead and heading straight for the water it seemed.

'Don't let him get away,' Cox shouted.

She wasn't quite sure what she meant by that. Was she telling Salman to shoot? He seemed to think so because a moment later he was slowing again as he raised his gun to take aim.

31

'Faiz, stop there!' Cox shouted. 'Please!'

Not even a twitch as he carried on sprinting.

She half-raised her own gun. At least if she pulled the trigger the decision was hers, no one else to blame if it went wrong.

But before she got the chance Salman fired. The boom so close to her ear sent a piercing pain through her head. She squinted as she saw Faiz stumble and fall. She wasn't sure where the bullet had hit. His leg hopefully. Perhaps his back.

She continued to close the distance. But Faiz was soon back on his feet. Moving more slowly but no less determinedly for the water.

'Faiz, stop!'

He didn't.

'Cox, get down.'

She realised she was in Salman's field of view. She stepped to the left. Another gunshot. She could just make out the burst of dust as the bullet sank into the tarmac. A miss.

Faiz kept going.

'No!'

He leapt as much as he fell over the edge . . .

Cox's heart missed a beat. She expected to hear the splash. As she raced forward, images flashed in her mind of Faiz drifting under the dark water, never to be seen again. She certainly wasn't jumping in there after him.

Was she?

But instead of a splash, there was a thunk. And then a groan.

Frowning, Cox darted up to the edge. She stopped with her toes just over the edge and looked down. She smiled as she stooped over, out of breath, and put her hands to her knees.

'Not quite what you were expecting?' she said as she looked down at the crumpled heap of Faiz who was sprawled and bleeding on the wooden gangway ten feet below.

Faiz glared back defiantly. Salman was soon by Cox's side, gun pointed at their man.

'Move, and I'll blow your balls off,' Salman said.

An unnecessarily macho comment, Cox felt, but she said nothing of it.

She took a few seconds to get her breathing under control. Mazin hobbled over.

'Bastard,' he said as he glared down at the man responsible for his split lip and the gash above his eye. Faiz simply continued to stare, said nothing.

'So what now?' Mazin said.

Cox thought back to the hotel. The mangled Land Cruiser and the car it was wedged into. And they couldn't exactly get all of them on Mazin's motorbike. And Nizwa, where they were supposed to be taking Faiz, was over a hundred and fifty miles away.

'Cox?' Salman said. 'What now?'

'It's a bloody good question.'

But at least they had their man.

She took out her phone to call Flannigan.

CHAPTER 5

Three weeks later

London, England

The box room Aydin Torkal was sitting in had only one, small square glass window, though there was little point to it because less than two yards beyond the glass a large grey-brick building loomed high. Even on a sunny winter's day like today, there wasn't a ray of sunshine in sight, the buzzing overhead strip light a necessity regardless of time of day or year it seemed.

Not that Aydin was bothered about having a room with a view. He was too focused, his fingers tapping away in a blur as his eyes flicked back and forth across the computer screen. The earphone in his left ear, the one facing away from the door, played a nonstop playlist of classical music, though Aydin had no clue what the compositions were or which composers wrote them, however familiar the sounds. Yet the melodic rhythms, the crescendos in particular, aided both his speed and concentration.

He stopped typing and sat back in his designer swivel chair that was apparently health-and-safety compliant, at least according to the over-keen head of HR for the small company he worked for, who'd recently insisted he use it for his own ergonomic benefit.

He hit enter then held his breath in anticipation as he stared at the screen, waiting for the result of his latest endeavours. When he received the error message his mood went from expectant to enraged in a second, as frustration and tiredness boiled over. He yanked the earphone out, clenched it tightly in his fist and thumped down onto the gloss plastic desk. He thumped again, growling in anger as he did so then slumped back, his heart racing, his head pounding, as the fruits of his efforts evaporated before his eyes with not a single item of tangible progress to show.

He heard a creak outside the door. Quickly closed down browser windows and logged out of all of the many applications he had running.

There was a light knock on the door before it opened and two curious eyes peeked through.

'Everything OK in there, old chap?'

Jim Waters. A peer of Aydin's at the software company they both worked for. At least they were peers in the sense that they were both the same 'level', and a similar age. Waters, however, was about as corporate as anyone could be in the world of software development, the idea of climbing the career ladder his clear life objective. That was fine with Aydin, he didn't begrudge Waters in anyway because of that, but there was a clear reason why Waters worked in an open plan office managing not just himself but others, while Aydin was content to be sitting in a glorified broom cupboard with nothing but hardware and software for company.

Well, there was more than one reason actually, and it wasn't just to do with career aims, or lack of them. Aydin *had* to work alone. How else could he get done what he needed?

'Yeah, I'm fine,' Aydin said.

'I didn't even realise you were still here. Not seen you come out of your hole in hours.'

'Just trying to get something done.'

Waters took a step further inside, glancing not very covertly at the computer screen as though trying to catch Aydin out.

35

He'd have to be quicker than that. Waters sighed. He actually looked vaguely concerned for Aydin. Really, he was a good guy. If Aydin hadn't been Aydin, then Waters would have been a perfectly normal person for him to be friends with.

But Aydin wasn't looking for a friend.

Waters glanced at his watch.

'It's getting on a bit. Just me, you and Bongo left.'

Bongo. A nickname for Will Long, though Aydin never understood how that had come about. Largely because he'd never bothered to ask anyone.

'We're heading out for a quick pint if you fancy it. Well, you know, pint or a Coke or a cranberry juice. Whatever.'

Waters looked slightly embarrassed at his own words, as though he wasn't sure whether Aydin had understood his base-level humour or not.

'Cranberry juice?' Aydin said. 'What is it, your period?'

It took Waters a second to figure that one out. 'Ah, yeah, *The Departed*, right? I never took you for the gangster movie type.'

Aydin shrugged.

'So you up for it?'

'Maybe another time,' Aydin said. 'I need to get this sorted tonight.'

Waters shrugged. 'Fair enough. See you tomorrow.'

He ducked out and shut the door behind him. Aydin released a long sigh as he stared at his blank screen, his brain whirring as he tried in vain to think of what next.

Several minutes later he was still sitting not really doing anything when he heard heightened chatter and footsteps outside the door. Moments after everything went quiet. Given his fruitless day he decided against trying anything more and finally got up from his chair, his legs and back aching as he did so.

36

Ergonomic? Then why was his body stiff as a board? Other than for the fact he'd been in the seat barely moving, and it was more than three hours since he'd last even stood up, that is.

He stretched his body out then moved to the door, opened it and peered through. The office floor outside was empty though across the far side there were still lights on in Meeting Room One where the two directors of the company were hosting some guy from Vodafone. Aydin didn't know the ins and outs of that one and didn't really care.

He turned off his machine, grabbed his coat and skulked across the office to the door for the stairwell, keeping his head down in the unlikely chance that one of the bigwigs would accost him.

They didn't, and Aydin was soon on the ground floor heading out. He glanced over at the sole security guard behind the front desk as he moved through the foyer but the guy paid Aydin no attention. It would be the same on the street outside, on the Underground too. That was the thing with London. Everyone was so anonymous all the time. Even in a small office building where probably fewer than two hundred people worked, people kept their heads down and themselves to themselves. Having worked there for the best part of eight months, Aydin reckoned he could pick out the faces of virtually everyone who worked there, and the security guards in particular must recognise his face by now, but no one ever engaged in chit-chat. It was rare even to get a smile and a hello.

The anonymity of the big city was, on the one hand, utterly depressing to someone like Aydin, who had no real friends or family. On the other hand it was utterly necessary for someone with his past, allowing him to blend in and carry on a life.

He got off the Underground two stops further from his home than necessary, like he often did on his way back from work, then made his way through the streets of Tottenham, heading a well-worn route which took him past his childhood home.

Set on a now crumbling residential street that was framed on two sides by soaring 1960s concrete towers, the apartment where he and his family had lived when he was a young and innocent boy was among a row of plain-looking four-storey red brick blocks dwarfed by their neighbours. He slowed his pace as he passed and a multitude of memories, good, bad and downright horrific crashed in his mind. He could see lights were on behind the thin fabric curtains of 12c. He often wondered who lived there now, and had been tempted more than once to go and knock and see, though what would his explanation to the new occupiers be?

Hi, my name's Aydin. I was brought up here as a child until my father kidnapped me and took me to Afghanistan to be trained as a terrorist insurgent. My sister was killed trying to find me, and the last time I was here my mother was brutally murdered because I tried to break free from that life.

Whoever lived there now, he somehow wasn't sure they would appreciate any of that too much.

Aydin didn't stop this time, just like he hadn't any other day. He picked up his pace again and ten minutes later he arrived on a street of handsome Victorian terraces where the wide pavements were lined with thick oak trees, though the cramped small front yards were largely filled with weeds and rubbish and discarded furniture, which together with the generally shabby-looking parked cars crammed together on the road showed the relative lack of wealth of today's occupants.

When he reached 190 he headed through the rickety gate that was wedged permanently open and took the key from his pocket as he approached the door. He put the key into the lock but then paused. Frowned.

An unexpected noise behind him.

Ever alert, one of the many skills he'd picked up as part of his 'training', he was certain he hadn't been followed back here. But he definitely wasn't alone now.

Of course, it could be anyone, a neighbour, but . . .

He pretended to be having trouble with the key. Groaned in frustration as his free hand slipped into his coat pocket where he had a four-inch flick knife. His fingers delicately wrapped around the handle. It would take him only a second to whip it out.

He took a breath and pulled the key from the lock and was primed and ready to attack as he spun round, the metal protruding from his clenched fist to act as a secondary and more rudimentary weapon while he surveyed the threat.

The figure was two yards away from him, but it only took Aydin a heartbeat to realise there was no threat here.

One half of her face was cast in the glow of the nearest street light. She looked down at his fist nervously. She knew what he was capable of, even if to most people he just looked like a guy trying to open his front door.

'You,' he said.

'Nice to see you, Aydin,' said Rachel Cox.

CHAPTER 6

Of course he didn't *have* to invite her into his home, but then, despite the unwelcome and unexpected visit he was intrigued on several levels as to her sudden appearance. Not just in how she'd found him but why.

'So is this what you call hiding in plain sight?' Cox said as she took a sip from her glass of water then set it back down on the coffee table that separated them – Cox in an armchair, Aydin on the sofa. He would have offered her tea or coffee had he felt the need to be properly hospitable, but he wasn't yet feeling that.

'Who said I'm hiding?'

'Then what? You've truly set up a new life for yourself as Mohammed Mhawi, software nerd?'

Aydin held his tongue. It felt like she was trying to rile him, but he wasn't sure why. Perhaps he was just being overly sensitive, though he also knew he was simply perturbed that Cox not only knew where he lived now, but knew of his new 'life'. But how much did she know of what he'd really been doing?

'I'm a little surprised you chose London,' she said.

'I grew up here.' Which wasn't exactly the entire truth. 'It's the only place I have happy memories of.'

She nodded as if that made sense to her. 'Honestly, I'm impressed with what you're doing,' she said as her eyes scanned the modest living space that quite clearly belonged to a young, single male. No ornaments or knick-knacks or photo frames or art in sight. Just a well-used sofa and non-matching armchair, coffee table filled with used cups and plates, and a TV on a stand in the corner with a seldom used games console underneath.

'I mean, after what you've been through, it's good that you're living so . . . normally.'

'Normal?'

'You've got a real job. You pay rent and tax. It's almost a strange choice to have made for someone in your position who could have just disappeared for a quiet life.'

'I could have taken your blood money you mean?'

Cox winced. She'd called it 'compensation'. He didn't want anything from the British government. Everything he had now from his new identity to his job was because of him.

He sat back on the sofa, arms folded, staring at Cox.

'I say strange,' Cox said, 'but really, to someone who knows you like I do—'

'You don't know me. Not really.'

Cox paused and held his eye.

'You really don't think I do? After everything?'

Aydin glared but didn't respond.

'Yet I know you well enough to be able to track you down. Granted it's taken me longer than I expected, but here I am.'

She paused again. Still Aydin said nothing.

'And I also know you well enough to figure out that your so-called job for an up-and-coming company specialising in anti-virus and anti-malware software probably isn't to fulfil your desire to be seen as a leading computer programmer.'

She stopped again and took another sip of her water, the silence in the room growing more uncomfortable – at least for Aydin – by the second. Which was likely Cox's entire reason for her dragged-out revelation, whatever it would be.

'In fact, I'd say your job for such a company is very possibly for an entirely different purpose.'

'Which is what?'

She shrugged. 'I mean, I'm nowhere near as clued up on these things as you are, so sorry if I struggle to explain this, but, hypothetically speaking, let's say we have an individual who's desperate for answers about something.'

'Pretty vague.'

'So far. And that something just happens to be steeped in mystery and lies and deceit of a . . . how could I put this . . . of an official nature.'

'You mean like lies and deceit told by a government?'

'I guess that works, right?' Cox said. 'A conspiracy theory, you could say. Then for someone who's already tech savvy, wouldn't working for a company whose whole purpose is to create barriers to back-door entry into the IT systems of large organisations be a perfect front for someone who was actually *trying* to gain back-door access to said organisations, in order to glean something from their classified data?'

'You mean like how said companies often hire ex-hackers to improve their systems?'

'Not exactly, because in this case the hacker is still a hacker, just no one knows it.'

'Except for you apparently.'

Cox smiled. 'So what have you found?'

Was there even any point in trying to deny it? He'd never taken Cox as being anything but astute and dogged. Clearly she'd already figured out his ruse. What that meant for him, he wasn't sure. Was she going to use it against him, or as leverage? Or was she simply trying to impress him with her research and deductions?

Perhaps she was there to help him in his never-ending search somehow?

'Aydin?'

'I've found nothing that you don't already know about,' he said.

Her eyes pinched at his curious response. What did that reaction mean? That she did know something key and was now worried he'd rumbled her?

'The thing is, Aydin, are you sure you don't already know everything there is to know about the Farm? What if there really isn't anything else to it all? You can't waste your life looking for answers that aren't there.'

Aydin now decided to stay quiet again. Largely because recently he'd also been coming to the same conclusion, though it still left a sour taste. In his eyes there remained so many unanswered questions as to who set up the Farm and why. Who was responsible for making him the man he now was. Responsible for his father's death. His mother's, his sister's.

His uncle's?

As far as Aydin knew, his uncle was still out there somewhere. Either in hiding, or as a captive of one side or another. What was his true story?

'No, there are still answers out there,' Aydin said.

'But maybe not to the questions you're asking.'

'What are you saying?'

Cox sighed. 'Take a step back to last year. We know the Farm came about because of operation Shadow Hand. An MI6 op, led by Edmund Grey—'

'You mean the murderous bastard who still works for the British government, despite everything, all of the misery and deaths?'

'Whatever his wrongs, his intention was never for the Farm to end up how it was.'

43

'No? But his plan was always for it to be a training camp where young boys would be taken away from their families and made into combat-ready machines.'

Cox sighed. 'Yes. I admit that appears to be the truth. But you know from everything you've found, and from everything I've found too, and believe me I have looked for the answers you crave, that Shadow Hand was supposed to be a counter-terrorism initiative. Your father believed that too. But it was hijacked.'

'By my uncle?'

Cox couldn't hold Aydin's eye now. 'That's what Grey has always claimed.'

'Except there's no evidence that was the case.'

'No. Not that I'm aware of—'

'And MI6 would rather sweep the whole sordid affair under the carpet now than to try to figure out who really betrayed them and why. Maybe you even have my uncle locked up somewhere so the whole embarrassing truth never comes out.'

'I wouldn't keep it from you if that was the truth. We've looked for your uncle. No one knows what happened to him.'

'That's not the same thing as finding out what happened with Shadow Hand.'

Cox sighed again. She looked both frustrated and fed up with the way the conversation had gone. Perhaps she was OK to move on with her life not knowing whether there was something they'd missed, whether the real bad guys behind the Farm were still out there, but he wasn't. He had to know. He had to find anyone who was still alive and free who had any responsibility. And he had to see them brought to justice.

'Why don't we drop the pointless debate,' Aydin said. 'You know I can't stop until I've exhausted every avenue. And I know that it's in no one's interest at MI6 to delve any deeper into its own murky past. So why don't you just explain why you're here.'

'Isn't it obvious?' Cox said. 'I need your help.'

Aydin scoffed.

'Help you what? Do the dirty work that MI6 can't do with its own agents?'

Cox squirmed slightly in her seat, which was pretty much an affirmative. Was it any wonder the intelligence services of Western nations had such a poor reputation in certain parts of the world?

'Please, hear me out,' she said. 'This does link, in a way, to what you're doing.'

He wanted to say no. But something about the sincerity in her tone caused him to rethink.

'You've got five minutes.'

She reached down to her bag and drew out some crumpled sheets of paper bundled together in a plastic wallet. After opening the wallet on her lap she flipped through until she found what she was looking for, and passed the piece of paper over to Aydin. He took it and focused on the black-and-white image of a man he didn't recognise.

'His name is Faiz Al-Busaidi,' Cox said. 'He's an Omani national and suspected terrorist now in our custody.'

'Lucky him. Should this face mean something to me?'

Cox shrugged. 'I can sense that it doesn't, and that's fine. I can fill the blanks in for you. For months we've been gathering intel on a new terror cell that has been on a recruitment drive. It's not another Farm, we don't think, but they're gearing up for . . . something. Al-Busaidi was one of the recruiters, for want of a better word.'

'But he's in your custody now. Why can't you get what you need from him?'

'We're trying. And we have got some information from him. Like the fact that this cell isn't based in the Middle East at all.'

'Here?'

'No. Actually we believe it's in the US.'

'I've never even been,' Aydin said, though he was strangely impressed with the audacity of the group. There were far easier targets to infiltrate than the US. In fact any target was easier, the UK included.

'Not yet,' Cox said.

'Not yet?'

'We want you to help us break into this group.'

Aydin frowned as a wave of anger bubbled up from his gut. 'Use me as a pawn?'

Cox looked a little embarrassed. 'No, Aydin. You'd be a truly key asset in this. We need someone to get on the inside. We don't have anyone who's anywhere near as . . . talented as you.'

'You mean as expendable as me.'

'You're not expendable. You're unique.'

'Did you really just say that?'

Cox grumbled and sighed. 'Aydin, seriously, get your head out of your backside. You more than anyone should know what people like this are capable of. You're in a unique position to help us. Help us before innocent boys get brainwashed, like you did. Help us before innocent people get killed.'

'Don't put this on me. I owe you nothing.'

'I know. That's true. You've already helped us, helped me, more than you could ever have been expected to. But we still need you. *I* still need you.'

'I'm sorry. I won't do it.'

Cox looked flustered now. Aydin checked his watch. Why had he given her as much as five minutes? This was a no deal. It didn't matter what she said next. It wasn't his job to run around the world stopping every terrorist plot.

She flipped through her papers again. Pulled out another picture. Aydin didn't take it this time, just scanned the image

46

before looking back up to Cox.

'I know you don't know him either. His name is Jamaal Rashid. He's British. Twenty-four years old. You have to admit, he bears a passing resemblance to—'

'Me?'

Cox didn't answer, but Aydin was beginning to figure where she was going.

'Rashid was captured over four years ago trying to enter Syria to join up with ISIS. He's been in our hands, in secret, ever since.'

Which Aydin took to mean the guy was rotting in some unofficial black site.

'You want me to pretend to be Jamaal Rashid?' he said. 'Do you realise how insane that sounds?'

'I do. But yes, that's what we need from you. Will you?'

'It's a ridiculous idea. Not a chance.' He checked his watch. 'Time's up.'

Cox shook her head despondently. 'Give me one more go.' Her eyes flicked to the bundle of papers again.

'I said no,' Aydin said. He got to his feet.

'Please. Just let me try.'

'Rachel. I said no. It's time for you to go.'

She got to her feet as she pulled another paper from the pile. Aydin wouldn't even look at it as she held it out to him.

'Go. Please,' he said, his tone terse, his body tense.

'Aydin, give me a break here. I'm putting my neck on the line doing this. This was my idea and I've worked so hard to get others on board.'

'But you're asking me to put *my* neck on the line for something that isn't even my problem.'

'Just look at the picture.'

'I said no.'

'We think this man is one of the ringleaders in the US, he—'

47

'Rachel, please—'

'Aydin, for fuck's sake!' Cox shouted. 'Just look at the picture.'

Both of them fell silent. Aydin held Cox's eye for a few seconds. He could see not only the determination, but the desperation that sat behind.

He put his hand out and took the paper then glanced down. Then frowned.

'Look familiar?' Cox said.

Aydin was lost for words. The man was thinner, had less hair both on his face and on his head. But the eyes . . . they were unmistakable.

'It's not him,' he said. 'It . . . can't be. He's—'

'You're right. Aziz Al-Addad is locked up in Z-site. And he'll never see daylight again. He's there because of you. And me.'

'Then what is this?'

'This might be the missing link in your search, Aydin. His brother.'

CHAPTER 7

Dearborn, Michigan

He knew they were following him as soon as he stepped out of the mall into the sprawling and jam-packed car park. Karim Hussein didn't panic. Not just yet. The men behind him were being discreet, staying well back as he headed north across the frozen space, away from the Fairlane Town Center Mall. He tried to be just as discreet with his increasingly nervous glances over his shoulder. From here it was a mile to his home. Would they follow him all that way?

Karim shivered as he walked, and it wasn't just from the blistering chill. The whole Detroit area was in the middle of one of its worst winters for decades. Apparently. Karim had only seen twelve winters here, though granted this one was by far the worst of those. The temperature today was hovering just below freezing, but it was the seemingly endless blizzards that had caused chaos. Two weeks ago over a foot of snow had fallen in less than forty-eight hours, and since then there'd been little thaw and plenty of new waves of white. Every street had mounds of snow piled high, sometimes as much as ten or twelve feet, from the constant clearing of roads and car parks and sidewalks and driveways. In most places those mounds were increasingly turning black around the bottom edges from the dirty slush splashed up from passing cars, and the grimy scene was nothing like a winter wonderland any more.

The poor weather also meant roads and sidewalks remained treacherous, and as Karim picked up his pace a little to try and move away from the men behind him, his inadequate Nikes slipped all over the place.

His heart rate slowly quickened with each beat. He cleared the end of the mall car park and was soon crossing the four lanes of Hubbard Drive. Once he was across the other side, he peeked over his shoulder again. Out in the open now, he could see the men more clearly. He'd thought there were three, but now he could see five, and they were closing.

Karim pumped his legs a little harder. Not full pace by a long stretch, but as fast as he could comfortably walk on the slippery surface. To his right was the glass-fronted AAA Michigan head office complex, to his left various low-rise buildings belonging to the University of Michigan. Like every commercial premises around here their car parks were unnecessarily huge. The city of Dearborn, within the metro area of Detroit, and much like its big brother, had been built on the motor trade, and every aspect of the city's design from the wide highways to the grid-like streets was predicated on the use of vehicles. On a wintry Sunday afternoon the vast swatches of icy tarmac around here were virtually abandoned, making Karim feel all the more isolated and vulnerable.

And his chasers all the more powerful.

'Hey, Karim, you fucking terrorist!'

'Saddam! Stop. We just want to talk.'

Karim clenched his fists. Of course their commonly repeated insults and heckles and slurs were just the start of the abuse that he and his friends regularly received. Abuse he'd received for years in fact, all through high school, and even now when they were supposedly adults.

For some reason Karim always took the brunt of the abuse compared to his friends. Was it only that these simpletons revelled in the fact that Karim shared his surname with Iraq's long-disgraced former leader, or the fact that he gave them as much shit back as they gave to him?

At least, he did when the odds were matched. But five against one?

He had no chance.

He looked back again to see two of the five were now jogging, and quickly closing. Craig – the ringleader and Karim's true nemesis – was at the front of the others as always.

'Shit,' Karim muttered under his breath.

He was still more than a half mile away from safety.

He broke into a jog himself.

'Hey, Saddam, don't go, we just want to show you something.'

Karim pushed himself a little faster, but every other step his feet lost grip. He glanced behind. They were only twenty yards away now.

He pumped harder still. Up ahead a car was approaching. A minivan, a woman driving. He kept his eyes on her the whole way. She didn't even once flick her gaze to him as she carried on past. Oblivious? Or just without a care?

'Stop now you bacon-hating piece of shit.'

That insult resulted in a guffaw from the others who were now following closely too.

Karim should have just let them have their say, in the position he found himself in there really was no need to retaliate . . .

He couldn't help it.

He slowed and spun round.

'No bacon for me,' Karim said. 'No sausage either. But your mom told me you love a chocolate lollipop. Wanna suck on this one?'

He thrust his groin back and forth as he said it.

The looks on their simple faces . . .

'I'm gonna fucking kill you!'

The chasing pack burst into a sprint now.

Karim did too. He raced the rest of the way up to Ford Road. Off to his left was St Sarkis Towers, his home. No. He wasn't going there. He headed right instead. Away from his tower block, away from the homes of the chasing pack too – more than one of the gang lived on the nearby and far more plush Fairlane Woods estate.

First looking left and right, Karim sped across the multiple lanes of Ford Road. He thought he'd judged the traffic, but panicked when a horn off to his right blared. He pushed himself harder and faster still. As he put his left foot down it didn't gain traction. Rather than try to slow and right himself, he quickly threw his other foot forward, but that slipped too.

Karim crashed down onto the icy verge at the side of the road, just managing to push his hands out in front of him to avoid a sickening contact with his face. He tried to roll into the fall. Got it all wrong and his knee, then his shoulder smacked painfully down.

With a cacophony of laughter behind him, he was as embarrassed as much as he was seriously hurt, though when he saw the looming figures now almost within touching distance, he was also scared.

Ignoring the aches and pains, he shot up to his feet, then turned hard right to run alongside the road. A few seconds later, having successfully cleared the main road with far more grace than he had, one of the buffoons actually made a dive for him, like the jock would have done in previous years on the high school football field when he was still a somebody.

His fingertips caught Karim's ankle. He stumbled, but managed to wriggle free.

A few more laughs from his friends, for once not at Karim's expense.

Karim raced along as fast as he could now, passing by a variety of fast-food outlets. Most of them were quiet. No one would come to his aid, he knew. He twisted left, hoping the quick movement would gain him a couple more yards. He entered the car park of a burger joint. At least this place, bustling compared to others, had a car park that was properly cleared of snow and ice, allowing him to build up speed again.

But not for long. Unless he headed right, and back to the road, up ahead he was fast approaching a seven-foot wooden fence marking the perimeter of the premises. He twisted his neck. They were right there behind him. He had no other choice . . .

He flung himself forward at the fence. Grabbed the top and scrambled over as one of the goons rammed into the wood panel with his shoulder, only narrowly missing Karim's legs.

Karim jumped down the other side and landed in a heap of uncleared snow. The icy white powder sank over the tops of his shoes, up his legs, down the top of his jeans, under his coat and jumper and t-shirt. He grimaced at the cold but was soon on his feet.

The car park in front of him was thick with snow. The unit here was abandoned now, though back in the summer, and for the fifteen years before that, it had been a convenience store owned by a friend of Karim's family. These were the times. Abandoned shops and other business premises littered the whole area.

Karim took heavy footsteps through the thick snow then headed round the far side of the derelict building whose doors and windows were all boarded up. Here, among rusting dumpsters was a small and curious clearing of snow, about twenty feet square.

Out of breath, exhausted, Karim finally stopped. He hunched over with his hands on his knees as he tried to get his breathing under control.

He was given only a few seconds' respite until the first of the goons – Craig – came careening round the corner in a flurry of snow powder.

'You fucking—'

'Oh, come on!' Karim said, straightening up and facing him off. 'You really wanna do this? Five against one?'

The guy's friends were soon lining up by his side. Expectant snarls on each of their faces.

'You asked for this you piece of shit,' Craig sneered.

As intelligent as these young men were supposed to be, in the eyes of the community at least, none of them had taken any notice of the fact that a square of this abandoned car park had been cleared away . . .

Two of the five edged forward, fists balled, faces screwed. The other three initially looked like they might leave their chums to it. Until Karim decided to egg them on.

'You always thought you were a chick magnet,' Karim said to Craig. 'But bringing all of these pussies with you?'

That was it. They all came for Karim now, shouting with anger and venom. He stepped back into a fighting stance, fists up and at the ready.

'Come on!' he shouted.

Not a battle cry. An instruction.

Shouts all around him now. Two men appeared from behind the dumpster to his left. Three from behind him. Two at the back of the group of jocks.

Eight against five. Karim liked those odds much more.

The jocks soon realised their predicament, but could do nothing about it now. Armed with bats and sticks, the ambushers raced into the melee. Karim burst forward too.

Saw a hook arcing for his face from Craig. He managed to half-block it, though the fist crashed through his forearm defence and grazed the side of his ear. It stung like hell but he was already in the process of delivering a response of his own. His balled fist swung up from his midriff. A perfect, unprotected uppercut caught the jock under his chin and Craig's head snapped back, looking like it might roll off his thick neck, before his body caved to the ground.

'Karim, take this.'

He looked to his left and caught the baseball bat as it flew through the air to him. He grasped it in both hands then turned and swung with force. The metal bat made solid contact with shoulder. The jock in front of him shouted in pain. Karim swung again and got him on the back, then went low and swiped away his legs.

Another one down and out.

The jocks had no chance.

For the next thirty seconds there were shouts of anger, shouts of pain and despair. Bangs and cracks, groans and grunts from the losers, and whoops of delight from the victors.

'Stop!' Karim shouted when he managed to catch his breath.

Panting, his face streaked with both blood and sweat, he looked over his friends. There were plenty of scrapes on them. The jocks had put up a good fight, under the circumstances, but not good enough. The five were each now sprawled on the ground, in various states of defeat.

One of them hurled an obscene comment about Muslim women. Prone on the ground it wasn't the wisest idea, but some people never learned. That misdeed got him the blast of a baseball bat in his stomach. A few more disgruntled comments followed, resulting in various warning shots, boots to the groin . . .

'I said stop!'

This time Karim's friends listened. They stepped back from their foes and as Karim looked over the scene he relaxed a little. The fight was over.

Karim crouched down next to Craig, grabbed him by the scruff of the neck.

'Remind me, what did you say about my mother?'

For once, the idiot had nothing to say.

'And my father? Something about bombs and Iraq if I remember rightly?'

Still nothing.

'You think I'm a violent terrorist, yet you still want to provoke me? Well this is what happens.'

Karim let go and Craig's head flopped back down onto the tarmac with a crack.

Karim straightened up and looked over to his friends with a satisfied grin on his face.

That was when he saw the flashing lights across the way on Ford Road.

'Shit! Let's go!'

He turned and ran.

CHAPTER 8

Thirty minutes later, shivering vigorously and his sopping wet clothes feeling like they were freezing solid to his skin, Karim finally looped back round to head home. He'd heard from his friends that they'd all successfully evaded the police too. Even the jocks had scarpered the scene as quickly as they could it seemed.

He reached the end of Westwood Street and scaled the chain-link fence into the partially cleared car park of the Islamic Center of America, the largest mosque on the continent, and the closest to Karim's home. Though it was also a Shia mosque. As Sunnis, Karim's family instead chose to travel to Jalalabad Mosque, a much smaller affair a few miles away.

There were a few dozen cars in the car park as he crossed through, and a group of men coming out of the back entrance of the mosque spotted Karim and glared. He nodded to them in greeting. He recognised a couple of them. They said nothing to him though he could feel their eyes on him as he moved away, head down.

Minutes later he was walking past Dearborn Academy and finally into the car park of St Sarkis Towers, a plain-looking eight-storey block of over 150 affordable housing units. His family took up a cramped three-bedroom apartment on the top floor.

He headed across the car park and did one last look behind him to check he was alone – he was, as far as he could tell – before he moved inside and headed for the stairs. Finally out of the bitter chill, his body was aching and he longed to be inside in the warmth. His stomach gurgled as he climbed, the myriad smells wafting out of the apartments that largely housed families from various ethnic backgrounds tickling his senses. On the top floor he headed to the second but last apartment, the key already in his hand as he reached the door.

He stuck the key in the lock and turned. Pushed the door open.

Saw his father standing there in the short and narrow corridor.

He did not look happy.

'Where've you been?' he snapped.

'Out.'

Karim went to close the door as his father lurched forward. Karim cowered. His father grabbed him by the shoulder of his coat.

'Get in here. Now.'

He resisted, but only a little, and was pulled along the corridor to the doorway for the open plan living area.

It was already clear he was due a severe rebuking from his father. Not particularly unusual. But this time, it was much worse than that, Karim soon realised. His father dragged him into the room. He let go and stood glaring at him with his arms folded.

'You've done it this time, Karim,' his father said.

Karim said nothing, but his heart sank when his eyes traced from his father to the figure sitting on the sofa across the room.

'You know Officer Riyad?' Karim's father said as the policeman got to his feet.

Luckily Karim did, which was likely the only reason the guy wasn't reaching for his cuffs.

'We were starting to get worried about you,' Riyad said.

Karim said nothing.

'Well? What have you got to say for yourself?' his father prompted.

'About what?'

'About the fight,' Riyad said.

'News to me.'

Riyad sighed. 'It's just as well those white kids have more to lose than you do,' he said. A strange comment. And one that for some reason Karim took offence to. 'Otherwise I'm sure they wouldn't have run away from the scene as fast as their little legs could carry them, like you did.'

Karim still said nothing. No point in incriminating himself. Better to just let this one ride out and see where it was going.

'You're lucky,' Riyad said. 'And you know I'll look out for you. That's why I'm here, alone. But if you make life hard for me, I can't always help.'

Karim nodded. Riyad looked to Karim's father as if questioning why Karim was suddenly mute.

'Say something you stupid idiot,' his father said.

'I understand,' Karim said. 'Thank you.'

'I'll be seeing you, Mr Hussein,' Riyad said to Karim's father before he headed across the room. 'No more shit,' he said more quietly to Karim as he passed.

A moment later Karim heard the front door open and then bang shut.

'You stupid little—'

Karim's father lurched for his son again, arm raised. Karim cowered down but his father somehow held his anger back. 'What were you thinking?'

'It was nothing.'

'Nothing? You beat those guys with baseball bats!'

'Those punks brought it on themselves.'

59

'Punks?' Karim's father said with obvious contempt. He didn't hold back this time. He swiped his palm across Karim's face. The slap stung like hell but Karim just stood there and took it. 'What kind of a word is that anyway?'

'You know what I mean.'

'I have no idea. So you want to teach some white kids a lesson? Is that it?'

'You know what they do to us. What they say.'

'Yeah? So you want to be the big man now? Is that it?'

Karim's father grabbed his son by the scruff of the neck and pulled him out of the lounge.

'Get off me!'

He didn't. He dragged his son into the master bedroom and threw him onto the bed then stomped to the wardrobe. Karim flinched when his father turned back round gripping a shotgun in his hands. He strode to his son.

'Go on take it!' he boomed.

Karim sat himself up on the edge of the bed, his eyes on the weapon, though he made no attempt to do as his father had instructed

'I said take it!'

The slap this time caught Karim unawares, the fingers rapping against his lip and splitting the corner.

'Take it!' The shotgun was shoved onto his lap. 'You want to teach those *punks* a lesson. Take this gun. Go and blow their damn heads off. Show them what a man you are. See where it gets you.'

Karim glared down at the weapon. His hand twitched but he made no move to pick up the shotgun.

'No? You don't want to now?'

His father grabbed the gun back off him and stuffed it back into the wardrobe.

'Just what I thought. You're not a real man. Just a stupid, stubborn kid.'

Karim went to get up.

'You're not in high school any more, Karim. Rather than getting yourself into stupid trouble, why don't you go out there and be a real man and get yourself a job.'

Did he think Karim hadn't tried?

'You do realise where we live?' Karim said, his tone as angry as his father's, a fact that was greeted by another more callous glower. 'This place is a shithole. There's nothing for any of us, which is why you get paid pennies for breaking your back.'

'I get paid *something*.'

His words were less angry now. Almost sorrowful.

'Yeah. Well that's not for me.'

'Get out,' his father said through gritted teeth.

Karim didn't need to be told twice. He turned and headed for the front door.

His clothes were still wet. He was tired and hungry and frozen. The family home should have been a place of solace for him. Instead it was a place filled with anger and hate, petty grievances and resentment. Kind of like how the whole of Detroit felt to him.

At least with his friends life was good, when they weren't being harassed, anyway.

The bus across town was quiet. Karim stayed in his seat, head down staring at his phone, until the bus was nearly at his stop, before he got up and moved for the front. Earlier on the journey there'd been a young woman with a headscarf on sitting there who he'd seen taking snide comments from two white female teens. Both the woman and the teenagers were gone now and there wasn't a white face remaining. In this part of town it would have been the teens who got the abuse. Such was life around here, always 'them' versus 'us', with battles drawn street by street.

Karim thanked the driver and stepped out into the cold night once more. He headed the short distance across a deserted road dominated by boarded-up retail units before he came to the entrance to the Jalalabad Mosque. The main hall was closed up for the night but Karim carried on round the side to the separate anonymous single-storey building at the back where there was a community centre which included a heavily used social club known more commonly as JL's.

There was no membership as such here. If you were a face people recognised, you got in. He knocked on the metal door and waited for it to be opened from the inside. The big guy who opened up looked like a nightclub bouncer, even down to his buzz cut and his black clothing. Karim recognised him, but he didn't know his name. Karim nodded and the guy stepped aside to let him in.

He headed on through the main foyer to the double doors at the end which opened out into a large hall with lino floor, plain walls and ceiling, the space filled with tables and chairs, sofas, armchairs, a pool table, foosball and groups of teens and young men milling around and smoking.

He spotted his crew over by the TV area, though the set was switched off and they were sitting in a cluster on the sofas nattering, clouds of vapour from their e-cigs spiralling into the air around them.

'Here he is!' chimed Hamza when he spotted Karim. 'The man of the moment.'

They beckoned him over and Karim greeted them each with a fist pump and a slap on the back.

'Could that have gone any better?' Hamza said.

'I still can't believe you made it back to us without getting your face smashed in first,' Omid said.

'It was close.'

'Yeah, Bambi here was skating all over the place,' Hamza mocked as he thumped Karim's arm.

'I was trying to make it interesting for them,' Karim said, trying to hide his embarrassment. He must have looked like a fool when he was slipping and falling all over. Still, the jocks bought the whole thing and it worked out so who cared.

'Oh-oh, that doesn't look good.'

Hamza indicated behind Karim and he turned to see Saad coming through the entrance, face like thunder.

'What's going on?' Karim said to Hamza.

'The muj are here.'

Karim grimaced. Muj was an ironic reference to mujahideen, the Arabic word for Jihadi guerrilla fighters. Originally slang used by the US army in particular for any Muslim or Arab male they fought against in the Middle East, Karim and his friends had taken the word muj for their own purposes, using it to refer to the top dogs within their community. Not men to get on the wrong side of.

As Saad came over the mood in the group deteriorated.

'They want to see you,' Saad said to Karim.

'Me?'

Saad shrugged. 'Come on. This way.'

Karim gulped as he stood up from the arm of the chair he was sitting on. No whoops or laughter or banter from his friends as he was led away. He didn't like this at all.

Saad led Karim back into the main foyer and over to the closed door for the kitchen. He knocked and the door was opened by another bouncer-type. This one Karim didn't recognise.

They stepped inside the kitchen, a big square space lined with silvery stainless steel units, a large counter in the middle where four men were gathered. As the door was closed behind Karim, three of the men parted to reveal the leader who was sitting on the counter, arms folded, his face covered in a deep scowl. Smartly dressed, he was a big man, could easily have passed as a bouncer himself. He had a thick beard and deep-set eyes, one of them with a jagged line of scarred skin cutting across it. A thick gold chain hung from his neck. Golden signets adorned several of his fingers.

'You're Karim?' the big man growled, his voice gravelly.

'Yeah,' Karim said, sounding way more confident than he had any right to be.

'You know who I am?'

Karim thought he did. At least he knew his nickname: *Namur*. Tiger.

'Yeah.'

'Good. That makes this a little easier.'

He nodded to one of the other men with him, a tall and wiry guy with a leathery face and a cleft lip – a scar? – that gave him a permanent sneer. He stepped towards Karim and reached forward. Karim stepped back and flung his arms up in defence.

'Don't fucking touch me,' Karim said

'Relax,' Namur said with an amused smirk on his face. 'He's just checking you.'

Karim didn't relax. Not fully, but he did drop his arms and let the man pat him down.

'We have to be careful here,' Namur said as if in explanation.

The man emptied Karim's pockets. Took his phone.

'Hey—'

'Unlock it for me.'

Karim hesitated for a second but he wasn't exactly in a position to say no, yet even before he'd agreed, the man grabbed Karim's wrist and pushed his thumb onto the screen to unlock it. Feeling ever so slightly violated, Karim snapped his hand back as the man scrolled through, looking for what, Karim had no clue.

64

After a few seconds the man turned and tossed the phone to Namur. 'All good.'

'Glad to hear it,' Namur said.

'You're not keeping that,' Karim said.

'Why not?'

'It's my—'

'You need to learn when to shut up,' Mr Sneer said.

Maybe he was right. But Karim was still about to retort when Namur butted in. 'I heard about what you did today.'

That was followed by silence as every person in the room now glowered towards Karim.

'And?' Karim said.

'And you sound like a complete idiot,' Namur said.

Karim slumped.

'Saad tells me you're nineteen years old?'

'Yeah?'

'Then stop acting like you're still fourteen.'

Karim scoffed. 'That—'

'You got a job?'

'No, but—'

'No job. You're not at university. But you do enjoy rounding up white kids and pummelling them with baseball bats out in the open. You must enjoy the prospect of a life behind bars.'

Namur rolled his eyes and received some grunts of acknowledgement from his crew.

'What's it to you, anyway?' Karim said.

Namur smiled. 'I heard you were like this. You're going to get on the wrong side of a lot of people you shouldn't be on the wrong side of with that mouth.'

Karim decided to button it. At least for now.

'But me?' Namur said, breaking out into what looked like a forced smile. 'I quite like it. Or maybe I'm just intrigued to see what trouble you'll get yourself into next time.'

Karim glanced around the group of men. With his initial bravado wearing off, he was starting to feel more anxious by the second.

'Intrigued, until your actions come back to harm *me*.'

'It's none of your business what—'

'If I say it's my business, then it is. Got it?'

Karim paused. He wasn't sure if he was supposed to answer or not.

'Yeah, I got it.'

'Good. So what do you like to do? I mean, you must have a lot of spare time.'

'I . . . I dunno.'

'You box?'

Karim's eyes pinched with curiosity. 'Used to.'

'You gave it up?'

'I guess.'

'You're a quitter?'

'I still do karate.'

'So you think you're a bit of a fighter then?'

'I can handle myself.'

Namur nodded, as if impressed. But by what? He turned to Mr Sneer.

'You think you could take down Benny?' Namur said.

'I . . . I—'

'Let's see.'

Namur nudged Benny and he stepped forward again, practically snarling. Karim stepped back, unsure what to do. Was this really happening? He looked at all the people around him, curiosity and expectancy on their faces. He looked behind him at the bouncer who was quite clearly blocking the door. Finally he looked at Saad whose face was creased with concern, though he certainly wasn't about to step to his friend's aid.

Karim turned back to Benny who was just three steps away.

Then Benny jerked forward and Karim flinched and shot his hands up into a defensive pose straight from the dojo. A move which resulted in a wave of laughter from the crew. Except from Benny who was in the zone.

The next second he barrelled forward. He threw a straight right punch. Karim stepped to the side, blocked and tried to grab the wrist but Benny pulled away too quickly.

The two men squared off, both in a fighting stance now, one hand up in front of their faces, the other closer to their chest, ready to unleash.

Without thinking why this was happening, Karim went for it. Better to get this over with, whatever the purpose. Benny saw the jab coming, but that was fine. Karim guessed his opponent would wind up for a counter punch, and he did. Karim easily blocked as he stepped to the side and forward, now alongside Benny, his intention to swipe Benny's leg away. Karim's leg swung out, he was inches away from achieving his aim . . . but Benny was a quick mover. He'd already read Karim's plan. He stepped out of the position and with Karim's body crouched and spinning, Benny crashed his elbow into the back of Karim's neck and he crumpled face first into a heap.

He was partially aware of the uproarious cheer as he lay sprawled on the tiled floor, and it took him several seconds to find the strength to move. He turned over and propped his torso up with his elbow. Benny, a crooked smile on his face, had already retreated and was standing over by his master once again.

'What do you think?' Namur said. His eyes were on Karim, but it was clear the question was for Benny.

'Maybe he's better when he's got a bat.'

That was received by a further chorus of sniggers.

'Seriously? He's got a bit of something,' Benny said.

'High praise indeed, coming from this man,' Namur said to Karim. 'Someone get him up.'

It was the bouncer from behind him who hauled Karim, shakily, back to his feet.

'Not so easy when you've got no weapons and you're up against someone who actually knows their shit,' Namur said.

Karim shrugged.

'What did those white kids do to you anyway?'

'What haven't they done? They've tormented us for years. They're racist pricks, all of them.'

'So you wanted to punish them?'

'Wouldn't you?'

Namur didn't react at all to the question.

'I know your father,' he said. Karim felt like rolling his eyes but somehow managed not to. 'He's a good man. Honest anyway.'

'He's an angry self-righteous prick,' Karim said.

Namur's face screwed in irritation now. 'You need to learn some respect. Or we're going to have a very short relationship. And *he's* angry? What is it they say about apples and trees?'

He let that question hang a few moments.

'Your father is honest, hard working,' Namur said. 'I'm sure he wants you to be the same, doesn't he?'

'Yeah.'

'Good. That's what I expected. You need a job, I'm offering you one. You'll come and work for me.'

Karim couldn't even think of a response to that one.

Benny stepped forward again. Karim flinched but soon realised it wasn't for another fight. Benny reached into his pocket, grabbed Karim's wrist and slapped a small bundle of paper into it. Karim looked down. Twenty-dollar bills. And quite a few of them.

'A down payment,' Namur said. 'You'll get more after you complete your first job for me.'

68

'What job?'

Namur smiled widely now, revealing a mouth of yellow teeth, one of which was capped in gold.

'Come back nine a.m. tomorrow, and you'll find out. Now go back to your idiot friends.'

Karim didn't need to be told twice. He was already turning before the bouncer grabbed him and pulled him out of the kitchen. The guy practically tossed him back into the foyer before the kitchen door was slammed shut, leaving Karim to anxiously wonder exactly what mess that fight with the jocks had got him into.

CHAPTER 9

Nurek, Tajikistan

Despite the sunshine in the clear blue sky it was blisteringly cold high up in the Tajik mountains, not helped by a biting wind, and Cox hunkered down into her wool scarf as she strolled away from the car to the edge of the monstrously high Nurek Dam. The deep blue water of the Vakhsh River twisted away several hundred yards below her. She headed over to the black BMW parked up in a small lay-by a few yards from the top edge of the dam wall. Outside the car, huddled into a thick ankle-length coat, Henry Flannigan was standing and looking out over the dam to the rocky valley below.

'Fancy seeing you here,' he said, glancing to Cox.

'Tell me about it.'

'The Soviets have a lot to answer for . . . but bloody hell, they could do engineering.'

Cox took a peek over the edge, taking in the scale of the over-three-hundred-yard drop. She gulped. She'd never been one for heights.

'Yeah, but it's basically just a wall, isn't it?' she said. 'What idiot can't even build a simple wall?'

Flannigan now faced her properly, one eyebrow raised. He held out a small plastic file.

'The clearance papers you need are in here. For both of you.'

'We could have just met in the city to do this,' she said, taking the file from him. 'I presume you haven't been to K-site today?'

'No. I only flew in last night. I wasn't exactly buzzing with anticipation about heading over there.'

'Long way to come just to say hi to me then.'

'I do have other business here, believe it or not.'

Cox waited for him to elaborate on that. He didn't, though it left her more than curious as to what business he could possibly have here. In the Tajik capital, Dushanbe, fifty miles away, that would be one thing, but out here?

'You've got a bit of a drive ahead of you still,' Flannigan said.

Cox shrugged. She knew that. This wasn't her first visit to K-site. Unfortunately, she'd been more times than she'd have liked, and it certainly wasn't a place she ever longed to return to.

Flannigan's eyes flicked behind her to her car in the near distance. She glanced over her shoulder, and could make out Aydin behind the glass, sitting in the front passenger seat, glaring at her.

'He doesn't want to come and say hello?' Flannigan said.

'If it bothers you, why don't you go and ask him yourself?'

Flannigan was mulling something over, Cox could tell, but he didn't say anything more as he continued to stare over to her car.

'I know you're not convinced by this—'

'That's not what I said exactly—'

'Actually I think you said, *are you fucking mental*?'

Flannigan snorted. It looked like he didn't know whether to smile or be offended by her tone.

'For anyone else, I wouldn't even have given this the time of day,' he said.

'But?'

'But . . . you and him. You seem to have a habit of making things happen. I just hope you haven't taken it all a step too far this time.'

'This plan is still a work in progress. Give me, and Aydin, a bit of time here—'

'You really think that's wise?'

'What?'

'You might be used to seeing places like K-site, but Aydin, whatever he's been through, is still just a civilian. If you ask me, getting him to sign up for your mad charade might have been more effective if you'd wined and dined him at the Ritz rather than bringing him out here.'

'No,' Cox said with absolute conviction. 'He has to see this. And he has to meet Rashid.'

Flannigan gave Cox a hard stare and it was clear he remained unconvinced.

He sighed. 'You want to hear a story?'

Cox's eyes pinched with curiosity. 'Only if it's a good one.'

'They're all good ones, if you think about the message properly. Now I never talk to anyone about this much, but you know I've been around the block.'

'And again.'

'Yet some things never change. Back in my younger days, when I was first starting out, we had an asset who everyone in the high ranks believed to be untouchable. A Russian. Actually Ukrainian, but this was when they were still part of the USSR. We were using him to gain intel on the KGB. He hated Moscow, had been hounded out of there in fear for his life . . . '

Flannigan's second mention of Russia and the Soviet Union since she'd arrived sent Cox's mind into overdrive. She'd often wondered what Flannigan had seen and done in his long career of espionage, and what he still did now on his mysterious outings . . .

' . . . I was only a junior analyst back then, but I knew of this guy because he was so important to us. Until he finally came unstuck. He was a known womaniser and playboy, and one night he went too far.'

Flannigan shook his head as though still in disbelief about whatever had happened all those years ago.

'What did he do?'

'What didn't he do? High on coke and with enough alcohol in his blood to open a distillery, he strangled his young Russian girlfriend to death. In a fucking central London hotel. And it was his young Russian girlfriend who also just happened to have family ties to the Kremlin.'

'Bloody hell.'

'Indeed. Everyone knew who was responsible. The Russians, despite our best efforts at keeping the crime low-profile in the public eye, were soon asking questions too. They wanted us to hand him over. But we couldn't just let an asset like that slip away, even after what he'd done.'

'So what happened?' Cox said, beginning to feel a sickly feeling in her stomach as she imagined the sordid affair. The political cover-up of the death of a young, innocent woman simply to save face.

'Obviously we never let the police near him. I was responsible for . . . looking after him. I interviewed him endlessly. We shared a hotel suite for weeks. I wrote a report to my bosses about him, what he'd done in his life, what he'd done for us, what had happened that night, and about the other times he'd been out of control on drink and drugs. Whether he still had any future potential as an asset for us.'

'And did he?'

Flannigan's face now screwed in disgust. 'Of course not. He was too tarnished. How could he ever get close enough to anyone that mattered again? The Russians knew it was him

73

who'd killed the woman. By now they'd even gone public themselves saying he was the murderer. They were demanding the British government either brought him to justice or extradited him. You don't remember any of this?'

'No,' Cox said, surprised by the fact. But then Flannigan had been in MI6 when she'd still been wearing nappies.

'And did they extradite him?'

'Are you joking? That wasn't even on the cards. But we also had no further official use for him. So instead, largely based on my own recommendation, we gave him a new identity and shipped him off to Liverpool.'

The story should have sounded outrageous to Cox, that her own government had knowingly let a murderer off the hook just to avoid political embarrassment, but really she wasn't surprised at all.

'I'm sensing that still isn't the end of this story,' Cox said when Flannigan remained silent, staring pensively off into the distance beyond the dam.

'Unfortunately not. We checked up on him regularly, as we knew the Russians would look for him, but a little over a year later he disappeared. Nobody knew where to. We thought they'd taken him or maybe just buried him somewhere. Until the operation I was leading to track him down finally came good.'

'You found him alive?'

'We did. But not for nearly two more years. Still in England. Back in London. Different name, different look, living the life in a lavish bachelor pad in Chelsea.'

'Seriously? How?'

'The Russians. Even though he was their enemy, they also knew we'd disowned him. Rather than assassinate him, they figured if we didn't want him any more, then they'd have him for themselves. Play him against us for a while.'

The bitterness in his voice was clear, though was he also embarrassed?

'Obviously at that point the whole position changed. There was a lot of anger, and certainly no more need to let him off the hook. He was finally arrested and charged with murder. And he would have gone down for life, no doubt at all . . . if he hadn't died on remand.'

'Died? I'm guessing—'

'We all knew he was assassinated. The Russians never cared for him, only that they had the upper hand. In many ways we didn't even care about his death. The biggest issue was that we had no idea the guy had run around London for those two years passing intel to the KGB. And he had been *our* guy originally.'

'Why are you telling me this now? What does this have to do with me? With Aydin?'

Flannigan flicked his eyes to the car again, then back to Cox.

'The only moral of this story . . . people are curious.'

'Curious? That's it?'

The story was strong, but was that really the best he could do to surmise it?

'You can never really know someone,' Flannigan said. 'You might think you know who they are, think you know where their loyalties lie. But that still won't stop them stabbing you in the back given the opportunity.'

Cox opened her mouth but she really didn't know what to say.

Flannigan put his arm on her shoulder.

'Let me know how it goes at K-site. If you do put Aydin through this, send him off to the US pretending to be someone he's not for *our* gain, don't let him off your leash for even a second.'

Flannigan took his hand back and turned away before Cox had a chance to respond. He idled back to his car. Cox stood

75

motionless for a few moments as his words reverberated in her mind, and his car was soon speeding away over the other side of the dam.

Shivering, she turned and headed for her car, still deep in thought. Aydin held her eye the entire way over.

She sank into the driver's seat and rubbed her hands together in front of the blower, trying to get some warmth back into them.

'He didn't want to say hi?' Aydin said.

Another shiver ran through Cox as the warm air inside the cabin took effect.

'I don't think he likes me much,' Aydin added.

'He doesn't need to like you,' Cox said. 'And neither do I. That's not why you're here.'

'So you don't like me?' Aydin said.

She looked over at him. She could tell he wasn't particularly bothered either way.

'Actually I do,' she said. 'But in my line of work that doesn't really mean much. What matters is that I need you.'

He seemed satisfied with that.

'He's not coming with us?' Aydin said.

'No.'

'He just happened to be in Tajikistan?'

'No. Not exactly.'

Given she knew so little of the story herself, she left it at that.

She pulled the car onto the road, her thoughts of Flannigan and his long life of espionage still rattling in her mind.

CHAPTER 10

Aydin had been to a so-called black site once before – thankfully as a visitor, not an inmate. Still he'd hoped he'd never see one again, and was more than apprehensive on the long journey through the cold and desolate mountains of Tajikistan.

After something of a rigmarole at the entrance, which had seen automatic weapons waved in their faces, Aydin, Cox, their car and their bags all thoroughly searched, and all of their electronic equipment confiscated, they were finally on the inside.

Inside the outer barbed-wire-topped chain-link fence at least.

Aydin stayed behind Cox as they were escorted through, keeping his eyes busy as he moved. He'd never been the trusting type, and there was nothing remotely comforting about the position he was now in, out in a wilderness he couldn't even see, with armed men who were edgy and unfriendly to say the least.

After a few yards the glow from the light on the guard tower by the entrance faded behind them and they were walking in near pitch black, no evidence at all of what lay in front except for the small arc of light from the torch on the guard's helmet.

'Watch your step here,' said the guard in front, who put his head down so his helmet torch lit up the stone steps that looked like they were carved directly into the hilltop – or was that just a trick of the eye in the dark?

They clambered down, and the blasting wind lessened a fraction with each step they took. Aydin could only guess they were heading down into a sheltered valley, though beyond the thin veil of light created by the guard's torch there was nothing he could see of the landscape around them.

Finally, after another fifty yards or so on the flat, they came to a thick metal door that was stuck right into the side of the rock they'd just climbed down. The guard knocked with the butt of his rifle. The clattering sound vibrated through the rock and echoed off into the distance for an almost unnatural amount of time.

The door opened. Another armed guard was standing there inside a more well-lit space.

'Follow me,' he said, ushering Cox and Aydin inside.

They both passed through and carried on in tow along a long, dank tunnel that gradually descended. Aydin peeked over his shoulder to see the guard from the gate still following. The narrow and barely seven-foot-high space was lit with archaic looking lanterns on one wall, the electricity wires powering them trailing along the wall between each light.

The tunnel carried on dead straight, and they passed closed doors on the left and right that gave no indication of what lay beyond – each of them looked like they were fitted straight into the rocks that surrounded them. Finally they stopped by a quite normal-looking door. Normal in the sense that it was a simple pine wood door with a handle and single deadbolt lock. Certainly not particularly secure.

The guard at the front knocked with his knuckles and within seconds the door swung open to reveal a casually dressed man in his thirties. With dark hair slicked back, he was tall, tanned, and athletic and looked more like a celebrity sportsman than a hermit who worked in a lightless bunker.

'Ah, Rachel, you're back,' he said with a wide smile of bright white teeth. He extended his hand to her before turning to Aydin. 'And you must be Aydin. I've heard a lot about you. I'm Rich Joyner.'

Aydin briefly shook his hand. Joyner gave a bone-crushing shake.

'Welcome to K-site,' he said. 'Or as we like to call it, the Warren. Come on in.'

How anyone in his position could be so cheery, Aydin had no clue. But he hated Joyner immediately.

Holding back his disgust at what he'd already told himself this man represented, Aydin calmly stepped inside.

Bizarrely, Joyner's living quarters inside the Warren reminded Aydin of the inside of a spaceship from the likes of *Star Trek*. Not that it was in any way ultra-modern, nor was it bright white and clinical, as was often the case in sci-fi imaginings of outer space travel. It was the fact that the room was so at odds with the barrenness that surrounded it. Not exactly a penthouse apartment by Central Park, but the large space had carpets on the floors and paintings on the walls and book-shelves filled with tomes and ornaments. The 'living room' Joyner showed them to had sofas, Hi-Fi equipment, a TV, an expensive-looking coffee machine.

Yet despite the trappings, there was nothing that could be done about the claustrophobic feel of the place – not just the lack of windows, but the very essence of the space. The way the sound didn't carry properly because of the solid walls. The smell of dankness and rock, and the texture of the machine-purified air that was thick and stifled.

79

'I know this isn't to everyone's taste,' Joyner said.

Aydin snapped from his thoughts and stared over at his host on the opposite cream leather sofa. Joyner and Cox had been deep in a conversation, firstly about goings on in London, and secondly about protocols and objectives and the like, and Aydin had more or less switched off from the whole thing.

'What isn't?' Aydin asked.

'How I live here.'

Aydin looked around him. 'I'd rather live in this part of K-site than where you keep some of your other guests.'

Joyner chuckled. 'Indeed. And I'd rather be on site, inside the Warren, where I can keep on top of business properly, than in some nice hotel fifty miles away, or even in one of the huts in the camp.'

Aydin hadn't seen the 'camp' yet, though he imagined a cluster of plainly built sandstone buildings in the valley outside the Warren, likely where the guards stationed here would stay. He also wondered whether there was more to K-site than just holding prisoners. Secret research or analysis of some sort, or was that just his overactive imagination?

'It's nothing to do with me how you live,' Aydin said. 'If it makes you feel more normal to surround yourself with material things, despite where you are, then that's your choice.'

Joyner glared, as though unsure whether he should be offended by Aydin's words or not. So far Joyner had come across as welcoming and cheery and confident – a persona which matched his looks. With his personality type he could have passed for a smarmy middle manager at any corporate company, but the fact he was actually running this place made Aydin realise with absolute conviction that Joyner's façade was nothing but a lie. What lay beneath was surely far darker and more sinister.

'Rashid knows nothing about you being here again,' Joyner said, turning his focus back to Cox.

The final word of his sentence sent Aydin's mind tumbling once more. He knew Cox had been here before. Not just because of Rashid, but Faiz Al-Busaidi too. But exactly how many times had she been? How instrumental was she in the men's treatment – or mistreatment – here? And what had the men told her?

He and Cox had held long conversations together en route, but he felt sure that she wouldn't have divulged *everything* to him. Not just because of her natural clandestine nature, but because he sensed she was, in many ways, embarrassed that the UK authorities were keeping the men in such an inhumane place.

Joyner, on the other hand, seemed to have no such qualms about K-site or what went down there.

'That's fine,' Cox said. 'How is Rashid now?'

'He's eating, but not talking much. Last time we got anything remotely coherent out of him was over two months ago. You may well have wasted your time and effort in coming here this time.' Joyner looked at his watch. 'It's late. I've prepared two beds for you in my guest rooms.'

He indicated the closed doors behind him.

'That might be a good idea,' Cox said, looking to Aydin. 'It's been a long day.'

'No,' Aydin said.

'No?' Joyner said.

'I want to see him now.'

'It's gone midnight. My guards need their rest too. As do I. And Rashid is probably sleeping. You'd—'

'Sleeping?' Aydin said. 'From what I understand you've had him in a windowless cell here for more than four years. He doesn't get an hour in the yard and three meals a day.

81

He doesn't see any daylight at all. I'm guessing he has no concept of day and night any more, and even if he did you'd probably concoct a *treatment* for him to simply disorientate that sense for your own gain.'

The room fell deathly silent except for the constant low whir of the air-purifying system. Even Aydin was a little surprised at where the sudden outburst of bitterness had come from. Did he really give two hoots how they were treating Rashid and Al-Busaidi, both suspected terrorists, here?

No. He didn't particularly. But he also didn't look favourably at men like Joyner who tried to normalise the mistreatment of such prisoners.

After initially looking pissed off by Aydin's mini rant, Joyner's face soon broke out into a wide smile.

'You're probably right,' he said. 'The guys we keep here haven't got a fucking clue what time it is. Most of them probably don't even know what year it is.' Joyner got to his feet. 'You want to do this now?'

He asked the question more to Cox than to Aydin, though she looked to him for reassurance still. He nodded.

'Yes. Please,' she said.

'Very well. Come this way.'

Joyner headed over to the door. Aydin took a deep breath, then rose to his feet.

'What was this place?' Aydin asked as he and Cox were escorted by Joyner through the twisting tunnels, past various guard posts, heading downward all the time.

'There's been a mine of some sorts in this mountain for over a thousand years,' Joyner said. 'Precious metals mostly, but also minerals. The Soviets finally exhausted what's easily accessible in the seventies. We were given the abandoned shell after Tajikistan gained independence in the nineties.'

82

'Given it?'

Joyner shrugged. 'Diplomats and their deals. What can you do?'

They passed by several more closed doors. The nature of these doors, made of thick-looking but worn down metal with small serving hatches in the centre, suggested the rooms beyond weren't lavish living quarters any more. They were cells.

'How many people are you keeping here?' Aydin asked.

'We've got space for nearly fifty,' Joyner said, glancing at Aydin, who didn't bother to seek clarification as to how many of the spaces were taken.

'This is the one,' Joyner said when they finally reached their destination. The door was much the same as the previous dozen or so that Aydin had seen. From behind a desk further along the corridor a guard stood from his post and came over.

'Open her up, please,' Joyner said.

'Yes, sir.'

The guard took the bulging keyring from his belt and turned the key in the sturdy lock. Then he knocked.

'Wakey, wakey,' he shouted as he opened the door.

The room was pitch black inside. Joyner flipped a switch on the outside and a gloomy orange bulb, recessed into the ceiling ten feet above, glowed. The walls of the cell, nine feet by nine feet, were bare concrete, scratched and stained.

The first thing to hit Aydin was the smell. Urine. Faeces. And an even more overbearing stench that Aydin couldn't describe, other than it was that of a caged human being slowly wasting away.

The cramped room was sparse, with just a filthy-looking bedpan in one corner – that was at least partly responsible for the smell – and on the opposite side, huddled in a heap on the cold floor, was a bag of bones that somehow resembled a man. Curled up into a ball, the bones of his spine were arced and protruded like that of an imagined sea monster.

The guard strode up and gently prodded the lump with his boot. Joyner, Cox and Aydin all remained on the outside looking in, as though none of them could bring themselves to enter the squalid room.

At least that was how Aydin felt.

'Wake up. You've got visitors,' the guard said.

The man didn't move at all.

The guard prodded a little more forcibly and the man moaned and shuffled.

'Jamaal, it's me. You remember me, right?' Cox said as she took a step inside.

Her smooth and almost comforting tone did the trick that the guard's boot hadn't, and the man uncoiled, his natural form taking shape.

'Leave us now,' Cox said to the guard.

He initially looked to Joyner for reassurance, who simply nodded before he retreated back outside.

'I'll leave you in Higbee's capable hands,' Joyner said. 'Anything you need, just tell him.'

Neither Cox nor Aydin acknowledged his words, both were too focused on the man in the corner. The door was closed behind them, the thud as the metal clanked into place made Aydin shudder.

Cox moved a couple of paces forward and bent down onto her haunches in front of the man who was by now sitting upright, though his head remained bowed, and Aydin could see little of his face. Wearing nothing but stained underwear, his skin was grimy. Was it bruised and bloody too in places? Aydin couldn't really tell exactly because of the filth. What was obvious, despite the mess of his skin, was that the man was painfully thin.

'Jamaal, I've brought someone to see you. He wants to talk to you.'

'*As salām 'alaykum*,' Aydin said.

A shuffle from Rashid now. He lifted his head a few inches.

'*Wa 'alaykum as salām*,' he mumbled under his breath, the words, a basic greeting, nearly incoherent.

Cox turned round and gave Aydin an impressed look, as though the basic return between the two men was some sort of triumph. They'd certainly have had others in there talking Arabic to Rashid to try and break through to him, so Aydin wasn't sure what the point of her gesture was.

'My name's Aydin Torkal,' he said. 'But my brothers used to call me Talatashar.'

Talatashar. The number thirteen in Arabic. Aydin's former identity within the terrorist cell he'd graduated with at the Farm.

Cox now gave him a more stern look, as though his mention of his former life was out of order, or would in some way spark an abrupt unwanted reaction from Rashid. But he wouldn't have a clue what Aydin was talking about. In the moment, seeing the young man so vulnerable, it just felt like Aydin putting himself back to a point of time in his own life of overbearing vulnerability was the right thing to do.

Rashid lifted his head further up and for the first time his eyes connected with Aydin's, whose skin prickled. Not because he was shocked at seeing the shell of a man before him, but because of what he saw in Rashid's defeated eyes.

Himself.

CHAPTER 11

Manistee National Forest, Michigan

'You've been up here before?' Karim said to Namur who was up front in the Jeep Grand Cherokee with the driver, who Karim knew only as Tamir.

Benny was sitting next to Karim in the back, along with Raf, who Karim likewise knew little about, but had decided was the least respected of the men who'd come along.

'Yeah,' Namur said.

Karim hadn't. For good reason. There was nothing here. They'd been in the car now for what felt like an eternity. For at least the last hour they'd been on a single-track road with nothing to see outside but snow-covered trees.

'So he knows where we're going?' Karim said. 'We're not just driving ourselves into desolation?'

A couple of amused grunts, but no meaningful response.

That was about the usual whenever he piped up with a question. Karim had only known these men for a few days, but he was still clearly the outsider. He was by far the youngest of the group, and in many ways he almost felt like he was Namur's plaything. Never quite brought into the mix about what they were doing or why, as though it made Namur feel all the more powerful to string Karim along.

Like today. Namur had said they were going hunting. That was it. No invitation exactly, no instructions about what to expect. Karim had simply been told to grab his coat and get in the car and off they went.

This trip had followed three previous days where Namur had likewise kept Karim close. Had had him carry out multiple random errands as part of his new 'job'. Dropping off or picking up people, or parcels. Getting food, drinks.

As pointless and at times as demeaning as it was, Karim went along with it all. For starters Namur had given him more than a thousand dollars so far for his 'help'. Plus, more than that, he remained intrigued as to what this group was about. He saw the way others within their community looked at Namur. Part envy, part . . . not fear exactly, but something close to it.

Is that how Karim wanted to be looked at by others too?

In some ways yes. In fact, he'd already noticed some of those similar looks coming his way from his own friends, though to a large extent they were mostly jealous that he was apparently now in with the big boys and they weren't.

'What are we hunting anyway?' Karim asked.

Namur turned round, an eyebrow raised. 'You've been in this car for over four hours and you suddenly decide you're interested in what we're hunting?'

'To be honest I hadn't realised we'd be so long. Otherwise I would have asked much sooner.'

Namur smiled and turned back round.

'Deer. Among other things.'

'Where are we going to put a deer? Tie it to the fender?'

'No. We've a pick-up truck too.'

That was the first Karim had heard about that. So where was the truck and who was in it?

Not long afterwards Tamir turned down a track that was barely wide enough for their vehicle. The following twenty minutes were tediously slow. The twisting trail wasn't just narrow, it was hellishly uneven too, the bumps sending all of the occupants shooting out of their seats, and more than once Karim thought they were well and truly stuck only for Tamir to somehow get the Jeep's wheels kicking again. Finally, in the near distance, in a clearing of trees where over a foot of fallen snow lay untouched except for a single set of tyre tracks, Karim saw a Ford F-150 parked up. No one was in sight by it.

Tamir parked next to the Ford. He shut the engine down and the non-stop whir of the car's heaters halted, and Karim was sure the temperature of the cabin dropped in that instant.

'Let's go,' Namur said, and each of the five men stepped out into the bitter cold.

Karim was shivering within seconds. Even with his over-coat on, gloves, hat, and more layers than he could count underneath, he was still freezing. The temperature here felt far lower than it had been in Dearborn that morning, and it had been damn cold there already.

'Karim, come here.'

Karim snapped from his morose thoughts and headed to the back of the Jeep where Namur was dishing out gear. Hi-vis jackets for each of them. A couple of rucksacks, the biggest and heaviest of which was shoved Karim's way. He also pulled out four rifles, each with scopes attached.

'I don't get a gun?' Karim asked, when it became clear he was the odd one out.

'Not this time,' Namur said.

'Then what am I here for?' He sounded as grumpy as he by now felt.

'To watch and learn.'

And to lug your damn gear around, he thought but didn't say.

Plus he really had no interest in learning about hunting. What was the point of it even? He'd much rather have been inside JL's with his friends talking shit.

What could he say though? *Sorry, I'll just sit in the car if you don't mind.*

'It's this way,' Namur said, leading them off towards an indistinct trail through the trees.

To make matters worse, after ten minutes of walking they passed over the crest of a hill and all of a sudden there was what felt like a hurricane blasting icy air straight into their faces.

'People actually pay to do this?' Karim said.

The fact he got no response whatsoever either meant the men were now ignoring his constant grumbles, or they just hadn't heard him because of the ridiculous wind.

Luckily, they soon turned and were heading down into a small valley and the wind died down to next to nothing. Which Namur took as his opportunity to explain to Karim about hunting. The main dos and don'ts. Essentially explaining how not to get his head blown off either by their own party, or by other hunters out there.

Other hunters? Was anyone else really mad enough to be all the way out here on a day like this?

'That's them,' Benny said, pointing off to the right.

Karim searched off in that direction. Could see nothing but tree trunks and snow to start with. But sure enough, in the near distance, he could make out the outline of two figures. Neither of them were wearing hi-vis though. In fact, as the five of them approached the others, Karim realised it wasn't two, but three people out there.

The figures finally became clearer. Two men. One older, one younger – a similar age to Karim. The third was a girl. Well, not a girl, a teenager. What the hell?

And Karim knew her. She was a junior at a school just outside Dearborn. She'd played in the same softball team as Karim's younger brother at one point.

'Aliya?' Karim said. She didn't react at all. Karim turned to Namur. 'What is this?'

Aliya was standing between the two men, were they holding on to her? She was shaking violently, though whether it was fear or cold or both Karim didn't know.

'This is the hunt,' Namur said with a satisfied grin.

They came to a stop a few yards away from the threesome. The men, the older one in particular, looked somewhat shell-shocked. Who were they? Aliya's father and brother?

'You told her?' Namur asked the older man.

He shook his head. 'She knows.'

'Good. Then do it.'

'No!' Aliya screamed.

She clearly sensed the inevitable and went to make a dash for it. To where, who knew, but her desperation was obvious. The younger man – her brother? – grabbed her arms, wrestled with her for a moment as she tried to writhe free from his grip. He managed to snake his hands around her, pinning her arms to her sides. Her father looked on, squirming. No, not squirming, Karim realised, he was ready to pounce. Karim saw what was in his hands. A clear plastic bag.

'Now!' the brother screamed and Aliya's father whipped the bag up and over her head and yanked the ends back, pulling the plastic tight around her neck.

Aliya's screams died down to muffled, choked yelps. The two men continued to jostle with her as she fought for her life. The bag was billowing in and out as she tried in vain to get a fresh breath of air. Condensation soon dripped down the inside of the bag, her oxygen-starved breath fogging over the plastic until her face all but disappeared.

Karim looked on, mouth open, eyes wide, but said and did nothing. When he glanced at Namur and the other men he saw the look of resolute determination on each of their faces, and he quickly tried his best to follow suit.

In front of him, in a final desperate attempt to free herself, Aliya kicked out. Then her legs went from under her and she and her father collapsed to the ground, her on top of him. He shouted in anger and pain as his arm came around her throat, and he choked the last breaths out of his daughter.

Her movements became more laboured. The father's face was contorted with effort, veins throbbing, his cheeks puffed, his teeth gnashed . . .

Finally Aliya went still.

'Get up,' Namur said after a few moments of quiet as Aliya's father tried to get his breathing back under control.

A tear escaped his eye — sorrow or just the effect of his exertion, or the cold? — and the father pushed the body of his daughter away and shakily got to his feet. He looked over at his son whose features were several shades paler now.

'You did what you had to do,' Namur said with little emotion.

'We only did what you asked,' the father said. He sounded broken.

Namur turned to Karim. 'Do you understand what you've just seen?'

Understand? Understand what? That a father and brother had just murdered a defenceless teenage girl?

'Family honour,' Karim found himself saying.

'Her actions caused this,' Namur said, nodding. 'Respect for our values, respect for your family, is everything. Without honour you are not a real Muslim.'

Karim looked at the two men. Had they really killed her out of honour though? Or because Namur had demanded it?

Did it make a difference?

'But these men are also murderers now,' Namur said. He spat on the ground. 'They killed a helpless young Muslim woman. God will not look favourably upon them for this.'

The father and son shared a look, both far more nervous now. They stepped closer together as though they'd have more strength that way.

Namur turned to Karim. He pulled a handgun from his coat and offered it to Karim.

'Shoot them,' he said.

'What?'

'Take the gun, and shoot these men. They are murderers. They have to be punished.'

'I . . . but you told—'

'They have blood on their hands. Not me.'

Karim couldn't think what to say.

'I thought you wanted to be a man?' Namur growled. 'I thought you wanted to punish non-believers? To punish people who bring disgrace to our way of life.'

'I . . . I do, but—'

'Take the gun.'

Karim did now, though he had to fight to stop his hand from shaking.

'Shoot them. Show them, show *me*, that you are indeed a man. A man deserving of my time.'

Karim tried his best to push rational thinking to the side. Frankly, if he refused, then what would Namur do to *him*? The chances of him getting away from this wilderness alive were zero.

There really was no choice.

He lifted the gun and pointed it at the father.

'No, please!'

Karim pulled the trigger.

Click.

He pulled again.

Click.

Nothing.

Click. Click.

There was laughing all around him now. Almost all around him anyway. The father and son certainly weren't in on the joke it seemed.

Namur stepped over and snatched the gun back.

'I can't believe you would actually shoot these two,' Namur said with a monstrous grin on his face as he pushed the gun into his pocket. 'These are good men, Karim! Honourable men. Look at what they did to protect our values?'

Namur stepped forward and hugged each of the men in turn. They didn't react at all to his bizarre behaviour. Clearly they were even more shocked by the whole experience than Karim.

Namur came back over to Karim now, put a hand on his shoulder.

'Of course I didn't want you to shoot these two . . . but the main point is, you would have done. For me.'

Namur slapped Karim lightly across the face. Then shouted over to Benny. 'Get him a shovel.'

Benny nodded and stepped over and behind the two men. Karim hadn't even noticed before but there was a pile of three shovels there, sunken into the snow. Benny grabbed them all. He handed one to the father, one to the son, and the last to Karim.

'You've not long until dark,' Namur said. 'Best get digging.'

CHAPTER 12

Nurek, Tajikistan

Aydin sat, jaw clenched in frustration, as Jamaal Rashid, whimpering like a small child, was escorted out of the interview room by the armed guard. The door was closed with a thunk, but not locked.

'You OK?' Cox asked.

Aydin sighed in response as his brain rumbled away. He and Cox had spent several hours of each of the last two days with Rashid. Sometimes in his cell, but more often in this much more pleasant, though still decidedly grim and claustrophobic interview room. At least the interview room had furniture and proper lighting and didn't stink of shit, though Aydin was still left to wonder what more sinister activities than 'interviewing' took place there. Judging by the initial look of terror on Rashid's face each time he was brought in, and the soft whimpering of relief each time he was taken back out unscathed, Aydin felt sure the room held dark secrets.

Although, were they really secrets, or just unspoken truths?

So far, all of the time and effort spent with Rashid had been for nothing as far as Aydin could tell. Rashid had given them nothing more than a few mumbled words. And Aydin honestly didn't believe that it was because he was holding out, but more because he was simply incapable now of conversing.

Rashid was broken, well and truly. Beyond repair, as far as Aydin could see. It hadn't mattered what tactic Aydin and Cox had tried, or what they'd tried to talk to Rashid about. At one time Aydin had spoken at length about his own horrific past, his time on the Farm, the aftermath, the death of his sister and mother and father, hoping that Rashid might see some sort of shared pain and torment in their lives. Rashid had said nothing in response. At least the retelling of the most harrowing moments of his life had, in some small way, had a cathartic effect for Aydin.

But it was to no avail, at least in terms of breaking into Rashid's head, and by the end of it all, Aydin was left with one predominant emotion. Anger. Though he wasn't quite sure who it was directed at.

'Don't look so defeated,' Cox said, snapping Aydin from his thoughts. 'We're not here to help him. We're here for you to learn about him, so you can impersonate him. That's it.'

Aydin looked over to her. 'I know that,' he said.

'I know what you're thinking,' Cox said.

Aydin was sure she really didn't.

'You see a lot of yourself in him. And you see how easily you could have ended up in a place like this, and in a state like he is.'

Was she right about that? It was true Aydin was shocked at just how damaged a young man had become in the care of the British government. Would Rashid ever even leave this place alive? Would there be any point in him leaving now, given his brain was mush?

'Rashid is a prisoner here for good reason,' Cox said. 'Please don't forget that. Outside of these walls you would have regarded him as an enemy. And I've seen what you're happy to do to enemies.'

'But he's no one's enemy in here. He's just a young man who's been broken beyond repair for no particular reason other than the satisfaction of Joyner and the other sadists who work here.'

'Rashid is a terrorist. Would you say the same thing about Wahid?' Mention of his 'brother' sent a wave of anger coursing through Aydin. 'Do you want us to move him to a nice swanky hotel where he gets room service every day just so he doesn't get too upset?'

Aydin ground his teeth rather than respond to that one. He could see her point, in a way. Though that didn't mean that he didn't still feel sympathy for Rashid.

Why was that though?

Nonetheless, to compare Rashid to Wahid was ludicrous. One was a murderous monster. As far as he could see, the other was a once-disillusioned young man who'd not even got so far as taking up arms before the British government had dragged him off to a black site to serve a life sentence of torture and abuse.

'I'm finished with Rashid,' Aydin said. 'I don't need to see him again.'

Cox looked as surprised as she was unconvinced. 'You're sure? You've got enough?'

'Enough what? What are we gaining here if he's not even talking to us? I've met him, I've spent time with him. Together with the information I already have I've got enough to be him.'

Cox still didn't look so sure. 'It has to be faultless,' she said. 'If there's any chance of you coming across someone who knew him, you *have* to be him.'

Aydin said nothing. He got it.

'But if you're sure?'

'I'm sure.'

She sighed. 'I must say the prospect of leaving this place is always a welcome one. I'll go tell Joyner. He'll probably be delighted to see the back of us.'

'But first . . . ' Aydin said. He opened his mouth to ask the question, but couldn't quite bring himself to do it. Instead he just sighed.

'What is it?'

'I want to speak to Faiz Al-Busaidi.'

Cox scoffed. 'No.'

'No?'

'He's not relevant to you.'

'Not relevant? He's the reason I'm here.'

'Rashid is the reason you're here.'

'This whole operation is based off intelligence from Al-Busaidi. It's because of what he knows that you've concocted this plan to send me to America.'

'Intelligence which you've already been party to. You don't need to see or speak to him.'

'Yet that's what I'm demanding.'

'Demanding?'

'I won't be part of your pet project unless you give me some time with him.'

'For what end?'

'Rachel, I just need to. You say he knows Aziz Al-Addad's brother, Nasir? The brother of the man who moulded me into *this*. Al-Busaidi knows the man I'm supposed to be tapping up in the US. How is that not relevant? And please, don't forget, but this is far more personal for me than for anyone else in this place.'

'Which is exactly why I said no. What good could come of you meeting him? It's *too* personal.'

'But you're going to let me do it anyway.' He paused. She said nothing. 'Please, Rachel. Don't let your plan fall apart over one little thing.'

She sighed, and was looking seriously apprehensive, though the fact she was even considering it told Aydin he was nearly there in convincing her.

'It's not my decision,' she said.

'Joyner?'

'Joyner. And I'm positive he won't like the idea. Faiz has only been here a few weeks—'

'What? They haven't had time to completely scramble his brain yet?'

Cox flicked Aydin a scolding look.

'Please?' he said. 'Will you ask him?'

'*We'll* ask him.'

Aydin smiled. 'Then what are we waiting for?'

'No fucking way,' Joyner said, waving the suggestion away with his hand as he sat back on his comfy sofa.

Cox, standing next to Aydin in Joyner's private living room, looked over and gave him a 'told you so' look.

'Why not?' Aydin asked. 'What difference does it make to you?'

'The difference is I'm in charge here. So what I say goes.'

'No. You're just a caretaker,' Aydin said. 'Not a decision-maker. You agree or we just take this higher up the chain.'

'You little shit,' Joyner said, now sitting forward and scrunching his face. 'You're in no position—'

'Aydin, reel it in a bit, please?' Cox said.

He bit his tongue at that, more irked that Joyner seemed to enjoy the reprimand than at Cox for giving it.

'But seriously, Aydin has a point,' Cox said, much to his surprise. 'I've known you a long time, Rich, and I don't want to have to go above you. We can be reasonable here surely?'

'Al-Busaidi, just like every other prisoner here, is my responsibility. I have a very strict process I like to follow with—'

'A strict process?' Aydin said. 'Is that the newest euphemism for torture?'

'No. It's a euphemism for we keep dangerous criminals here who if they were let out onto the streets would kill countless innocent civilians, and the purpose of them being here under my care is so that we can learn everything they know so we can identify more rotten apples on the outside and protect more innocent lives.'

He looked smug with his own response which only riled Aydin further.

'The point is,' Joyner said, looking back to Cox now, a show that he was done with Aydin, 'if you want us to continue getting good intel out of this guy then we can't derail what we've started. How is that in anyone's interest? It's simply too soon to be throwing fresh fish at him.'

'Fresh fish?' Aydin said. 'I've been called a lot of things . . .'

'I'm sure you have.'

'Aydin, button it,' Cox said.

He rolled his eyes but decided to do as he was told.

'Come on,' Cox said. 'One meeting with me and Aydin—'

'No,' Aydin said. 'Just, me—'

'Aydin, will you just let me deal with this.'

'Careful, boy,' Joyner said with a smug smile. 'She'll send you to your room if you're not careful.'

Aydin felt like flinging himself at the guy, but he managed to hold himself back, and his irritation inside. Just about.

'No need, Joyner,' Cox said in her strictest headmistress tone. It got Joyner's attention again. 'I'm trying to compromise here. Give me and Aydin an hour with Al-Busaidi. I've seen him before and you didn't get your knickers in a twist then. There's little difference in Aydin being in there with me. One hour. Then we're done here.'

It was far from what Aydin wanted, but he supposed it was better than nothing.

'One hour?' Joyner said.

'One hour. In the interview room. You can sit and watch through the one-way mirror in the adjoining room if you like. Hell, bring all your friends and some popcorn. Let us do that, then we get out of your hair for good.'

Surely he had to like that idea?

Joyner sighed but said nothing. He looked from Cox to Aydin and back again.

'I heard a lot about you,' Joyner said, turning his focus back to Aydin once more.

'Yeah?' Aydin said, sounding calm and nonchalant though really he was pissed off with whatever Joyner was trying to insinuate.

'You're one messed up kid.'

'And I didn't even have to be put through your process to get me there.'

'No. You didn't. But you've teetered pretty damn close to earning yourself a position here. It's only because of the respect I have for Cox that I let you onto my site in the first place. And it's only because of the respect I have for her that I'm going to give in to her request. This time.'

'Thank you,' Cox said.

Aydin wasn't feeling quite so thankful himself.

'So you've both got your hour. But listen to me, Aydin. I *don't* trust you. Not even a little. And I like you even less. You say one thing in that room I disapprove of, do one thing that I don't like, and I'll haul you out of there and into your own little welcome cell myself. Is that clear?'

'Yeah,' Aydin said. 'Whatever you say, *Boss*.'

'Aydin, just quit while you're ahead, yeah?' Cox said. She turned back to Joyner. 'So when? We're ready now, and I know you can't wait to see the back of us.'

'Not yet. He's bang in the middle of . . . therapy.' The way he said the last word made Aydin's skin crawl. 'Give me two hours.'

'Fine,' Cox said. 'Thank you. We'll go and get some prep done.'

Joyner nodded as he continued to glare at Aydin.

'Come on, Aydin.'

Cox grabbed his arm to pull him away. One thing was for sure, Aydin would sorely love to give that man a taste of his own . . .

CHAPTER 13

Some of the prisoners had been inside the Warren with no sunlight or fresh air for years. Aydin had only been inside for a few days, yet he was already feeling disorientated, his body and brain losing sense of night and day. There was nothing a digital clock screen could do about that. With time to spare before they met Al-Busaidi, he decided to get some much-needed natural light and fresh air.

Getting out of the Warren was as much a task as getting inside, with numerous guard posts to pass through until finally that thick metal door was opened and a swathe of bright orange light burst into his face. He squinted from the brightness as he stepped outside, Cox right behind. The temperature drop as they moved from in to out was as extreme as the light levels. It was freezing. Possibly as much as minus ten or fifteen, and with no overcoat on, Aydin was soon shivering vigorously.

Still, the mountain air tasted damn good.

Mid-afternoon, the sun was already creeping behind the rise of rock directly in front of them. Within a few minutes it would be gone for the day and the temperature would dip further. At least in the enclosed valley they were spared the wind.

Aydin cupped his hands to his mouth and blew.

'We'll be away from this place soon enough,' Cox said.

Aydin looked across to the bottom of the valley to the mini-village there that consisted of a series of basic stone-built shelters now used by the guards and other 'workers' at K-site. The dwellings looked like they'd been there for hundreds of years, probably dating back to when the mines in the area were still heaving.

'Forget about the prisoners here,' Cox said. 'I don't exactly envy the workers much either.'

'You mean because they have to see Joyner every day?'

He could tell she was trying not to smile at that.

'No. I meant stuck in this wilderness, nothing to see or do. Might as well be the surface of Mars. And I know you've taken a disliking to Joyner, but he's really not that bad.'

'You think?'

'He's not dealing with nice people here, Aydin.'

He didn't bother to respond to that. Really he wasn't sure himself why he was suddenly so against the interrogation methods used at K-site. Cox had intimated herself that it wasn't like he wanted his own enemies to be put through a 'normal' judicial process. He wanted them to suffer. He wanted them dead. Yet what he was seeing at K-site was still hard for him to take on so many levels, largely because he saw so much of himself in Rashid, and he could quite easily imagine, having been essentially imprisoned for much of his childhood at the Farm and brainwashed there, what it would be like to be in Rashid's shoes. In fact, maybe he would still end up like that one day if he got on the wrong side of the wrong people at MI6. He would never truly be one of them, that was for sure.

'Come on, let's get inside,' Cox said.

Up ahead the last glimpse of darkening sun disappeared behind the mountain sending a renewed shiver through Aydin.

'Yeah, come on,' he said.

After eating and resting and re-reading some of the notes he'd been given on Rashid, it was soon time for Aydin and Cox's final meeting at K-site, and they were both once again travelling back towards the interview room, Joyner taking the lead.

'You'll be alone in the room with him,' Joyner said. 'Like you requested. But I'm watching from next door, and I'll have a guard right outside the door at all times. It won't be locked.'

'I don't understand the significance,' Aydin said. 'Are you expecting him to attack us?'

'I'm just being prepared.'

'Aydin's got a point,' Cox said. 'Has Al-Busaidi been violent in here before?'

'These are just necessary precautions,' Joyner said. 'Nothing to get wound up about.'

Though Aydin didn't quite buy that. Why such a different protocol for Al-Busaidi than it had been for Rashid? What was Joyner not telling them? And what did that mean for his own plan? He'd already had to compromise by having Cox in there with him, now Joyner was right there watching and listening too.

They reached the room and Joyner knocked. The unlocked door was opened from the inside by one of the ubiquitous armed guards. Joyner leaned forward and muttered something into the guy's ear. He nodded, then stepped out of the room.

Joyner turned to Cox and Aydin. 'He's all yours.'

Aydin stepped inside first, then frowned when he saw the man behind the desk, sack covering his head.

'He's had a shot of adrenaline to wake him up,' Joyner said as Cox headed in behind Aydin. 'I'll let one of you two do the honours.'

With that Joyner slammed the door shut. The noise made Al-Busaidi jump. No locks were turned. The first sign of anything untoward and the guards would descend in a flash . . .

Cox and Aydin shared a look as they stared at Al-Busaidi. Aydin nodded, then tentatively stepped towards the man. Much like Rashid, Al-Busaidi was also semi-naked, wearing only dirtied underwear and a once-white t-shirt that had ridden up over his protruding potbelly. He was more obtrusively shackled than Rashid had been; the cuffs on his wrists and ankles connected by a chain so that he couldn't even reach his hands up far enough to have them on the desk.

Aydin reached out and Al-Busaidi flinched when his fingers brushed the fabric of the hood. Aydin gripped the sack and hauled it off in one swift movement. He'd seen pictures of Al-Busaidi, though his once-thick beard had been recently shaved off, as had the hair on his head, leaving painful-looking scuffs and scratches all over.

Al-Busaidi's angry eyes were on Aydin immediately. His face contorted in distaste, his lips puckered before he spat a mouthful of phlegm. The glob landed on Aydin's chin and dripped down onto his sweatshirt.

'You fu—'

'Aydin!'

He paused, fist clenched, and had to try really hard to hold the anger in when he saw the smirk on Al-Busaidi's face.

'Sit down,' Cox said.

Aydin wiped away the remnants of the spit with his sleeve, took a deep breath then went and sat next to Cox, his keen eyes never once leaving Al-Busaidi.

'You,' Al-Busaidi said in his native Arabic as his eyes locked on to Cox.

'Hello again, Faiz,' Cox said, herself switching to Arabic seamlessly.

105

'You bitch.'

Cox said nothing to that. She looked to Aydin, as if to prompt him to begin. After all, it was he who wanted to be in the room with this man.

The initial back and forth conversation over the next ten minutes told Aydin that Al-Busaidi was a different proposition to Jamaal Rashid. Granted, this man had only been at K-site a few weeks, versus Rashid's more than four years, and while there was clear evidence of his physical abuse there – bruises on his torso, arms and face, the heavy black bags under his eyes a sign of severe sleep deprivation – he remained lucid, mostly, possibly helped by the shot of adrenaline Joyner mentioned.

That said, he wasn't exactly fully coherent, nor one hundred per cent with it. His speech was slurred. He got spaced out easily, his attention span was like a child's. But he wasn't a broken man. Yet. An air of contempt and anger remained throughout.

Despite his apparent togetherness, Cox and MI6 had already forced useful intelligence out of this man. About the plotting taking place in the US under the watch of Nasir Al-Addad. At least, that's what Cox had told Aydin, though he was beginning to question now whether this man sitting before him really was the source. He didn't look much like a man on the edge who was willing to sacrifice the most secret information. How had they persuaded him to talk?

Regardless, Aydin was in the room with Al-Busaidi for one clear reason. And he wouldn't get a second opportunity.

'How do you know Aziz Al-Addad?' Aydin asked.

By now Al-Busaidi was in a momentary lull, his head bowed. Aydin's question did nothing to stir him.

'You've heard of Aziz Al-Addad, haven't you?' Aydin said again. 'People know him as the Teacher.'

Al-Busaidi mumbled something under his breath. Aydin could feel Cox's eyes burning into him. He'd told her this was the reason for him wanting to speak to Al-Busaidi. To learn what the man knew of the Al-Addad brothers. She'd warned him it would be fruitless. That Al-Busaidi would either lie or obfuscate.

But Aydin wasn't so sure about that. After all, he hadn't explained to Cox exactly what he was planning to say – or do – in order to get what he wanted.

'Faiz, can you hear me?' Aydin asked.

'Yes.'

'Tell me what you know about Aziz Al-Addad?'

A snort. 'He's dead.'

'Except he isn't.'

A shuffle from Cox, though she said nothing.

'He's locked up in a place just like this. Vermin, just like you. He's locked up because I helped MI6 to catch him.'

Al-Busaidi now lifted his head.

'Have you heard of the Farm?' Aydin asked.

Another snort from Al-Busaidi.

'I was brought up there.'

A strange flicker in Al-Busaidi's eyes now. Respect? Fear?

'I was taken from my home by my father to that place. Al-Addad is responsible for the man I've become.'

Al-Busaidi said nothing now.

'Tell me what you know about that place,' Aydin said.

Al-Busaidi closed and opened his eyes but no words passed his lips. Aydin could sense Cox was getting restless, as though she believed the tame questioning was pointless.

Which it mostly was. So far.

'This is the only time you and I will see one another,' Aydin said. 'So you need to tell me what you know now.'

Al-Busaidi raised his eyebrows and looked away.

'Aziz's brother, Nasir, is now in the United States?'

Nothing from Al-Busaidi. He was staring at the wall at the side of the room.

'I'll be going there soon to meet him,' Aydin said. 'I'm going to infiltrate his gang. I'm going to tear them apart from the inside. And, hopefully, by the time I'm finished, they will all be dead.'

'Aydin?'

He looked over at Cox. She looked pissed off. Because of the veiled threat or because he was giving away intel? But what was Al-Busaidi going to do with it?

'I'll kill them all myself if I have to,' Aydin said, bitterness dripping from every word. 'You know why?'

Still nothing from Al-Busaidi, who now struggled to keep his head up. The last thing Aydin needed was the guy drifting.

'Because I made a promise to myself. A promise that I would seek out every single person responsible for the Farm. And that I would see them punished. Are you one of those people, Faiz?'

Aydin glanced at Cox who was now looking a little more nervous than before.

'Faiz. Listen to what I just said. I'm a product of the Farm. Do you know what that place did to boys like me? Have you any idea what we're capable of?'

Aydin stooped down to try to catch Al-Busaidi's eye, but the guy looked away. Time for a different tactic.

'I heard what you did to your wife,' Aydin said. 'Now that was cold.'

Aydin dug into his pocket and took out the folded printouts. His eyes flicked to Cox. He could sense her unease but she didn't say anything.

'This is your son, I believe?'

Aydin pushed the photo across the table. With his hands and ankles shackled together underneath, Al-Busaidi had no way of picking up the picture, but his eyes soon found it.

'Five years old. What do you think will become of him now?'

Aydin could tell Al-Busaidi was gritting his teeth.

'Last I heard he was going to be adopted by an American-born family. That must really sting.'

Again, Aydin knew Cox was staring at him. For good reason. She hadn't told him any of this. He'd had to figure it all out the hard way. His own research, back in London before they'd left for Tajikistan.

'And I know that Rachel is clued in to this part. But, Rachel . . . ' Aydin now turned to face her. 'Did you also know that Faiz had a mistress?'

The look on her face suggested she didn't. He turned back to Al-Busaidi again who had lifted his head, his glare set on Aydin.

'I'd show you a picture of her too, but I'm afraid I didn't bring one. You see, doing so would have tipped off MI6 as to her identity. But I'm going to keep that one to myself.'

Al-Busaidi's cheeks and his neck were reddening. Anger.

'I'm presuming, therefore, that MI6 also don't know about your *other* son and daughter.'

Aydin shoved that picture across the table. He was surprised that Cox was remaining tight-lipped at this point.

'Ibrahim and Habiba. Six and nine years old. You really kept that quiet very well. Although not quiet enough.'

Al-Busaidi still said nothing, but the way the sinews in his neck and shoulders were now bulging told Aydin that he wasn't just angry, he was livid, his every muscle tensed, ready to explode.

'Ask yourself one question, Faiz. Why haven't I given this information to MI6 already?'

Al-Busaidi's eyes met Aydin's once again.

'It's really quite simple. Leverage. Tell me what you know about the Farm. About the Al-Addad brothers. Tell me everything now. Or when I leave this place, guess who I'm going to pay a visit to?'

'Aydin, come on—'

'Rachel, stay out of this,' Aydin said, his voice only raised slightly above normal. He was still remarkably calm, despite the torment in his head, though his foot was now tapping furiously as his inner rage took hold.

He knew he couldn't hold it in for much longer.

Particularly if Al-Busaidi had his head set on keeping his mouth shut.

'Shall I tell you what I'll do to them when I find them?' Aydin said. 'Some tricks I learned back at the Farm. Tricks that would make your treatment here seem like a pleasure cruise.'

'I've never seen those kids before,' Al-Busaidi said, though it wasn't even slightly convincing.

No, enough was enough. No point in fighting it any longer. He'd never expected Al-Busaidi to just open up. In fact, he'd kind of hoped the meeting would come to this.

Aydin burst to his feet. Both Al-Busaidi and Cox reeled back. Aydin grabbed his chair, hauled it above his head and swung it in an arc with as much venom as he could muster. The wood smashed against the wall. The back of the chair carved off from the seat.

'Aydin!'

He ignored Cox's plea. Still holding the back, he rushed to the door. Could hear the shouts and the footsteps outside. He grunted as he jammed the broken wood under the handle, wedging it against the floor. Not a second later there was a slam on the outside of the door. A clattering thump, then another, as one of the guards – most likely – tried to charge

110

the door with his shoulder. The door remained firmly shut. They weren't getting in that easily.

Aydin spun round. Cox was out of her seat.

'You need to stop this,' she said, her tone of authority. She'd need more than that to get Aydin to listen now.

He flexed his wrist and the flick-knife hidden in his sleeve poked out. He grasped it with his other hand, flicked out the three-inch blade.

'Aydin, no! This is crazy!'

'Rachel, just shut up,' he shouted, pointing the knife at her. The fury in his voice was enough to cause her to take a half-step away from him, sheltering behind her chair and the desk. Aydin kicked the desk over. Al-Busaidi was shaking with fear now. So he should be.

Another thump on the door. Aydin could hear Joyner screaming profanities. It almost made him smile.

In the corner of his eye Aydin saw movement. Cox coming for him. Did she really expect she'd be able to tackle him? Aydin side-stepped and lashed out with his free arm. The bottom of his open-palmed hand connected with the bundle of nerves at the base of Cox's neck and she collapsed into a heap on the floor.

Aydin looked down at her for a second. He hadn't wanted to hurt her. But she should have known better.

Aydin turned and launched his boot into Al-Busaidi's midriff, sending him and his chair backwards and he clattered to the ground. Aydin jumped on top and stuck his knee into Al-Busaidi's windpipe. He dug down until the prisoner rasped for breath and his eyes bulged.

'If you want your woman and those kids to live, tell me what you know.'

He released the pressure just enough to give Al-Busaidi room to speak. The guy should have taken the opportunity.

'I don't . . . know anything!'

'Wrong.'

Aydin grabbed at Al-Busaidi's hands. Already clasped together by the cuffs, he had his fists curled tight. Aydin thumped his elbow into Al-Busaidi's chest to help convince him to release the grip and he managed to prise them open.

He took hold of a finger.

'Tell me about Al-Addad!'

Al-Busaidi said nothing.

Aydin yanked back as hard as he could until he heard the crunch of bone. Al-Busaidi screamed in pain. Aydin tugged again and the skin and tendons tore with a sickening squelch, the digit more or less cleaved off.

Aydin took another finger.

There was another boom at the door. This time it gave an inch and as Aydin looked up he could see the strain of the chair-back. Before long it would splinter and the door would fly open.

'Were you involved with the Farm!'

'No!' Al-Busaidi shouted.

Aydin twisted the finger and heard another crack. Then he took the knife. He pushed the blade down onto the web of skin between thumb and forefinger. The sharp edge dug straight through and blood oozed as Al-Busaidi's body flinched and bucked.

'Tell me!' Aydin screamed. 'You want me to do this to your children?'

'Aydin, please, stop.'

Cox. Her voice was desperate and pleading. Aydin glanced at her. She was propping herself up on her elbow but she looked out of it and didn't have the strength even to get to her feet. Even if she could, Aydin wasn't sure she would

112

have tried anything stupid again. Unlike Al-Busaidi, she knew exactly what Aydin was capable of.

Another crash at the door. This time Aydin heard the wood cracking. He only had seconds left.

He cursed Joyner. If he and Al-Busaidi had been afforded time alone together, it would surely have been a different story. Perhaps now Cox understood Aydin's request.

Aydin removed his knee. He dug his hand under Al-Busaidi and hauled up his torso before he wrapped his arm around the prisoner's head, yanking it back to expose the neck. He pushed the tip of the blade up against his skin.

'Do the honourable thing,' Aydin said. 'Save your children. What do you know?'

Al-Busaidi was now whimpering. 'The Farm. It . . . it was . . .'

A crash the other side of the room and the wood from the broken chair gave way and the door finally flung open.

'Drop the knife!' came the shout of the first guard who barged through. He was closely followed by two others. No sign of Joyner.

'It was what!' Aydin shouted.

'It . . .'

'Drop the knife!'

Aydin didn't. A moment later gunfire erupted. Except it wasn't like normal gunfire. More muted. Like a put-put. There was a stabbing pain in Aydin's neck. In his arm. Two. Three. Four shots. He let go of Al-Busaidi. Not because he wanted to, but because he realised he didn't have the strength to hold him.

'Drop it!'

The knife was still in his hand. He looked down. Another stab of pain in his abdomen. The knife clattered to the ground. He hadn't even intended to release it.

He looked up. His vision was blurring. He went to charge for the guards. Made it two wobbly steps . . .

His legs went from under him and he plummeted face first to the concrete floor.

CHAPTER 14

'This is a complete bloody shit-show!' Flannigan blasted, his voice all the more grating because of the tinny speakers of the K-site satellite phone, sitting in the middle of the coffee table in Joyner's living room.

Unfortunately, it wasn't the first time Cox had heard Henry Flannigan scream those words at her, though it was possibly the first time that she actually agreed.

The one saving grace was that he hadn't brought his own boss, Roger Miles, onto the call. His presence would surely have been even worse news, and could even have spelled an end not just to Cox's operation, but her career.

'I completely agree,' Joyner said, much to Cox's annoyance. She hadn't wanted him on the call at all, but at K-site it seemed nothing was allowed to take place without his knowledge or presence. 'Which is why I had rejected the request for Torkal coming here in the first place, and why I vehemently opposed the idea of Torkal and Cox interviewing Al-Busaidi.'

Flannigan was silent now. Cox didn't like that. Sitting in an armchair opposite Joyner she was trying not to look into his eyes. She couldn't stand to see that smug look a moment longer.

'Rachel?' Flannigan prompted.

'Yes, Joyner did oppose the idea, but not because he felt Aydin was a risk, but because he felt Al-Busaidi was too . . . I don't know what. Too volatile? Or was it just that you hadn't broken him down enough yet?'

She glared at Joyner now, and was pleased to see he had clearly taken offence at her words.

'So which was it?' Flannigan said.

'It was for more than one reason,' Joyner said. 'But certainly because Aydin Torkal doesn't belong here.'

'Yet you didn't kick up a fuss at me and Aydin spending time with Rashid?' Cox said.

'That was for a completely different purpose,' Joyner said.

'The most worrying aspect of this is not only what Aydin did in there but that he was armed,' Flannigan said. 'And not with something he'd picked up inside K-site.'

'We check visitors, but—'

'Well obviously you didn't check thoroughly enough. I'll have to have a think about what message I pass to my superiors about that, but I can assure you they won't be very impressed. K-site is supposed to be more than just secure. What if Aydin hadn't been attacking Al-Busaidi but there to attack you and the guards, to help those prisoners escape?'

Joyner had no response to that one. He simply remained sunken into the sofa, his face screwed in distaste.

'OK, Joyner. We'll get back to the issues of security some other time. I need to speak to Cox alone.'

'Got it,' he said.

It was now Joyner's turn to avoid Cox's eye as he got up and headed for the exit. At least his rebuking was over, for now.

'Are we alone?' Flannigan asked after a few moments.

'Go for it,' Cox said, already dreading what her boss might say next.

'You must see how this looks?' Flannigan said.

116

'I'm not stupid,' Cox said. 'But what exactly do you want to happen? Are you suggesting we now lock Aydin up here with the others?'

'That's not what I want at all.'

'It's what Joyner wants.'

'Joyner has no say in this. But you must see that this is more than just a dent in your planned operation?'

Cox sighed. He was right. And this was truly a crossroads for her now. For her whole life, perhaps. The easiest path by far was to concede the point. To see the operation curtailed even at this early stage. To have Aydin sent packing, outside the clutches of MI6 for good, and for her to desperately try to find another way to break open the terror cell she was sure was currently plotting in the US.

But was that the right answer? Did it get anyone to the desired end point?

The other option was that she dug her heels in, but she really didn't know if she wanted to stick her neck out for Aydin any more.

It wasn't really about him though. It never had been. The bigger picture remained. They had to find out more about the cell in the US. They had to quash it before the attacks began.

'The other day in the car,' Cox said, 'after I'd met you by the dam—'

'You mean when I told you that story? About how you can never really know someone.'

Cox winced at that comment. How apt.

'Yes,' she said. 'That day. Afterward, I sensed that Aydin had taken offence at something you did.'

'At me?'

'To be fair you were glaring at him nearly the whole time. Have you two ever even had a conversation with each other in all the time he's helped us?'

'So he decided to attack Al-Busaidi in retaliation for me not talking to him? What on earth is your point?'

'My point is that in the car afterwards, he commented that you don't like him much. And I told him that it didn't matter whether we, me included, liked him or not. What mattered was that we needed him.'

Flannigan sighed. 'You're right. It doesn't matter if we like him or not, but it does matter whether or not we can trust him.'

'I do trust him.'

'How can you say that!'

'I trust that he's doing this for a purpose.'

'To bloody kill and maim anyone he doesn't like!'

'No! To help us catch terrorist scumbags who'll kill innocent people unless we intervene! His goal is the same as ours—'

'But his methods are off the chart of sanity—'

'OK! Yes he's a complex character, his head is messed up in more ways than I can count, but think about where he's come from. Think what *they* did to him.'

'We'll never be able to truly rein him in.'

'We don't have to. We just have to . . . '

'Watch him like a hawk?'

'Be open and honest with him.'

'You're saying we haven't been?'

'We never are, fully. The most striking thing about all of this is that Aydin already knew more about Al-Busaidi than we did.'

Silence now. That had to be a good thing?

'Aydin isn't a civilian,' Cox said. 'Far from it. And neither is he just some combat-ready mercenary. He's so much more than any of that. In the space of a few days he somehow uncovered all of this information, this *leverage*, against Al-Busaidi—'

'Yes, for his own sick purposes. Come on, Cox, threatening to kill those kids?'

'Words. He would never do that.'

'Do you really know that? Of a man who wouldn't think twice about breaking a man's fingers and slitting his throat?'

Now it was Cox's turn to be silent. She really didn't know how to respond to that one.

'Al-Busaidi is the scum of the earth,' she said. 'There's a reason he's at K-site, so it's pretty damn hypocritical of us to complain that Aydin hurt him.'

Another sigh from Flannigan, though the fact he didn't argue that point suggested to Cox that it had hit home. Who were they to take the moral high ground? They'd already elicited intel from Al-Busaidi and however many countless others at K-site and beyond through supposedly inhumane interrogation techniques. Aydin's techniques were certainly far more graphic and direct, but still MI6 weren't really in a position to criticise.

'I sense you're going to try to persuade me that we go ahead,' Flannigan said.

'If we don't go ahead, now that we've planted this seed in Aydin's head about Al-Addad, do you really think he's going to go back to his quiet life in London?'

'You're saying if we ditch this operation, he'll still go over there anyway?'

'You know he would. Even if we tried to stop him. Wouldn't you rather we had some control over what he does? Until that meeting with Al-Busaidi, we'd got everything we needed here. We were ready to go. To put a stop to this operation now . . . I really can't say that we'd get to where we need to be in time.'

'If Aydin goes over there under our authority, he's on the shortest leash imaginable.'

'He will be.'

'And if he does a single thing, however small, that I think compromises us—'

119

'I understand. We'll disown him. Pretend it was never anything to do with us.'

'That or we lock him up for good.'

Cox squeezed her eyes shut for a moment. She truly hoped matters would never get to that point.

'So we're agreed?' she said.

'We are. You'd better go and explain the bad news to Joyner.'

Cox smiled. 'On it.' She leaned forward and pressed the button to end the call before Flannigan could get another word in.

Her smile didn't last long.

There was no doubt what she'd witnessed in that room had truly shaken her. Not just what Aydin had done, to her and to Al-Busaidi, but the way he had flipped so quickly and so completely. In the time she'd known him, she'd never quite figured Aydin Torkal out, but now . . . she realised she was truly afraid of what he was capable of, and of what made him tick.

But she still needed him. She had no doubt about that.

Ten minutes later Cox was following Joyner through the Warren. Even looking at his back she could tell he was angry. Other than the expletive he'd thrown at her, he'd said nothing since she'd explained the situation to him. When they reached the cell door, Joyner pulled two guards over. They both had their weapons raised as Joyner unlocked then swung open the door. The lights in the dank room were already on, quite a luxury afforded to the man inside compared to others at K-site.

Aydin was sitting in a corner, knees up to his chest, his head sunken, his eyes bleary; no doubt the continuing after-effects of the high dose of tranquilliser that had been shot into his bloodstream hours before.

120

Cox's eyes found the speckles of blood still on his hands and wrists. As she looked up, his gaze met hers. Somehow he looked different to her now.

She'd certainly learned one thing from this experience; she'd never let her guard down around Aydin Torkal again.

You can never really know someone.

Those same words from Flannigan swam in her mind once more

'Come on, Aydin,' she said, nervously holding his clothes out to him. 'We're getting out of here.'

CHAPTER 15

Dearborn, Michigan

The set-up in Namur's Grand Cherokee was almost identical to the day in the woods, at least in terms of the car's occupants, though Karim was more than a little glad that the drive today was going to be much shorter, with them heading just a few miles from Dearborn to downtown Detroit for this 'meeting'.

The journey east on the I94 would only take them a few minutes, not that there wasn't enough time for Karim's nerves to take hold for what lay ahead. He'd already been feeling edgy even before he'd left the apartment.

As they drove along Karim looked down at his hands on his lap. His fingers were still raw and blistered from having helped dig the shallow grave for Aliya's body in the frozen forest several days ago. An experience he'd tried his hardest not to think about since, though one that flashed in his mind every few minutes. Particularly the pleading look of the dead girl's glassy eyes, as he shovelled snow and dirt onto her . . .

He shook the image away. Pushed his hand to his side where the Beretta was stashed in his waistband. A present from Namur. And yes, it was loaded. And yes, he did actually know how to use the damn thing now, thanks to a few trips to the local firing range at Namur's invitation.

Would he get the chance to use the weapon today? Strangely, he was conflicted as to whether he wanted the answer to be yes or no.

'Why are we dealing with these people anyway?' Karim asked.

'Because they have what we need,' Namur said.

Karim grumbled under his breath. He hadn't even been told what it was they needed. Apparently he wasn't important enough for that.

'How long have you lived here for?' Namur asked.

A strange question to ask just then, Karim felt, but he didn't say anything of it.

'Since I was seven,' he said.

'I've been here thirty years,' Namur said. 'I never saw Detroit at its peak, but I've still seen three decades of decline . . .'

Karim had his eyes on the outside as Namur spoke. Somewhat fittingly he watched the various industrial buildings alongside I94 flash past. Small ones, large ones, gargantuan ones, all in various states. A few were still being used for their original purpose – largely suppliers to the automotive plants – some were refurbished as trendy apartments and offices, but many were abandoned. Karim hadn't lived through thirty years of decline like Namur, but the state of Detroit was clear for anyone to see.

' . . . and you know what comes out of decline?'

'What?' Karim said.

'Desperation.'

'We're desperate?'

'No. Not us. We're opportunists. Before you joined me, *you* were desperate. I could see it in your eyes, could understand it from your actions.'

'I'm not an opportunist too?'

'You are now. You took the opportunity I gave you, didn't you?'

Took it? Was he given a choice?

'My point is,' Namur continued, 'you need to learn to see when others are desperate. Clever men use the desperation of others to their advantage.'

'Like back home,' Benny chimed in.

'Exactly,' Namur said. 'Think about what's happened over there. The Arab spring. Revolutions in countless countries, the rise of the Caliphate a direct consequence.'

'Because they took advantage of desperation?' Karim said. 'But that's completely different from what we're doing here.'

'But it's not. The end result is different, but seizing the moment is the same.'

'So we're dealing with these guys because they're desperate?'

'They hate us. Truth is they hate everyone—'

'We don't like them much either,' Benny said.

'No,' Namur said. 'But who gives a shit. And we do have common interests.'

'Money?' Raf said.

His comment received a few sniggers.

'You could say that money is one thing that binds us all,' Namur said.

'Money and power,' Benny added.

Namur nodded, clearly satisfied that the men all seemed to be on the same wavelength. Except Karim, who was pretty much lost.

Not long afterwards Tamir pulled the car off the exit of I94 and they headed the short distance down a long straight road with shrivelled and cracked tarmac freshly iced over. Off to their left was the sprawling and long abandoned Fisher Body Plant 21 factory. Karim knew little of the detail of Detroit's past, but he'd passed by this building and plenty of others like it countless times, and such places essentially told the whole story of the city all on their own. Nowadays these abandoned shells weren't just eyesores, they were permanent scars.

Tamir rolled the car to a stop. Beyond the broken chain-link fence, the factory building stretched for what seemed like several hundred yards into the distance.

'Looks like we're good,' Namur said after a few moments of spying in his mirrors and out of the windows.

Tamir nodded and pulled the car onto the factory grounds through a large gap in the poorly maintained security fence. The empty car park of the factory was covered in thick snow though there were tyre tracks and footprints here and there. Looters, vandals, graffiti artists, perhaps young couples looking for a quiet place to make out – the factory and its grounds still had a variety of uses for the locals, whatever the weather.

The Jeep was soon round a corner and out of sight from both the entrance road and the I94, and Tamir pulled over and shut down the engine.

'You think they're here already?' Karim asked. 'No sign of any cars.'

'They'll be here. This is their spot more than ours.'

Namur sounded ever so slightly nervous about that.

Still, moments later the four men – Tamir had stayed with the car, both to keep watch on the outside and to provide a quick getaway if needed – were traipsing through the snow alongside the decrepit structure.

Looking up at the factory, Karim was filled with a strange sensation. Part despair for what it and the whole area had become, part admiration for the engineering that had gone into the building's original design and purpose nearly a hundred years ago. Despite decades of neglect and looting and vandalism, the shell of the structure remained largely intact, even down to the water towers on top.

'In this way,' Benny said, leading the way.

Heading in through an old loading bay they were soon out of the snow and standing among wood and brick and concrete debris in a mammoth open space, six storeys high. A lattice-work of rusted steel girders above dripped icy red liquid into puddles on the floor around them.

'I don't see them anywhere,' Namur said, looking about the place.

None of the four had their weapons drawn, though Karim could see each of the others had their hands at the ready.

Benny took out a piece of paper from his pocket which had a crudely drawn map on it.

'It's over that side,' he said, pointing over to the far corner where the open factory floor ended and the individual storeys of what might once have been offices rose up.

The foursome traipsed over, Karim at the back. He was surprisingly calm still, almost revelling in the moment of the unknown now he was here, even despite the fact that the others seemed be getting more nervous with each step.

They reached a large internal doorway, wide enough to get a truck through, and Benny slunk through first, hand on his hip. He looked around.

'Found them,' he said.

Karim noticed Namur relax now. The other three followed behind Benny. The space they walked into was some sort of workshop. The once-rendered walls had large gouges exposing the red brick underneath. The concrete floor was covered in debris much like the main factory floor. The ceiling was a mess of crumbling plaster and rusted metal, huge holes in it giving a view of the floors above.

Over at the far side of the room were three men. One of them was sitting at a basic foldout table. His two sidekicks, bulky black clothing, their heads covered by baseball caps covered by hoods, were standing either side, weapons in their hands. Karim didn't know much about guns but he was sure they were Uzis or something similar. Certainly far more lethal than the handguns which his own crew had brought.

Across the scarred wall above the threesome was a ten-foot-high spray-painted image of a man Karim thought he vaguely recognised – a hip-hop star? The red bandana on his head signified his gang affiliation, as did the splashes of red on the thick clothing of the three men across the room, signifying them as being part of the Bloods.

'Karim, wait here,' Namur said.

Karim nodded and Namur, Benny and Raf headed over. Somewhat surprisingly it was Benny who stepped forward from the group of three and began a muffled conversation with the seated man.

As the others talked, Karim kept his eyes busy as he looked over the three gangsters, around the room, up through the gaps in the ceiling, and back out to the main factory floor which thankfully remained empty.

Across the other side of the room the conversation continued. Karim still couldn't make out any words but he was sure it was sounding less friendly by the second.

Benny turned round and indicated to Raf who stepped forward and plonked the holdall he'd been carrying onto the table. Karim could take a pretty good guess what it contained. Money.

The leader of the gangsters unzipped the top and rummaged inside. He seemed satisfied. He turned to the man on his left who ducked behind a wall and came back carrying a small cardboard box which he set down on the table. Benny flipped the lid and looked inside. He turned to Namur who stepped over to take a closer look. He peered inside for a few moments. The conversation became more heated still.

'Where's the rest of it,' Benny said, his voice now raised.

At least that's what Karim thought he'd said. The gangster boss gave his response, still calm, though Karim had no idea what he'd said. It didn't seem to please Benny much who turned to Namur as if to question what to do next.

That was when a flash of movement up above caught Karim's eye. His gaze flicked to the broken ceiling. Was that a boot? Someone standing on the floor above?

He glanced back and forth between the meeting in front of him and the spot above his head – nothing there now. Across the room one of the two henchmen by the gangster boss was staring over to Karim. Did he know what Karim had seen?

Then his friend glanced up too.

Karim's eyes shot up again. This time he saw it more clearly. A black boot. The outline of a jeans-clad leg. The arm of a puffer jacket. The hand, fingers encircling the trigger of a large black gun. The barrel pointing down towards the group below.

'Namur!' Karim screamed.

Too late. The gangsters in front were already raising their Uzis.

Karim had no choice. He pulled the Beretta from his jeans, lifted it up, and fired.

CHAPTER 16

The bullet from Karim's gun clanked into a steel girder just a few inches from the sniper's foot. Within a heartbeat every other person on the workshop floor had their fingers on their triggers. Firing erupted everywhere.

'Get the money!' Namur screamed.

The sniper was already letting loose with his weapon, seemingly oblivious to the near miss. Benny and Raf and Namur scattered as best they could and returned fire both against the sniper and the three gangsters in front of them.

Karim, surprisingly focused in the melee, adjusted his aim and fired again. Again and again. Finally he hit home, a leg shot. The sniper up top yelped in pain and somehow lost grip of his gun which clattered down and smacked onto the floor with a billow of dust. Karim adjusted his aim for a killer shot, before a cascade of bullets raked against the wall next to him. Fragments of brick and dust burst into his face. He shouted in surprise and hauled his body down and back towards the doorway. Namur went racing past him. Skidded to a stop beyond the doorway and swung round to provide covering fire for Benny and Raf, who were both retreating too, intermittently crouching and shooting behind them at the gangsters who were all now in cover. Raf had the holdall, slowing him down somewhat.

'Karim, you moron, help us!' Benny screamed.

Karim realised he was zoned out. Maybe for only a couple of seconds as he took in the scene of chaos. Benny's angry instruction, together with another bullet which whizzed so close to his ear he felt the air pressure caused by the projectile, brought him back to reality. He took aim again. The three men across the room were well covered. The sniper? No sign of him now.

Karim realised why. He spun round and looked up, into the main factory floor.

'Over here!'

Not one, but three more guys with big guns were up high, readying themselves to ambush. Karim fired at them without taking the time for proper aim. Another miss, but he wasn't far off. As the men opened fire, Karim edged his barrel to the right. Fired again.

A hit.

The bullet caught the shooter in his shoulder. Karim adjusted and fired another shot. The bullet sank into the guy's neck . . . he wobbled, then toppled over the edge of the barrier he was up against.

Karim winced when the body splatted onto the ground a few yards from him. But he was given no chance for respite. Bullets rained down. He and Benny and Raf and Namur were all hunkered close to the doorway, which provided them little cover from the three men still inside the workshop on one side, and the two remaining shooters up high. And they didn't have an endless supply of ammo.

'Raf, you run for it,' Karim said. 'Take their fire. We'll pick them off.'

'You fucking run!'

'Just do it!' Namur shouted as another bullet clattered into the metal beam an inch from his face. 'Now!'

With the bag still over his shoulder, protection of sorts, Raf got up and sped for the exit, shooting up and behind him as he went, without even looking. But at least his movement, and his firing, had the desired effect, giving Benny and Karim the chance to properly take aim at the remaining two snipers. They fired almost in unison. Shot after shot as they tweaked their aims on the fly. A few misses, but also two direct hits.

Both of the shooters slumped down.

'Go!' Namur shouted.

They were soon all rushing for the exit, Raf still in front. Then a shot from behind them. The men on ground level.

'Raf, help us,' Karim shouted.

Raf reached the loading bay to the outside. It looked like he was going to keep on going to safety, leaving the others to it, but at the last second he skidded to a stop to hide round the corner and pulled his gun round. He provided covering fire as Karim and Namur and Benny sprinted towards him.

Then Raf's face surprisingly broke out into a broad smile.

'I got one!'

'Just keep firing!'

He pulled the trigger again. Nothing happened. He looked down at the weapon. He was out. Karim was too. But he was also already at the exit. He raced outside and screamed over to Tamir who was behind the wheel with the engine running. When he saw Karim he floored the accelerator and the Jeep lurched forward, its tyres skidding all over the place.

Karim glanced over his shoulder. All four of them were on the outside and away from the exit. The shooting inside had stopped, but there were still at least three of the gangsters inside, with superior weapons and possibly far more rounds.

Tamir swung the Jeep round and to a stop just a yard from Karim's feet. He pulled the two side doors open.

'Come on!'

Namur was already there. He jumped into the front passenger seat. Benny jumped into the back. Raf launched the holdall to Karim who tossed it into the back before he jumped in too.

Raf was only two steps away . . .

Karim saw the flash of movement by the loading doors. Then the flash of light. The boom from the gun came at the same instant as the wet thwack. Raf jerked forward. Karim reached out and grabbed him and somehow managed to haul him into the Jeep.

'Go!' Namur shouted.

Tamir swung the Jeep round again before he stomped his foot down. The car shot forward just as Karim managed to fully haul Raf inside. The door swung shut on its own a moment later when the Jeep bounced up over a piece of debris on the forecourt.

Karim glanced behind. He could make out two figures outside by the loading bay now. Weapons by their sides. They were no longer firing, nor were they giving chase.

But Karim wouldn't feel relief just yet . . .

Raf, who was practically in his lap, was screaming, his face contorted in agony. Karim tried his best to prop him up. Doing so left a smear of thick dark blood across the tan leather seats.

'Those pieces of shit!' Namur raged.

'Which way?' Tamir asked hurriedly. 'I94?'

Would the police be closing in already? There must have been a hundred rounds fired back in the factory, but then who the hell else was around there to hear it and phone the cops?

'Namur, which way?'

Tamir slowed the car as they approached the junction. Certainly Karim saw no sign of flashing lights. Could hear no sirens. Did that mean they were in the clear?

'I94,' Namur said.

Tamir nodded and pulled the Jeep right to head for the slip road. No sooner had he done so than up ahead they saw the blue-and-red strobes.

'Fuck!' Namur growled. 'Slow down. Keep it steady.'

Steady. Calm. Except for Raf who was still howling in pain.

'Raf, quieten down or I'll finish you myself.'

Namur's strangely placid tone did the trick. Raf pulled back on his shouting, but continued to whimper. Karim looked over at him, could see he was trying his hardest both to keep a lid on it and to look relaxed, though if they were stopped by the police it wouldn't take them a second to see the blood.

Up ahead the police car . . . no, two police cars, were fast approaching. The Jeep was tucked up behind a pick-up truck, and they now had a sedan close behind them too, helping them to blend in.

'Indicate,' Namur said.

Tamir flicked the right indicator on, showing their intention to head onto the I94. The first of the police cars blasted past, the officers inside paying no attention to the Jeep. The second one was almost past them too. Karim's eyes followed it. The passenger glanced over at the Jeep. Was he staring right into Karim's eyes? The policeman did a double-take, Karim held his breath, his body froze . . .

The police car sped past. Karim still didn't breathe yet. Didn't dare look behind him either. The car was deathly silent for a few seconds except for the low murmurings of Raf.

'We're good,' Tamir said, eyes flicking between the road and his rear-view mirror.

Karim closed his eyes and exhaled. Seconds later they were picking up speed on the I94. Karim looked out of the window on his right, kept his eyes on the Fisher building in the near distance as they passed. He saw the police cars approaching the factory. Too late. Unless the gang bangers were stupidly still there.

'What are we going to do?' Karim said.

'About what?' Namur said.

'Raf. He's bleeding real bad.'

'We go home. I know a guy.'

Not much of an explanation, but Namur didn't seem too bothered by the fact that one of his closest associates had been shot and was badly wounded. Strangely, that did help Karim to relax.

'What happened?' Benny said. He sounded seriously agitated.

'You saw,' Namur said. 'They played us. They never had any intention of giving us what we asked for.'

Karim felt like asking exactly what they'd been trying to buy in the first place. He realised now was highly unlikely to be a good time.

'You told us they were good,' Benny said. 'This is on you.'

Karim was shocked at Benny's outward criticism of the boss. He willed him to back down in fact, he'd seen enough fighting for one day. He could see Namur clenching his jaw in anger at the front. The last thing they needed now was for him to lose it.

'Namur, you told us they were good,' Benny said, not reading the signs. Or perhaps he could read them just fine and wanted to egg the big man on anyway. 'We almost lost the money. We almost got killed in there!'

'I know what happened!' Namur slammed. 'Those bastards will pay for this.'

Which to Karim sounded like a really bad idea. Regardless of what had happened, what had gone wrong, was drumming up a further beef with a local Bloods gang really in anyone's interest?

'They won't get away with this,' Namur said. 'A fucking alarm clock? That's what they tried to give us. A fucking alarm clock.'

Karim puzzled over that for a moment. What the hell was he getting himself involved in here?

'And you think we're angry,' Benny said. 'We just killed at least three of their guys. They're after us now, not the other way around.'

'They wouldn't dare come after us,' Namur said. 'We only stepped onto their patch to conclude this deal out of courtesy. Never again. The lines are drawn now. We'll find another source.'

'We don't need a source,' Benny grumbled. 'We can do it ourselves. I told you that already.'

Namur said nothing to that.

Karim looked over at Raf who had gone quieter and quieter on the short journey.

'No . . . no! Raf!'

His head was lolled to the side. He wasn't even murmuring now. Namur turned round in his seat. Karim tried to lift Raf's head but it just flopped back down again. He wasn't breathing, no movement in his chest. No breath coming from his lips when Karim placed his hand there.

'He's dead,' Karim said, sounding as shocked as he felt.

'No need for the doctor then, I guess,' Benny said.

The heartless comment drew a deathly glare from Namur.

'No need for the doctor,' Namur said. 'But there's going to be more blood because of this, I can guarantee you that.'

Karim sensed Benny wanted to argue the point on that one, but instead the car went remarkably quiet the rest of the short journey back to Dearborn, the mood solemn. Karim felt ghastly the whole way, sitting next to a dead body. But it wasn't just the dead body that had him feeling so rotten now, it was the aftermath of the fight, the thoughts of what they'd just been through. What he'd done too. He'd killed a man today. Possibly two.

Five minutes later they pulled up into the car park of a small disused office block a mile away from the mosque. Namur checked his phone.

'They'll be here in five,' he said.

No explanation of what that meant. Did Tamir and Benny understand? They both nodded.

Namur turned round and looked over Raf, before locking eyes with Karim.

'You did good,' he said. 'You kept your head. You got us all moving. They would have taken our money, and they were planning to kill us all if we tried to stop them.'

Benny slapped the back of Karim's head as if to congratulate him.

'We're alive,' Benny said, 'and we have our money because of you.'

'Except for Raf,' Karim said.

Namur snorted. 'Yeah, except for Raf. But you also nearly saved him too. I always want people who are calm under pressure. You . . . Karim, you're special.'

Karim didn't quite know how to take that. On the one hand he was thrilled with the compliment, on the other he was shocked at how natural he'd felt in that moment.

'You sure you were never a soldier?' Benny said.

'Too many video games,' Karim said with a wry laugh. No one else laughed or even smiled.

Namur turned back round. Not long after, a black BMW X5 came screeching into the car park. Two men Karim vaguely recognised got out and Namur headed over to speak with them. Neither Karim nor Benny nor Tamir said a word.

When the conversation was done, the two men got back into the X5 and the vehicle was already spinning out of the car park when Namur plonked himself back into the car.

'They've got everything we need,' he said. 'Let's go.'

Karim gulped at the thought of what that meant. Were they heading right back to Detroit now to take their anger out on the Bloods?

'Where are we going?' Karim said. 'I'm sitting next to a corpse here! We can't just take him everywhere we go.'

'We won't. This is his final journey.'

'What? But—'

'We've got a dead body we need to get rid of,' Benny said. 'We've got four unlicenced firearms involved in a shootout in the city that need to disappear too.'

Karim got it even before Namur provided the confirmation.

'I hope you've been polishing your digging skills as much as you have your shooting,' Namur said. 'It's time for another visit to the woods.'

CHAPTER 17

Two weeks ago, Aydin had been quietly going about his business in London. A week ago he'd been at the horrific place known as K-site in a remote and inhospitable corner of Tajikistan. For the last two days he'd been in Dearborn, Michigan, acclimatising himself to a brutal winter in a foreign land. Quite a turnaround, even for someone with a life as surreal as his.

Two days in Dearborn, Michigan. Although not two days purely in the small city that was so intermingled with its larger neighbour, Detroit. He'd also spent some of that time in the big city itself, as well as roaming around neighbouring areas. One thing he'd figured out in his short time here, was that it wasn't hard to find trouble, if you happened upon the wrong place at the wrong time.

Or the right place at the right time, if you were intent on looking for it . . .

Having left K-site under something of a cloud, Aydin and Cox had spent the subsequent few days further preparing for Aydin's new role. Learning what they could about the place and people who Aydin needed to ingratiate himself with. Cox had all sorts of weird and wonderful ideas about how Aydin should go about that. He'd been non-committal with her the whole time, much to her agitation, but in his own mind he already knew exactly how he'd play this first step.

The diner he headed to in Dearborn Heights, yet another distinct city – apparently – right next door to Dearborn, was just like those Aydin had seen on TV. On a busy main road, the area outside was lined with single-storey red brick retail units, the vast majority of which were boarded up or looked so grotty they may as well have been. The diner, from the outside, looked just the same as those other establishments, though on the inside it was quaint and well kept, if several decades out of fashion. There were a dozen booths with high leather-backed benches, a few other tables lining an inner walkway, a long open plan kitchen where there was a sole cook in chef's apron and hat, and two waitresses dressed in red-and-white chequered dresses.

Aydin found himself a seat at the nearest empty booth to the door, plonked his heaving holdall one side and sat down on the other. Within a minute, one of the two cheery wait-resses came over with a pot of coffee.

'You want one, darlin'?'

'Please.'

She turned over his coffee cup and filled it almost to the brim with the thin mixture.

'You eatin'?'

'Pancakes please.'

'No bacon I'm guessin'.'

'No. Thank you.'

She winked at him then tootled off back to the counter.

Aydin looked about the place. At nearly midday the diner was a little more than half full, a wide range of patrons from young to old, singles, couples, groups. It hadn't escaped Aydin's attention that his entrance had received a few ques-tionable glances from people he could only assume were regulars. But particularly from a group of four young men sitting across the other side of the door from him. Two of them had the remnants of bruises to their faces. Aydin had seen them the day before too, had actually quietly followed one of them for a few hours.

With Aydin mostly keeping his head down, the waitress was soon back with his pancakes which he added a few splashes of maple syrup to. As he ate, a police officer in uniform walked inside and headed up to the counter where he took one of the stools. Aydin glanced outside at the patrol car where the driver was still sitting playing on his phone. Aydin noticed the emblem on the car. Dearborn Heights Police Department. He was yet to figure out exactly the purpose and responsibilities of the many overlapping law enforcement agencies in Michigan, though the local police in each city were basic peacekeepers and first responders as far as he could gather.

Aydin chewed through another mouthful of pancake as he strained his ears to try to listen to the overly friendly chat between the officer in the diner and the younger of the waitresses – the one who'd served Aydin. No, he couldn't hear them, but as he was trying, his gaze caught one of the foursome across the way who was glaring over.

This was almost too easy.

Aydin kept eye contact until all four of the twerps were scowling at him. He swallowed and wiped his mouth with his napkin then got up from his seat and walked over. The conversation among the four died down. Aydin looked left and right. From the policeman who was still flirting with the waitress, paying Aydin no attention at all, and back to the lads who couldn't take their eyes off him.

As he neared them, the one on the end facing Aydin shuffled in his seat like he was debating whether or not to stand up and accost him.

Aydin drew alongside and slowed and bent down slightly and whispered, 'Your mum's a stinking fucking whore.'

Not nice, and certainly not subtle. Aydin would even have gone so far as to say he was ashamed of himself for using such grotesque language. But he had to make sure he got the response he wanted.

The guy jumped up from the booth, closely followed by his chums. Aydin kept moving.

'What the fuck did you say?'

The diner went silent. Aydin stopped and turned. Everyone was now looking. The policeman included.

Aydin put his hands up, looked nonplussed.

'What did you say you fucking raghead?'

'Hey, Craig, watch it,' the policeman said as he took a few steps closer.

'I was just asking for the toilet,' Aydin said, not just acting innocent, acting a little scared too.

'Bullshit, you f—'

'Craig, enough!'

Craig. The leader of the clan? The policeman came over. Craig's friends, as agitated and angry as they looked, took their seats. He didn't. He looked like he wanted to smash Aydin's face in.

'What's going on?' the policeman said, stepping in between Aydin and Craig.

'I'm sorry, officer, I was just after the toilet.'

'You lying son of a—'

'Sit down, Craig. Now.'

The guy clearly didn't like being told what to do, but he did take his seat, grumbling under his breath.

'Toilet's that way,' the officer said to Aydin, not particularly cordially. He indicated behind Aydin.

'Thanks.'

141

Aydin headed off to do his business. When he came back out the four lads were still there, heads down now. The policeman was back at the counter, on his stool, though his flirty conversation with the waitress was well and truly over. He was glaring over at Aydin, and his eyes followed him all the way until Aydin had taken his seat again.

He only managed one more mouthful of pancake before the policeman walked over.

'You're not from around here,' the policeman said, glancing at Aydin's bag, though he guessed it was more likely his English accent which had given his origin away.

'No. England.'

'What are you doing around here?'

'I came for some pancakes.'

The policeman's eyes narrowed. 'I mean what are you doing in Dearborn Heights? Business? Pleasure?'

'Hopefully a bit of both. I've relocated here.'

'Relocated? Here?'

The way he said it made the scenario sound ludicrous.

'What's your name, son?'

'Why do you need to know that?'

'Because I asked you.'

'Have I done something wrong?'

The policeman was by now becoming agitated, Aydin could tell, which hadn't exactly been his intention, but he really wasn't sure why the guy was so interested in him all of a sudden.

'Show me your ID please.'

Aydin realised now that more than a few eyes were on him. Including the table of four.

'Probably one of them damn illegals,' one of the four said, just loud enough for everyone else to hear.

'You get many illegals coming over from London?' Aydin said, before facing the officer with a smile.

142

'Just show me some ID.'

Aydin grumbled but reached over for his bag and dug inside for the passport in the name of Mohammed Akhbar, which also had a valid visa – a necessary further layer to Aydin's ruse in order to give him credence to those he was trying to get close to. The policeman flipped through the pages of the passport, his face sour as though disappointed there was nothing he could pull Aydin up on.

'Enjoy your time in Michigan,' the policeman said as he placed the passport on the table.

'I will.'

'You take it easy. We've got enough problems around here already with your lot and their lot.' He indicated over to the four lads.

'Noted,' Aydin said. 'I'll do my best to keep my nose clean and the Muslim faith beyond reproach.'

The officer's face twitched as though he wanted to say or do something else, but before he could, the waitress shouted over for him. Aydin glanced to see her holding up a bag of food and a tray with two coffees. The policeman said no more before he turned and walked over and took his order from her. As he headed out of the diner it was Aydin rather than the aggressive foursome who received the policeman's keen eye once more.

Whatever.

The policeman got back into his car and soon they were out of sight. Aydin took his time with the rest of his pancakes. The foursome left in the meantime, though not before they'd each given Aydin a complimentary glower. He watched them through the window as they walked away in the opposite direction to that Aydin had arrived from.

Less than two minutes later he paid for his food and drink in cash, thanked the waitress, grabbed his bag and headed off in the same direction.

He'd moved less than a hundred yards down the road when he saw them. Hiding round the corner among the snowy frontage of a closed-down liquor store.

'You got something else to say, raghead?'

Aydin stopped and turned to face them. Craig was standing at the front of his posse.

'I think I said all I wanted to earlier.'

That earned Aydin a few sniggers from the imbeciles. One of them repeated his words, exaggerating his English accent and making him sound like an old-school upper-class toff.

'I never heard a raghead sound like the queen,' one of them snorted.

'That's because you've probably never even left this state, you inbred prick.'

That comment was the spark they needed. The four growled in anger and raced forward, Craig remaining front and centre. Aydin had to try hard, really hard, not to properly react, not to take them on and snap each of their necks in quick succession. It would have been so easy . . .

Instead he dropped his bag, cowered and put up a pathetic defence as Craig barged into him and sent him crashing to the ground.

Aydin landed painfully, his head taking the brunt of the fall onto the concrete below, and dazing him far more than he'd hoped. Craig rained punches down. Aydin did his best to block so as to not take the full brunt of the blows, but put up little by way of counter. Within seconds he'd taken several big hits to his face. His eye throbbed, his nose and lip were bleeding.

'Jesus Christ! Get off him!'

A female voice. Craig's blows slowed down some, but he didn't stop.

'Get off him now or I call the cops.'

A different female voice this time. Older, hoarser.

'Craig, come on, he's had enough.' One of the lads now. He grabbed Craig by the shoulder and pulled him up and the beating was over.

Craig stood over Aydin, snarling, chest heaving.

'You stupid idiot!' The young woman was right by his side and she shoved him with both hands, causing Craig to stumble back.

'Whatever,' he said before he glared down at Aydin again. 'Next time I see you, keep your damn mouth shut.'

Aydin said nothing. He propped himself up on his elbow as the four turned and walked off, fist-pumping each other and whooping like idiots.

'You OK?'

Aydin looked up at the two women. One older, one younger. Both had wavy brown hair, green eyes, freckled skin. Mother and daughter. The young woman held her hand out to Aydin to help him up. She must have been in her early twenties, and remarkably pretty in a clean-cut and natural way.

'Mister, are you OK?'

Aydin grimaced in mock pain as he took her hand and got to his feet.

'Damn. I think my ribs are broken.'

'Jesus, Kate, we need to get him to a doctor,' the older woman said.

'Come on, it's just around the block,' Kate said. 'My car's over here.'

'Thank you.'

'What's your name? You're not from around here, are you?'

'No,' Aydin said, stifling a smile as best he could. Could his plan have worked out any better than this? 'No, I'm not. My name's Mohammed. Mohammed Akhbar.'

CHAPTER 18

The restaurant Rachel Cox found herself inside in central Detroit had something of a clash of personalities. Recommended to her by her host, from the outside the block-like high-rise, once a factory of some sorts, had clearly undergone recent and trendy refurbishment, with a propensity of huge graphite-coloured metal window frames interspersed with the original red brick-work. The inside of the restaurant though, which took up the whole ground floor of the building, looked like someone couldn't be bothered to finish it off. Reclaimed floorboards, actually on the floor, were peppered with splashes of paint and oil and huge gouges. Similar floorboards were bizarrely stuck to the walls in some sections. The remainder of the walls were bare brick, the same as on the outside, except on the inside rather than clean pointing there was messy mortar and render slopped all over the place.

As for the ceiling . . . well there wasn't really one. Just a tangle of chrome and matt grey air-con ducts, wires, gas and water pipes.

If this was intentional modern design, Cox really didn't understand exactly what it was trying to show. Certainly not that the establishment was down to earth and reason-ably priced. Cox blinked a few times when she opened the embossed menu to see the prices of the mains, which largely comprised a variety of steaks and not much else.

A white-gloved waiter came over, his formal clothing yet another oddity compared to his surroundings, though looking around at the generally well-dressed clientele, perhaps they simply got what Cox didn't.

'Ma'am, would you like to order anything?'

Cox looked at her watch. Twenty minutes late now.

'Just another sparkling water please.'

'Certainly.'

The guy sauntered off, doing a really good impression of someone whose spine had fused into a single metal rod.

Across the far side of the restaurant from her circular booth that was big enough to seat five, Cox saw a smartly dressed man step in from the cold. He stripped off his long black overcoat to reveal a nicely tailored suit. With neatly coiffed dark hair and a spattering of thick stubble on his face he looked the part. Though a little young for Cox. Not that she was in Detroit for anything of that nature in any case.

She was surprised when the stiff-walking waiter pointed the man over in her direction and he strode over confidently.

'Miss Cox?' the man said when he reached her table.

'Er, yeah?'

He held out his hand. 'Sorry I'm late. There was an accident on the interstate. I'm Special Agent Tarkowski.'

'Rachel Cox. UK Secret Intelligence Service.'

'I thought you were called MI6? Or is it five?'

'SIS is both.'

She shook his hand, then he reached into his pocket and pulled out a business card.

Homeland Security Investigations. Cox could understand his slight confusion as to the difference between SIS, MI5 and MI6. She was more than slightly baffled as to who exactly her

US counterparts were these days. Homeland Security had been created in the wake of the September 11 attacks back in 2001, for the specific purpose of overseeing anti-terrorism activities, but its remit since then had mushroomed and everything from the coast guard to the issuing of visas came under its control. Cox's confusion partly stemmed from the fact that despite Homeland Security's remit, several other federal agencies also retained their fingers in the counter-terrorism pie, including the FBI, DEA, USSS, ATF, USPIS, USMS, FAMS, DSS, NCIS, CID, OSI, and pretty much any other acronym that anyone could think of.

Tarkowski sat down on the chair opposite Cox, leaving the four-seater bench all to her.

'Sorry if I seemed a bit confused,' Cox said, 'it's just I was expecting to meet with Agent Dixon today.'

She looked at her watch again. 'He was due here nearly half an hour ago.'

'Yes, sorry for the short notice . . . '

What notice? Cox thought.

' . . . but Special Agent-in-Charge Dixon had more pressing matters to attend to.'

Cox had never been one for using archaic formal titles every time someone's name was mentioned. She couldn't even remember her boss's formal title.

'More pressing?' she said.

Tarkowski nodded before he scrutinised his menu.

'Sorry, but what was more pressing than meeting with me?'

Tarkowski looked up from his menu as though insulted that Cox had interrupted his thought process.

'I'm sorry, that's really not for me to say.'

His eyes went straight back to the food and drink choice. Cox's irritation was piqued.

'But it's something that's more important than the national security of the US?' she said.

Tarkowski looked taken aback by this, as though Cox had just seriously offended him. The waiter appeared by their side. Conveniently or inconveniently?

'Have you had a chance to decide what you'd like?'

'I already ate,' Tarkowski said, putting his menu down and looking smugly at Cox, 'but get anything you want.' He turned back to the waiter. 'Just a regular cappuccino for me please.'

'Certainly. And you, Ma'am?'

She thought about that one for a moment. Clearly Tarkowski was trying to cut this short.

'Some bread and olives to nibble on please,' she said.

'Of course. And for your main?'

'Then I'll have the tempura prawns to start please, followed by chateaubriand.'

The waiter looked a little put out. 'Ma'am, that's for two to share.'

'There's two of us.'

'Really,' Tarkowski said. 'I'm not that—'

'OK. Ditch the prawns. I'll go straight for the steak. Medium rare, please. And a side of winter greens. And a side of dauphinoise. And I'll get the raspberry sidecar mocktail.'

The waiter rapidly scribbled the ever-growing order before he took the menus and scuttled away.

'Sorry about that,' Cox said. 'But I was expecting lunch. I haven't eaten since I got off my flight. Dixon told me on the phone the chateaubriand is the best in the city. He also offered to pay.'

'That's fine,' Tarkowski said, waving it away in such a fashion as to show that it wasn't fine at all. 'I'm sorry that your plans were spoiled.'

'They haven't been spoiled. I'm still having steak. But you were saying, Dixon has something more pressing than a matter of national security? I—'

149

'No, Agent Cox, that's not what I said.'

Cox sipped her water. 'It's not? Sorry, what did you say then?'

By now, Tarkowski was beginning to look vexed. Cox couldn't care less. She was the one they were trying to play.

'I said he had something more pressing than meeting with you.'

'And meeting with me isn't in the interests of national security? Have you even read through the intel briefing I prepared?'

'I glanced through it, yes. I understand you've supplanted what you call an asset in Michigan, and I know Homeland Security helped to organise his papers, but . . .'

'But what?'

'This isn't an active case for us. We have no recourse on it. Frankly, I think you've ruffled a few feathers already with your plans—'

'Which is why I've come through official channels, and why I had arranged to meet with your boss. To make sure we all understand each other.'

Tarkowski sighed and took a moment to compose himself. Cox too took the chance to calm. She knew there was no benefit in getting het up, but she could already sense that for whatever reason Dixon had decided that this investigation was a waste of his time. At least, she supposed, they hadn't tried to curtail what she was doing here. Yet.

Tarkowski pulled his satchel onto his lap and dug about.

'The thing is, Agent Cox, we do know about some of the individuals you're looking at. To put it simply, we keep a close eye on every religious group in the state, one way or another, but particularly we're close to the mosques in the area. We talk to people who visit them, gauge the mood, try to see the warning signs . . .'

Cox bit her lip as Tarkowski pulled a small bundle of photos from the bag and looked around the room before he placed them on the table.

'You said you were particularly interested in the Jalalabad, and I'd say there are some interesting characters there. This is Ahmed Akhwabi, known locally as Namur. Tiger.'

Cox looked at the pictures. She knew who he was from her own research.

'Are you trying to tell me something?' she asked.

'Namur isn't a terrorist, not even an extremist. None of the guys around there are. If anything he's a wannabe gangster. They make money from extortion, racketeering, gambling, theft.'

'You think that's OK?'

'Of course not, and believe me there are federal agencies in Michigan that have him and others on their radar for good reason. But he's far from a big player, and he certainly isn't concocting the next 9/11—'

'How on earth do you—'

'We just do.'

Was there even any point in arguing? Tarkowski, and his absent boss, had clearly already made up their minds, and while Cox was privy to more information on the cell she believed was in place in Michigan than had been included in the briefing pack sent to Homeland Security, she wasn't about to declare her full hand just yet. Not until she had something more concrete. Though she firmly believed Namur was part of that cell, and part of the operation that Faiz Al-Busaidi had been affiliated to from Oman.

'What about Nasir Al-Addad?' she asked.

Tarkowski flipped his hands to show the name didn't really mean anything. 'I saw that name in your briefing, but we don't know him at all.'

'Nasir is the brother of Aziz Al-Addad. A man who was largely responsible for nearly bringing Europe to its knees—'

'Miss Cox, I'm aware of what happened in Europe. I've heard about the Farm, and I've heard rumours about your role—'

She held a hand up to halt him. She couldn't care less what he thought he knew about her role in quashing those attacks. She grabbed her phone and scrolled her emails to find the grainy image.

'This is him. Nasir Al-Addad. It's not the most recent, but we believe this man is here, in Michigan. In Dearborn. And if he is, that's a big problem for you.'

'*Possibly* it'd be a big problem. *If* he was here, in Michigan. But . . . there's no evidence that he is.'

'We have intel from a very reliable source—'

'What source?'

'I can't tell you that.'

Tarkowski sighed. The waiter came over with the drinks and a single portion of bread with the tiniest bowl of olives.

'Your food will just be a few minutes,' he said before heading off again.

'They're building up to something. The chatter we've intercepted, we know this cell isn't working alone. They're in contact with groups in several other US locations . . . '

'This wasn't in the pack. Where exactly are you obtaining intercepts from?'

Cox sighed. 'I'm not here to debate the process or bureaucracy. The fact is I'm relaying to you what we have.'

'Thank you. And perhaps if you want me to help properly you can share the full details of that. But from my current position, you have to believe me, we've checked everything we have access to in relation to these people. We know about this Namur, we know his close associates. Some were born here, some are legal immigrants, some *were* immigrants but are now naturalised. But we have no records of Nasir Al-Addad. No birth records, marriage, death, tax, immigration, asylum—'

'OK, I get it.'

'So there's not much more we can add in that regard. You and your man are welcome to stay here and see what you can dig up, and I'd appreciate updates as to what you find, but you certainly don't have carte blanche. As long as your work here stays within certain bounds, we'll help you however we can . . .'

Cox wouldn't bother to ask what he meant by that. *Short leash* would probably have been an equally apt description as *certain bounds*.

' . . . But you have to remember this city is in turmoil right now. Have you been to Detroit before?'

'First time.'

'You've probably already seen evidence of the decline?'

Was he referring to the interior decor of the restaurant?

'Yeah. And I've heard plenty about it.'

'And you can surely imagine that in such a big city, with so many people fighting for so few jobs, there's a lot of poverty here, and with poverty we get a lot of anger and resentment. Crime, gangs. In the metro area we already have the highest proportion of Muslims of any big city in the US. It's been that way for a long time, but in recent years it's become a source of deep-rooted grievances from all sides, and I'm sure you can imagine what happens when you add power struggles into the mix.'

'What are you saying exactly?'

'I'm saying at times it feels like this city is in the middle of a civil war. Muslim gangs, African-American gangs, more and more white folk are being pushed to extremism too, the goddamn KKK are having a resurgence here. The police, the Feds, Homeland Security, we all do our best to keep control, and we do care about rooting out the bad guys. But what you're saying about this cell led by Al-Addad is just not what we're seeing or hearing.'

'Except the same conditions you just mentioned are the exact conditions that breed terrorism. Terrorism comes from hate.'

The waiter arrived with the food and Tarkowski quickly pulled the pictures back together and put them in his satchel.

The gigantic steak looked and smelled amazing. Cox noticed Tarkowski eyeing the meat longingly.

'Would you like a plate, sir?' the waiter asked him.

'No, really, I'm fine. I need to go.'

He was already clipping his satchel back together as Cox picked up her knife and fork.

'If you find anything more concrete,' he said, 'then please let us know as soon as you can, and we can talk again.'

'Got it.'

'I'll get the staff to put the food on our account.'

He glanced at the food once more before he got to his feet.

'Have a good day, Agent Cox.'

'You too, Special Agent.'

He turned and headed for the door. Cox stared at the meat for a second before she tucked in.

Her full belly grumbling with satisfaction, and the waistband of her suit trousers pushed to the limit, Cox stepped out of the restaurant and into the cold and waved down a taxi. The quality of the food certainly justified the hefty prices. The only thing missing from the meal was a glass or two of red wine. Actually, a companion would have helped. A companion who gave a shit about her investigation would have been even better. As it was, she'd managed two thirds of the mammoth steak. At least she wouldn't need much food tonight.

She stepped into the taxi. 'Regent Hotel, please.'

The driver of the Prius nodded and they moved off. Cox checked her phone. Nothing from Flannigan since she'd landed. Nothing much from anyone. She needed to make contact with Aydin. Perhaps he'd already had more luck in uncovering Al-Addad's whereabouts. He'd been in the country for more than two days already, though she was yet to hear from him in that time. They'd set up various means of secure electronic communication to use to contact each other, and once she was inside her room and warmed up she'd try to reach out for an update.

The taxi ride only took three minutes. She guessed she could have walked. It might have done her good to burn some of the food off. She paid in cash and stepped from the car and was moving towards the revolving doors of the hotel when she spotted a figure off to her left. He pulled away from the lamppost he was leaning on just as Cox turned to him.

'Aydin,' she said, shocked.

'Jamaal,' he corrected her. 'Or is it Mohammed? I forget.'

'What are you doing here? How did you know—'

He shrugged like it was nothing, which only turned her surprise into anger.

'Seriously, how did you find me here? And what's happened to your face?'

His left eye was badly bruised and swollen. There was dried blood caked inside his bulbous nose and he had a thick lip.

'Just getting to know the locals.'

'A fight? Are you kidding me?'

'It's just a first step to getting me where I need to be. Don't worry.'

'Don't worry? I . . . '

She lost her words. He looked around himself now. As though he was nervous about being out and about with her. She certainly wasn't going to invite him inside. She was more than a little disconcerted that he'd already tracked her down.

Inviting the stalker in for tea was a step too far. But she was also shivering from the cold.

'We need to communicate through the official channels,' Cox said. 'We talked about this. It's why we set them up. And I won't be staying in Detroit the whole time.'

'But you're here in Detroit now. What's the harm?'

'What if someone saw you with me?'

'Nobody that matters knows me. Yet.'

He seemed despondent. Like he had something he'd come to say but didn't know how.

'Do you want to talk?' she asked.

He glanced behind his shoulder again. It was her who'd mentioned about them being seen together, but it was Aydin who was all jittery. Or was that just his natural self?

'I can't stop thinking about that place,' he said.

'K-site? Aydin, come on, we talked about this. You don't need to think about what happened there. You don't need to think about Rashid at all.'

'Are you serious? I have to think about him every minute of every day. I *am* him.'

She knew he'd taken the experience at K-site badly. Worse than she'd expected. The connection that Aydin had felt to Rashid . . . she could never have anticipated that.

'I called her,' he said.

Cox's heart sank.

'Called who?' she asked, though she already feared she knew the answer.'

'Jamaal's mother.'

'Fuck's sake, Ay— what are you trying to do?'

He'd said he wanted to. She'd clearly told him it was among the dumbest things imaginable.

'I had to,' he said. 'I'm playing her son. Won't it seem weird if these people check me out and get in touch with her to say I'm living in Michigan, safe and sound, after all this time, and I didn't even contact her to tell her I'm OK?'

'Who gives a flying crap what she thinks?'

'Her son's alive and she doesn't even know.'

'Yes, but you're not her son!'

They both went silent. Aydin looked troubled. It didn't fill her with confidence at all, particularly after the waste of time meeting with Tarkowski earlier.

'Remember what you're doing here,' Cox said. 'This isn't about Jamaal, his family, any of that. It's about you and me catching some sadistic terrorist scumbags.'

Some sadistic terrorist scumbags who according to Homeland Security didn't even exist.

'I know that,' he said.

Cox's phone vibrated in her bag. She didn't answer.

'Tell me what happened to your face?' she said. 'Who were you fighting with? More importantly, if that's the state of you, what happened to them? You mess up here and they'll sling you straight in jail.'

'It was just a bunch of kids. And they're fine.'

Cox sighed and was about to try to find out more, but her phone rang again and this time she took it out and saw it was Flannigan calling. The fact he'd called twice in a row suggested it was important.

'Just give me a sec?'

She pressed answer and turned away, but soon realised the call had already rung through. When she spun back round Aydin was gone. Cox turned left and right, looked up and down the street. He'd simply vanished.

An uneasy shiver ran through her as she redialled Flannigan, and this time it was little to do with the cold.

CHAPTER 19

Saad and Hamza were already inside JL's when Karim arrived back from his latest run of errands for Namur and his underlings. Three days had passed since the deadly shootout in central Detroit. A deadly shootout that Karim now knew had left three members of the Bloods dead, and Raf's body buried somewhere in the frozen forests further north, along with a stash of weapons of no further use. It'd been three days of heightened anxiousness for Karim, who'd been jittery every time he was outside, and in bits anytime he'd heard a siren or seen a police cruiser nearby. Surely it was only a matter of time before the cops came knocking?

Or so he'd expected. The fact the three days had passed without any incident at all was nothing short of a miracle, he believed. Even stranger was that despite his looking, the only reference in the public domain to the fact the shootout had taken place at all was a brief and little-read news article on a local news website.

Karim hadn't known those gang-bangers at all, but were their lives really worth so little?

Not that it was bad news of course. Most importantly there was nothing at all in the news about the involvement of Namur and his crew in the deaths of the Bloods, which had simply been categorised as drug-related violence to the few media outlets who'd even bothered to run with the non-story.

Still, Karim felt somewhat worn down by his constant state of alertness, and it was on weary legs inside JL's that he headed over to Saad and Hamza who were standing at the side of the pool table, cues in hand, though the balls weren't set and they were deep in a conversation about something.

Saad must have noticed Karim approaching because the conversation stopped and he turned to Karim with a smile.

'The delivery boy returns,' Saad said. 'You didn't bring any take-out for us?'

'Very funny,' Karim said before giving each of them a slap on the back.

Saad and Hamza had no clue about what Karim had seen and done over the last few days, which wasn't bad, all considered, though in a way he was actually a little embarrassed that they only saw him as an errand boy for Namur.

If only they knew what had happened . . .

'So?' Karim said, aware that he'd butted in on something.

Saad and Hamza glanced at each other, as if trying to decide who would tell.

'We've got fresh meat,' Hamza said, indicating over Karim's shoulder.

He turned and set his eyes on the back of a guy's head, over by the small TV in the corner that was connected to an ageing PS3 console.

'Who?' Karim said.

'Exactly,' Hamza said. 'Turned up at prayers two days ago. He's been hanging around here ever since.'

'How'd he get in here?'

'I invited him,' Saad said.

'And?'

'And he's creepy as hell. Barely says a word to anyone. Just comes, prays, sits, plays, prays. Either a fanatic or a lunatic.'

'Give the guy a break,' Hamza said. 'Maybe you're just not his type.'

That received a scolding look from Saad. 'There is something else,' he said.

'Yeah?' Karim said.

'Go and take a look at his face.'

'Do I know him?'

'No. But you could say you two have something in common. You'll see what I mean.'

By now Karim's intrigue had got the better of him. He moved away from his friends and headed up behind the new guy who was tapping away on his controller, in the midst of blasting neon-tinged aliens to hell on the crappy TV all of two yards from his face.

Karim stepped to the front of him, not quite obscuring his view of the game, but making it clear he was there to talk. Karim saw now why Hamza and Saad had taken such an interest in the new guy. Scrawny and probably in his early twenties, he had deep purple bruising around his eye, a fat lip.

Karim expected the guy to stop playing, but he just carried on oblivious. Karim shuffled sideways a few inches and the guy just shifted in his armchair to keep his eyes fixed firmly on the TV.

'What's your name?' Karim said.

No response at all. Karim sidestepped again, this time fully blocking the view.

'Looks like you've been getting into some trouble,' he said.

The guy hit pause on his controller and the sound of laser guns blasting stopped. He glared up to Karim. 'Can you move?'

'No,' Karim said. 'You're English?'

'You don't say? Can you move so I can finish this?'

'I already said no. What's your name?'

'None of your business.'

'Except it is.'

'Because?'

'Because you weren't invited into this club to be a dick.'

'Nor was I invited by you.'

Karim gritted his teeth. This was not what he'd been expecting. Saad and Hamza hadn't warned him the guy was an asshole. He turned round and pulled the plug on the console and the TV went blank.

'What the f—'

He turned back to see the guy shooting up from the chair.

'Sit down before I even that face up for you,' Karim said.

The guy paused. He did what he was told. Good choice.

'Why the attitude?' Karim said, trying to keep himself calm and give the newbie the benefit of the doubt. For now.

'Attitude? You're the one who just came over and screwed my game up.'

'Are you fifteen? Who gives a crap about a video game?'

That comment received a sullen glare.

'Who did that to you?'

'What?'

'What do you think? You've taken a beating.'

'Why does it matter?'

'Because not everyone around here is as nice as I am. It might be that we have some common problems.'

'You reckon?'

Why else were Saad and Hamza so interested?

'Let me guess,' Karim said. 'Their skin was a bit paler than mine?'

The guy said nothing but the way he sighed suggested Karim had hit the nail on the head.

'You're not the only one around here who gets harassed by them,' Karim said. 'But we give as good as we get. In fact, if you show me who—'

'I'm not interested in playground grievances.'

Karim squirmed at that. The suggestion that he *was* bothered about playground grievances. Which, when it involved the likes of Craig and his friends, he was.

'I can think of far better ways of getting my own back on racist pricks,' the guy said.

'Yeah? You'll have to tell me about that sometime.'

'Is there a reason you came over?'

'There are plenty of reasons. Like why are you such a—'

'I'm just minding my own business. I don't see why you can't do the same.'

Karim took a deep breath. Perhaps it was time for a different approach. He held out his hand. 'Why don't we start again? I'm Karim,' he said.

The guy looked like he was contemplating whether to accept the simple gesture or not. He did.

'Mo,' he said as he shook Karim's hand.

'Why don't you come over and shoot some pool with us?' Karim said, nodding over to Saad and Hamza who were staring with intent, still no sign of any game going on.

Mo looked over too, then at his watch. 'Maybe another time,' he said as he got back to his feet. 'Nice meeting you.'

Just like that, he turned and walked towards the doors.

'Yeah. A real pleasure,' Karim said.

He stayed where he was until Mo had opened the doors and stepped out. Then he headed back over to Hamza and Saad.

'So?' Hamza said.

'So he's an asshole.'

'You see what the jocks did to him though?'

'I saw. Hardly surprising. I felt like punching him myself.'

162

Saad and Hamza both smirked until they realised Karim wasn't joking at all.

'Let's find out what we can about him.' Why had a young English guy suddenly appeared there?

A nod from Hamza, but Saad wasn't really listening. A flash of concern swept across his face. Karim followed his friend's gaze to the doors, half expecting to see Mo there again with an AK-47 in his hands, ready to unleash like the closeted gun-toting psychopath he probably was.

Instead it was Benny, glaring over at Karim. He knew what the look meant. He was wanted again.

'No rest for the wicked,' Hamza said.

Karim said nothing. He turned and walked towards the exit, thoughts of the new guy and what the hell he was all about evaporating in an instant, as he wondered what Namur had in store for him next.

CHAPTER 20

As Aydin stepped out of JL's and headed across the foyer towards the outer doors, his attention was grabbed when the wide door off to his right for the kitchen opened and out stepped a rough-looking man with a sneer plastered to his face.

But was it a sneer or just the shape of his features?

Aydin gave him nothing more than a flashing glance, avoided eye contact, and therefore only managed to get a brief glimpse inside the kitchen beyond as he passed. A whole group of rough-looking men were gathered inside, and there was certainly no sign of cooking at this time of night.

Intrigued as he was, Aydin carried on out into the cold. Given the awkward conversation with Karim moments before, he was surprised when he strolled along the eerily quiet street outside the Jalalabad Mosque for a hundred yards with no indication at all of anyone following him out. He'd felt sure he'd laid enough of a seed to get Karim and the other youngsters inside the centre both curious and uptight about his sudden appearance in their mosque and their club.

Apparently not.

Oh well. He'd have to turn it round on them instead. He doubled back on himself and was soon across the street from the mosque, in the shadows down a dark alleyway next to a closed-down restaurant. From his position he had a glimpse of the back-door entrance to JL's, the only community centre he'd ever seen that was manned by beefy bouncers, who he'd also noticed were armed with concealed weapons. As if that in itself didn't raise a huge question mark as to what was taking place behind closed doors.

Not that there was anyone around here who was taking an interest. There were no houses in this area, and most of the business premises were permanently shut down. Even those that were still in use were closed up, with the time now past ten p.m. Certainly there were no passersby here, and the local police were nowhere to be seen.

Factors which would hopefully make this all the more easy for Aydin.

The only question in his mind as he waited in the freezing cold was who was it best to follow tonight? He'd already figured out from his multiple visits to the mosque that the majority of the young men there were likely nothing more than down-on-their-luck early twenty-somethings who had little better to do with their time than to hang around with their own crowd day in, day out. He also had some basic intel from Cox on who some of the apparent players in the community were, in particular one man known as Namur, who Aydin was sure he'd seen in that kitchen.

Certainly no sign of Nasir Al-Addad yet in his time around the mosque, but Aydin had to believe his way in to the group, and to finding Al-Addad, lay with the men, rather than the boys. That said, his brief run-in just now with the guy who'd called himself Karim suggested he was something of a go-between, as was Saad, the kid who Aydin had first met inside the club, who from what Aydin could gather was a messenger of sorts. Neither of them was one of the big boys, exactly, but certainly they were pretenders, and without doubt they were more of a contemporary for Aydin at this stage of the game, despite Aydin having been deliberately obtuse earlier.

Namur would have to wait. Aydin was standing in the cold for only ten minutes before Karim came out of the back door. Alone. He headed for the Jeep Grand Cherokee parked up in the near empty car park. Aydin hadn't known whether he'd be on foot or not, but the fact Karim had the vehicle wasn't the worst-case scenario. His rented Ford was twenty yards down the street. The city's roads were largely marked out in the classical grid system, and the Jalalabad Mosque was on a long straight stretch of main road mainly taken up by large commercial units without a turning within a hundred yards in either direction. As long as Aydin got over and into his car quickly enough, he fancied his chances of following, and remaining unseen doing so.

He waited until the Jeep had swung out into the road and passed him by before he crept out from the darkness and, head down, scuttled along the street for his car. As he was moving forward, his eyes fixed on the Jeep moving away in front, he was aware of more movement across the way at the mosque. He glanced over to see the back door open once again, and three men stepping out. The same man with the sneer he'd seen earlier, one man he didn't recognise, and a big man. Namur?

Aydin, five yards from his car, was in plain sight of them, and once again didn't leave his eyes on them for long. Suddenly he was caught in a conundrum. Should he sit and wait in the car and follow them instead? Or had them seeing him led them to being spooked, in which case did he actually need to make a quick getaway?

The last thing he wanted tonight was a confrontation.

Those thoughts were still circling in his head as he unlocked the car and got in. He peeked over his shoulder as he did so, back to the mosque. Thankfully, the three guys were paying him no attention at all, and were laughing and shouting as they stepped into a large black SUV.

It was tempting to follow them but . . . no, stick to plan A.

Aydin turned the key, and initially left the lights off on the poorly lit street as he pulled into the road. The Jeep was still ahead of him though moments later it turned left and Aydin now flicked his lights on and put his foot down to try to close the gap. He glanced in his rear-view mirror to see Namur's vehicle head out of the car park in the opposite direction. At least they weren't following him

He carried on behind the Jeep, getting no closer than fifty yards to it as Karim took lefts and rights, heading into Dearborn Heights. At one point they passed within a single block of the small apartment building where Aydin was now staying, and right past the still bustling diner where Aydin had received a beating the other day.

Soon crawling down a residential street, Aydin pulled the car over to the side of the road when the red brake lights of the Jeep further ahead flicked on and stayed on.

Aydin could see from the fumes rising up from the Jeep's exhausts that the engine was still idling. Moments later two figures emerged from the house the Jeep was parked by. Not quite what Aydin was expecting to see, the two young women, both with bleached blonde hair, were swaggering giddily, arm in arm. They stuttered and scrambled across the icy driveway on heels several inches high. Both wore long overcoats but their legs underneath were bare. It was clear even from where Aydin was that the women were both drunk and seriously dolled-up.

In a fit of giggles, one of the women opened the back doors of the Jeep and they both pretty much fell inside before the door was closed and the brake lights went off and the Jeep was on its way again.

Initially sticking to the busier inner-city streets, Aydin followed more closely now, his vehicle less suspicious than on the deserted roads near the Jalalabad Mosque. But the Jeep only travelled a short distance on the main roads before heading back across into Dearborn and deep into suburbia, causing Aydin to once again fall back so as to stay unseen. As a result, more than once he'd thought he'd lost Karim, only to catch up again by flooring it every time the Jeep was out of sight, and finding a bit of luck here and there. With each turn he made now, the houses got a little bit bigger, and a little bit smarter, and the cars outside them a little newer and more expensive.

Finally the Jeep stopped again and Aydin initially slowed down, contemplating whether to drive by to get a closer look. No. The brake lights remained on. Once again the Jeep wasn't stopping long so Aydin decided to do the same and he pulled to the side as the back doors of the Jeep opened and the drunk women stumbled out.

Laughing and calling, they headed on up the driveway of the house that Aydin couldn't quite see from his vantage point. The Jeep pulled away and Aydin followed suit. He went slowly as he passed by the large and modern executive house. The two women were still at the front door. It opened just as Aydin was alongside.

Mr Sneer.

And there was the black SUV from the mosque, parked up on the drive.

Mr Sneer glanced over. With a sudden rush of adrenaline, Aydin put his foot down a little harder, trying to get out of the line of sight as quickly as he could. He risked a glance. Was sure the guy was staring over at the Ford.

'Shit,' Aydin said out loud. He whipped his eyes to the front, his eyes flicking between the road and his rear-view mirror as he moved away. He sighed in relief when he realised the man and the women had gone inside and the front door of the house was closed again. Then cursed under his breath a second time when he realised he couldn't see the Jeep up front.

He put his foot down further and the car shot forward, then he braked heavily, nearly losing the back end of the Ford in the process, to stop at the T-junction he was racing towards. He skidded to a stop at the head of the junction and allowed himself a smile of relief. The road layout had been kind to him once again, and the Jeep was right there up ahead on the long straight road.

Quickly calming himself, Aydin headed out after it, managing to keep a safe distance. Less than three miles later the Jeep turned off a main road just past a gargantuan mosque and headed up a twisting lane. Aydin pulled over onto the verge of the main road. At first he thought the Jeep was heading for the mosque, but he soon realised it was going into a car park for a block of apartments next to it that was partly obscured from the road by a run of trees.

Aydin lost sight of the Jeep and was about to follow further in when he spotted Karim on foot, heading across the cleared car park towards the entrance to the apartments. Finally it looked like the bizarre journey was over. So was this Karim's home?

Aydin decided to wait it out. Once Karim was inside, he'd head over and park up and take a look around the place.

At least that was the intention, but then Aydin heard the single blip of a siren, saw the flash of blue-and-red in his side mirror and realised there was a police car approaching right behind him.

No need to panic. Aydin was sure the police car hadn't been following him before. He would have spotted it surely?

He quickly pulled out his phone and began an imaginary conversation as the police car pulled up alongside him. Aydin glanced over and ended his phone call before he opened the window.

'Evening, officer,' he said as he looked over at the policeman. He was surprised, and a little comforted, when he saw the complexion of the policeman, and the name tag that read Riyad.

'What are you doing?' Riyad said. 'There's no stopping here.'

'Sorry. I was on the phone.'

'So? You can't stop here.'

'Sorry, officer. Force of habit. Back home you can't use the phone and drive.'

Riyad looked a little miffed by this, and Aydin knew his accent had once again only further raised suspicion in the local. He glared at Aydin, then his eyes passed behind Aydin to the apartment block beyond.

'What are you doing here?' Riyad asked.

A pretty vague question, and not at all dissimilar to what his colleague from Dearborn Heights police had asked him in the diner the other day.

'I'm just on my way home,' Aydin said.

Riyad looked further puzzled by that.

'I'm pulling over,' Riyad said. 'I'll need to see your licence and registration.'

This was all Aydin needed. But he'd cooperate.

At least he would have done, but Riyad's radio crackled to life and he turned away from Aydin to listen. Aydin couldn't hear the details of the request, or Riyad's response, but he got the gist.

'You're off the hook,' Riyad said, turning back to face him. 'But no loitering here. You go straight home. I'll be keeping an eye out for your licence plate.'

Aydin nodded. Time for a new car tomorrow then. Riyad flipped a switch and his siren blared. He closed his window and the police car shot off into the distance. Aydin thought about the police officer's words for a moment as he watched the flashing lights fade into the distance. He again looked over to the apartment block.

No. There was no need to go up there tonight. He had plenty to go on for now. It was getting late and there was still one more place he wanted to check on before he called it a day.

He took the phone from his lap and opened the map app. Typed in the address. It was less than two miles from where he was. This wouldn't take long. He'd be back in his apartment soon enough.

Quietly satisfied with his progress, Aydin pulled back onto the road, and set off for his final waypoint of the night.

CHAPTER 21

Cox was sitting on the bed in her hotel room, curtains open on a cloudy start to a freezing morning in Detroit as she waited for the call on her laptop to connect. Ever conscious of eavesdroppers, the voice over the IP line itself was as secure as it could be, though Cox had her earphones in so that on the very off-chance that somehow someone was listening to the conversation from bugs in her room, they'd at least only be able to hear half of it.

The high-pitched voice of Leslie Kaufman, the senior analyst assigned to Cox's operation from within GCHQ, finally burst into Cox's ear. Cox had known Kaufman for more than two years, and together with the team underneath her, Cox believed she was among the best in the world at intercepting electronic communications of targets. In fact, Cox thought it seriously unnerving just how deep into the everyday lives of targets GCHQ were able to go without them being any the wiser, even after the backlash the secretive government organisation had faced in recent years following the revelations by the whistleblower Edward Snowden related to the mass collection of online and telephone data.

'So what time is it over there?' Kaufman asked.

'Just gone seven a.m.'

'Ouch. Busy day ahead.'

'Aren't they all? So where have you got to?'

'We've made some really good progress these last few days.'

'I'm glad to hear it.'

'But we're going to need more help from your end if we're to really make sense of it all.'

Cox sighed, though it wasn't entirely an unexpected comment. There was only so much that cyber intercepts could provide without other corroborating intel, and only so deep that GCHQ could go without some sort of physical intervention – as in gaining direct access to people or their devices.

'Give me the snapshot then,' Cox said.

'We've concentrated in particular on Akhwabi, or Namur as you said he's more commonly known, and aside from regular communications, which I'm not seeing much interest in, we have traced quite a lot of activity we believe to be him from within the dark web, particularly on the KOLO and Gresta messaging sites.'

Two sites which were widely known to be used by criminals from all walks of life, all around the world. In some ways, the existence of such sites, although layered in secrecy, made it easier for law enforcement and security organisations. The simple fact alone that Namur was messaging across those sites was a huge red alert.

'As you know, this process is quite hit and miss,' Kaufman said. 'People use the dark web for good reason, and even with our best efforts it's often the case that with a real-time message string, it disappears from existence before we ever see it. But for the more meaty conversations over hours or days, we have a better shot at interception.'

'I get that. So you've got some of the meaty conversations, you're trying to tell me?'

'Yes and no. Yes we've captured quite a few back and forths, and we're building up a picture of who Namur has

173

been corresponding with. Or, at least, the IP addresses of those people.'

'I'm sensing a but here.'

'Several actually. As you can imagine, these guys are using all sorts of relays to mask their true locations.'

'So you've no idea where they really are, or who they really are?'

'I didn't say that. It's not an easy process, but it's not impossible to unpick the layers and work along the chain to figure out the true locations. From there, the identities, with any luck.'

'And where are you on the chain?'

'There are ten key contacts we're looking into currently. For six of them we've figured out the original destination IP address. And . . . I'm not sure if this was what you were expecting, but they're all in the US.'

Cox's face screwed as she thought about that one for a few moments. Was it what she was expecting? Not exactly. She'd certainly thought, based on Al-Busaidi's intel, that Namur's cell would still be in regular contact with someone within the Middle East. Why weren't they?

'Which locations in the US?' Cox asked.

'All over really. Eastern Seaboard, Midwest, California.'

That really didn't help Cox much. Although the fact there were several locations was worrying. Largely because at present the operation wasn't geared to target anyone other than the cell in Michigan.

'We need to identify these people as soon as possible,' Cox said. 'If the threat spreads out from Namur and Michigan, we need to know as soon as possible.'

'Of course. We're working on it, day and night. Though you didn't let me get to my other but.'

'Which is?'

174

'The messages themselves. They're all encrypted.'

Cox sighed, but what had she expected really? 'You can't break it?'

'We haven't yet. But from all of the attempts we've run, it looks like they're running a particular type of cypher that we're not familiar with. Perhaps something bespoke that changes randomly after every message.'

'Is that a problem?'

'Nothing's a problem given enough time, but if you want quick results, we just need access to the key.'

'The encryption key?' Cox sighed again as she thought through Kaufman's unspoken words. 'Let me guess, there's only one way to get you that?'

'Well, I imagine there's multiple ways you *could* get it, right from knocking on their door and asking nicely, through to—'

'Through to finding some way to steal it without them knowing.'

'That would work too.'

'But there's no way you can get this without physical intervention, is what I think you're saying.'

'Of course we could try to plant malware to obtain the key, but that could take time, as we need to go phishing first.'

'No, no, that's fine. Let me see what I can do.'

Cox already had more than one idea about how she would get that key, and who she would target to do so.

CHAPTER 22

Cox rubbed her gloved hands together then cupped them to her mouth and blew through them in a vain attempt to try to get some feeling back in her iced digits. She'd been sitting in the car with the engine off for the best part of two hours now. From the base-level intel she already had on the players in Namur's gang, and the little Aydin had so far relayed to her from his own efforts, she'd already started to build a picture of what the roles of some of the various people around Namur were. It was apparent to Cox that the young men within the group, Saad and Karim in particular, were relative newcomers, and overtly keen to win plaudits and to be taken under the wings of their elders. While it appeared Karim was already allowed to roam with the big boys, Saad remained little more than an errand boy. A messenger. Yet even if he didn't have the answers Cox needed, he might well have access to those answers, even if he didn't know it himself.

He was the easiest first target for Cox, no doubt about it. The easiest to get to and the easiest to manipulate. Which was why she'd been sitting in her car outside the downtrodden bar in central Detroit for more than two hours, despite the unfamiliar territory and the freezing temperature. Saad had definitely gone inside this place. Cox had followed him here from his home in Dearborn. Quite what he was doing inside, she had no idea, but he'd definitely not come out, at least not out the front, and his car remained parked in the lot across the street from where she was sitting.

Cox checked her watch. It was gone ten p.m. The bar wasn't thriving, far from it. Cox had seen barely a dozen people go in over the last two hours, and none that she recognised. So who was Saad meeting with?

The answer to that question remained a mystery when not long after, Saad emerged from the front door. Alone.

Except he now had a laptop bag over his shoulder. He'd gone in empty-handed.

And he didn't turn left out of the bar, to head for his car, but hunkered his neck down into his coat and moved off to the right and walked away on foot.

Now Cox was really in a quandary. The last thing she wanted was to be outside traipsing around for who knew how long in the freezing cold, yet she could hardly follow Saad in the car now.

She could call it quits for the night, or . . .

Cox was made of tougher stuff than that. She went to open the door.

Then paused when she spotted the darkened figure across the street, emerging from an unseen spot within the bar's small car park. Thanks to a thick coat on top, and a hood covering the figure's head, Cox could see nothing of the person's face. She was sure their sudden appearance wasn't coincidence. Even after just a few seconds she could tell from the way the person moved, so carefully, zig-zagging to keep in the shadows, switching from short slow steps to big fast steps, that they were moving from cover to cover.

Saad was being followed by someone else. How had Cox not noticed before?

She waited a few seconds until both Saad and his stalker were out of earshot before she quietly opened her door and set off into the night in tow.

As she ever so carefully followed, she became more and more spooked as the stalker continually disappeared before her eyes, moulding into the darkness that surrounded them. This was no amateur, and it made her hold back further. Someone so good at stalking would surely be just as good as spotting when they were being watched?

Even more disconcerting, though, as Cox intermittently picked up her pace to catch up, was that the stalker wasn't just stalking. He, or she, was steadily closing the distance to Saad, even though the young man seemed to have no idea whatsoever that he was being followed.

Cox didn't know what to do. Should she deliberately create some noise to give away her own position? Or she could even shout out a warning to alert Saad? But alert him to what exactly?

Then, with Cox's mind still searching for an answer, it happened.

As Saad stepped across the mouth of a pitch-black alleyway, the stalker shouted out.

'Hey, Saad!'

Saad stopped and turned, his face was obscured by shadow. The stalker pounced. Cox, open-mouthed, held back a gasp. A second later, in absolute silence, both of the figures in front of her had disappeared from view into the blackness of the alley.

Cox's heart raced. What the hell was she supposed to do now? Of course she could run headlong into the alley after them, save Saad from whatever was happening. But was he even the good guy in this? Who was attacking him?

Plus, she shouldn't really even be there.

She could call for help?

Instead, she found herself looking around nervously as she crossed the road to try to find a secluded vantage point. She tucked herself away behind a dumpster in an alley opposite. No sign of Saad or his attacker. No sounds either. And the street was otherwise deserted. More than once Cox had to hold back the urge to charge forward . . .

No need. Moments later she saw shadows moving within the alley, the faint sounds of a scuffle . . . then a figure took shape. Saad? Or the attacker? Cox couldn't be sure. She held her breath. The figure continued to gain definition as it came forward to the head of the alley, like an image buffering on a computer screen. The person was hunched over, almost limping . . . a man . . . as he stumbled away, his partially obscured face was caught in the thinnest veil of light from the orange street light above.

It was Aydin.

And he was now walking, or more like scurrying, away from the scene carrying the bag Saad had earlier had when he left the bar. He was hurt. Cox had no doubt about that, it was obvious by the way he was hunched over and shuffling along.

And what about Saad? Confusion swept through Cox. Did Aydin need help? But she and he weren't supposed to have direct physical contact here in Michigan. What if someone saw? And how would she explain to the police or to the paramedics who they both were?

No, one way or another, she'd catch up with Aydin soon enough. She had to trust he would look after himself. He certainly had a propensity for survival.

So instead, Cox checked left and right, then darted out from cover and, keeping her feet as quiet and soft as she could on the icy ground, she headed straight across the street to the alley.

She heard him before she saw him. He was groaning and moaning. Then she noticed the writhing figure on the floor. She took out her phone to light him up.

Saad was crumpled in a heap on the frozen tarmac, an arc of blood was spreading out from his body.

'Shit,' Cox said as she hunched down and turned him over onto his back. He was barely conscious and clutching at the oozing wound on his belly.

He needed an ambulance. And fast. Cox lifted her phone up . . .

No, she couldn't use hers. She delved into Saad's pockets and found his, then grimaced as she grabbed his limp wrist and used his thumb to unlock the device. She called 911 and in her best fake American accent gave the basics. The dispatcher told her to wait there. Told her to stay on the line.

Cox ended the call and dropped the phone to the ground.

'Help is on the way,' she said to him, though got no response at all, other than his continued groaning, which was weakening by the second.

Whatever state Saad was in, she certainly didn't want to be there when the ambulance arrived. But she couldn't leave just yet. Taking away the horrible situation of a man dying in front of her, this was now a case of damage limitation. Was there anything here that could tie Aydin, or her, to the scene? She shone the light from her phone around the area. She saw no sign of a knife of any other weapon, nothing at all that Aydin had left behind.

Cox froze when she heard footsteps and voices nearby. She switched the torch off and held her breath. Saad continued to groan, though the sound was weak and almost inaudible now even to Cox and she was right next to him. She held her breath as long as she could as she listened. Her eyes keenly watched as two shapes appeared at the end of the alley. They

180

didn't stop. Didn't seem to take notice at all. They were merry and oblivious and soon out of sight and Cox heaved a sigh of relief as quietly as she could.

The relief didn't last for long. As she turned the torch back on, and shone the white beam over the body in front of her, it didn't take her long to realise that Saad had already stopped breathing.

Cox closed her eyes for a couple of seconds as she fought against the sense of despair. Then the sound of a distant siren caught her attention.

There was nothing more she could do here. With a well of guilt and worry swelling in the pit of her stomach, Cox straightened up and headed out into the night.

CHAPTER 23

At the tender age of twenty-four, Aydin had enough scars from battle wounds to last anyone a lifetime. Despite the experience and familiarity, the agony remained as overwhelming as any other time he'd had to self-stitch a gaping wound.

He took two deep breaths then bit down on the leather belt between his teeth before he squeezed the folds of skin tightly together and sank the needle into the flesh. He weaved in and out, in and out, in fluid motion, knowing that it was best not to prolong the ordeal a second longer than necessary.

By the end he was woozy from the pain and he opened his mouth and the belt clattered to the floor as he dropped the bloody needle into the sink. He stared in the mirror of his closet bathroom for a few seconds, trying to focus on his reflection. He'd been lucky. If the knife had penetrated a few inches further down then Aydin would have been in big trouble. As it was, the wound on his side, near the base of his rib cage, had caused a nasty-looking gash that had bled badly, but the bones had done their duty faithfully, protecting his organs from the blade that Saad had stabbed him with. The same blade that Aydin had, somewhat reluctantly, turned against Saad moments after.

That was a mistake, Aydin knew. An instinctive reaction. It had never been his intention to so badly hurt Saad, but in a grapple like that, best intentions are rarely relevant.

And Aydin knew Saad hadn't been as lucky as he had. The wound he'd delivered was highly likely to have been fatal, barring a miracle medical intervention.

As sullen as he was anything else at his own mistake, Aydin grabbed a small hand towel and wrapped up the debris. He'd burn it all. The knife he'd already disposed of. He was in the bedroom looking for a clean t-shirt when his laptop pinged. He headed over. Cox. It was nearly midnight, what was that about?

He thought about ignoring her. He didn't need a babysitter. He'd only been in Michigan a few days and was content to be finding his feet still and doing things his own way, and he'd already rebuffed more than one attempt from her for an update. He'd contact her when good and ready. But when Cox sent another nudge barely two minutes later, then another, Aydin decided to bite the bullet.

It took a couple of minutes to connect the encrypted call, though when Cox answered he almost immediately wished he hadn't bothered with the lengthy procedure.

'I know what you did,' she said, each word edged with anger and bitterness.

'Do you?'

'He's dead, Aydin. You killed him . . . you bloody idiot.'

Aydin didn't say anything to that.

'I was there. I was following Saad.'

How could that be? He hadn't seen anyone else around. But then . . . Cox wasn't exactly just another chump.

'Aydin. You killed a man. I know it's not the first time, but . . . Saad? He was barely even out of his teens. He was no criminal mastermind. Haven't you got anything to say?'

183

No. He didn't.

'You might get lucky,' Cox said. 'Perhaps the police won't care too much about him. And perhaps even if they do, you managed to get away from there without leaving much of a trace. Best get rid of that knife though.'

Aydin frowned as he toyed with her sudden change from accusatory to pragmatic.

'I already did that,' Aydin said. 'And the knife wasn't mine.'

A momentary silence.

'He attacked me first,' Aydin said, now feeling the need to justify his actions. But was that for his benefit or Cox's. 'Or maybe you didn't see that part.'

'You grabbed him and pulled him into a dark alley.'

'To talk to him.'

'That's not how you talk to someone, Aydin.'

'Says who? And you were following him too. Why?'

Another silence from her now.

'I wanted to put some pressure on him,' Aydin said. 'I've seen what he's about. He's a bloody informant. I thought . . . I thought I could play him.'

'An informant?'

She sounded shocked now. Clearly she hadn't known. So why had she been following him then?

'I don't know at what level, but I saw him earlier. Fed types.'

'Jesus, Aydin, then you're really in the shit.'

He could imagine her in that moment, head in her hands in her hotel room.

'No. I'm not,' Aydin said. 'If it is the Feds, it's nothing to do with why we're here, and they can't exactly now blow open that they had someone on the edge of Namur's gang. They'll need to keep this quiet.'

'You've thought this through already.'

184

'I'm offended you would have thought otherwise. Saad was one of the best targets for getting direct intel. You obviously thought the same thing, as did the Feds.'

Another silence, which this time gave her answer clear enough. But why was she trying to get direct intel from Saad?

'I'm going to need the laptop,' Cox said.

'What laptop?'

'The one you stole from him. Saad was a messenger. An errand runner. That laptop could have evidence of communications, or perhaps more importantly, evidence of the methods of communications the cell are using. We need it to—'

'Whoa, Cox, I see where you're going. But there was no laptop.'

A pause. Then, 'What?'

'There was no laptop,' he said again. 'The bag contained money. Ten thousand dollars. He took it from the Feds in the bar.'

'Shit.'

Aydin's brain whirred.

'You're saying they're communicating via the Internet.'

Cox said nothing.

'You need an encryption key.'

Again nothing. But Aydin didn't need an answer, he was already planning his next step.

'Leave it with me,' he said before he killed the call.

CHAPTER 24

The mosque was filled with men of all ages, the vast majority of them wearing traditional dress, though Karim was in simple cotton trousers and shirt. The address by Imam Ibrahim had been solemn yet profound, though Karim could already remember little of it, hadn't even attempted to comprehend the sentiment. He wasn't in mourning as such, though the loss of his friend Saad had hit him hard. He was angry and filled with a thirst for vengeance, and for some inexplicable reason the focus of his ire throughout the address had been on Mohammed Akhbar. The young Englishman had sat towards the front of the room, and was clearly enthralled by the Imam, given the fact that now, as the room was slowly clearing, Mohammed was up at the front having a private word with the religious leader.

'You OK?' Hamza said as he came up to Karim's side.

'Why wouldn't I be?' Karim said.

'I mean . . . you know.'

'Look at him.' Karim nodded over to Mohammed.

'What?'

'What's he up to?'

'Maybe give him a break,' Hamza said, shrugging. 'Probably just a devotee. I've spoken to him, even got a few words out of him. I can't figure him out at all but one thing is for sure; he knows the texts like the back of his hand. Maybe he's an Imam in training or something.'

Karim said nothing to that, though it was certainly a different vibe altogether that he got from the guy.

'Come on, let's go,' Karim said.

Hamza nodded and the two of them made their way to the doors. Not for the first time recently, Karim was sidetracked before he got there, when he saw Benny approaching off to his left.

'You're wanted,' was all he said before he spun on his heel and headed off.

Karim rolled his eyes.

'I guess I'll see you around then,' Hamza said before Karim scuttled away.

He caught up with Benny who led them though the community centre and into one of the sparse meeting rooms decked out in cheap pine furniture where Namur was already sitting and waiting at the table. A teapot was sitting on top with three glasses, thick black tea already poured. Karim got a waft of the fragrant mix, topped off by a fresh stick of cinnamon in each glass.

'Have one,' Namur said, indicating the glasses.

The three men each took a glass and Karim and Benny a seat. This was certainly a bit different. About the most informal set-up that Karim had ever seen his new boss in. He couldn't figure in his head whether that was a good or a bad thing.

'I'm sorry about your friend,' Namur said.

Karim nodded but didn't say a word.

'He was a good kid. He would have been a good addition here.'

Karim still said nothing. He wasn't sure if he was supposed to or not.

'I'm only going to ask you this one time,' Namur said. 'So whatever answer you give, that's the one that sticks.'

Karim nodded. His palms were sweaty now and he tried to sit still and keep himself composed for whatever Namur threw at him.

'Why was Saad down there? And why was he alone?'

'I . . . I have no idea.'

Namur scoffed. 'I thought you'd say that. Seems to be the answer everyone gives. Whatever the reason, and I will find out, it's clear to me what happened there.'

'It is?'

'Bloods. That was their turf. He shouldn't have been that side of the divide.'

Karim had thought the same thing. Was Saad's death the first retaliation by the Bloods? It made sense, but the question remained as to why Saad had been there at all, and he really didn't know the answer to that one.

'I can keep our people safe,' Namur said. 'Loyalty to me breeds loyalty back to you. It's a two-way thing. You go behind my back . . . you can see for yourself the kind of trouble you can get yourself in.'

'I won't go behind your back,' Karim said. 'I don't even know how you think I'd do that, or why?'

Namur held Karim's eye as if waiting for the young man to say something else, but Karim really didn't have anything to add. Was Namur calling him out? But Karim had done nothing wrong, what else could he say?

'The new guy,' Namur said. 'Tell me what you found.'

'Not much so far. His name's Mohammed Akhbar. He's English. Apparently he's on some sort of secondment here.'

'Secondment?'

'He's got a twelve-month visa. He's going to be working at the University of Michigan, though from what I can tell he hasn't started yet.'

188

Most of this intel hadn't come from Karim's work, as such. Rather Namur had introduced him to a couple of contacts who termed themselves 'private detectives'. Whatever that meant these days. They weren't even based in Michigan. From what he understood they basically just scoured the Internet and police and government databases, by who knew what kind of access, to gain intel on people.

'This was just preliminary,' Karim said. 'It'll take a few more days to get everything they can. If you really think it's worth the cost?'

The PIs charged a couple of hundred dollars an hour. Karim certainly had no interest in footing their likely exorbitant bill. Couldn't they just have asked Mohammed for this stuff?

'The white kids beat him up?' Namur said.

'That's what I heard. Outside Rosie's diner. You know—'

'Yeah, I know where it is. He was beaten up, only to be saved by two women. The question is, what the hell was he doing?'

'How do you mean?'

'How did he get into that fight?'

'Who knows? Craig and his boys—'

'You're saying it was them?'

'Around there? Most likely, yeah. They're probably looking out for any brown kid on his own to beat up on after . . . after what we did.'

Karim hung his head as he said the last part. Not that he was ashamed of what he'd done exactly. Mainly he was happy and proud about it in fact, but when talking to Namur he saw that disapproving look and he was sure his boss saw his actions as immature and ill thought out. Particularly if the jocks were now out seeking reprisals. Where would it end? Did they have a hand in Saad's death? It would have made some sense, had it not been for the location of Saad's demise.

Namur said nothing now as he continued to glare at Karim while he took a sip from his tea. Karim hadn't touched his. He was too nervous, and his hands so clammy the glass would probably slip from his grasp.

'We've organised another deal,' Namur said.

Karim looked from the boss to Benny and back.

'Yeah?'

'And you're coming with us.'

'I . . . yeah . . . of course.'

'Just the three of us for this one. We need to keep it quiet.'

Karim nodded. He realised Benny was giving him a death stare but daren't look in that direction.

'Are you gonna tell me this time what we're looking to buy?' Karim said.

'Why do you need to know?'

'Why? I mean . . . because . . . '

'You don't. The less people know, the better. But I want you there with me. After the last time . . . you're a big part of this.'

What was *this* exactly?

'Thank you,' Karim said. 'Just tell me what you need me to do.'

'Benny'll fill you in. Clear any plans you've got for the weekend. And get your sunglasses out. We're getting away from this dump and this shitty winter.'

Benny sprang to his feet. The simple gesture made Karim jump. He relaxed a little when he saw Benny was only indicating for him to get up. The meeting was over.

'And let me know what else you find on Akhbar. Get someone on him too if you need. It was you who came to me about him, and I can't make a decision if I don't even know what I'm looking at.'

'I will.'

Benny grabbed his arm and shepherded him towards the door.

CHAPTER 25

It was no understatement to say that Aydin's mind was in turmoil as he drove away from the mosque, and it wasn't just because he'd had to sit through an address in honour of a man who he'd killed the night before. The fact was, on each of the last few days now, Aydin had spent several hours either in the mosque or the community centre that accompanied it, far more time than he spent in his home mosque back in London where he'd been working long hours for months on end, and where he'd never really warmed to the lacklustre Imam. Here, though, Imam Ibrahim . . . Aydin struggled with the comparison somewhat, but Ibrahim reminded him of his Imam Hadid back at the Farm.

Horrific memories to dredge up at any point.

Yes, the years spent there, largely under the cruel tutelage of Aziz Al-Addad, were the darkest and most painful of Aydin's dark and painful life, but he'd always held respect for the Imam during his time there. A man who'd not just taught Aydin about Islam, but who'd guided him through his formative years.

Since his escape from that place, Aydin had long considered whether the Imam at the Farm really was good and moral, or whether that impression of him was simply because he was such a stark contrast to the other far more oppressive elders there. Having only spent a few days with Ibrahim, Aydin realised it was probably worse than that. Imam Hadid at the Farm was, in all likelihood, simply a wolf dressed in sheep's clothing. In his own kindly and fatherly way he'd helped to show Aydin and the other boys at the Farm down a path of violence and hatred, all wrapped up as if it was God's will. Yes, he'd done so in a smooth and caring and comforting manner, as opposed to Al-Addad's brutishness, but nonetheless his purpose and presence at that place had been clear.

Despite all that, in Aydin's mind, he still felt warmth at the thought of the conversations and the debates that he had had with Imam Hadid about Islam, and about life. A warmth that he was once again feeling with Imam Ibrahim.

Surely he couldn't be blinkered again after everything he'd been through?

Aydin shook the conflicting thoughts from his head. He didn't have the time to dwell now. He checked his mirrors then pulled the newly rented Chevrolet Cruze off the main road and into the car park for the Islamic Center of America. The car park for the mosque was equally as huge as the building it served, though mid-afternoon during the week, in between prayer times, it wasn't even a fifth full. Aydin parked the Cruze in the middle of the spaces, near to another cluster of cars, and facing away from the mosque and towards the neighbouring apartment block known as St Sarkis Towers.

Of course, he could have parked closer to the apartments – his destination – but if this went wrong, the last thing he wanted was for his car to be parked right outside and visible to witnesses. From here, he felt a safe distance, but also still had a good view.

He couldn't sit and wait too long though. He knew Karim Hussein wasn't in, as he'd seen the guy at the Jalalabad

Mosque, and when Aydin had left there, Karim had been in the middle of a meeting with Namur. There was a chance though that he could be back soon enough.

Aydin took his phone from his pocket and dialled the number. It went straight through to voicemail. He cancelled the call, waited a few seconds for the voicemail to reset, then called again. Still no answer. No guarantee that the apartment was empty, but it was as good as he could hope for.

Aydin stepped out from the Cruze and pulled his near-empty backpack over his shoulder as he did a quick take all around him to make sure he wasn't being watched. He wasn't. Hood up and head down, he set off across the car park, aware that both the mosque and the apartment blocks had CCTV. He took a direct route across the snow to reach the adjacent lot for the apartment block. No one was around, though as he approached the building he could hear noises from the homes within. A few TVs, some shouting, a baby crying.

The plain-looking apartment block was basic and generally well kept, though security, as with most affordable housing wherever in the world, was lax. In that there really wasn't any. Aydin was able to head straight onto the stairs and up to the top floor without hindrance and he soon found himself standing in the corridor outside the Husseins' apartment. From the research Aydin had done the night before, he knew Karim lived with his parents and younger brother. The brother was at school, and both parents worked in low-income jobs and wouldn't be back until early evening. Aydin was taking no chances though. Satisfied he remained anonymous on the corridor, he knocked on the door then held his ear close to the wood. He could hear nothing from the inside.

He knocked once more for good measure, though was already fishing in his coat pocket for his balaclava this time. Still no sounds from inside as he pulled the fabric over his head. Then he went to his other pocket for his tools. Two locks to go through. They took him less than a minute and he was soon slowly pushing the door open.

No alarm. Not that it'd have been a big problem if there was one. He'd been prepared for it.

One last glance over his shoulder then Aydin stepped inside and closed the door softly behind him.

Other than the apartment being dingy and cramped with a narrow entrance hall and low ceilings, the first thing he noticed was the smell. A nice smell. Spices, both from cooking and from incense. Everything about stepping inside was like . . . stepping into his family home back in London.

He shook those memories away. The last time he'd been in his London home, he'd inadvertently led the sharks to his mother's door. She'd been killed that same day. Whatever happy memories might have been locked somewhere in his head about his early childhood, before he was taken to the Farm, he wasn't letting them out today.

Feeling a rush of anger, exactly what he needed to see him through, he started his search.

The apartment, although three-bedroomed, was cramped and cluttered, with little spare space in any of the rooms. Aydin popped his head round each doorway, initially satisfying himself with the layout of the place, before he headed to Karim's bedroom, a box that was barely ten feet by ten feet. A quick targeted search led Aydin to exactly what he was looking for: a laptop computer and a tablet. He'd brought two USB drives with him, each pre-loaded with imaging software. Plug and play devices that would automatically copy the hard drives of the machines without him even needing to log on. He plugged the drives in and set the machines on the top of the unmade bed. It shouldn't take more than thirty minutes for the imaging. Plenty of time to continue his mooch around.

Aydin only spent a little time in Karim's brother's room, and in the master bedroom too, where the only items of interest he found were a loaded shotgun, a shiny Remington revolver and more rounds than were feasibly necessary for home invasion purposes. Whatever the explanation and intent of those, he left the guns and the ammo in place and after a brief search of the open plan living area, he finally turned his focus back to Karim's room.

The rest of the apartment had been exactly what he would have expected. The furnishings and the knick-knacks . . . the look and feel and smell of the place was undeniably a family from the Middle East – Iraq, he believed the family had come from. Yet the apartment also had all of the mod-cons and pop culture items one would expect in consumer-driven America, from the large LED TV to the various electronic devices in the small kitchen area, to the diet cookery books, to the dust-covered spin bike in the corner of the lounge.

Karim's bedroom though was quite a stark contrast of clashing personalities. In many ways it could have been the room of any American teenager, with glitzy fast cars on the walls, local sports heroes, posters of big budget sci-fi movies. But the closer he looked, there was a strange and conflicting undertone, with various titbits related to his family's faith and home country, topped off with partially hidden paraphernalia glorifying Middle East violence. The most overt of those items was a printed picture inside a drawer showing a group of mujahideen, their heads and faces covered with shemaghs, large weapons in their hands.

People Karim knew, or just something he'd pulled from the Internet?

Aydin didn't know much about Karim Hussein at all, but what he could see was that this was a young man who really didn't quite know which direction he should be taking in life. And if the wrong kind got their tendrils wrapped around him . . .

But Aydin wasn't there to explore the psyche of the clearly conflicted young man, he was there for intel. While his software was still doing its work, he continued to rummage through drawers, the cupboard, under the bed, between the bed frame and mattress, behind posters and picture frames.

He hadn't expected any sort of smoking gun, and didn't find one, but it was worth the effort to make sure.

The green light on the drive in the tablet blinked on. It was done. Aydin pulled it out, stuffed it in his pocket then put the tablet back on the drawer unit where he'd found it.

He heard a noise outside the room . . .

A key in the lock on the front door.

'Crap.'

He glanced down to the laptop. No green light yet. He could pull the drive out and hope he'd already got most of what he needed . . . or . . .

The front door opened.

He grabbed the laptop and slung it into the backpack which he'd just thrown onto his shoulders again when he saw the shoe move across the open doorway in front of him. Karim appeared and nearly jumped out of his skin when he spotted Aydin standing there.

'Motherfucker.'

Anger. The worst reaction Aydin could have hoped for.

Yet Karim still spun and went to dart away. Aydin bounded forward, initially confused, until he realised Karim wasn't going for the front door, to run away. He was going to his parents' bedroom. Aydin could think of only one reason why he'd do that.

No point in getting into a gunfight. Particularly as he didn't have a gun himself.

Aydin slammed Karim's bedroom door shut and clicked the lock. He turned and raced over to the window which looked out onto the small balcony accessed through the lounge area.

A bang on the door.

'You fucker. I'll blow your head off!'

Aydin pulled open the window and slunk out onto the balcony. He looked over the edge, eight storeys below. Nothing as handy as a drainpipe here, though the balconies, stacked one on top of the other provided a route. Of sorts.

There was a boom behind him. A shotgun blast that would surely devastate the bedroom door lock, though Aydin didn't bother to look. He only had seconds before Karim was standing there with a clear shot. Grasping the top of the balcony screen, Aydin swung his legs over, let his body dangle, then one hand at a time reached down until he was hanging from the lip of the balcony floor. His feet were only inches from the screen of the balcony below.

'You piece of—'

Aydin dropped. His feet fell inside the balcony below and he pushed his body forward and clattered down onto the concrete. He heard thudding upstairs.

'I'm gonna kill you!'

He waited a couple of seconds. Karim couldn't see him at all. Would he assume Aydin had headed into the apartment?

He heard the footsteps above moving away, back inside. Most likely Karim wasn't finished, but at least he wasn't going to sit on the balcony and take potshots.

Karim had eight flights of stairs to clear. Aydin had seven balconies. A more direct route, in a way.

He moved to the edge and looked up to make sure it was all clear, then grasped the balcony screen and swung himself over again. He dropped down to the next level, cleared another floor, then another in quick succession without any problem.

Soon he only had two floors to go, though he was out of breath from exertion and his arms were beginning to ache and feel numb from the effort.

As he went to drop down once more, he messed up the landing angle of his feet, and his right foot, rather than dropping inside the balcony, smacked on top of the screen. Aydin, hands already free from the balcony floor above, had nothing to grasp and his body tipped back and he tumbled . . .

In the split second before he landed on the ground below, he somehow managed to twist his body side on, at least avoiding a potentially horrendous landing on top of the laptop. Instead his elbow and his shoulder and his hip took the brunt of the blow as he smashed down onto the snowy grass below. Even frozen solid, at least it was better than concrete, though he was sure the stitches in his side ruptured even if he didn't dare to look just then.

Ignoring the immense pain, Aydin groaned as he hauled himself back to his feet. Looking up, there was more than one balcony where the surprised occupants were now leaning over, watching the spectacle and wondering what the hell was happening.

Not good.

'What are you doing!' one person shouted.

'I'm calling the cops,' said another.

The police were the least of Aydin's worries right now.

He glanced across the car park. His car was forty yards away. The entrance to the apartment block was only twenty. He had to expect Karim would be out in the open any second, and certainly before Aydin made it to the car.

Decision made. He raced across to the entrance as best he could manage with his banged-up body. He was only three yards away when Karim burst out into the open, pulling the shotgun up to his chest at the same time. But, as Aydin had hoped, he obviously wasn't expecting to see the masked intruder barrelling towards him.

Karim's face burst with surprise and the shotgun boomed, but Karim had fired out of panic, and Aydin was well clear of the firing line as he crashed into him. They both tumbled to the ground. Aydin landed on top, knocking the air out of Karim's lungs with a *whoomph*. The shotgun clattered away.

Aydin, even more dazed now from a second, albeit more cushioned fall, fought through the pain and the fog in his mind and jumped up to his feet. He launched a boot into Karim's chest, further compounding his efforts to find his breath. Aydin grabbed the shotgun and legged it. He headed straight over for the mosque car park, in two minds whether to take the car or not. When he was just a few yards from it he looked over his shoulder. Karim wasn't giving chase. He was still on the ground, although he was sitting up and being attended to by a kindly neighbour. But there were still people out on the balconies, their eyes following Aydin's escape. More than one had a phone in their hand, taking photos or videos.

No, it was too big a risk. If anyone got his licence plate it would be the simplest task ever for the police to trace the robbery to Aydin – or Mohammed Akhbar at least. He'd have to come back for the car later.

He tossed the shotgun away, then carried on sprinting.

CHAPTER 26

Karim had to say he was impressed with the response. The police arrived within five minutes of him being laid out on the ground outside his apartment block by the mystery intruder. Not that he'd called the cops. Apparently one of his well-intentioned neighbours had done him the courtesy. His intention, of course, had been to blast the bastard's head off with his father's shotgun, not to call 911.

Dazed, and with his chest feeling like a lead weight was still pressing down on it, Karim was still fuming only minutes after the police had arrived when the cavalry turned up. Namur, Benny, and three others in Benny's X5.

Until now the only times Karim had really seen Namur out in the open had been when he'd had a gun in his hand on a mission to kill. This time Karim got to see another side to him altogether. After initial heightened suspicion from the police with regards to Karim's 'story', Namur had soon helped to smooth things over with the cops. They had now firmly decided that Karim wasn't a suspect in any kind of assault or attempted murder. He was the victim of a robbery. Namur had collected the shotgun and put it back where it belonged. That wasn't police evidence here. He and Benny had then been around some of the other apartments, talking to the residents and calming them . . . and likely persuading them what to say to the police when – or if – they ultimately bothered to speak to them.

Which seemed unlikely less than an hour after the incident when it was clear the only two officers on the scene wouldn't be joined by any others and were themselves preparing to leave.

Karim was by then back in the apartment. His father too. His mother had taken his brother out for some food to get him away from the chaos.

Sitting opposite his father in the lounge, Karim could tell the older man was angry – as ever. But at what exactly? The intruder, or at Karim? Or was it Namur he was angry – jealous? – with for the way he was successfully managing the situation and keeping his son out of trouble?

'OK,' Officer Sanchez said as he came back into the lounge, followed by Namur. For now their apartment had an open-door policy it seemed. 'We've done what we can today.'

'You've spoken to everybody?' Karim's father asked before glaring at Namur.

'Everybody we need to for now,' Sanchez said. 'If we need your son to make a further formal statement we'll let you know.'

'What about fingerprints? DNA?'

'We'll have to arrange fingerprints. Hopefully it'll be later today.'

He looked at his watch, as if indicating he was out of time.

'My son could have been killed. This is a serious matter.'

'Of course it is, Mr Hussein. We'll do everything we can. You have a good day now.'

Sanchez turned and walked out. Karim craned his neck to follow him and saw him pause momentarily in the corridor as he stared down to the door to Karim's room that now had a four-inch hole gouged out where the shotgun pellets had obliterated the lock. He shook his head then carried on out without a word.

'There's nothing for you to worry about,' Namur said.

It wasn't clear who he was speaking to.

'Nothing to worry about?' Karim's father said, his face screwing up. One thing was for sure, Karim had to admire his balls. Did he know what Namur was capable of? 'That's easy for you to say.'

'We'll find who did this,' Namur said.

'That's not your job.'

Namur glared at Karim's father now and the older man took the hint to back down.

'Karim, do you think I could have a word?' Namur said.

Karim looked to his father for reassurance but the man just sat there with a petulant scowl on his face.

He went to stand up.

'Oh, don't you inconvenience yourself, son. I'll go.'

Karim's father stood up and stormed towards the exit, nudging Namur's shoulder as he passed by, a move which caused Karim to wince, but Namur looked faintly amused. Karim's father headed to his bedroom and slammed the door shut.

At least Namur hadn't risen to it, Karim was glad to see. Unless he was planning bloody revenge for later, he thought with a shudder. Though he felt he knew, and could to some extent understand why his dad was so angry. It wasn't like everybody didn't know Namur's notoriety. Until today, his father had no clue that Karim knew the Tiger, nor that he was now part of his crew. He would surely be in for a rough ride over that as soon as Namur left.

Or was Karim himself untouchable now?

'I've smoothed this out for you,' Namur said, looking down at Karim, who all of a sudden struggled to hold his boss's eye.

'But you could have been in big trouble here. Firing that gun? Running out into the street swinging it around like Rambo? What if you'd killed the guy? In broad daylight? What if you'd hit someone else?'

'I get it.'

'I'm not sure you do.' He took a long inhale then sighed as though he was seriously fed up. 'You act on impulse too much. If you wanna be with us you need to cool it. There's a time and place for everything. A duck shoot in your own apartment block is not—'

'I said I get it.'

'I hope so. Because I won't bail you out again if you're in trouble because of your own stupidity.'

'Yeah, thanks.'

Namur's eyes drifted around the room for a few moments as if he was surveying the place.

'Do you know who it was?' he said when he'd finished.

Karim had already told the police he had no clue. That there was no one who had a beef with him. That he hadn't seen anyone hanging around the apartments suspiciously today or any other day, and he couldn't think of any reason why he would be a target specifically.

Which was partially true. Certainly there was no reason why a simple burglar would target their top-floor apartment rather than any other on the block. They weren't rich in any sense. Their apartment had no better or worse security than any other.

'I don't know for sure,' Karim said, 'but who's been causing trouble for me recently?'

'The jocks?'

'Makes some sense, doesn't it?'

'Not really. Why would they want to break in and steal your laptop? They want to punch your face in, not find out what porn websites you've been surfing.'

Karim tried not to look embarrassed at that comment. 'So what do you think?'

Namur thought about that one for a moment. Karim too had another thought as to who the culprit could be, but he didn't want to share it just yet, as he didn't really understand what it would mean if he was right.

'Yesterday Saad was killed. Now this.'

'You think the Bloods again? They wouldn't dare come over here.'

Namur humphed. 'Maybe you're right. And why the fuck would they want to steal from you?'

'Plus, Saad wasn't robbed, was he?'

'No. He wasn't. Phone and wallet were still on him.'

'Then maybe this is two completely different things.'

'We'll figure it out,' Namur said. 'I know people across the road at the mosque. We'll get their CCTV. From here too. We'll find who did this.'

'Are the police not going to get there first?'

Namur scoffed as though that was a ridiculous proposition.

'You might want to lower your expectations about how much of a shit they give about you, me, any of us.'

He already had low expectations, so that would be hard. Except they did care when Karim and his peers were the supposed bad guys, just not when they were the victims.

'Thanks for your help,' Karim said. 'I appreciate it.'

'We stick together. No loose parts. There's no other way this can work.'

Karim nodded.

'I'll leave you to it. I sense your old man wants to have a word with you. Be straight with him. About me.'

Karim just nodded again. Namur obviously sensed he'd figured out the dynamic between the Hussein men pretty well. Which it looked like he had.

'But I do need to see you later.'

'Yeah?'

'Mohammed Akhbar.' The way Namur said the name was like he was at that moment imagining how he'd kill the guy. Karim's interest was naturally piqued.

'A problem?'

'That's what we're going to find out.'

CHAPTER 27

After flooring Karim, Aydin had legged it from St Sarkis Towers, across the mosque car park and over a fence onto a quiet residential street. There he'd stripped off his balaclava, which he'd dumped in a bin, before carrying on at a slower and less conspicuous pace. It was soon clear there was no chase on from Karim, nor was there a swathe of police cars coming to hunt him down. Though he did still decide it would be better if he could change his appearance, even a little, so before he even attempted to return for his car, he first headed on foot from the quiet suburban streets to the bustling Fairlane Town Center Mall. Perhaps a strange choice for someone looking to lay low, but inside in the warmth it meant he could lose his thick black coat that was surely part of his description for anyone looking, and after stopping for a refreshment he purchased a bright red parka as a replacement before heading out into the cold again.

By the time he made it back outside the Islamic Center of America, there was no sign of the police across at the apartment block. No sign that an incident had taken place at all in fact.

Although what he did see was that same black BMW X5 that belonged to Namur's right-hand man in the car park for St Sarkis Towers.

Not bad for Karim to have the big man on his emergency call list.

Aydin didn't dwell. He kept his head down as he jumped into the Cruze and was soon heading away on the main road without incident.

He checked his watch. Nearly five p.m. Following the somewhat botched burglary, he at least now had a complete copy of the hard drive from Karim's tablet, plus the laptop in its entirety. Karim was just the starting point for Aydin. There were bigger fish to go after, but this would do for now, and with any luck he might be able to glean the information Cox needed to break the code to whatever communications the British government had intercepted. He'd need some time, days, to properly sift through the data for his own purposes, to see if there was anything of relevance.

Once inside his apartment Aydin first went about checking on his side, to find that the stitches were mostly fine despite the earlier tumble from the balcony. He re-dressed the wound before setting up his computer equipment to start the initial processing of the data he'd stolen. Once he was satisfied, he headed out for some supplies.

Aydin was back in the car park outside his apartment, pulling the bags from the boot of his car when he heard her voice.

'Mohammed.'

He left the bags of shopping in place and spun round to see Kate – the young woman who'd saved him outside the diner the other day – standing there, a meek smile on her expectant face.

'Hi,' Aydin said as he quickly tried to compose himself.

'It's Kate. You remember?' She hunkered down in her check scarf as a blast of wind caught them both off guard.

'Of course I do,' he said. 'How could I forget?'

'You're looking . . . ' Her face screwed with concern as she looked him up and down. He was in pain and it was a struggle to properly straighten up.

'As bad as I feel, to be honest,' Aydin said. 'Do you live around here?'

She looked a little embarrassed now. 'No . . . I er . . . I work nearby. My dad owns an art shop.' She was shivering, but he wasn't going to invite her inside. Was that what she wanted?

'I was thinking, about the other day . . . ' she said. 'That was hardly a nice first impression for you here.'

'I won't judge you all because of it.'

His stifled smile brought an uneasy pause to the already stilted conversation.

'You only just arrived in Detroit, right?' she asked, before rolling her eyes and shaking her head. 'Sorry, I'm so rude. I didn't even ask anything about you the other day.'

'You didn't need to. You helped me more than I could have expected. But yes, I've only been here a few days.'

'You're working here?'

'I will be. At the university.'

'Oh, you're a researcher? A professor?'

'Not exactly. IT analyst. I work on developing security systems. It's a funded project . . . not very interesting really.'

The way she was already slowly nodding suggested she really didn't care about the finer details at all. Which was good, because the finer details would be nothing but bullshit.

'You haven't started yet?' she asked.

'No. I'm just getting settled still.'

Another awkward silence.

'That's kinda what I thought,' she said. 'I mean, if you want . . . maybe I could show you around some?'

The pause as his brain whirred seemed to go on for an eternity. Aydin's heart drummed in his chest. Her meek smile was back again. It was as endearing as it was alluring, even to a man like Aydin who was so inexperienced when it came to matters of courtship. Inexperienced? He had *zero* experience. But that's what this was, wasn't it? She was asking him on a date.

'Sorry,' she said. 'I know you're not—'

'I'm just really busy,' Aydin said, and she looked even more embarrassed now than before.

He was about to give some other lame excuse, when behind her he saw a car pulling to a stop in the car park. Karim emerged.

What the hell?

'But . . . if you give me your number,' Aydin said, 'I can call you?'

She sensed his unease and glanced over her shoulder as he took his phone out. She rattled the number off and he typed it in as Karim idled over suspiciously.

'I'll call you, yeah?' Aydin said.

'I hope so,' she said before she turned and moved away.

'What was that?' Karim said as he reached Aydin and flicked his eyes to Kate then back again.

'What do you think it was?'

'Whatever,' Karim said.

Aydin went to move back round to the driver's door. No way he was heading up to the apartment now, not with Karim in tow while his stolen laptop was whirring away inside.

'You're looking worse for wear,' Karim said.

'Yeah,' Aydin said. 'From when those arseholes kicked the crap out of me.'

'Seems worse than the other day.'

Did he know? About Saad? About the laptop? If so . . . It was quiet here. Kate was already out of sight. No one else was around. Aydin could attack. But what then? There was surely no need to kill the kid and dump his body just to hide the fact he might know Aydin killed his friend, and robbed him. Two dead bodies wasn't going to make his life any easier.

'You're off somewhere?' Karim said.

'I was.'

Aydin paused, hand on door.

'Whatever it was, it'll have to wait. You're wanted.'

Aydin was by now coiled and primed, ready to explode into action.

'Wanted?' he said as he turned back to face Karim.

'My boss wants to talk to you.'

'About what?'

'Didn't tell me.'

'Who's your boss?'

'Namur.'

Aydin shrugged.

'You've not met him yet. But believe me, if he wants to see you . . .'

'OK, then where is he?'

'At the mosque.'

'Fine. I'll see you there.'

Aydin went to turn round again.

'No,' Karim said, holding his arm out to stop him. 'I'll drive you.'

Aydin didn't like the sound of that at all.

'Let's go,' Karim said, indicating the way.

Aydin sighed, deciding it was best to go along for the ride. Literally. They headed over to Karim's Jeep. Despite his hesitation, Aydin got in and moments later they were off. Aydin tried his best to stay calm at least on the outside, though his head was filled with conflicting thoughts as they drove along. At least Karim did seem to be following a path to the mosque.

If it looked at any point like he was going anywhere else, without explanation, Aydin would throttle him.

'Nice car,' Aydin said, wanting to break the awkward and somewhat ominous silence.

'Thanks,' Karim said.

'Not bad for a . . . ' Aydin nearly said nineteen-year-old, but stopped himself when he realised he had no reason to know that, at least in Karim's eyes. 'How old are you exactly?'

'Nineteen. Why?'

'Wish I had a car like this when I was nineteen.'

'When you were nineteen? Not that long ago, is it? And from what I hear, you were up to a whole lot more when you were my age.'

Karim gave him a knowing look. Aydin pretty much knew what it meant now, but he said nothing.

Oh, Karim, if only you really knew what I was doing when I was nineteen, Aydin thought. *You'd have run a mile from me by now.*

When they arrived at the mosque, Aydin wasn't at all surprised to see the car park nearly full, given the time of day, and the shiny black X5 was once again parked up right next to the back doors. Karim parked in the one spot that was curiously still available next to the X5, as though the space was reserved especially for him. They both got out and Karim led the way to the back entrance, and the doors were opened by a bouncer before they reached them. Karim led them through the foyer and to the closed doors to the kitchen.

'I am pretty hungry actually,' Aydin said as Karim knocked on the door.

'Very funny,' Karim said.

The doors were opened by a big bulky guy Aydin hadn't seen before, and Karim indicated for Aydin to step through. He did so and flinched a little dramatically when he saw the entourage inside, mostly clustered around the central island like they were a bunch of mafiosi plotting the demise of a rival family.

Intimidating? Not much to Aydin. Yet his bubbling nerves were real as there was still little he liked about the position he found himself in, even if he was quietly confident of getting out of it if he had to.

The door was closed behind him. Aydin looked around. Karim remained standing somewhere behind.

'Do you know why you're here?' came a deep and husky voice.

The underlings in front parted to reveal Namur, resting his wide backside on the countertop, a snarl on his face.

Aydin shrugged. 'You can't figure out how to do your pop tarts?'

A flicker of a smile from Namur. 'Do you know who I am?'

Aydin sighed. 'Kind of.'

'Good. Saves me some explaining. Now ask me.'

'What?'

'Ask me the same question.'

As the words passed his lips Aydin was grabbed from behind. Thick hands grasped both of his arms and twisted the limbs behind his back. He squirmed as the elbow and shoulder joints were strained to bursting, but he didn't fight it.

'Go on then,' Namur said. 'Ask.'

'Do you . . . know who I am?' Aydin said.

'No,' Namur said, getting off his arse and sauntering over. He dipped his head down to look into Aydin's eyes. 'No. And that's the problem. I don't know who you are. But believe me, one way or another, you're going to fucking tell me.'

CHAPTER 28

Cox checked her phone once more as she sat in the car outside the looming Fisher Body Plant 21 factory shell. No calls or texts to her number since she'd left the hotel, but more frustratingly nothing from Aydin since they'd spoken the previous night. His elusiveness was one of the key reasons Cox would remain in Detroit, with Flannigan breathing down her neck from three thousand miles away. He remained as unconvinced as ever that Aydin was going to break through here, and unfortunately Cox was increasingly coming round to the idea, particularly given events so far. Perhaps this time her boss was actually right. What was Aydin up to? She wasn't far off going on a stalking mission and following him around personally to figure it out.

Yet his unconventional methods and lack of communication wouldn't stop Cox from doing what she could on her own in the meantime.

She sighed and stepped out of the car into the cold. She was already fed up with the freezing temperatures, the ice, the snow. Come back dreary rain of London. Hell, come back the oppressive heat of Muscat.

She looked up and down the frozen street then over to the long-abandoned monolith in front of her. There was no one in sight.

Cox moved away from the car and through what was once a gate onto the factory grounds. She headed round to the far side of the building and easily spotted where she needed to be because one of the old loading bays, now just a big open hole in the wall of the factory, had several runs of police tape pulled across it. No sign of any officers here though, the tape was as much a relic of the factory's past as the rest of it.

Beyond the lines of tape Cox found herself inside a huge expanse where decades before the main production line would have run. Now it was a puddle-filled dingy mess. With thick cloud outside and only an hour or so before darkness, it was eerily gloomy too and Cox took out a torch to help find her way.

It wasn't too hard. The further mess of police tape was obvious, and even among the debris and puddles on the floor, the spots and pools of blood were clearly visible. In the near distance, white chalk marked off where one of the three dead bodies had been found. Cox wondered where the other bodies had lain. She took a few minutes to carefully inspect what remained of the scene, moving into a graffiti-filled workshop area where pride of place was a giant mural taking up most of one of the walls. Cox had already spent some time reading the police reports of what had taken place here. A drug deal gone wrong. The *bland* police reports, she should say, because it was clear the matter was hardly being treated as a priority, and the level of investigation was minimal at best.

As one policeman had told her many years ago, 'We don't mind so much when vermin eat each other.'

Yet what the police had seemingly failed to pick up on was the fact that rumours abounded that the other party to this drug deal was a group of Muslim men from Dearborn. A massive blip on her radar, even if it wasn't on the police's.

214

Satisfied that she'd dwelled enough on the scene, and that there wasn't any useful evidence left behind, Cox headed on out and back to the car. She was yards from her vehicle when she looked up the street again and saw two figures not far away, coming towards her. The two men were wrapped in winter gear. Both had baseball caps on their heads, covered by hoods from both their sweatshirts and their coats.

She was shivering. They looked like they couldn't care less.

Maybe she simply wasn't wearing enough layers.

Each of the men had a headphone in one ear with a wire trailing down into the neck of their coats. They were casually chatting. In fact nothing about them was particularly threatening, except for the fact that the street was otherwise deserted and Cox was on her own.

She moved into the road and up to her car door as they approached.

One of the men looked over and caught Cox's eye before he nudged his friend with his elbow. They both glared at her suspiciously. She'd already noticed the flashes of red in their clothing, and as they swaggered past her muttering, the red bandana hanging from the back pocket of one of the men's jeans further cemented her deduction.

'Hey,' Cox said, moving back round to the pavement.

The men stopped and turned, looking somewhat surprised that they'd been accosted.

'You heard about what happened here?' Cox asked.

They looked at each other but said nothing.

'I'll give you a hundred dollars if you tell me what you know.'

Cox pulled two fifties from her purse and held them up in the air.

One of the men scoffed as if offended by her offer. The other edged forward.

'What are you, lady? A cop?'

'No.'

'Why you here?'

'Do you want the money or not?'

He continued to slowly walk over, looking back to his friend every now and then who remained where he was, sullen-faced.

'What do you wanna know?'

'Three men were killed here. Did you know them?'

He pursed his lips.

'I'm interested in who else was here. And why.'

He snorted. 'You are a cop.'

'No, I'm not.'

'Then why do you care?'

'Because it's important to me.'

She held the money out for him. He went to take it and she whipped it back. 'You'll tell me what you know?'

He grunted and rolled his eyes. 'Yeah.'

She handed the money again and he quickly snatched it.

'So?' she said.

'I don't know anything about it. Wasn't here.'

He smirked as his friend guffawed, then turned to walk away.

'Another hundred for the truth,' Cox said.

He paused.

'Please.'

She took the money out. Had it up in her hand when he turned back round with a cocky glint in his eye. He idled over.

'What is this?' he said.

'I'm just after information.'

He chewed for a few seconds.

'Two hundred dollars,' Cox said. 'Who was here? What was for sale?'

He went for the money, but Cox pulled it back again, a move which she could tell agitated him. What did he expect?

216

'Damn hajis wanting something no one around here got,' he said.

'What does that mean? What did they want?'

'Give me the bills.'

Cox lowered her hand and he snatched them off her.

'Dumb bitch.'

He turned again. Cox wasn't surprised, but she was disappointed. She'd tried to give the guy the benefit of the doubt.

She lurched forward, almost losing her footing on the slippery surface.

'Hey, man,' the guy's friend shouted to his friend a split second before Cox reached forward.

She grabbed the guy and twisted his arm behind his back, then threw him up against the side of her car with a thud.

'What are you doing!' he shouted.

'Hey!' the friend said, coming forward.

With her free hand Cox flicked the bottom of her jacket up to reveal the holstered handgun. She turned her gaze to give the friend a determined scowl.

'Step back,' she said.

He got the message.

She pulled the money from the guy's hand and stuffed it back into her pocket then rummaged in his. She took the hundred dollars back then grabbed his wallet.

'I knew you was a cop!' he shouted.

Cox said nothing now. She flipped the wallet open to his driving licence. He was only eighteen. She almost felt bad.

'D'Andre?'

'Let the fuck go of me!'

'Next time someone offers you a good deal, you should take it.'

She hauled her knee up into his groin then let go and stepped back. She saw the friend flinch again and her hand whipped to her side.

'Get out of here, both of you.'

The would-be trickster scuttled to his friend with his hands over his crotch. They were both mouthing off as they moved away though Cox paid little attention to their insults. She was too deep in thought.

She sat down in the driver's seat and sighed.

Had the trip here been a complete waste of time?

Mostly, yes. Except for one thing D'Andre had said. *Damn hajis wanting something no one around here got.*

As vague as it was, that actually meant something. For starters it meant that D'Andre knew more than he'd told her. A part of her felt like going after him and forcing the information out. But she wouldn't do that. There was another way, even if the idea of it filled her with trepidation.

She checked her phone again. Still nothing from Aydin. If she wanted some answers, she didn't have much choice but to try to find them herself. She pulled the car into the road and set off.

CHAPTER 29

'Who are you?' Namur said.

'Mohammed Akhbar.'

'Mohammed Akhbar. A twenty-four-year-old English guy from London who just wants to spend a bit of time in this shit dump.'

'What's your point?' Aydin said, before squirming when his decision to ask a question caused one of the henchmen behind him to twist his arm further.

'My point is I don't buy it.'

'Buy what?' Aydin said, sounding just a little desperate.

'You don't know me,' Namur said, straightening up and turning. He slowly paced back and forth. 'Whoever you are, and why ever you're really here, you sure as hell don't know me. Because if you did . . . you would know I'd find out.'

'Find what!'

'A secondment at the University of Michigan? You really thought anyone would buy that crap? Though I am intrigued how you managed to get over here with that visa stamped in your passport.'

Aydin squirmed again.

'I know how to find out about people,' Namur said. He stopped pacing and stared at Aydin again whose genuine concern was now growing by the second. His brain fired with thoughts of how he'd get out of this if they'd really rumbled his true identity. He even wondered if Cox would somehow suddenly spring to his rescue with an assault team if she knew his cover had been blown. Would she, if she knew?

But how would she know?

'If you knew anything about me,' Namur said, 'you would have known how good I am at finding the truth. At finding what people don't want to be found. And I know everything about you . . . Jamaal Rashid.'

Aydin felt like smiling. He didn't.

Namur's sidekick wandered over with a piece of paper which he stuck under Aydin's nose. It was a printout of an article from the *Daily Mail* website from more than four years ago. He didn't need to read it, he'd seen that one before, and all of the others. Plus, Namur was kind enough to help him out.

'Jamaal Rashid. A nineteen-year-old from London who disappeared two months ago and hasn't been seen since.'

Aydin said nothing as he held Namur's eye.

'He hasn't aged very well,' Benny said, smiling at his own quip.

'No. He hasn't,' Namur said.

Benny shuffled the papers to reveal another story underneath. Same outlet, two weeks later.

'Jamaal Rashid believed to have been groomed online by radicals. Police are looking into the possibility that he's attempted to travel to Syria to join with ISIS fighters.'

Aydin still said nothing as he switched his gaze between Namur and Benny. Strangely, this was exactly where he wanted to be, though he did wonder how they'd uncovered the fact he was actually Rashid – kind of – so quickly. Was there a worry that if they kept on digging they'd uncover that Rashid was just a ruse too?

'After that point, the stories soon dried up,' Namur said. 'Seems nobody cared about you enough to keep on looking.'

Aydin wasn't sure why, but he felt genuine offence at Namur's snide remark. He clenched his jaw as he worked the anger over, thinking through what would come next. What he'd do next. One of his biggest worries right then was what if they found the stab wound on his side? How would he explain that?

'So tell me, Jamaal, where have you been for four years?'

'You want to know where I've been? What I've been doing?'

Namur's eye twitched slightly.

Aydin was ready.

He pushed away thoughts of his damaged state. He could show no weakness here. In one swift movement he lifted his right knee up to his chest then used the leverage in his leg to propel his heel into the groin of the goon behind him. The guy grunted in pain and his grip relaxed just enough for Aydin to slip his arm free. With only one arm now in a lock, he was able to twist his body round, unwinding out of the hold. He yanked his arm free and spun round.

The guy he'd hit was still squirming, so Aydin went for the other one first. He launched himself forward. The guy looked like an overweight boxer and he moved like one too. Big arms, big fists that would cause some serious damage, but he was flat-footed and Aydin skipped to his side, grabbed his arm and twisted round and back as he pulled. The momentum caused the big man to lose his balance, aided by Aydin's outstretched leg. He followed the guy down, still twisting the arm as they went, and by the time the guy was on his back with Aydin's knee pressing down on his face, Aydin had a wrist lock engaged and several ways to quickly switch into an arm bar if he wanted.

221

Aydin glanced over to Namur, seeing whether he needed to follow through or not. The fact he saw the other goon was coming for him gave him the answer.

He pushed down and there was a crunch as the bones of the wrist snapped. The guy screamed in pain.

Prone on the ground, Aydin had to move quickly with the on-rushing goon almost on him. He roared in anger as he sprang forward and grabbed the ankle of the charging brute. He pushed up and sent him toppling backwards. Aydin landed on top, but he had no hold this time, and without one it was unlikely he'd have the superior strength to overcome the heavily muscled henchman.

Best to end this quickly then.

Aydin threw his elbow down, using the weight of his upper body to increase the power in the blow. The pointed joint smashed down onto the goon's nose and a spray of blood erupted. The guy threw a wayward fist towards Aydin's head. Just what he needed. The fist glanced his face and Aydin grabbed the arm and hauled his body off and to the side, pulling at the same time. The man's body rolled with the motion. Aydin clasped his legs shut. These limbs at least had muscles that were easily as powerful as the goon's thick arms.

The guy was face down in Aydin's groin, sandwiched between Aydin's thighs, the arm Aydin had hold of wedged against the side of the neck, aiding the constriction of the carotid artery and the blood flow to the brain. Strangulation, rather than choking. Unconsciousness would take only a few seconds. Death would come quick enough if Aydin held on that long.

Aydin, his face contorted from the effort of maintaining the tight hold, glared at Namur who looked as surprised as he did angry.

222

Then the man between Aydin's legs went limp. He was asleep already. Aydin was about to let go when he sensed someone else coming at him from behind.

But the only person there was Karim.

He had no time to react before the object – a gun? a rolling pin? – was smashed against the back of his head. He saw stars and let go of the goon and went to get back to his feet. Another blow and it felt like the skin on the back of his head had torn open and he was on the brink of unconsciousness himself.

Aydin tried to fight through it, but seconds later others had joined the melee. Outnumbered, Aydin was dragged across the floor as fists and boots pummelled him. He intermittently tried to protect his head, then the wound on his side. If they saw blood there . . .

'Enough!' Namur roared.

The beating stopped.

Aydin coughed and groaned. He was on his side. A knee was pushed down onto his neck. The barrel of a gun pressed into his temple.

'I just . . . wanted to show you . . . what I've been doing for four years,' Aydin slurred as his lips turned up into a bloody smile.

'What? You've been causing me problems?' Namur said.

Aydin's smiled broadened further as blood dribbled down his chin.

'You've got five seconds to convince me not to skin you right here.'

Aydin struggled for the words now. Would anything he said really get him out of this or did he need to find a way to fight back once more? However improbable, he wasn't in an *impossible* situation yet.

'Just tell me why the fuck you came here,' Namur said, snarling. 'Last chance.'

'I'm looking for someone.'

A few moments of silence.

'Who?'

'Nasir Al-Addad.'

The silence now was thick with suspicion and curiosity and confusion. Most faces gave away that they had no clue what Aydin had just said, but the look on Namur's face . . .

'Get off him,' Namur said.

The gun was pulled away. Then the knee. Aydin coughed and spluttered on the blood that was pooling in his mouth, then took a deep breath as he lifted his torso up before groggily getting to his feet. The aches and pains he'd already had were of another magnitude now.

'I came here looking for Nasir Al-Addad,' Aydin said. 'In fact, I was sent here.'

'By who?'

Aydin looked around the room. A lot of angry faces. A lot of men though who quite clearly didn't know what Aydin was saying.

Which was interesting.

'Everyone out,' Namur said as if cottoning on to Aydin's thoughts. A few murmurs of disapproval but slowly the men shuffled away, aiding the two injured as they went.

'Take them to the doctor,' Namur said. 'Karim, Benny, you stay for this.'

Aydin glanced at the two chosen ones. Karim looked seriously surprised to be included in the clique. Benny looked seriously pissed off. As always.

The room was soon cleared except for the four men and the smears of blood on the floor.

'Who sent you,' Namur said.

'No,' Aydin said. 'I need to see Al-Addad. I'll tell him.'

'It won't work like that.'

'Says who?'
'Says me.'
'Because?'
'Because Nasir Al-Addad is dead.'

CHAPTER 30

Cox didn't have to travel far. The police reports she'd read, sent to her through a series of 'contacts', had given her the names and addresses of each of the three men who'd been killed at the factory. Ranging in age from twenty-one to twenty-eight, the young men were all African American and all lived within two hundred yards of each other on the streets clustered around Nyland Avenue. Interestingly D'Andre was a close neighbour too, judging by the address Cox had seen on his driving licence.

Cox knew little about gangland America, and less still about the inner workings of specific gangs like the Bloods, who apparently had associate members spread through the whole country. She did know though, from what she'd gleaned over the last two days, that Nyland Avenue was a known hotspot for the Bloods, and she headed there with an open yet alert mind.

The streets around Nyland Avenue were lined with single-storey houses, wooden constructions, tightly crammed together, the dwellings mostly in disrepair. To describe the area as down at heel would be an understatement. Even on a drive-by the level of poverty was clear, and was stark compared to the glitz in certain parts of nearby central Detroit. While certainly not every person who lived here was gang affiliated, it was also obvious that with residents so impoverished, the area was a natural breeding ground for gangs who found it easy to get their claws into the disgruntled young men and women who grew up here.

Cox drove along slowly, taking in what she saw. Front yards were in general unkempt, many filled with rubbish. Rusted and abandoned cars were left both on housing plots and on the road. Though every now and then there'd be a house where clearly the residents had tried their damnedest to make their home presentable and neat and tidy.

Despite the cold, small groups of people, mainly teenagers and young men, hung around on corners. Outside some houses there were groups huddled sociably in the cold around BBQ drums, orange flames glowing as they drank and ate.

Cox got a few curious stares as she drove on past but nothing more. After a few minutes she'd driven a short circuit around the houses where each of the dead men had lived. No signs of action at any of those, but one of the groups who were busy barbecuing meat, just a few doors away from one of the victims' houses, had taken her interest. She circled back around to that street and parked on a quiet corner. Daylight was now done for and within minutes of her turning the engine off and sinking down into her seat, the street lights all along the road flicked on, their dim orange bulbs doing a pretty bad job of providing illumination. Which was partly OK for Cox. At least it meant she was less visible.

She kept her eyes busy as she waited. Her heart quickened every time anyone approached the car, but other than a few questioning glances, no one paid her much attention. The group of men in front of her, fifty yards away, ebbed and flowed with new arrivals and others leaving, but as much as she could, Cox focused on one man in particular.

With the engine and the heaters off it wasn't long before Cox was shivering from the cold again. She could see her own breath, and slowly the windows of the car were steaming up, making her presence all the more obvious. She carefully wound down both of the front windows an inch to try to help, resulting in even more cold air pushing in.

Thankfully, she didn't have to wait too much longer. A little over thirty minutes later, the man she had her eyes on pulled away from the group with another. They came in her direction. The man Cox was spying on was limping badly, the bottom half of his left leg was covered in a white bandage, his jeans leg rolled up over it.

Cox stayed low in her seat as they passed by on the other side of the street, then she followed them in her mirrors as they headed off to the right and further away.

She took a deep inhale as she prepared herself, then she got out of the car to follow. Hat pulled low, head down, hands in her pockets, her left around the butt of her now unholstered weapon, she followed behind the men across two blocks.

Soon the injured man was all alone after his friend went inside one of the houses. Cox closed the distance. When the guy turned up a driveway, she pushed her pace further.

There was no one else around . . .

Wait, no, there was. A hundred yards further up the street, two people had just turned in.

Shit.

But Cox was already closing in, almost within touching distance, and the man had realised. He turned round . . .

She had no choice. She leapt forward. Pulled the gun out. The guy was two steps away from his front door, but he didn't go to head inside. His hand went behind him. A weapon.

Cox crashed her gun down onto his arm, putting paid to his attempts to reach for whatever he had. She swiped his

228

legs away – a not too difficult task given his injury – and helped him down to the ground. She pushed a gloved hand over his mouth to muffle any shouts, grabbed the gun from his waistband and tossed it away. She shoved the barrel of her own gun in his eye and forced her knee down onto the bandage on his leg which caused him to buck and whine.

'I'll take my hand away from your mouth,' Cox said. 'But if you shout . . . I'll put a bullet in your other leg too.'

He glared at her defiantly.

'Do you understand?'

No sounds now. Cox carefully pulled her hand away from his mouth.

'You stupid crazy bi—'

Hand back in place she ground her knee into his leg and she was sure she saw tears in his eyes.

'Not nice.'

She quickly looked behind her. No sign that anyone had been alerted. Yet.

'I've only got two questions for you. Answer them and you won't ever see me again. You got it?'

Nothing from him. That was kind of a yes.

'Who were you and your gang trying to sell to. I need names.'

A look of concern in his eyes now.

'You're going to tell me. Nod, to show me you're going to tell me.'

She pushed her knee against his wounded leg just slightly this time. Enough to get a response. He nodded.

She lifted her hand from his mouth.

'I don't know any fucking names.'

Cox growled and pushed down with her knee once more.

'Wait . . . wait,' he said, squirming. 'I don't know his name. Just they call him Tiger.'

'What were you selling them? What did they want?'

He gave a funny sort of snort that Cox read as incredulity.

'We were playing them.'

Which Cox had figured. They just wanted the money. Given three of theirs had lost their lives, was it really worth the subterfuge in hindsight?

'But what did they ask for. What did they want?'

The man snarled and shook his head.

'We ain't got nothing like that. Even if we did, why'd we sell to *them*.'

There was genuine disgust in the final word.

She heard shuffling behind her. She glanced to see two men approaching on the street. One of them looked over. Cox was partially shrouded in shadow but they must have spotted the glint of her gun or something.

She dug her knee down as hard as she could and the man yelped. 'Tell me what it was!' she shouted, her voice now desperate.

'Hey,' one of the men shouted over. 'Hey you!'

'What are you doing?' the other said.

Looking down she saw power returning to the man's eyes. She was done. She had to get out of there.

Cox jumped to her feet and turned the gun round, double-handed grip.

'Step back,' she said with enough conviction to get the bystanders to halt their progress.

'What the fuck?'

She could see them both hesitating. Weighing up their options. These could be gang-bangers too, or just two normal guys. In the dark, she couldn't really tell. She couldn't take any risks though.

She sensed movement behind her. Half-turned as she side-stepped to realise the injured man was lurching towards her. He swung and missed and Cox scuttled further back, switching the gun from him to the two others.

'Just stay back. All of you.'

'All right, miss. You just put that thing away. Before you do something really stupid.'

'Stay the fuck back.'

All three of the men were clustered together now. And they didn't look too daunted by the position they found themselves in. No, none of these were just normal guys.

'You chose the wrong neighbourhood,' one of them said with a sneer.

Cox dipped the gun and fired. The bullet smacked into compacted snow by their feet, sending up a plume of powder. The three men jumped in surprise. Cox turned and ran.

She sprinted as fast as she could. More than once her boots skidded on the icy surface but she didn't slow her pace. Behind her the men were barking and calling, all manner of profanity thrown her way. She fired another warning shot at the two men giving chase, the injured man somewhere behind. Soon her car was in sight. She skidded up to it. Swung the door open and dove in. Her hand fumbling, it took an age to get the key in the ignition. By the time she'd managed it and the engine rumbled to life the two men were only yards away.

She floored it.

The tyres skidded and screeched and eventually found traction and the car shot off, swerving left and right as Cox battled to stay in control. She glanced in her rear-view mirror to see the two men, one of them with a gun in his hand. He raised it.

Cox braced herself . . .

The shot never came.

She swung the car round the next corner and they were out of sight. Two more turns and she was heading for the main road leading in and out of the city, and she finally heaved a sigh of relief.

CHAPTER 31

Cox's already patchy night's sleep was painfully interrupted a little after four a.m. by the incessant vibration of her phone on the bedside table. The noise in the hushed room was like an industrial saw. Cox's head shot up off the pillow. Her tired and weary brain took a couple of seconds to figure out that she wasn't being attacked by some crazed idiot with a chainsaw. She groaned and slammed her head back down as she grabbed the phone. Flannigan.

The call rang off. Not because she'd decided to ignore it, but because it had taken her so long to pull her sleepy self into shape. No matter, it was soon ringing again.

'Good morning,' she said. 'Kind of.'

'Which part?' Flannigan said. 'You sound half asleep.'

'Not half.'

'Where are you?'

'Still in Detroit.'

'Detroit . . . Damn. Sorry, Rachel. I'll call back later.'

'No need. I'm awake now.'

He sighed. 'You didn't tell me you were staying.'

He went silent. Was she supposed to say something to that?

'My optimistic side would say you're still there because you've already had some huge breakthrough that meant you

232

never got a chance to leave,' he said. 'My realistic side, together with the fact you hadn't already told me you were still there, suggests something altogether different.'

'You could have been a detective.'

'Not too early in the morning for wisecracks, eh? Talk to me.'

'I think I got something.'

'*You've* got something? Not our man?'

She ignored that comment. She turned on the side light to try to ignite her brain, then properly sat up in the bed, giving herself a couple of seconds to come up with the words. 'Aydin's doing fine. Actually, we're hoping for something of a breakthrough imminently. A cypher key that could give us direct access to our cell's dark web communications.'

The revelation was met by silence and Cox was more than a little disappointed by that.

'We've got several key contacts from our Michigan cell spread out across the US.'

'Key contacts? What is that supposed to mean.'

'We don't know yet. Best case is it's just a bunch of guys spreading information around. Worst case . . . worst case is our cell has its claws right across the country, and is planning to utilise that reach.'

'You're suggesting coordinated attacks?'

Was she suggesting that? She certainly hoped that wasn't the case, yet that was exactly what Aydin and his fellow graduates from the Farm had planned across Europe two years previously.

'There's no direct evidence of that yet, but we have to bear that possibility in mind.'

Flannigan sighed. 'We need to know, Cox. If that's what you're saying then we, and the Americans, have to be geared up. We'll need far more help to quash this if we've—'

'I know, I know. We'll get there. There's something else too.'

'Go on.'

'Six days ago there was a shootout at a disused factory building in central Detroit. Three men were killed, though the police here labelled it as gangland violence and it's pretty much a non-story both with the law and press despite the fatalities.'

'I'm seriously hoping you're not about to tell me this was Ay—'

'Of course it wasn't him,' she said, almost a little too quickly. It wasn't as though Aydin wasn't capable of such an act, and he had already got blood on his hands in the US, not that she was about to mention that now. 'The three dead men were all believed to be members of the Bloods—'

'Then what the hell has that got to do with—'

'I've heard directly from two Bloods members that their guys were meeting with a group of . . . Muslim men. To put it more politely than they did.'

Flannigan was silent now, which meant he was thinking, which was far better than him either berating or arguing.

'The thing is,' Cox said. 'I'm convinced this wasn't a drug deal, which is what the police assumed.'

'Then what?'

'The men I spoke to—'

'Hang on, Cox. Back up for me. Who on earth have you been speaking to? Under what authority? Aydin is supposed to be the one out there on the streets, not you.'

Cox sighed. There was no easy way to answer that one. 'Can I just explain what I've got first?'

'I suppose you'd better.'

'I was told by two different gang members, one of them a man who was actually shot and injured at the supposed deal, that the other guys wanted something the Bloods didn't even have to sell.'

234

'What are you talking about?'

'The Bloods set them up. The whole deal was a ploy so the Bloods could rip off the other guys.'

'Then what did they *think* they were buying?'

'I don't know. Weapons maybe. Bomb parts. I really don't know. But one of the Muslim men was Tiger. Namur. He's one of the crew down at the Jalalabad Mosque where Aydin is.'

A long sigh from Flannigan now. 'Cox . . . I just . . . where's Nasir Al-Addad in all this?'

'We've found nothing about him so far, but—'

'Cox, you need to give me some clarity here. You have this Namur guy communicating across the country, but you've no idea what about. They could be long-lost cousins talking about baseball. You've got a blown nefarious deal which could have been simple drugs. You've got no evidence whatsoever on Al-Addad, who is our one and only link back to Al-Busaidi and extremism. At the moment, I'm really not seeing—'

'We just need a breakthrough.'

If Aydin could get that encryption key. Or if he could get in front of Al-Addad . . .

'But, if I'm right, you're telling me this Namur is responsible for the deaths of three Bloods members?'

'Yes.'

'So give the information to the police. They'll have him and his gang arrested for the murders. Whatever this crew are up to, we quash it just like that.'

Cox didn't say anything to that straight away. She was too taken aback by the proposition. 'Are you serious?'

'Tell me why not?'

'Because that's not why we came here. You know as well as anyone that if you cut off an arm from these cells, another one grows back. You have to hit at the centre to stop them.'

'Maybe Namur is the centre.'

'He's not. Al-Addad is.'

'You don't even know where he is!'

'Neither do you! He could be right here, in the final stages of attacks right across this continent.'

'My point is,' Flannigan said, his tone more sharp, 'you're operating over in the US, one of our biggest allies, with no jurisdiction, hot in the middle of a murder investigation. You have potentially significant information in that murder investigation which so far, I'm guessing, the police and the Feds and whoever else that matters know nothing about. Not only could this take—'

'You're worried about form-filling? Is that it?'

'Would you please stop interrupting me?'

'Fine.'

'No, I'm not *only* worried about the official clean-up process that might be needed here, but that is a factor because it's me rather than you who has to do it. More importantly, though, you have evidence that a key target in our operation is responsible for three murders, and with such a lack of anything more concrete about these guys, why on earth would we not take what we can and get these men off the streets and into a jail cell?'

'Please, don't do that,' Cox said as an unexpected wave of emotion washed over her. What was that? 'I promise you it would be a huge mistake. Namur is just a link. You've seen the intel from K-site. We know Al-Busaidi was a recruiter, and we know he worked with Al-Addad. We know they've been trying to target the US. Nasir Al-Addad is—'

'Is a goddamn urban legend for all we know.'

'Now it's you interrupting.'

Silence.

'We've only been here a few days,' she said. 'Aydin is already neck deep getting on the inside. Give him some time.

236

If we find nothing more, then of course we give the police here everything we have to allow them to bring Namur and anyone else involved in those shootings to justice. But we can't jeopardise what we've started here so soon, especially when there's a chance that there's a bigger plot building up here that stretches beyond this cell.'

Another much longer silence now. More than once Cox opened her mouth to add something else but thought better of it. She was genuinely nervous about what he'd come back with.

'My biggest concern here,' he said, 'is your continued use of the term *we*. Aydin is the asset, he's the one we put in place there with the knowledge and assistance of the US authorities. He's the one tasked with getting us intel on this group.'

'I know. I'm sorry b—'

'I wasn't finished. I know he's only been there a few days but I also know how sceptical Homeland Security and other people that matter in the US are about this operation. And so far, based on what they've shared with us, and what you're telling me now about this failed drug deal, or whatever it was, I'm becoming increasingly sceptical too. I'm not saying you're wrong, but I do need to see progress. Progress related to Al-Addad and credible evidence of a terrorism threat. Without that, there's no point in this exercise. And on the flip side, if you do think there's a bigger plot here, and you have actual evidence of that, we need to alert the US authorities immediately, because we can't possibly stop such a thing on our own.'

'I understand. I've—'

'You'll give Aydin forty-eight hours more before we make the next call.'

'Forty-eight hours! That's—'

'That's what you've got. Forty-eight hours. I want to see something tangible by then, something that tells me this isn't

237

a huge waste of everyone's time and that there's more to these characters than gang-related crime. It should be plenty long enough for Aydin to tell us whether there's legs in this, and plenty of time for you to make your way back to London.'

'But—'

'Cox, do you understand?'

'Yeah. I get it.'

'Good. Sorry to have disturbed your sleep.'

The call clicked off before she could say anything more.

She looked over at her bedside clock. Her brain was on fire now, but her tiredness underneath was real. She grabbed her phone again and set the alarm for six thirty. A quick breakfast and she'd be ready to head out before seven thirty. First stop, figuring out what the hell Aydin was up to.

She lay back down and closed her eyes, though Flannigan's nagging tone and accompanying images of his well-practised pissed-off face wouldn't stop playing over in her mind. She kept her eyes shut though.

She'd try her best to get some more rest before the day started. She needed it, because her time was literally running out now.

CHAPTER 32

Aydin had rarely been a sound sleeper in his troubled life, and last night was no exception. By seven o'clock it'd been clear he wasn't getting any more sleep so he'd taken a quick shower before getting to work reviewing the data he'd stolen from Karim the previous day. A quick browse soon turned into two hours before Aydin's grumbling belly got the better of him and he headed to the kitchen to fix himself some cereal, hobbling as he did so.

The run-in with Namur and his crew the previous day had ultimately ended surprisingly well, in some respects, Aydin considered as he tossed some cornflakes into a bowl which he then filled nearly to the brim with ice-cold milk. He sat down at the crappy little dining table with a grimace. The aches and pains in his body were even worse this morning, with several large golf-ball-sized welts on his arms, legs and torso from the beating he'd taken, to add to the knife wound and other injuries he had.

At least he'd fared better than those two goons . . .

And he'd fared better than he would have done if Namur had been intent on doing him serious harm. Luckily for him, that hadn't been the case. Aydin mentioning Nasir Al-Addad had, for now, cemented his safety, even if he wasn't exactly on the inside yet.

Namur claimed Al-Addad was dead, but had given zero information about when or how that had happened. What he had said, however, was startling to say the least. Namur had claimed to be Al-Addad's cousin. He was quite literally one of *them*.

Aydin had dropped the name of Faiz Al-Busaidi as the man who'd sent him – Jamaal – to Dearborn. The name didn't seem to mean much to Namur, which was a surprise, and made Aydin all the more nervous. If Al-Addad really was dead, and they had no clue who Al-Busaidi was, then was Aydin's purpose in Dearborn null and void?

No, because the fact Namur didn't just know of the Al-Addads, but was related to them, was huge.

Regardless, Namur had dismissed Aydin not long after, telling him to come back and see him after the weekend to talk further, and making it clear that if Aydin wanted any future involvement with the group, other than them torturing him to death, he'd come back prepared to be open with them about why he was in the US.

Fine with him. The door was open. He'd wait. He also knew they'd be keeping a close eye on him, and in all likelihood would be doing what they could to look further into both Aydin's story, and his past. Jamaal's past, at least.

In the meantime, with Karim's stolen laptop and the image of his tablet, Aydin had plenty to keep him occupied. In fact, in the two hours he'd spent scouring the data that morning, he'd already had a good find; the reason Namur was so keen to keep Aydin out of his hair until after the weekend . . .

Not wanting to waste any time, Aydin quickly finished his cereal then headed back to the desk in the far corner of the open plan living space where his computer equipment was still busily whirring away.

An hour later and he was again in the midst of a deep dive when he felt the sudden urge for a break to keep his overly absorbed mind from scrambling too soon. He shot up from his seat to make himself the second coffee of the day, and to finally open the blinds and let some sunlight into the apartment. He'd long ago learned that five-minute breathers every now and then were the only way to make it through endless hours of staring at computer screens, though it was a good intention that often went by the wayside.

He was staring out of the window to the street below which had a fresh covering of dusty snow when his phone buzzed. Cox. He'd expected her to be in touch following his earlier message to her, but wasn't it her who the other day had been so keen to remind Aydin outside her hotel of their carefully arranged protocols for making contact with each other, which certainly didn't include direct telephone exchange?

He didn't answer. The call soon rang off and he remained standing and staring at the phone to see if a voicemail would come through. One didn't, but a moment later there was a knock on the front door at the far side of the open space. He whipped his eyes round, then froze as he stared over at the inanimate object as though waiting for it to come to life.

A few seconds later the same soft treble-rap came again.

Aydin walked quickly but quietly across the room to the kitchen where he grabbed the largest of the knives from the wooden block. He held it behind his back as he crept towards the door.

Another knock.

'Aydin, please, it's me.'

Cox? No use of any red words to show she was under duress.

Aydin strode over and peered through the peephole, not something he did lightly.

Sure enough she was standing right there, alone, with an expectant and slightly nervous look on her face.

He unbolted the latches, turned the lock then pushed the handle down and opened the door.

'What are you doing here?' he said.

'Can you just let me in please?' she said, then looked over her shoulder anxiously.

He stepped aside and she headed through. He glanced into the empty corridor before he shut and relocked the door.

'You complained to me about turning up at your hotel?' he said. 'Now this?'

'Nobody followed me here,' she said. 'And there's no indication of anyone staking you out so I think we're in the clear.'

'Does that mean I'm OK to break protocol whenever too?'

'No,' Cox said. She huffed and took off her hat and unwound her scarf. She was stopping, apparently. 'So stop being a dick and put the kettle on, will you?'

Thirty minutes later Cox was sitting comfortably on the sofa having finished her coffee, while Aydin was facing her on his desk chair already wanting another. She remained pensive, even though they'd talked openly for half an hour about what each had been up to. Openly in the sense that he hadn't lied to her at least. She'd already explained how some team of analysts stuck in a small room somewhere in England were beavering away trying to break the encrypted messages that they'd intercepted in cyberspace. The big hope was that the data from Karim – which Aydin had transferred into a secure cloud server to give GCHQ direct access – would hold the encryption key, though Aydin was a little sceptical about that. Karim was on the inside with Namur, but there was no doubt he was a newbie. How far into the circle of trust was he really? Would he have been the one sending and receiving encrypted messages about the group's terrorist plotting? Aydin wasn't so sure, but that didn't mean that what they now had wasn't a useful stepping-stone, and Karim's data did at least give them a glimpse into the operations.

Aydin said nothing of what he'd found that morning about the crew's plans for the weekend, though he couldn't quite figure in his own head why not.

'We know from what we've already intercepted that he's communicating with people all over the US,' Cox said.

'You think their cell stretches that far?'

'Or there are multiple cells. Or it could be something else entirely.'

'Like what?'

She briefly explained about the failed deal with the Bloods in Detroit several days earlier. Aydin had known nothing about that. That had been his first day on the ground in the US.

'Do you have any idea what they were trying to buy?' Cox asked.

'No,' Aydin said. 'But like you, I'd say it wasn't drugs. Weapons? Perhaps. Parts for bombs? Who knows?'

'Do you really think Al-Addad is dead?' she asked. 'The Feds here won't acknowledge that he's been here at all.'

'I don't know. The fact Namur admitted to knowing him is a huge sign though. It shows this isn't just a hunch of yours.' She winced a little at those words, though he'd not meant to offend her. 'Even if he is dead, Namur knew Al-Addad, they're related, and I'm convinced therefore that he knew *what* Al-Addad was. That's enough for me, for now. You just need to give me more time to figure what this group is up to.'

Cox sighed again. She looked like she was holding on to something, but she didn't say a word.

'Something's troubling you,' he said.

'Something always is.'

There was a flash of weakness in her demeanour which he rarely saw.

243

'What is it?'

'Do you ever think about what life must be like for normal people?' she said.

The question took Aydin aback. Where had that come from?

'Normal people?'

'People who just have their own small world problems. Relationships, jobs, debt, whatever.'

Perhaps unfairly, he thought of her a little like that. Yes, she was an intelligence agent and had undoubtedly seen and been through some tough experiences, but to compare that to his life . . .

'No,' Aydin said, a blunt answer which garnered a look of further disappointment from Cox. She was struggling with something. Why now, he didn't know, but her question had set something off in Aydin's mind. Was that what she'd intended? 'But I do wonder about . . . me. About what my life is. Whether it will ever change.'

'Change how?' she asked.

'What future do I have?' he said. 'The thing is . . . you have a job. A real job. A career. I know it's not an easy life, you travel to the cesspits of the world, you deal with horrible shit. You don't have a partner or anyone else back home to return to—'

'Fuck, you make my life sound so miserable and lonely.'

'You're good at your job, but if there's ever a point where you've had enough, you could get out. But for me? Can I ever break free from my past? Do I even want to?'

'Bloody hell,' Cox said. 'Shall I fetch the nooses?'

The sarcasm in her words perhaps didn't come through as strongly as it should have done.

'You might not believe this, Aydin, but I admire you,' she said.

'Next you'll tell me that deep down I'm really a good person. You've told me that before. That it's not my fault how I am.

But what if it's you that's wrong? I've already killed a man here. I didn't want to, but it happened with barely a second thought. What if this really is the real me?'

Cox looked uncomfortable now. She shifted in her seat, as though she'd just glimpsed something behind Aydin's façade that terrified her.

He glanced at his watch.

'You need me to go?' she said, picking up the signs. Or perhaps she just needed a get-out from the gloomy conversation.

'No,' he lied.

'Don't worry,' Cox said, getting to her feet. 'I do have plenty to do myself, believe it or not.'

She put on her coat then grabbed her hat and gloves and scarf.

'Seriously though, Aydin. I believe we're both here for the right reasons. We just need to stay strong, and together. *You* need to stay in touch. Otherwise this op will be pulled, and if that happens we're out of here, regardless of what the bigger picture is.'

'Understood,' he said.

She nodded then turned for the door, pausing for a split second as she did so. Aydin cursed himself when he realised what she'd seen. His packed cabin bag.

'You off somewhere?'

He gave her a nonplussed look.

'The bag?' she said.

'Oh, yeah, fishing with some friends.'

She raised an eyebrow.

'Joke,' he said. 'I just haven't packed it away yet. I've only been here—'

'A few days. Yeah, OK.'

She didn't seem to fully buy it, but she continued on to the door regardless, before she turned back to him one last time. 'Just remember what I said.'

He nodded, though he couldn't be sure which part of their conversation she was referring to.

Nonetheless she was soon gone, and the door was once again locked and bolted. Aydin looked down to the bag again, then at his watch. The unexpected diversion had cost him a bit of time, but it wasn't a huge deal. He still had a little under an hour before he needed to head for his flight.

He moved back over to the desk to continue his work.

CHAPTER 33

Los Angeles, California

It wasn't a hot day in the largest city in the Golden State, not by a long stretch, but at sixteen Celsius, when Aydin stepped outside the airport into the sunshine, it felt like the tropics compared to the big freeze in Detroit. With his winter coat in his hands, and just a jumper and t-shirt on top, Aydin was stifling as he was standing waiting for a taxi, but it couldn't have been clearer in his mind which climate he preferred. That said, and although he hadn't yet booked a return flight, he was hoping his business here would be wrapped up in no time, and he'd be back in Detroit before the end of tomorrow.

He was only in the taxi for two miles. He needed his own transport for this expedition, though he wouldn't hire a car from one of the big companies at the airport. He wanted something a little more discreet, not that he was expecting anyone to try to unpick his travel route retrospectively. At least not if everything in California went smoothly.

He paid in cash to hire a rusting Toyota Camry from a single-office rental company that carried out as few checks on their cars as they did on their customers, then immediately hit the road and headed south. He was soon on I5, that for its most southerly portion clung to the rocky coastline of the Pacific like a creeper on a tree trunk. To his right the rocky outcrops dropped down into the crystal blue of the Pacific Ocean. To his left the rolling mountains of Cleveland National Forest rose into the distance. The views, particularly on a clear day with a deep blue sky, were nothing but spectacular.

Aydin was close to the middle ground between LA and San Diego when he pulled off the highway and found a motel to check into. Forty dollars later he was back on the road, cabin bag and winter clothes discarded and just his backpack of provisions for the job ahead.

He left the highway again when he was a little under two miles from his destination, at the turning for a scenic viewpoint with breathtaking views down to the waters below. Several other cars – couples, families of various ages – were there taking advantage of the views. Aydin took a quick albeit appreciative glance, but then was on the move once more, this time on foot. He traipsed across the rocky ground away from the viewpoint and was soon out of sight from the people there. The undulating and to some extent unplanned route took him on a twisting path, at times only a few feet from the beach below, others at heights of what felt like fifty yards or more with jagged and sheer drops just inches away.

He frequently checked his handheld GPS. One of several new purchases for this trip. The majority of the land he was on was Federal, though every now and then there'd be a string of private properties where he trod with an extra bit of caution to make sure he stayed unseen and undisturbed. It took nearly an hour to reach the high outer fence for the property he was looking for.

Standing on its own at the edge of a secluded bay that had sweeping cliffs all around it, the mansion known as Los Olivos had a plot of more than forty acres that included manicured gardens, a mini pine forest, multiple swimming pools, sand dunes, not to mention the sheer rock faces.

Aydin had scoured aerial photos of the grounds on the Internet before he'd arrived and had a detailed mental image of the layout, albeit in real life the sheer scale of the place was quite different from on a computer screen. He'd already determined though that the best way to access the property unseen would be from the beach and up the rocky cliffs, rather than from any of the accessible routes onto the property, or over the secure fence and through the gardens which were closely monitored by CCTV.

The clamber down was treacherous. Not that Aydin was scared of heights, but he also wasn't a mountaineer, and more than once on his scrambling descent, he lost his footing and nearly his life with it. He somehow made it down to the bottom with only a few skin scrapes to add to his growing list of ailments. With the sea lapping away behind him, he headed on into the bay and was soon scaling the rocks again, but this time on the inside of the mansion's grounds.

When he reached the final ledge he pulled himself up and peered over. Just beyond the rocks was the southwesterly edge of the white-painted mansion. Although only two storeys tall it was huge and extravagant and in pristine condition and . . . glorious. There was no doubting that whoever owned such a home wasn't just rich, they were filthy rich. Although the owners clearly still had a certain amount of taste to go with it, Aydin mused.

He carefully pulled himself up into a safe spot, away from the cliff edge, and in the midst of prickly undergrowth sprouting up from the bare rocks to provide him with cover. He pulled binoculars from the backpack and brought them up to his eyes. He scoured around the mansion and the grounds. As well as the main building there was a separate stable block. Perhaps once a building actually used for its apparent purpose of holding horses, it was now converted into an elaborate garage and Aydin could see three cars parked on the outside, each worth several hundred thousand dollars. Off on the northerly side of the mansion was the main pool. The biggest of three. One side of it was built right up to the cliff edge. Every now and then Aydin caught noises – voices, giggling – and he could see now there were two women sitting by the edge of the pool, clothed but with their bare legs in the water, and in among the splashes bouncing up every now and then from the pool were at least two young kids who were braver than their mothers at getting into the water on a mild though far from hot day.

Aydin carried on searching. There was a separate pool house further along that was bigger than most millionaires' mansions. A tennis court. Tables and chairs and loungers by the pool, on lawns, in among palm trees.

Finally Aydin found something of interest. Two men. Both were dressed casually. Linen trousers and shirts. They were sauntering along together through the grounds, chatting and smoking. Assault rifles dangled by their sides on straps off their shoulders.

Aydin pulled the binoculars away. He could just make out the armed guards still, though from his position they surely couldn't see him. Aydin pulled the binoculars back into place as he looked over each of the windows of the mansion visible from his position. A moment later two French doors at the back of the main building flung open and out stepped a pot-bellied and heavily bronzed man in colourful shorts, massive aviator sunglasses covering most of his face. Even with the sunglasses and at a distance, Aydin still recognised him from his research back in Detroit. Emilio Torres was the owner of the mansion, and the reason Aydin was here.

Not that he looked like much with his swim shorts on, but this was not just a rich but a very powerful man.

He called over to the pool and there was heightened excitement from the kids in the water as the man raced over and dive-bombed in. Much to the delight of the kids, but to the annoyance of the women, given the tidal wave that nearly wiped them out. Aydin smiled to himself at the sight. He checked his watch. Just under an hour to go until the guests arrived. It didn't look like the host was feeling particularly nervous about what lay ahead. And neither was Aydin. He was in the zone. He pulled the binoculars down then, with the warming early evening sun on his face, he sat back and waited for the others to arrive.

CHAPTER 34

Detroit, Michigan

Frustratingly, Cox had spent much of the day in her hotel room. Aydin hadn't been back in touch since the morning, though she could hardly badger him all day, she realised she needed to give him space, but with Flannigan's forty-eight-hour window quickly winding down, the pressure on Cox was growing all the time. They needed a breakthrough. With little action in Dearborn, she was hoping it might come from GCHQ, and had been counting down the minutes to the recently scheduled call with Kaufman.

'You received the data OK?' Cox asked once the call was connected.

'All downloaded, processed and in the midst of analysis now.'

'Any luck on the key?'

'Nothing.'

Cox slumped.

'The user, Karim Hussein, has plenty of correspondence with your target list, but it's nearly all uncoded, unencrypted communications. No evidence of the encryption key, and also no evidence that he's been a party to any of the dark web conversations.'

'Great,' Cox said. 'So we've got nothing.'

'I didn't quite say that. In fact, we've made some real tangible progress. The thing is, Hussein's devices are all linked together; phone, tablet, laptop. He receives a call or a text or an email on one, and it comes through on all three.'

'It's the modern way.'

'It is for the younger generation. The name of the game is convenience, but it's also a huge shoo-in for operations like this.'

'OK, I'm liking the sound of this.' Finally, some good news.

'Essentially, from the data we've captured, we've been able to gain real-time access to Hussein's devices. Calls, messages, whether SMS or through apps like WhatsApp, email, the lot. We can track his communications, his movements in real time now.'

'That's good. But it doesn't help us if he's not privy to the information we need.'

'Actually it does. Because we don't just have read access on his devices, but write too. We can send messages, emails. We can be him if we wanted. But, more importantly, we can use his devices to do direct phishing, with the devices he, or we, connect with.'

'That sounds more promising.'

'It is. And we've already hit gold. We now have full access to Ahmed Akhwabi's home computer too.'

Namur. This was huge. Cox's heart thudded in her chest as she waited with anticipation for Kaufman to carry on.

'He's not as technologically advanced as his younger counterpart,' Kaufman said, 'so it is just the computer we're talking about. But we've got it. The key.'

'Seriously?'

'Seriously.'

Cox would have high-fived her if she'd not been stuck alone in a gloomy hotel room.

'We've managed to decrypt everything we've intercepted so far. I'm uploading the decrypted transcripts into the data room now.'

'This is . . . I can't believe it. Give me the snapshot.'

Now there was a sigh, and Cox felt like her bubble was about to be burst.

'It's pretty bland, on the face of it. Lots of talk about people going places, but it doesn't seem to mean much. The names aren't names on your list, the places aren't the same places the IP addresses are located.'

'Can you give me an example?'

'Give me a second . . . OK, this one. Sent three days ago. "Osbourne planning to visit Milwaukee on twenty-third. Make sure he gets in the pool."'

Cox's face screwed. What on earth was that nonsense?

'The twenty-third is today,' Cox said.

'But the rest is . . . '

'Coded?'

'Yeah, pretty basic coding, but that's what it seems like. We can run some analysis, the more intercepts we get the better it'll be, and see if we can decipher some of the code just by breaking down the patterns. That becomes much easier though the more we can overlay real information on top. The best way to understand the code though is to find someone who knows it.'

Was that an option? The only way to do that would be to capture and interrogate one of Namur's gang, but Cox felt that they were a long way from that being the best course of action.

'What about your man?' Kaufman suggested.

'Aydin?'

'He doesn't know this cell, but—'

'But he might still understand the coding. Or at least have some clue as to its design.' After all, Aydin had spent plenty of time on the inside of a terrorist cell in his dark past. 'OK, leave that with me.'

Cox ended the call and sat back in her chair with a sigh that was part content, part frustration. Finally they were making progress, though they still needed more, and it seemed everything now came down to just one man. Aydin.

She tried several times to call him, but he didn't answer at all. She left a message before she ordered yet another room service meal. She was barely halfway through it when her phone lit up with a call. She'd hoped it was Aydin, though saw it was a local number she didn't recognise, which turned out to be Agent Tarkowski of Homeland Security. Which was interesting to say the least. And more likely to be bad news than good, Cox decided.

'I've got some news for you on your targets,' Tarkowski said.

Cox frowned. 'Which targets?'

'Ahmed Akhwabi, aka Namur. His sidekick Benyamin Dawood, and Karim Hussein.'

Cox held her breath. As cynical as she was as to why Tarkowski was looking into her 'targets' at all, her biggest fear on hearing the names was that Tarkowski was calling to tell her that an attack had already taken place, and they'd been nowhere near to stopping it.

'Agent Cox, are you still there?'

'Yes. What have you got?'

'Just passing on some intel for you. I had an automated alert from the TSA earlier—'

'TSA?'

'Transport Security Administration. An agency within Homeland Security, they deal with . . . well, transport security.'

Cox rolled her eyes. Agencies within agencies now. How on earth did anyone keep up with it all? Was someone in the government paid just to come up with three letter acronym agency names all day, every day?

'I know we're not taking any active role in your operation but as a courtesy to you, and for our own security purposes I guess, I had the TSA set a tag on the IDs of all those individuals you're interested in.'

'Sounds sensible,' she said, even though a part of her wondered why Tarkowski hadn't mentioned to her the first time they'd met that the US authorities would be taking an active role in watching her 'targets'.

'This morning those three boarded a flight at Metro Airport, heading to LAX.'

'Los Angeles?'

'That's the one.'

'Have you got eyes on them?'

'No, Ma'am. The TSA doesn't have the resource or capability for that, and like I said, those individuals are not part of an active investigation for us.'

Cox huffed.

'This is literally just an automated message from a computerised tag,' Tarkowksi said. 'It's not much, but I thought you might want to know.'

'Yes, of course. Thank you.' She looked at her watch. It was gone four p.m. now. Apparently the computer wasn't exactly speedy at sending its automated messages.

'And your Mohammed Akhbar?' Tarkowski said.

'Yes?'

Cox's heart beat faster and louder all of a sudden.

'He didn't travel with them, but he was on a later flight. He's in LA now too.'

Cox didn't say anything to that. Just clenched her fist and ground her teeth.

'Obviously we have a tag on him too, given . . . his background.'

'Understood,' Cox said. 'And you'll let me know if they go anywhere else?'

'As soon as I hear.' Which could be several hours after the event, apparently, but it was better than nothing. 'You have a good day, Agent Cox.'

The call was dead before she could respond, and Cox was left to finish her half sandwich with anger bubbling away, and thoughts of what the hell she would do with Aydin when she caught up with him next.

CHAPTER 35

Pacific coast, California

Playtime in the pool didn't last too long. After a quick splash with the children, Emilio Torres was soon out and towelling himself dry. By the time he was heading inside the house again, the kids were out too, and moments later they and the women had all disappeared inside the huge mansion.

Aydin didn't move from his spot among the rocks as he lay in wait. As much as he'd prefer to be closer to the house, there simply wasn't anywhere else he could see which would offer as much relative cover and safety. He checked his watch and his phone intermittently. He had numerous missed calls from Cox. What was that about? Aydin wasn't given much time to dwell. The French doors at the back of the mansion opened once more, and two men strolled out. They were casually dressed and both had big weapons, but they weren't the same two guards Aydin had spotted earlier.

How many were there?

The two men did a thorough recce of the area around the pool. So it looked like that would be the spot, which was perfect from Aydin's perspective. He'd assumed, given the weather, and the fact that men like Emilio Torres were naturally hesitant to hold private rendezvous indoors for fear of eavesdropping devices, that the meeting would take place outside, and it looked like he was right.

The boss man himself was soon back outside too, now wearing cream linen trousers and shirt, those same aviators still covering his face. He took a seat at a table overlooking the pool then began a casual conversation with the two guards in view to Aydin, who were standing either side in front of their employer.

Minutes later the distant growl of car engines drifted over. The noise got the attention of Torres and his guards, the two armed men all of a sudden looking less casual and more uptight. Aydin could see nothing of the approaching cars coming along the road beyond the mansion, though the sounds of their engines were getting louder by the second. Then came the crunch and grind as tyres hit loose gravel, and before long a peaceful silence returned when the cars stopped and their engines were turned off.

Torres didn't move from his seat. Apparently he wasn't part of the welcoming party.

Aydin, binoculars up, flicked left and right, from Torres, to the house, to the space at the side of the mansion. The latter being where he finally saw movement. Two more armed guards in front. Two men in the middle. One was a smartly dressed man Aydin hadn't seen before – one of Torres's guys? The other was Namur, all suited up like an office worker. Behind him Karim and Benny – both also in tight-fitting suits – strode along next to a final armed guard.

Karim and Benny were both sullen and serious, compared to Namur who was relaxed and smiley. Soon Torres was on his feet and he and Namur shared an uncomfortable-looking embrace. A show, more than anything else. From what Aydin could see there was certainly no familiarity in the gesture, nor genuine closeness. Had these two men even met in person before?

Namur was offered a seat opposite Torres. Karim and Benny remained standing at the side, their eyes busy as they glanced from one guard to another. At five against two, they were seriously mismatched, even if they did have handguns under their suit jackets, which Aydin was sure they did, given the bulges he could see.

As Aydin was staring, Karim glanced in his direction for a beat longer than necessary. Aydin froze. Too late to duck down. If he did that the movement, even at distance, would catch the eye too easily. Karim eventually looked away and didn't say a word to Benny, so Aydin could only assume he remained in the clear.

The conversation between Namur and Torres was animated, in an over-the-top friendly kind of way. The entire set-up seriously puzzled Aydin. What would a kingpin of Venezuelan drug trafficking have in common with Namur, a local thug and something of a wannabe Islamist – apparently? Yet the two men certainly seemed cosy enough together.

Torres nodded over to one of his guards who scurried away to the garage block. He used a clicker to open the right hand of the multiple retractable doors, then stepped inside. He came back out carrying a large cardboard box. Not so large or so heavy that it wasn't easily carried though. What the hell was Torres selling?

The box was placed on the table between Torres and Namur and both men got to their feet. Namur ripped the tape off the box and lifted the flaps and peered inside. His face remained expressionless. He glanced back up to Torres and said something. Torres, himself now looking more serious, gave a lengthy and not particularly friendly response. Aydin braced himself. It appeared all niceties had worn off. With a meeting like this, only one wrong word could lead to carnage, and Aydin could see all the other men tensing as they awaited the verdicts of their bosses.

Eventually Namur indicated over to Benny who stepped forward. His hand went to his side, causing all of Torres's guards to whip their assault rifles up, aiming at all three of the guests. Benny paused, looked more angry than worried, and after a little explaining by Namur, Benny reached for his pocket again and took out a large phone. Guns were lowered. He typed away and then showed the screen to Torres, who nodded, satisfied.

Then, somewhat surprisingly, the box was removed from the table and the guard who'd brought it out strode back to the garages with it and by the time he was back out, empty-handed and walking towards the group again, the meeting was over, business concluded, without anything actually changing hands. Other than a few germs perhaps from that strange initial embrace.

Torres and Namur shook hands and moments later the three guests were being escorted round the side of the house. Torres remained by the pool, chatting to his remaining guards. Aydin heard the car engines fire up again, and only when the sounds had faded into the distance did Torres move back inside his home.

And then all was blissfully quiet and beautifully serene. Not that Aydin appreciated it much. He worked over what he'd just witnessed in his head. Clearly a transaction of sorts had just taken place. Benny and his phone the payment? The box from the garage a sample of what was being purchased? A sample that couldn't be taken by Namur today because how would he get illicit goods back on a plane?

That all made some sense. But then why had Namur paid at all if they hadn't yet taken any goods?

Most importantly, what was Namur buying?

Aydin had to find out. That box was still in the garage . . .

Aydin only waited ten minutes more. Off to the west the sun was nearly beyond the horizon, the villa and the grounds in front of him were lit up by thick orange rays. Although it would be easier to do this next part at night, the thought of traipsing back across the rocks to his car in the dark didn't fill him with joy in the slightest. He needed to do this now.

All remained quiet outside, and there was no indication where in the villa Torres and his crew were.

Did any guards remain on the outside?

Aydin would soon find out.

He pulled the balaclava from his backpack and put it over his head then stuffed the binoculars away. He took out the sheathed hunting blade which he strapped to his side. With only his fake UK ID to travel with, he had no means of acquiring a gun in the US, at least not legally, but there were no restrictions on knives, and Aydin was comfortable enough that his choice of arms was fit for purpose, for now.

Aydin slipped the backpack over his shoulders then stayed low as he moved forward through the thick mess of rocks and bushes, heading along the side of the property, aiming to come up to the garage block from the back.

He made it there within a couple of minutes. Most likely his movement had been caught by at least one of the many CCTV cameras on the buildings and around the grounds, but given their sheer number he was betting there wasn't someone sitting in a dark room staring at the multiple live feeds all day every day.

Aydin pulled up against the white painted back wall of the garages and took a few seconds to get his breathing nice and slow and relaxed and as quiet as possible. He peered round the corner, looking back to the pool area. No one there. But a moment later he heard the gentle crunch of footsteps on gravel. Two sets. The men were right the other side of the garage walls.

262

They certainly didn't sound like they were on alert. Probably just a routine walk around. Could this play exactly into Aydin's hands? It would be much easier to enter the garage if he had that clicker, but he had no way of knowing if whoever was the other side even had one.

Better to wait this out and find another way in he decided.

He remained where he was as the footsteps initially got louder. Every now and then the two men shared the odd word or two but there was no deep or meaningful conversation.

Aydin stole a glance . . . whipped his head back when he saw the figures a little more than ten yards away, but they had their backs to him, and they were already heading away from the garages, over to the pool area. Aydin peeked twice more. The men paused a few moments near the pool, perhaps admiring the view and the last remnants of sunlight, before they carried on their stroll towards the other side of the mansion.

When they were finally out of sight, Aydin moved. Not to the front of the garages, to the doors, but to the single side window he'd earlier spotted.

He glanced over to the house as he moved. A CCTV camera on the corner was pointed more or less directly at him, red light blinking, but it was too late now to worry about those. He just had to hope he could do this quickly.

He peered through the window. No lights were on inside the garage and with the fading daylight it was hard to make out what lay beyond. The window had a simple latch lock on the inside. Not overly secure, but then it was only the garage. Aydin took his knife from its sheath and wedged it into the gap between the window opening and the frame. He heaved down. Had a split-second image in his mind of the blade snapping in two . . .

There was a crack and a crunch. Aydin looked in relief to see it wasn't the knife failing, but the internal lock. He looked around him. No indication anyone had been alerted to the sharp and abrupt sound. He slipped the knife away then pulled the loose hanging window open and slunk inside.

Without any lights on, and one single window at either end of the large open space, it took his eyes a few seconds to adjust. There were three expensive-looking cars in the garage, but the end Aydin had entered was lined with shelving and filled with tools, garden equipment. Boxes. Which one was it?

He took out a torch and moved over to the ones closest to the door. Some were sealed, some weren't. Some had logos and lettering printed on the outside giving away what they contained. Fertiliser, lawn feed, chlorine, other household chemicals. Aydin's brain throbbed with confusion. Yes many of the items could, in theory, be used for crude explosives, but why would Namur come all this way to buy fertiliser for an IED? Most likely this was all simply supplies for Torres and the lavish grounds his home was set in.

So where was the box that had been shown to Namur?

His frustration and anxiousness growing, Aydin swung the torch around, flicking it here and there.

He found it. He was sure that was the box, over in the far corner. No labelling at all on the outside of it, and the remnants of tape on top where Namur had peeled it open. Aydin moved forward quickly . . .

Then froze dead when there was a mechanical whirring. The garage door behind him began to retract upward.

Someone was coming in.

CHAPTER 36

Aydin spun round. The window he'd come in through was three yards away. The opening door, and whoever was beyond it, was five yards away. The box he so desperately wanted to see was barely even two yards behind him.

The garage door was already open a couple of feet, two shoes visible the other side. So just one man out there, but Aydin knew there were several more armed men on the grounds. To fight, if he could avoid it, was ludicrous.

Aydin took perhaps the least satisfying option and launched himself for the window. He barrelled out as quickly and carefully as he could, making minimal noise. At least he hoped the sound he did make was drowned out by the retracting door, and as he touched down on the ground outside he quickly reached up and grasped the window and did his best to push it gently back into the frame.

As he did so he peered back through the glass, over to the door, which was now almost fully up, and the man's face — one of the guard's from earlier — was in full view.

Aydin threw himself down.

Had he been seen?

He held his breath as his heart drummed in his chest. He heard footsteps inside. Still on his haunches, Aydin side-stepped like a crab. He'd made it to within a yard of the corner of the garage when he heard the man's exclamation.

'Qué?'

Had he spotted the broken window?

Aydin flung himself round the corner out of sight, just as the window was pushed open from the inside. The man started shouting in Spanish. At Aydin? Or was he speaking into a radio, to his companions? Either way, Aydin had to scarper. Except he could already hear the man's footsteps approaching, outside now. Aydin rose to his feet. He pushed his body against the side of the garage as he thought through what he could do.

The footsteps slowed.

No. He couldn't stand and fight. At least not here. Aydin burst forward, away from the garage and for the nearest thick palm tree in front of him. He made it before the guard was in view, but had the noise given him away?

The main thing was that he try to draw the man away from the garage and the house. The closer Aydin was to the mansion, the bigger the problem he had.

He scuttled across to another tree. Then another. Peered round the side. The guard, assault rifle held up at the ready, was at the back of the garage now, rummaging around there.

Aydin pushed forward again and skidded to a stop behind a thick hibiscus bush that was bursting with purple flowers.

But this time Aydin's movement did catch the man's eye.

He shouted at the top of his voice. Aydin didn't catch the Spanish words but he was sure it was a rallying call. Aydin moved again. Barely breaking pace now, he quickly moved from tree to rock to shrub until he was back near the rocky outcrop where he'd earlier spied from.

He flung himself to a stop, pulled himself close to the ground to give him cover and looked back. Bright white spotlights

266

burst to life at the back of the mansion. Two, three, four guards were there, assembling themselves. Not coming in search of Aydin – yet – but protecting the property it seemed. At least that was a positive, Aydin thought.

He didn't have long to bask in his relief though. The guard from the garage was closing in, and was now only five yards away. He hadn't yet seen Aydin's hiding spot, because if he had he'd be shooting already, but it would only be seconds before he did.

Keen to remain out of sight from the house, Aydin pulled himself further into a crevice between two rocks then waited. He could hear the guard approaching. Could hear the man's angry breathing.

Then he saw the man's shoe, on the rock above him. Aydin paused. When the second shoe came into view, moving forward, Aydin reached up and grabbed it and hauled down. The man yelped and tumbled forward. He let go of his rifle and lifted his arm to prevent a sickening crack between his face and rock. It was still a horrendous fall though, as he thudded down onto the craggy surface. Skin was torn, blood oozed. He was already dazed as Aydin lurched forward.

The man tried to regain his feet. Tried to get hold of his gun again . . . he managed the first task, but not the second. Aydin yanked on the rifle and the strap came loose and the gun clattered away down the cliff to the unseen bay below. As they scrambled, Aydin had the speed and strength to pull the guard into a reverse headlock. He squeezed hard, trying to choke him, using his free arm to pull the hold even tighter. The man was injured from that initial fall, but fighting for his life he had plenty of strength left in him and he writhed and bucked and threw elbows and fists into Aydin's sides.

Aydin flinched and grimaced, both from the pain to his already bruised body, but also to try not to make a sound.

From where they were, behind the rocks, they remained out of sight from the guards gathered by the house and Aydin wanted to keep things that way as long as possible.

But the guard wasn't going to make things easy for Aydin – he was desperate. He made a last gasp grasp for Aydin's knife. Aydin had to release his left arm from the hold to fend off the wandering hand. He managed it, but with his weakened grip around the guard's neck, the guy's power and focus in his fight was suddenly raised several notches. Aydin took a painful strike to the groin. Then the guard dug his fingernails into the dressing covering the knife wound on Aydin's side and raked across. Aydin growled in pain and pulled his arm away from the man's neck as he inched back.

The guard, freed, looked like he was about to square off and resume his fight. Aydin didn't want a fight. He needed to finish this and to scarper.

He lifted his heel and drove forward. His foot connected with the guard's gut. Enough power to cause him to stumble back. Except there was nothing for him to stumble back to. His trailing foot connected with thin air . . .

The panicked look on the guard's face showed he'd figured out his predicament. Aydin helped him on his trip anyway. He reached forward and shoved. The guard, wide-eyed, flung his arms out, tried desperately to grasp hold of Aydin. But Aydin wouldn't be this man's saviour.

The guard plummeted out of sight as he screamed in despair. There was a thud, then another, then a third and final one as his body came to its final resting place somewhere below, beyond where Aydin could see.

By now, even disguised behind the rocks, the commotion was sure to have got the attention of the other guards. Sure enough, as Aydin peeked round the rocks he could see two of them closing in, though moving cautiously.

He couldn't fight them all.

Aydin looked over the edge of the cliff. Tried to push the thoughts of the daredevil descent from his mind, then began the dangerous clamber downward.

Thankfully the angle of the jagged rocks meant he was soon sheltered from view from up above. Should the guards look over they wouldn't see him. He carried on his downward scramble and soon the guards' voices above were drowned out by the crashing waves behind him. Somehow the adrenaline coursing through his body gave him better grip and focus than when he'd earlier gone down, and Aydin made quick work of the task at hand.

He was almost at the beach below when he passed right by the body of the guard. Splayed across the top of a small ridge, his limbs were twisted at horrific angles, the white of broken bone visible, his spine surely snapped in several places given how his torso was arched round the curve of the rock beneath him.

Not a nice way to go.

Aydin carried on. Soon his feet hit sand, to his huge relief. He looked back up. He was all alone. None of the guards were brave enough to give chase. At least not this way, it seemed.

As Aydin looked across the bay and to the water, he realised the tide had gone out several yards since he'd arrived. With any luck it would mean he could make it some of the way back to his car on the sand rather than across the rocks. Pushing the grim thoughts of the sight of the dead guard out of his mind, together with the frustration at having been so close to that damn box before his plans were scuppered, Aydin burst into a sprint.

CHAPTER 37

Dearborn, Michigan

'You OK?' Namur said to Karim.

Karim turned to his boss across the other side of the back seats of the X5, their ride back from Metro Airport. Tamir was up front driving, Benny his passenger.

'Why wouldn't I be?'

'This has been a lot for you to take in. I know that.'

It was something of an understatement. As out of his depth as Karim at times had felt, at least the trip to California had been less dramatic than the previous one to the factory in Detroit. The meeting with Emilio Torres had gone by without incident, without gunshots, without bloodshed, and without any dead bodies needing to be disposed of. That had to be some sort of plus point.

All considered, Karim would have felt quite relaxed heading back home to Dearborn had it not been for the conversation he and Namur had had on the way to LAX that morning.

'I'm fine, really. Just looking forward to some rest.'

'Rest?' Namur gave a mocking laugh. 'You kids really are something.'

Karim didn't have a response to that. He turned back to look out of his window again and his mind was soon back twisting away at recent events.

Before the meeting at Torres's glorious villa – which, if that wasn't an advert for the benefits of an illicit life, then what was? – Karim had once again been told little about what the supposed deal between the Venezuelan and Namur involved. He still had little inkling even coming away from the villa. Namur had simply told him Torres was a man who wouldn't let them down, not like the Bloods had. A man who literally could get you anything you needed, if you paid him in kind.

Which was the strange thing, because as far as Karim had figured out from the meeting in California, nothing had changed hands. Namur had paid nothing other than a token transfer to a charitable trust in Torres's wife's name, and Namur had come away with literally nothing at all, other than a glimpse inside that box and a promise that what he'd asked for would follow.

At least since their conversation earlier in the morning Karim now understood what all that was about, and what Torres was sourcing for them.

Strangely, he wasn't sure what scared him more. The thought of what Torres was giving them, or what they had agreed they'd do for him in return . . .

'I chose you for this because I believe in you,' Namur said.

Karim faced him again though he struggled to hold eye contact.

'You didn't even know me until a few days ago.'

'Of course I did. You didn't know it, but I know everyone. That's my job. Call me a talent scout, whatever.'

'All you knew was that I beat up a bunch of jocks.'

'No. That was the tipping point, but you've been on my radar a long time. I talk to people. A lot. Imam Ibrahim always had good things to say about you.'

So was that it? The Imam had set Karim on this collision course? Karim had always seen the religious leader as a wily

271

old man, but it had never really crossed his mind he had such an ulterior role among the community.

'Anyway. We're all set now. You've got two days, then we go again,' Namur said. 'And this time—'

'I'll be ready for it. I'll do whatever's needed.'

Namur nodded in appreciation, but the truth was Karim just wanted to end the conversation. Not that what he'd said to Namur wasn't true, because it was, but he just needed a bit of space now.

'You missed the turning,' Karim said, whipping his head round to Tamir who was driving.

'You're not going home just yet,' Namur said.

'Then where?'

'Let's just say, there's someone who's been looking forward to meeting you. Karim, this is it. You're one of us now.'

The words sent a shudder down his spine.

CHAPTER 38

Aydin spotted her the moment he stepped through the automatic doors into the arrivals hall at Metro Airport. Despite the seriously unfriendly look, he headed over to her.

'I've never had a welcoming party before,' he said. Cox didn't say anything to that. 'Except I'm not sure it's very welcoming really.'

'Cut the crap, Aydin. This way.'

That told him. Even though he really wasn't in a mood for a grilling, he did as she'd asked and they were soon in her car heading away from the airport.

'Just tell me where you've been,' Cox said.

'I figure you already know the answer, otherwise how were you waiting for me there?'

He looked over and could tell she was seething. But why was she? So he'd not told her about the trip. So what? He didn't need a nanny.

'So how did you figure it out?' he said.

'Because I'm a bloody spy. I'm surprised you forgot that.'

Aydin humphed.

'Please, can you just tell me.'

'I was going to anyway. I would have done once I got back. I'm sorry that I didn't realise you needed updating every time I breathed.'

'Don't be so damn pedantic. You sound like a child.'

He gritted his teeth but said nothing to that. Was that how she saw him?

He briefly explained about the trip. About the meeting with Torres.

'I've looked into him. He's something of a South American criminal kingpin.'

Cox was open-mouthed now.

'What on earth was Namur buying.'

'I tried to find out. I nearly got killed doing so. The other guy wasn't so lucky.'

'Aydin, please don't—'

'Don't tell you I killed someone?'

'Again.'

Aydin said nothing to that. He stared out of his window at the bleakness of wintery Detroit. California seemed a million miles away.

'You lied to me,' Cox said. 'How can you expect this to work if you won't even be straight with me about what you're doing and what you've found.'

'I am straight with you, but that doesn't mean I have to call you every time I find the smallest piece of information.'

'Why wouldn't you?'

'Because . . .' He sighed. He didn't know how to answer that.

'I get it,' she said. 'Kind of. You hate being tied to us. To me. You want to be free from it all. Maybe one day you can be.'

'But not today, right?'

'Not today. What do you think happens if you push too far? If the op gets pulled and I'm dragged back to London, where does that leave you?'

Aydin didn't answer.

'A bogus identity in a foreign country?' she said. 'No job, no money, no way home.'

274

'Is that a threat?'

Cox glanced at him but didn't answer the question. Aydin held his tongue.

'We've been through so much together and I want to be on your side,' Cox said. 'But not everyone in SIS does. The decision of what happens to this op, to *you*, won't be mine, but if you push too far . . . '

'And what if you push *me* too far,' Aydin said. 'What do you think happens then?'

He saw the look of disquiet in her eyes at his thinly veiled threat.

'Didn't you tell me you wanted to break free from your past?' Cox said. 'From the violence and the hatred?'

'Yes, I said I wanted to. I said I wasn't sure I ever could.'

Strangely, in that moment he had a flashing image of Kate in his mind. He'd texted her since the day she'd stopped him in the car park. More than once he'd questioned in his mind whether agreeing to going out with her on a date was something he needed to do. Why couldn't he do normal things?

He hadn't taken that step yet. As ludicrous as it seemed, such a seemingly small step felt far more difficult than everything else he was doing in the US.

'In a way you're actually lucky I found out about your trip,' Cox said. 'The fact you'd trailed Namur there, for whatever purpose, was enough to keep Flannigan off my back, off *our* backs, for now. But you should have told me your plans.'

'Why?'

'I could have helped you. We could have set up proper surveillance.'

'Your suggestion being my surveillance wasn't good enough.'

'You just told me you killed a man, Aydin! Who cares if he was good or bad, he was still a man, and you can bet there'll be repercussions. What if Torres blames Namur?'

The thought had obviously already crossed Aydin's mind.

'It's one thing acting gung-ho on your own time, but here you're not on your own time. You're working with me.'

'With? Strange choice of word from where I'm sitting.'

Cox tutted. 'Aydin, let me make this as clear as I can for you. This is the last time. The last time you lie to me. The last time you withhold from me. Do you understand?'

'Yeah,' he said.

'And you might be wondering why I've been trying to get hold of you.'

'I guess.'

She explained to him about the encrypted messages. About the coding that sat behind.

'Do you think you can help with it?'

'I can try. We used something similar. It's often not too difficult to understand the context, it's just that keywords are interchanged. A person could actually be a place, or vice versa. An object could be a specific action. That sort of thing.'

'So if I said to you, "Osbourne planning to visit Milwaukee on twenty-third. Make sure he gets in the pool." Does that mean anything at all to you?'

Aydin worked it over in his head for a few moments.

'No,' he said. 'I'd need more. Osbourne could be a person, but it could also be a thing. Milwaukee could be a place or a person. The pool?' He thought back to Torres's villa. Was 'pool' some sort of reference to that? The date would match. 'The best I can do is to take a look through it all. The more I see, the more I can try and unpick it.'

'OK, I'll get it all to you as soon as I can,' she said as she turned the car onto the street where his apartment was located. 'Perhaps we could even go through it all together?'

He heard her words but he didn't respond. As they approached his building, he was too busy eyeing the group of men milling outside. Cox slowed the car.

'Keep going, keep going!' Aydin said before ducking his head down.

'Shit,' Cox said, obviously realising the issue.

Aydin kept his head low until they'd headed past, then glanced in his side mirror at Namur, Benny, Karim and Tamir.

'Did they see us?' Cox said, staring into her rear-view mirror.

'I don't know,' Aydin said.

'We'll come back later,' Cox said. 'If you come to the hotel I can show you the—'

'No. Just take this turn then drop me off. I want to know why they're here.'

'You think it's a problem?'

Aydin didn't answer. Cox took the turn and then pulled the car to the side of the road.

'You need to keep me in the loop. OK?'

'OK,' he said, though he wasn't really sure what he was agreeing to. 'I'll leave my bag with you. No point in inviting suspicion as to where I've been.'

Cox mumbled a sarcastic response, but Aydin was already stepping out into the cold.

He shut the door and strode away and round the corner and soon had Namur and the others in his sights again. Karim prodded the boss to get his attention as Aydin crossed the road towards them.

'Where've you been?' Namur said in a kind of a growl as Aydin reached them.

'Out. And you? Not seen you lot for a couple of days.'

'We've been busy.'

'Sounds interesting. You can tell me all about it if you like.'

'We need to talk.'

'OK.'

Namur indicated behind him to the apartment block. 'Inside.'

'I'm not sure we'll all fit, but let's go.'

Aydin led the way. As they idled up the stairs he had a momentary panic about his computer equipment. He'd left the search software running while he'd been away, which was fine, but where was Karim's laptop? He was sure he'd put it into the desk drawer before he'd left for California, but was now having a niggling doubt as to whether he'd just thought it.

When he opened the door, the first thing he did was to stare over to the corner. Sure enough the laptop wasn't in sight. All good, as long as no one went snooping.

He let the motley crew inside. Karim and Tamir and Benny remained standing, milling about, inspecting the place. Namur and Aydin took a seat in the lounge area. They all declined drinks. Whatever this was, it wasn't a friendly social gathering, which was why Aydin had made sure to take a seat with his back to the wall. He didn't want any nasty surprises, and he'd also previously stuffed a hunting knife into the crevice between the cushion and the frame.

He casually stuck his fingertips down there now, making sure the blade was still in place.

It was.

'Why are you here in Dearborn?' Namur asked.

'Haven't we been through this before?'

'And the last time you gave me some bullshit answer about some guy sending you here to see Nasir Al-Addad.'

'It wasn't bullshit.'

Aydin glanced over to Karim who was edging closer and closer to the computer equipment that remained whirring away.

'Not many people would be brave enough to mention those two names to me,' Namur said. 'Nasir Al-Addad. Faiz Al-Busaidi. You're playing a dangerous game, whoever you are.'

Aydin sighed. 'Have you got a point to make?'

278

Karim was now right by the desk. He reached out to press on the space bar on the keyboard.

'Don't touch that,' Aydin said, the authority in his tone enough to make Karim pause.

In fact, enough to make everyone in the room pause. All four men glared at Aydin. Namur raised an eyebrow but said nothing. He looked over to Karim and nodded. The young man didn't look too happy but he stepped back from the computer. Well, stepped towards Aydin actually, as did Benny. One of them either side. Both of them glaring.

'I've known Faiz Al-Busaidi a long time,' Namur said.

Aydin's nerves were building now, not least because of the way he all of a sudden felt surrounded. He pretended to scratch under his leg. His fingertips brushed the handle of the knife again.

'How long have *you* known him?' Namur asked.

'A few months,' Aydin said.

'A few months? And when did you last see our good friend?'

Aydin shrugged casually. 'A few weeks ago, perhaps.'

'You knew him well?'

'Depends how you define that.'

'You've been to his home?'

'Which one?'

'Met his family?'

'Which one?' Aydin said, this time with a wry smile. It looked like Namur didn't get the joke. Which perhaps meant he didn't know quite as much about Al-Busaidi as he was pretending to. 'You can try to trip me up if you like. Ask me to name his wife, his kids, his mistress, whatever. I know him. Maybe not as well as you, maybe not for as long as you. What are you trying to prove here?'

Aydin's confident response halted Namur for a few moments. Aydin looked left and right to Benny and Karim. Both were giving him the evil eye still. The truth was, as bolshy as Aydin was being, he didn't like this position one bit. It felt like they were just one nod of Namur's head away from carnage breaking out.

'Faiz Al-Busaidi is missing,' Namur said.

'Missing?'

'No one has seen or heard of him for weeks.'

'I didn't know that.'

'You haven't tried to contact him?'

Aydin pursed his lips and shook his head.

'You meet a man. He persuades you to travel across the world to start a new life, and you don't even try to reach out to him to say thank you? To say *I'm here*. You just forget about him for good?'

'I didn't say that.'

'But you haven't tried to contact him?'

'I already answered that.'

'And you had no idea he's missing.'

'Why would I?'

'Missing. Kind of like how you were. For four years.'

'I was only missing to the people who didn't know where I was. I knew where I was.'

'People like your mother, you mean? Who still has no clue where you are now. What kind of a son does that?'

Aydin glared at Namur now as he tried to keep his raw emotion in check. Yes, he was playing Jamaal Rashid here, but any time mention was made of family, it was his own family he pictured in his mind, and his own life and mistakes that he saw and felt.

'You've nothing to say about that?' Namur said.

'About what?'

'A teenager goes missing for four years—'

'I'm not a teenager any more.'

280

'Missing for four years. Suddenly he turns up across the world, asking after a dead man, and claiming to have been sent there by someone else who also just happens to now be missing.'

'Have you got a point to this?'

'You don't think any of that is strange? The one person who could corroborate your story . . . can't.'

'There's no story.'

'I guess I just have to take your word for that.'

'You either do or you don't.'

'Or you could properly explain to me where you've been all this time. Places, people you knew. What you've done. Evidence to back up what you're telling me.'

'You're right. I could do.'

'So?'

'Now?'

Namur nodded.

Aydin took a moment to compose himself. This wasn't entirely unexpected, of course. He spouted off a few well-prepared names that he and Cox had carefully put together as part of Jamaal Rashid's backstory of the past four years. Some real, some not. The real ones were all dead – ISIS fighters and the like whose existence it would be easy to prove, but whose whereabouts and fate were less difficult to uncover. Other names were fake, but with the amount of detail Aydin had for them, they would at least hopefully keep Namur beavering away a little while if he was really intent on following through.

By the end of Aydin's pre-planned regurgitation, during which Namur had asked for plenty of sensible and probing clarifications, the boss man was looking a little more relaxed, if a little disappointed that he hadn't managed to fully trip Aydin up. Was that his intent?

'Do what you want with that information,' Aydin said.

'I will,' Namur said. He looked over his cronies. 'OK. We're done here.'

Namur got to his feet. Aydin followed suit, though he was still tense and primed and ready for a sudden ambush. As they huddled towards the door, he made sure to stay a couple of steps from them, and with them all in his sights. He wasn't leaving his back exposed.

'I know about Al-Busaidi's role,' Namur said as he reached the door and turned back to face Aydin. 'I know what he does for the cause. And if he sent you here, I know why.'

Aydin nodded.

'Come and see me at the mosque at eight a.m. tomorrow. I'll get you started.'

'Thank you,' Aydin said.

'And call your mother,' Namur said. 'She's worried about you.'

Aydin flinched at that comment. Namur opened the door and the four men filed out. When the door was closed and locked and bolted, Aydin sighed with relief before he took the knife from behind his back and peeked into the spyhole.

They were gone. For now.

CHAPTER 39

The next two days, Aydin's first two on the inside of Namur's gang, were far less eventful than he could possibly have imagined. He'd never expected to be seen as a glorified errand boy, but apparently that was what Namur had his heart set on for Aydin. In some respects, it wasn't necessarily a bad thing, although he did wonder whether his almost meaningless role was because Namur still didn't trust him, and was simply playing him along.

After a day spent mostly driving around Dearborn and Detroit, Aydin was back relaxing in JL's, sipping a coffee and reading a car magazine, when Karim showed up. He strutted in, walking tall, a confident pout on his face like he now owned the place. He said a few words with his little league chums before he headed over to Aydin.

'Jamaal,' he said, before sticking his hand out for a fist pump.

Aydin responded, however foolish it felt.

Karim sat down on the arm of Aydin's sofa. Aydin went back to his magazine.

'You been busy today?' Karim asked.

Why did he care? 'Not really.'

'But you were busy last night, I heard.'

Aydin pulled the magazine down. Karim wanted his attention, now he'd got it.

'Yeah. I was,' Aydin said.

'That Kate Dickson. Nice looking lady.'

Aydin tried not to rise to it, but his temperature was already increasing. He'd finally persuaded himself that it would be an OK thing to do, for him to go on a date. He and Kate had spent a few hours in bars in central Detroit. Although initially awkward, he'd enjoyed the time, and thought she had too. Now he felt a little dirty about it, knowing that others knew. But how did they know?

'Don't look so angry,' Karim said. 'One of my boys saw you two out together, that's all.'

'You had someone spying on me?'

'Spying?' Karim laughed sarcastically. 'No. Why'd I care about you enough to do that? Seriously though, I get why you're into her.'

Aydin thought he probably really didn't.

'But you should be careful with girls like her.'

'She's not a girl. She's a woman. And what do you mean, *like her*?'

'White girls. Non-Muslims.'

'Well which is it? One isn't dependent on the other.'

Karim's eyes narrowed. 'I'm just saying. Maybe that's your taste, but around here, it could cause you some problems.'

'With you? With Namur? Or do you mean with *her type*.'

'If you bring along that attitude too, then with everyone.'

'OK. Thanks for your advice. I'm guessing you'll be telling our mutual boss the same thing next time he's entertaining prostitutes at his home.'

Karim was fuming now, and not doing a good job of hiding it.

'How'd you—'

'I'm his new errand boy, remember.'

Which was true, but Aydin hadn't yet been asked to escort any young ladies to Namur's crib. He was of course referring to when he'd spied on Karim doing that, but so what.

'I get what you're saying, though,' Aydin added, deciding perhaps it was better to try to diffuse the situation a little. 'I'll bear it in mind.'

Karim made a strange sniffing noise in response.

'I hear you're off on another trip,' Aydin said.

Which was partly true. Actually GCHQ had gleaned this from the access they now had to Karim's cyber life. Though they didn't yet have details of where the trip was to, or who it was with, despite their best efforts.

'You heard about that?' Karim said.

He looked a little nervous now, his bullishness disintegrating in an instant.

'Of course. Namur was just saying, after your trip to California, this was the big one.'

'California?'

'Maybe I'm more clued up than you realise.'

Karim huffed. 'After this trip . . . ' Karim looked around him. Making sure no one was in earshot. 'Truth is, I'm . . . '

'Nervous?' Aydin said, picking up on the vibes. 'Who wouldn't be. I might be new around here, but I'm not new to this process, nor what you're going to need to do now you're with Namur. He's been building you up. Sooner or later it'll be your time to shine.'

Aydin winked at him. Karim was nodding now, as though all of a sudden Aydin wasn't a threat but a source of great wisdom.

'Before you came here . . . what did you have to do?' Karim asked.

'What do you think? I was in Syria for over a year. In Iraq too.'

'You were a fighter?' Karim whispered, before mouthing 'ISIL'.

Aydin nodded. 'It's not as glamorous as what you might want to believe. Yes, there was a time when we were on top, but those days are over now.'

'What do you mean?'

Aydin straightened up as though finally willing to take the conversation seriously. Karim wasn't the dumbest person he'd ever met, but he was certainly easy enough to string along, if the right buttons were pressed. 'The coalition forces . . . once they upped their game, we stood no chance.' He went on to describe some of the battles he hadn't been in. Karim was in raptures. 'The thing is, anyone who's left now, who wants to live, is looking for a way out.'

'Which is why you came here?'

'We all have to go somewhere. And we can't go home.'

Karim nodded again.

'But the fight isn't over,' Aydin said. 'It's just different now. I'm sure you'll find that out soon enough.'

'In two days, I'd say,' Karim said.

Aydin's heart skipped a beat at that. What was he alluding to now? He would try to pry, albeit with subtlety.

'You've shot a gun before?' Aydin said.

'Of course,' Karim said. He looked offended.

'You've killed?'

Karim looked around him again, then nodded. 'But this time . . . this will be different.'

'Damn right it will be,' Aydin said.

'You know since we arrived here when I was a kid, I've never even been out of the country.'

'Seriously?'

'Seriously.'

'You've never been back to the Middle East?'

'Too difficult. Most of our family there is now dead or somewhere else anyway.'

Was that where they were going? To the Middle East?

'I always wanted to go back,' Karim said. 'Maybe one day.'

'Maybe.'

'But I never once thought about this fucking place,' he said with a smirk. 'Wouldn't even have been able to find it on a map. Not until a few days ago anyway.'

He winked, slapped Aydin on the back, then got up from the arm of the chair and walked away. Aydin remained on his seat, trying to act as calm as he could. He returned one eye to his magazine but really he was concentrating on Karim talking to his friends. They only stayed for a few minutes more before Karim led them out.

Aydin didn't hang around. When he was sure the coast was clear, he tossed the magazine down then got up from the sofa and bolted out of there.

He wasn't sure what he'd just stumbled upon, but he was certain this time he needed to speak to Cox.

Two hours later Aydin was walking with Cox along a pleasant-looking though horrifically cold promenade on the Detroit river, in the centre of the city. The other side of the water was Canada. Aydin had never been. What was life like over there? It was so close he could nearly touch it, yet in his mind it felt like a world away.

'I'm hoping this is good timing,' Cox said. 'I was looking at booking my flight out of here when I got your message.'

'Your boss is dragging you back to London?'

'Maybe not now.'

Aydin explained the little he knew. Karim's planned trip to some 'fucking place' he knew so little about.

'But you don't think it's the Middle East?'

'No,' Aydin said. 'Remember we were talking about the coding they use, how the words they use could be an object, a person, a place, an action.'

'Yeah, and?'

'I've seen plenty of mentions of Hawaii, but Hawaiian too. It's hard to explain but the latter always makes it sound like they were talking about food. Like a Hawaiian pizza.'

'Pineapple on pizza. They should be locked up just for that.'

Aydin held back a smile. 'The references to Hawaii seemed more obvious, like it was a place.'

'But you don't think it's actually Hawaii?'

'No. But I do think I know where.'

'Where?'

'Venezuela. Hawaiian is code for Torres. Hawaii is Venezuela.'

Cox stopped walking and stared at Aydin.

'When?'

'Two days.'

Cox huffed. 'There's a tie-in here we're not seeing. Why Torres? Why Venezuela?'

'You mean because it's hardly been a hotbed for Islamist contempt in the past?'

'That's exactly what I mean. Why on earth would they be planning an attack there?'

'Maybe they're not.'

'Then what?'

'It's a good question.'

'And you still don't know what that deal was about? What Torres sold them?'

'Nothing at all.'

Cox looked disappointed. 'OK. You did good here, Aydin,' she said, despite the look. 'But the pressure's on you now. This feels like we're almost at the tipping point. Plus, you're on the inside, but they're probing into you. It'll only take one slip . . .'

'I know that. And I've no doubt I'm under close scrutiny.' He thought about telling Cox about his date with Kate the night before, and how he'd been spotted, but he really couldn't figure how he'd explain it all. 'They also called my . . . Jamaal's mother.'

Cox sighed. 'I know.'

Aydin gave her a scathing look.

'We've had a tag put on her phones,' she said. 'We're looking out for you, Aydin. You had to expect this dissection of your supposed past. But the fact Karim is talking to you like he has done today suggests we shouldn't be overly worried. Yet.'

'Unless they're simply setting a trap for me.'

'Which perhaps they are. Which is one of numerous reasons why I'm going to insist you stay here the next few days rather than trying to follow them again.'

'How did I know you would say that?'

'It's for everyone's good,' Cox said. 'If it's Venezuela they're off to, I'll go. I might even be able to pull in some extra help. We'll stay close to Namur and we'll figure out what this is all about.'

'And if he doesn't even go there? If it's all a smokescreen?'

'Let's wait and see. We'll be ready to react.'

Aydin stared off into the distance, over the water to Canada again.

'I'm glad you're being honest with me this time,' Cox said.

Aydin nodded. 'See you around.'

He turned and walked away.

CHAPTER 40

A strange concoction of emotion wormed around Aydin when he awoke the following morning. The significance of the day ahead wasn't lost on him. Namur and the others were due to head to Metro Airport at midday, at least according to Karim's texts, though Aydin hadn't yet seen any information mentioning exactly which flight they were taking, and Venezuela as their destination remained little more than an educated guess. If he, and MI6, couldn't glean that information in the next few hours, Cox would just have to do her best to follow.

With a few hours to spare until the boss was away – Namur, rather than Cox, that was – Aydin had a busy morning planned which would largely involve him staring at his computer screen as he continued his deep dive search. He'd hit blanks so far with the obvious – there were no mentions of Nasir Al-Addad, or planned attacks or anything as revelatory as that. To his growing frustration he was now casting the net wider and wider in the hopes of uncovering something of interest. So far to little avail.

Still, by the end of the day, he'd hopefully have far more data to add into the mix, once he'd been on his roam around Dearborn.

To give a little light relief to all of that, he'd also proposed lunch with Kate. Now that the seal had been broken . . . So far though, he'd not received a response from his message the previous night. He sent another text then set to work.

Three hours later it was nearly noon and Aydin finally lifted his head for air. He sat back, head spinning, his vision bouncing as his eyes tried to focus beyond the computer screen to the window and the view outside. Once he'd managed that seemingly simple task, he got up from the chair and stretched out his aching body, checked his phone. Nothing yet from Cox, though by now she would be on her way to the airport.

Nothing from Kate still either. He'd been so engrossed he'd forgotten his invitation was still in the air.

He called her. No answer. Called her again. Same.

As much as he realised how off-putting his badgering might be, his naturally pessimistic mind was whirring. Karim, and by extension Namur, knew Aydin had been out with Kate. If anyone wanted to punish him, wasn't she an obvious target? He tried to keep the morose thoughts from building. He found the number for the art shop she worked at and called.

'Good morning, Dickson's Fine Art.'

Kate. So why didn't he feel relieved to hear her voice?

'It's Mo.'

'Oh, hi. Mo, sorry, I'm . . . I was just with a customer. I'll call you back?'

'Of course.'

She ended the call. She was safe at least, but he still didn't like the situation much. Why was she ignoring him?

He tried to relax as he waited for the call back. Went over to the computer screen again but couldn't concentrate. After an hour more he'd had enough. In that time word had come through from Cox that she was at Metro Airport, tailing Namur and his team – six men in total. At least that part of the day was going to plan.

Aydin had work to do. He grabbed his things and headed out.

His initial intent had been to go straight to Namur's house – the big executive home where a few days ago he'd spied Karim taking two young prostitutes for Benny's and Namur's pleasure. Aydin had been back a couple of times since then to properly survey the property from the outside, understand what he could about the layout and the security. Knowing Namur was away should make this a cinch now.

That confident feeling was perhaps why, as he was driving across Dearborn, Aydin decided on a slight detour first.

He parked up behind the art shop, which was the end unit on a run of single-storey premises on a busy highway. As he approached the front door he spotted Kate through the window, behind the desk. She was all alone now. Yet she still hadn't called him back over an hour since he'd spoken to her?

Already dubious, but wanting as far as possible to give her the benefit of the doubt, he opened the door and stepped inside. She looked up. Barely a smile. In fact, something of a grimace.

'Mo?'

'I was just passing. I wasn't sure if you'd had my messages. About lunch? Fancy a break?'

She looked down. 'Sorry. Look, I . . . I'm too busy today.'

But her tone was all off.

'What's going on?' he said.

She looked back up but couldn't hold his eye.

'I'm allowed to say no to a date,' she said, her tone cold, which only further irritated Aydin.

'But you didn't say no. You ignored me.'

'Please. Don't make this more difficult.'

'Make what more difficult?' He took a couple of steps towards her, which caused her to become all jittery. 'You were fine the other day.'

'I know but . . . '

'Tell me what happened.'

She looked petrified. What was she expecting him to do? He stepped forward again

'Kate?'

She didn't answer. He'd wanted to stay calm. He really had.

'Just tell me!' Aydin shouted.

'One more step and I'm calling the police!' Sheer panic in her voice. 'You want to know what the matter is?'

She sounded angry now, though her fear remained. She grabbed something from the desk and chucked it towards Aydin. The piece of paper wafted down to the floor by his feet. He picked it up. Tried his hardest not to explode when he saw what it was. The *Daily Mail* article. The one accusing the missing Jamaal Rashid – quite rightly, as it turned out – of having fled the UK to join ISIS.

'Is it true?' she said. 'Is that really you?'

'How did you find this?'

'It doesn't matter. Is it true?'

It wasn't even close to the truth. Unfortunately, the truth was probably far more frightening for her.

'I want to know how you got this,' he said, unable to hide his irritation now. 'Someone gave it to you?'

'It doesn't matter, Mo! Or is it Jamaal? Who the hell *are* you? How can you expect me to want to date you when . . . this!'

'Who gave it to you!' he boomed.

The sheer rage in his tone shook her. She picked up her phone. Her hand was shaking.

'Get out,' she said. 'Please. Just go.'

Somehow he managed to control the rage. It wasn't really directed at her after all. He dropped the piece of paper and turned for the door.

CHAPTER 41

Cox's day had started out with far too many loose elements for her liking, but everything was finally falling into place now. The intel from Aydin had simply been that Venezuela was the destination for Namur and crew, and despite his best efforts the only other information he'd found on the trip was that they were leaving from the mosque at midday. Enough to make a start, but pretty vague all told. For that reason, she'd been parked outside the mosque since ten a.m. Ready and waiting for . . . anything really.

Agent Tarkowski had provided a massive helping hand, and had already confirmed earlier, with help from the TSA, that there were no flight itineraries in any of the names of Namur or his gang to Venezuela, nor to anywhere else that day from any US airport.

Which initially caught Cox off guard. Yet as midday came around, the six men filed out of the mosque, climbed into two cars, and drove off. Cox followed. Sure enough the group headed to Metro Airport. Cox followed them inside. With no direct flights to Venezuela from Detroit, the most sensible routes from Cox's research showed the group would most likely have to change in Colombia or Panama en route. It would be an arduous journey.

Led by Namur, the men headed over to the check-in desk for Copa Airlines, the flag carrier of Panama. Cox stayed back and spied on the men from across the departures hall. When they were each quickly processed, Cox realised they already had tickets. How the hell hadn't the TSA's searches picked up the itineraries then?

Cox took out her phone to call Tarkowski and explained the situation. The men walked away from the desk towards security and were soon out of sight. Cox didn't follow. She headed over to the check-in desk, circumvented the queue and walked up to the woman who'd served the men. Much to the annoyance of the waiting passengers. Cox ignored their grumbles and questioning comments.

'Please, you need to take this,' Cox said, handing her phone to the bemused and slightly perturbed attendant. She didn't say a word as she listened to whatever it was Tarkowski had to say to her to convince her of his bona fides. She nodded a couple of times then handed the phone back to Cox.

'All sorted,' Tarkowski said. 'Let me know how it goes.'

Cox put the phone away and smiled at the attendant. She didn't smile back. She indicated for Cox to lean over to see the screen then typed away on her keyboard.

'These are the names of the passengers.'

Cox stared at the screen. At the names. She didn't recognise any of them.

'You're sure these are the same men?'

'Of course I'm sure,' she said quite snottily.

'OK. I need a ticket to match theirs please.'

The woman grumbled but got on with the request. When she was done, Cox turned to the waiting groups behind her and muttered an apology before scuttling off, phone to her ear again.

'Tarkowski,' he said when he answered.

'I found them,' Cox said. 'Six bogus identities. None of them American.'

'Shit. We can pull them. You don't have to let them leave the US.'

Cox had already thought about that one, but she mulled it over some more now.

'How do you even know Venezuela is their final destination?' Tarkowski said when Cox didn't respond. 'Maybe it's a stop-off to somewhere else. With bogus non-US IDs they could be heading to Iran or Syria or any one of a host of other sanctioned countries.'

'They could. But that wouldn't necessarily cause you a problem at home, would it?'

'And what if they turned up in London? Would that be a problem to you?'

'Yes. And no. As long as I'm still with them then I'll be ready for that.'

Tarkowski sighed. 'The choice is yours, Agent Cox. You have enough for us to detain them here.'

'No. It would defeat the purpose,' Cox said. 'But at least if I give you the names you could do some searches. See if it brings anything else up.'

'Shoot.'

Cox reeled the memorised names off, then thanked him and ended the call.

Cox moved to the back of the security queue and made another call. Kaufman answered on the third ring. Cox explained about the bogus names.

'I'll run them through the system,' Kaufman said. 'Maybe we'll get lucky.'

'Thanks,' Cox said. She went to end the call . . .

'Sorry, before you go. I do have some other news. A bit of a frustration really.'

297

That was the last thing Cox needed. 'Go on.'

'The encryption. It's changed.'

'You're joking?'

'I'm afraid not. Perhaps because of the stolen laptop, or some other reason, but the key we have doesn't work now.'

No, it had nothing to do with the laptop. But Cox could think of one clear reason why they'd change now.

'They're almost ready,' Cox said.

'How do you mean?'

'They're into final prep. The change in encryption was always planned to take place now, in the final run-up, to thwart any attempts up to this point.'

Kaufman said nothing to that.

'We need to break it. You *have* to.'

'We're trying, believe me. And one last thing, we finally backtracked all of the IP addresses.'

'Please don't give me another but.'

'Sorry. You must know my tone too well. Every one of the designation IP addresses is a public building. Mostly libraries. You could set up surveillance or request CCTV, but right now we have no other way of identifying the people on the other end.'

'But you do at least know the destinations?'

'Yes. Six US cities.'

Could they all be targets?

'OK, thank you. Let me know if there's anything more at all.'

'I always do.'

Cox put her phone away and tried to calm her growing anxiety as she waited in the queue. With Namur and the others out of sight, was it possible they'd already given her the slip and done a U-turn?

But why would they do that?

Once she was through security Cox rushed across to the departure gate and, much to her relief, they were all there,

298

sitting in three separate groups of two. Cox took a seat well away from them, but with them all in sight, and waited.

Karim, of all the six, looked the most apprehensive, his eyes darting about, his foot tapping on the floor. More than once he glanced at Cox momentarily, but there was no alert in his mannerisms as he did so. Cox blended, and Karim had no clue who she was. She'd need to keep a low profile though, as it was a long way to Caracas and sooner or later Karim and the others would become suspicious of the increasingly familiar face.

As she was waiting for the soon-to-depart flight Cox received another call. Aydin. Hopefully this was some good news finally. She tried to stay relaxed as she got up from the seat.

'Was it you?' he said.

There was a lot of background noise. Was he driving? Yet even with the noise she could tell he was angry.

'Was what me?'

'Who told her? Who told her about Jamaal's past?'

'I've no idea what you're talking about.'

A snort. 'If it was you, Cox . . . '

'Are you serious? I—'

'You and me . . . we talked about what I want from life. About how can I put the misery and the violence behind me. Maybe it was stupid of me to think I could.'

'Aydin, would you listen to me!'

'You might have thought it was ridiculous me seeing her . . . but she showed me. She showed it was possible for me to be different. And now it's all fucked.'

The call ended.

Cox realised she was shaking. The anguish and desperation in Aydin's voice . . . she'd not heard that before. The last thing she could afford right now was for a man as fragile,

299

and as deadly as him, to be pushed over the edge. She tried
to call him back. Tried several times. He didn't answer.

What the fuck was going on?

For several minutes she tried to reach him again with no
success. She lost track of where she was. When she turned
back round and moved over to where she'd been sitting,
she realised the flight was boarding. Karim and three of
the others were near the front of the already dwindling
queue.

But where were Namur and Benny? Already on board?

Cox, in a momentary panic, looked around. She saw them
in the distance, walking off in the opposite direction. Back
towards security.

'Shit,' she said out loud.

She tried to call Aydin again. He still didn't answer. She
left a message.

'Aydin, I don't know what's happened with you, but listen.
Namur and Benny aren't getting on the flight. I don't know
why. I have to go . . . be careful.'

She ended the call as she rushed after Namur and Benny.
Were they going for a different flight?

No, it didn't look like it. They back-tracked right out of
security. Cox looked at her watch. Looked up at the departures board. The gate for her flight was closing.

She turned and sprinted back the other way and left garbled
messages for both Flannigan and Tarkowski as she went. If
Namur and Benny were flying somewhere else, they had to
find out where.

And if they were heading back to Dearborn . . . What did
that mean for Aydin?

Too late to worry about that now.

Cox showed her ticket to the attendant at the gate.

'You need to be quick,' the woman said to her.

Cox nodded then raced down the gangway, phone pressed to her ear again to try to reach Aydin one more time. Once again he didn't answer. What more could she do? Cox stepped over the threshold onto the plane.

'Ma'am, we'll be leaving soon, you'll need to switch the phone to airplane mode.'

Cox nodded to the flight attendant. She found her seat and reluctantly turned the phone off, already thinking through the worst of what could happen over the next few hours.

CHAPTER 42

Aydin's mood had hardly calmed as he performed his second drive-past of Namur's home, though he was trying his hardest to remain focused. More than anything he needed someone, or something to vent his anger on. Part of him wanted to see Namur, or perhaps one of those jocks, walking down the street right now so he could jump out of the car and turn them over.

No. That was ridiculous. Juvenile and ill-thought out. He slapped his head, as though doing so would release his pent-up rage. It didn't really work.

Just like the first time he'd driven past, there was a plain-looking car on the driveway. Not a car he'd seen before today, it was certainly too small and old and cheap for a man like Namur.

His confused thoughts bubbling away, Aydin set up a spotting position further down the quiet street. The minutes of calm solitude gave his mind little respite, but when he saw the front door of the property open, it was like a fog suddenly cleared. This is what he needed. To be lost in the moment of action.

A diminutive woman in a blue-and-white dress stepped out of the house, coat over her shoulders, and scuttled to the car. A cleaner or maid? Well, with the man of the house away for a few days, hopefully she wouldn't be back any time soon.

She reversed off the drive and drove away in the opposite direction to where Aydin was sitting. He waited another few minutes. She didn't come back, and there were no other signs of life at the house. He started up his engine and did one last slow drive-by.

No indications at all that anyone was home now. He took a left up ahead then parked the car and moved back to the house on foot. No need to invite suspicion if anyone on Namur's street had already seen his car hanging about.

Aydin, with his backpack over his shoulders and a cap pulled low over his head, walked along the partially cleared pavement, eyes flitting about to try to spot any onlookers. There were none. The street was deserted.

He headed straight up the driveway, bypassed the front door and moved across to the side gate. It was locked. Aydin glanced behind him. He was sure no one was watching. He jumped the gate and landed softly the other side, an area which opened out in a large mainly lawned garden that was covered in untouched snow. Aydin kept his head low, avoiding the cameras he knew were above him, as he walked along the side of the house and to the back.

There were three doors that gave access to the house; one into a utility room, and sets of double French doors into both the lounge and the kitchen/diner.

The utility was the best choice, he decided. The two sets of patio doors had leaded windowpanes, and both were fitted with anti-snap tumbler locks. It was possible to pick them, but the utility door was a plain-looking composite door with a single deadbolt and a single lever mortice lock. Again, locks that could be picked, but Aydin didn't need to. The double-glazed window in the centre of the door was easily big enough for a man to fit through.

Aydin slipped his hand into his pocket and took out the radio transceiver. As was often the case, the security company who'd fitted their alarm system to Namur's home had been kind enough to leave stickers plastered all over the property. Some online research had allowed Aydin to familiarise himself with the company's wireless products. High-end systems that were easy to fit, easy to use, had plenty of functionality and various anti-tamper features to account for issues such as loss of Wi-Fi, loss of electricity, or someone trying to physically adjust any of the many infra-red and magnetic contact sensors.

But Aydin didn't need to worry about any of that. Not uncommonly, the central control unit for the system communicated with each of the components via simple radio waves. When the motion sensors were triggered, they sent a signal to the control panel which in turn triggered the alarm. All Aydin had needed to do on his previous planning trips was to intercept that data, decipher the commands, and now play them back at will.

He took a moment to make sure the transceiver was doing its job. It was. He put the device back in his pocket then took out the knife. He pushed the tip of the blade into the rubber seal at the edge of the windowpane and drew it all around the glass, cutting right through the seal. When he'd gone all around he used his gloved hands and shoved at the top of the pane. It took some effort, but eventually the top of the pane was pushed inward, and the bottom flipped out the tiniest fraction. Enough to allow Aydin to slip the knife under and lever the pane further out and free from its mounting. He placed the intact pane of glass carefully onto the slabs behind him, then repeated the process for the second piece of glass which came out with even more ease, without the suction effect of the previously sealed unit that was now no more. So much more easily in fact that the pane almost toppled inward and out of Aydin's grasp, though he just managed to rescue it before it crashed to the ground, and soon it was lying safely next to the first one.

Aydin slipped in through the now gaping hole. Once inside his eyes fell on the sensor in the corner of the room. The red light was blinking away, picking up on his movement, but there was no alarm. He smiled to himself, then got to work.

The downstairs of the house proved fruitless. Garishly decorated, everything black and gold and over the top, it was some sort of bachelor's pad, topped off with an extravagant entertainment room with huge TV and sound system and several reclining chairs laid out around the centrepiece screen. Looking around the place made Aydin despise his new boss all the more, and it was nothing to do with jealousy. Mostly he hated the hypocrisy of the man who was clearly so materialistic and . . . Westernised.

Aydin headed upstairs to the grand central landing. There were six doors off it. Five bedrooms, and a main bathroom he assumed. He found nothing of interest in the first three bedrooms, which all appeared little used. The next room he headed to was the master, judging by the once again horrific decor which included an unnecessarily large bed with a mountain of cushions on it and a mirror on the ceiling that filled Aydin's mind with images that repulsed him.

At least in the master bedroom events got a little more interesting. He found two handguns, a couple of boxes of ammo. Plenty of materials, books, related to Islam.

There was also a safe built into the bottom of the wardrobe. One that Aydin believed he could crack, but it wasn't his priority just yet.

He took some items of jewellery for good measure. Expensive watches, rings, chains, hoping the missing items would help convince the homeowner that the invasion was nothing more suspicious than a robbery.

He continued his search to the next room, which in fact turned out to be a home office. This was more like what he'd been looking for all along. He set his thumb drives going on the tablet and desktop computer he found. He rifled through the single three-drawer filing cabinet. He wasn't much interested in tax returns and the like, and found little else of interest. He performed a rudimentary search across the bookshelves. Nothing of note. Finally, he headed back to the desk where there were five side drawers, all locked up. But the lock was crude and a screwdriver and a bit of force was all Aydin needed to get inside.

Most of the drawers contained little except for routine correspondence, bills, bank statements. Aydin scanned them, but nothing jumped out. It was right at the top of the final drawer that his interest was finally genuinely piqued for the first time.

He pulled out the bundle of light blue papers. Duplicate copies of waybills, each of them issued by a freight company called Blue Swift Transport Inc.

Aydin had come across the company name previously, before he'd left for California, when he'd been researching Emilio Torres. The company was real, and one of many that were linked to investment vehicles controlled by the Venezuelan. Aydin scanned the waybills. There were more than a dozen deliveries due to different locations in and around not just Detroit but the whole American Midwest, beginning today, and ending in two days' time. Aydin looked at his watch. The first delivery had already been made, apparently.

The nature of the goods listed were more or less meaning-less to him, the descriptions abbreviated beyond recognition. Whatever the consignments included, the use of a genuine company to transport the goods Namur had purchased was sensible, given the vast distance and the number of states the trucks had to cross to get from California.

But what the hell was in the shipments?

Aydin took pictures of each of the waybills then placed them back in the drawer.

He glanced over to the desktop and the tablet. His thumb drives were still working away. He'd leave them to it. He still had one more bedroom to go, plus that safe.

He moved back onto the landing and over to the final bedroom. The door was shut. He turned the handle and pushed and there was a whooshing noise as the bottom of the door dragged slightly against the thick pile carpet below. Aydin stepped into the room, his mind still working over those waybills.

He froze, heart pounding, when he saw the figure lying in the king-sized bed across the room, white sheets tucked neatly around him.

Aydin stared over. The old man beneath the sheets, nothing but his head and shoulders sticking out, was asleep. Or at least his eyes were shut, and he hadn't flinched at all at Aydin's sudden entrance.

Quietly, Aydin sighed in relief.

But the relief didn't last more than a fleeting second. He continued to stare at the man. Pale and frail, his skin was mottled and wrinkled, the wispy hair on his head was wiry and grey. He looked much older and quite different to the pictures Aydin had seen. Looked different from his brother too. But there was no doubt who Aydin was looking at.

Nasir Al-Addad.

CHAPTER 43

Aydin took a step closer, moving silently. His hand reached down to the knife. The old man groaned, then sighed. His eyes didn't open. He was still asleep. Aydin's fingers wrapped around the handle of the knife as his brain tried to make sense not just of what he was seeing, but what he was doing.

Before him was Nasir Al-Addad. Brother of Aziz Al-Addad. The man who'd stolen Aydin's childhood, who'd turned him into a killer.

What was Nasir's role in that?

The answer to that question was why Aydin had come here in the first place. In fact, he had so many questions to ask this man, yet he was struggling to fight against the primal urge to pull out the blade and slice Al-Addad's neck wide open.

He took another step forward. The smell of the man in the bed caught in Aydin's nose. A musky, damp smell. A remarkably bland yet altogether unpleasant smell. The scent of . . . death.

Aydin drew the knife out. His hand was shaking, a combination of pure rage at what he believed this man represented, and his continued struggle to control his own actions and hold himself back.

It would be so easy to take Al-Addad's life while he slept. But did Aydin even want that? Or did he want this man to suffer?

No. He didn't even know what his involvement in the Farm was. Not with any certainty. That was what Aydin had to find out.

A noise somewhere outside the room pulled Aydin from his inner quarrel. He stopped moving. Stopped breathing. Just stood and listened as his heart thumped in his chest, his stare fixed on Nasir Al-Addad still.

A bang downstairs. A door opening or closing. Someone was home. Al-Addad shifted in the bed and murmured, as if his sleep had been disturbed by the noise, though his eyes remained closed.

Or was it Aydin's presence that had roused him?

Thudding footsteps echoed up from the hallway below. Aydin grimaced in despair. He sheathed the knife, turned and padded across to the door. He turned round to check Al-Addad. His eyes were half open now, though he was staring straight up at the ceiling. Did he know Aydin was in the room with him?

Aydin could do little about it either way now. He chastised himself, though wasn't sure why, then stepped out of the room and crept over to the banister. He saw a shadow moving down below, could hear movement in the kitchen. He'd closed the door to the utility room before he'd come upstairs. Would whoever was down there go in and see the broken window?

Aydin crept further along the landing and peered out of the small front window to the driveway below. His heart jumped and his head pounded when he saw the black BMW X5 outside. He'd thought it was the maid returning. Or was she a nurse for Al-Addad? Either way, this was far worse.

Movement in Aydin's periphery caught his attention. He spun round to see a figure downstairs, coming out of the kitchen.

Namur.

He had his head down as he stared at his phone. Aydin darted out of view.

Then had a sudden further cause of panic. He'd left the thumb drives whirring away in the office. He couldn't leave those. He shuffled over there as quietly as he could. Heard talking below now. Not just Namur. Benny was there too. Aydin slunk into the office. Pulled the thumb drives out. Neither had been ready but he had no choice.

He quietly moved back over to the open door. Flinched when he saw the shadow glance over the carpet right outside. One of them was already upstairs . . .

Aydin whipped his body out of the way and pulled himself into the gap behind the door. The soft footsteps outside on the landing stopped. Aydin could hear shallow breathing, could almost feel it, the breaths were so close, right the other side of the wood.

Aydin, on the other hand, wasn't breathing at all. He couldn't. It took him a few moments to realise his hand was once again on the handle of the knife.

Given his position, his predicament, shouldn't he just burst round the corner and gut whoever was standing there? Take out both Namur and Benny and then do what he needed to do with Al-Addad?

Strangely, it was Cox's nagging voice of reason in his head that was pulling him back from doing so.

He heard more footsteps from outside the room now, though that soft breathing remained.

'What are you doing?'

It was Namur.

'Nothing,' Benny said, his voice so close the sound reverberated in Aydin's ears and he was sure he could smell the man's coffee breath.

Then, just like that, the footsteps – two sets – moved away and the breathing was gone.

'You're awake,' Namur said, his voice more distant, and Aydin heard the muffled response from Al-Addad, but couldn't make out any of the words.

Realising they were gone – kind of – Aydin finally let out a long and slow and silent exhale. Then he stuck his head round the door and looked over to Al-Addad's room. The door was pushed to. Aydin couldn't see any of them. And they couldn't see him.

He moved out onto the landing. His eyes never left the bedroom door as he moved across and then down the stairs.

He raced across to the utility room. Sure enough the door was still closed. Aydin opened it and stepped inside then shut the door behind him. He paused again when he heard creaking right above him. The sound soon stopped, though he could tell from the continued muffled voices that they were still up there.

Aydin climbed outside, jumped the fence and quickly darted down the drive and to the pavement, not once looking back to the house as he headed away. Namur would find the broken window soon enough. Would he believe he'd simply been robbed?

Aydin was soon in his car and driving away as the significance of what he'd found still sloshed away in his mind, fighting for prominence against his bitter disappointment at having fled the scene rather than tackling the monster there. Or was it monsters?

He was so engrossed in his own thoughts that he barely heard the first few rings of his phone. He pulled himself back to reality, grabbed the phone and looked at the screen.

Namur.

Aydin answered as his heart once again drummed away.

'Yeah,' he said, sounding surprisingly nonchalant.

'It's me,' Namur said. 'What are you doing?'

'Just driving.'

'Well drive over to JL's. I'll see you there in an hour.'

The call ended. Aydin only realised a few hundred yards later that he was still driving one-handed, the phone still in his grasp as he stared at the road ahead in confusion.

He looked at his watch. One hour. Just sixty minutes to decide what he should do next. To decide on the actions that would likely shape the rest of his life.

Fifty-seven minutes later and Aydin's brain was sluggish and weary from overuse as he played over and over with the various scenarios for what would happen if he did indeed turn up at JL's as requested.

The timely nature of the phone call from Namur, with Aydin still fleeing the scene, certainly hadn't escaped his attention. Namur would surely know by now that his home had been broken into, wouldn't he? If so, did he know Aydin was the culprit? Did he know Aydin's subterfuge?

Plus, what was the story of Nasir Al-Addad? And why was Namur still in Dearborn anyway, when his crew were on their way to Venezuela?

Aydin had so many questions. Each was hugely significant, yet he didn't have a single answer.

He'd already sent pictures of the waybills to Cox, but had received no response. If she passed those to GCHQ, they might be able to overlay the details against the coded messages and hopefully glean some useful intel. Aydin had more pressing matters right now than those deliveries though. He checked his watch for the hundredth time as he sat in his car outside the mosque. No sign of Namur yet, but it was almost time.

Aydin got out and moved over to the back doors, his eyes busier than ever. He didn't bother to knock. Instead he took out his phone and played around with it while he leaned against the wall. It was freezing out, but he'd much rather be in a position to make a run for it if he needed.

The X5 pulled into the car park two minutes after the sixty was up. Only Namur got out. That was a good starting point as far as Aydin was concerned. If this had been an ambush surely Namur would have arrived tooled up with a mini army?

He didn't look happy though. He strode over to Aydin, face like thunder.

'We need to talk,' Namur said.

'That's why I'm here,' Aydin said.

Namur knocked on the door and it opened a second later and Aydin hesitantly stepped through after the big man, checking behind to make sure there wasn't anyone else there.

There wasn't.

The inside of the community centre was strangely quiet. Aydin followed Namur across the foyer, towards the kitchen. Aydin was well prepared to walk into the room to find it filled with goons holding knives and bats and guns, ready to turn him inside out. In fact, he found it almost disturbing when Namur opened the door and Aydin stepped inside to see it was spotless and entirely empty.

Did anyone ever actually use this place for cooking, though?

Namur closed the door behind him. Stood across it as though blocking Aydin from making a run for it. Aydin, cool on the outside, glanced about the room again, half expecting men to jump out on him from some unseen corner.

They didn't.

'You're looking nervous,' Namur said, glaring at Aydin.

Aydin wasn't sure he did, was Namur fishing?

'Just curious,' Aydin said. 'You seem pissed off about something.'

Namur snorted.

'I thought you were out of the country,' Aydin said.

'Did you now?' He wasn't trying to hide his suspicion.

Aydin shrugged. 'You told me you were going away for a few days. Karim told me the same.'

'Don't believe everything you hear,' Namur said.

Sound advice.

'You know I managed to speak to a good friend of Faiz Al-Busaidi.'

'Yeah?'

'I was asking about you.'

Aydin nodded. 'Who?'

'Doesn't matter.'

'Did I check out?'

Namur didn't answer that, just continued to glare at Aydin until the younger man looked away.

'There's something I need you to do for me,' Namur said after a few tense moments of silence.

'OK.'

Namur dug his hand in his pocket. He took out some folded papers. Aydin thought he knew what they were even before Namur straightened them out.

'We're almost at the end now,' Namur said. 'But there's still time for you to be part of this.'

'This?'

'You know.'

Namur passed the waybills over to Aydin.

'The final building blocks. One shipment has already arrived. Two more are due in Detroit tomorrow. The first one at seven a.m. The address is on there.'

'Shipment of what?'

Namur rolled his eyes. 'You'll be there to accept the goods.'

'Of course. Just me?'

'Well who else would you bring? The cops? The Feds?'

314

Namur held Aydin's eye for a little too long. As cool as Aydin was, there was no doubt he was rattled standing there in front of Namur with so much deceit hanging in the air.

'I'll be there,' Aydin said.

Aydin tensed when Namur reached to his side, but he was only putting his hand into his trouser pocket. He pulled out a small bundle. Something wrapped in paper wrapped in elastic bands.

'The keys and the combination for the alarm,' Namur said.

Aydin took the bundle off him and stuffed it away without looking.

'Call me when it's done.'

Aydin nodded. Namur opened the door and moved aside. Aydin hesitated until Namur indicated for him to leave. Aydin stepped out and flinched at the noise of the door slamming shut behind him.

Trying not to show his obvious relief at walking out of the room in one piece, he headed towards the outer doors, a large part of him shocked that he was still walking at all. He had no idea if he'd just dodged a bullet, or if he was now simply being set up for his own gruesome downfall.

One thing he did know, in a few hours, he'd have a lot more answers than he did right now.

CHAPTER 44

Caracas, Venezuela

It was no understatement to say that Cox had been to some of the most dangerous and least pleasant places on earth. Caracas wasn't the worst of them, not by far, yet as she was driven in the taxi to the hotel, there was no doubting that there was an air of hostility in the nation's capital and an ever-present threat of violence bubbling away. Factors which weren't helped by the heavy-handed military presence throughout the city – the ailing government's desperate attempts to keep a growing civilian unrest at bay.

From what Cox knew, the Venezuelan economy had been in free fall for years, to the point where the entire country was on the brink of implosion. Millions had already fled, many millions more were living in abject poverty, and masses were now embroiled in constant inner fighting, whether in political circles or in bloody encounters on the streets.

Despite the economic and social turmoil, the relative wealth of the sovereign state which was responsible for the largest oil reserves in the world was still evident in fits and starts within the capital city, not least in the glitzy glass-rich skyscrapers that peppered the centre of Caracas, and the plush five-star hotels that catered to diplomatic dignitaries from home and abroad, and to prosperous business travellers – largely those involved in the stripping of the country's fossil fuels.

The poverty of the many couldn't have been more stark. Much of the city was little more than a shanty town, and the two sides of the divide were given little breathing space from one another, the Eden Hotel where Cox was headed being a prime example.

The wide five-storey glass-fronted hotel had perfectly mani-cured front lawns with palm trees and water features, and the whole façade was immaculate and glitzy and expensive-looking. It could have been a five-star hotel in any big city in the world, except off to one side, beyond the hotel's grounds and a ten-foot-tall stone wall topped with barbed wire, the ramshackle huts of the masses rose up into the distance on a prominent hill. Hardly a view to die for.

Having passed through the outer armed security gate, the taxi stopped by the hotel entrance and an eager bellhop opened the door for Cox. The heat hit her as she stepped outside. She'd almost got used to the blistering cold of Detroit now, and thirty degrees Celsius felt like a furnace.

Cox paid the driver and wrestled her baggage from the bellhop.

'It's fine. I can manage,' she said.

He muttered apologetically then left her to it.

She headed on inside, welcoming the cool air-conditioned interior. She bought a room for three nights. She was more than an hour behind Karim and the others. Her 'asset' in Caracas, a man named Carlos Valencia, who worked for SEBIN, Venezuela's equivalent to MI5, had already set up a tail on the four visitors from Detroit from the airport in Caracas, and confirmed their hotel of choice. In fact, he'd even relayed to Cox the numbers of the two rooms that they'd checked in to, and she was able, on request, to secure the room right next door to them.

There was no sign of the four men now as Cox headed across the marble-rich foyer to the lifts, though a squat suited man standing against a thick decorative column did catch her eye and give a slight nod.

Not Carlos Valencia, but perhaps the man Valencia had sent to snoop. Cox ignored him. She didn't want to draw any attention to herself. The fact he was stationed there though was a good thing. If he spotted anything, she'd get the word soon enough.

She headed on up to the fifth floor and walked slowly across the corridor, her ears straining as she passed the two doors for Karim and the others. She could hear muted voices but nothing more as she passed, and she was soon inside her own expansive twin-bed room. She poured herself some water. Opened the net curtains and stared across the confused cityscape.

She could still hear muffled voices from the room next door, but couldn't make out what they were saying, even when she pressed her ear up against the thin wall. Still, she'd keep alert for the sound of any of them leaving the rooms. Quietly she took out her phone and connected to the Wi-Fi and was finally able to get access to her messages and emails. She'd already passed on details of Aydin's findings – the waybills, and the fact that Nasir Al-Addad was alive – to the various interested parties; Flannigan, Kaufman, Tarkowski. She'd not yet heard anything in response other than confirmation the information had been received. Nor was there anything new from Aydin.

She called him.

'You're OK?'

'So far. I saw him, Nasir Al-Addad. I was standing right in front of him.'

He sounded tormented by the fact.

'You spoke to him?' she asked.

'No. Not yet. He's an invalid or something, or maybe just seriously ill, but he's here, and definitely alive.'

'Aydin, what's happening there? I don't like this.'

He didn't respond.

'I can get help for you. I'll find someone to come and assist if you need.' Her thoughts turned to Tarkowski. Would he be prepared to dial in reinforcements if Aydin now had proof that Al-Addad really was there? Or perhaps it was too early for that, before they'd even figured out any of the story.

'What are you going to do?' Cox asked. 'Will you get to speak to him?'

'They don't know I know.'

'You're not making much sense.'

'I think it's almost time,' Aydin said. 'I can sense it. I'm going to end this.'

'Aydin—'

The line went dead. Cox put a hand to her head in despair. She was rattled. Not for the fact that Nasir Al-Addad was alive and in Dearborn, but because she was blind as to what Aydin was planning next. And also what Namur was planning next, following his seemingly abrupt change of plans at the airport.

She tried to call both Tarkowski and Flannigan again. Neither answered, though Flannigan had a better excuse given it was already well into the night in the UK. She left a brief message for each of them explaining her concerns. Perhaps they had a better idea of what they should do next.

Cox was still in deep in thought over that complex point when she heard a door opening in the corridor. She jumped up and raced across her room. She looked out of the spyhole to see Karim and Tamir saunter past. Cox held her breath for a few moments as she listened to their movements fade into the distance. She opened her door and peered out. At the far end of the corridor Karim stepped into a lift. Cox headed out and was soon travelling down after them.

She cautiously stepped out onto the ground floor. Her eyes found the short man almost immediately. He'd changed positions now, and was standing closer to the bar area. He indicated to his left and Cox glanced across and saw Karim and Tamir sitting on two armchairs in the bar. They were talking to someone on a sofa opposite though from her angle Cox couldn't see who it was.

She moved across, bypassing the spook without acknowledging him and headed to the bar. She ordered a soft drink and took a stool and swivelled slightly so she was at a right angle to the bar, giving her full view of the area beyond. She took her phone out and placed it on her lap.

Karim and Tamir were speaking to a middle-aged man. He looked local, with dark brown skin and jet black hair. He had a handlebar moustache like a military man from days gone past, and his smart casual clothing was well fitted and expensive looking. Although Cox couldn't hear a word, she could tell the conversation was clipped and formal.

As she looked across the room she noticed the spy was on his phone now, and looked a little agitated. He finished the call and motioned to Cox apologetically before he sauntered off towards the exit.

What the hell was that about? She supposed she'd find out from Valencia later. For now, the disappearance wasn't a problem, but it might be if Karim and the others split up or if they headed out of the hotel quickly before Cox could follow.

Hopefully events wouldn't come to that.

She sipped her drink for a few moments as she took in her surroundings. The bar area was about half full, though there were small groups of people milling through the reception area beyond too. Mostly she could hear English voices, and

American accents. She'd noticed there were two conferences underway at the hotel. One was for a Venezuelan management consultancy group, the other for a US think-tank related to the oil industry, which likely explained the presence of so many Americans.

Cox looked back to Karim. The moustached man reached to his side and passed a thick manilla envelope across. He looked more nervous as Karim lifted the flap and peered inside. It wasn't money, but documents of some sort, Cox thought. Wads of white paper.

The next moment, with barely a word more said, the moustached man got to his feet. No handshakes or any other niceties before he walked off.

Cox hadn't noticed them before, but as the man strode out, two other men, in smart suits and with expressionless faces, appeared from either side of the hotel reception area and followed him out. Not on his tail, but his protection, Cox realised, only adding to her curiosity as to what she'd stumbled over here.

When she turned her attention back to Karim and Tamir she realised they too were ready to leave. She averted her gaze as they got up and headed back over to reception. She willed them not to go outside. She really didn't want to have to be trailing about after them through Caracas on her own . . . but then why had she come here if not to do just that?

Still, she was relieved when they moved back to the bank of lifts and they were soon inside one and out of sight. Cox quickly finished her drink. Then she herself got up, her phone with the pictures of the moustached man she'd just taken clutched tight in her hand.

With any luck she'd soon have a name to put to the face.

CHAPTER 45

Seven a.m. was simply too far away, Aydin had by now decided. Having left JL's and headed straight to his apartment, he'd spent a few hours setting up his equipment to read and catalogue the data he'd managed to swipe from Namur's devices earlier — before he'd been rudely interrupted. Not enough time to actually get stuck into reviewing the data, unfortunately. Doing so would have to wait. Because he was now in his car and heading across to the other side of the city to the warehouse Namur had given him the keys for.

No, seven a.m. was far too long to wait. Aydin wanted answers tonight. He'd already spotted that this was the address that the first shipment had already arrived at. Perhaps the goods were even still there.

Of course it hadn't escaped his attention that maybe Namur was setting him up with the supposed delivery in the morning, which was another reason to go now, rather than tomorrow when Namur was expecting him there. At the very least, if he properly scoped the place out tonight, he was less likely to be scuppered come the morning. In fact, the whole thing could play to his advantage.

The time was nearly midnight when Aydin pulled up outside the chain-link fence. He left the engine running as he got out and headed over to unlock the padlock, his breath in the cold night lit up by his car's headlights and billowing around him as he worked. He swung the gates open, got back in the car and drove through, leaving the gates open behind him, should he need a quick getaway.

The warehouse and the grounds around it were pitch black. On a street full of other industrial units and warehouses, many of them permanently closed down, there was little illumination here save for the sporadic street lights, the closest of which was more than twenty yards away, though the headlights from Aydin's car showed him that there were no other vehicles parked on the forecourt.

He shut the engine down, plunging him into near darkness, then got out, torch in hand. He grabbed his backpack and headed over, past the single set of loading doors, and to the adjacent entrance door. One thing he had noticed as he walked was that the grounds were cleared of snow. This place had definitely seen recent use, even if it was deserted right now.

Aydin used the key from the chain Namur had given him and unlocked then opened the door. An alarm blipped away. He spotted the control box on the wall next to him and typed in the six-digit code. He flipped the lights then shut the door behind him.

He found himself standing and looking into a large open space. At the far side of the warehouse was a door and a window into a cheaply built office area, but the rest of the inside was open, with corrugated steel walls and roof, no windows. Largely unused shelving cluttered one wall. Most of the smooth concrete floor was empty, except for four large pallets with plastic-wrapped crates on top.

Aydin headed straight over, ripples of anticipation ebbing away. There were delivery sheets stuck to the sides of the crates and just a quick glance showed Aydin these were the goods that had formed the delivery earlier that day from Blue Swift. He took out his knife and sliced down through the plastic wrap covering one of the pallets. He pulled the covering off to reveal two large wooden crates. No kind of description on the outside to give an indication of what lay within, except for a seemingly random string of letters and numbers that made no sense to Aydin.

Anticipation and nerves growing further still, Aydin slipped the edge of the knife under the lid of one of the crates and levered the nailed-down board off.

He stared inside at the weapons. A cluster of neatly packaged AT4 grenade launchers. He stepped aside and prised the lid off the second and larger crate. This one was filled with twelve-inch high-explosive artillery shells. Heavy duty munitions for sure. He looked across at the other crates. No doubt they too contained arms of various sorts. Explosives, grenade launchers, shells, guns, ammo. This was a mini arsenal, and not what Aydin had expected at all.

One thing was most stark though. Aydin knew plenty about weaponry, and even just from a glimpse inside the first two crates, he knew these weren't any old weapons that Namur had somehow persuaded his drug smuggling friend to cobble together. These were all goods specifically designed and made for the US army.

Aydin took out his phone. He had to speak to Cox. He moved over towards the second pallet as the call rang.

'Like what you're seeing?' came the voice behind him.

Aydin spun round. Namur. He was standing right there by the warehouse door. Aydin hadn't heard him at all. How? Had he been so engrossed in what he'd found?

The biggest problem was that Namur wasn't alone. Behind him Benny stepped inside. Weapon in hand.

A set-up. He'd suspected it, yet he'd walked right in. Aydin's mind raced with less than perfect options for how to fight them.

He didn't get long to mull it over. Benny lifted the weapon and fired.

There was no bang. Aydin had already noted it wasn't a regular gun in Benny's hand but an X26 Taser. The barbed darts burst through the air. Aydin couldn't move quickly enough and the darts pierced his clothing around his sternum.

A huge surge of electricity coursed through Aydin's body. He collapsed to the ground. His muscles spasmed involuntarily. It was pure agony. Aydin felt like his brain would explode, like his heart would give up on him. Like he was being cooked from the inside out.

After several excruciating seconds the surge of electricity stopped. Benny and Namur walked forward. As much as Aydin fought against the paralysis, he simply had no control over his still twitching body.

'String him up,' Namur said.

It was the last thing Aydin heard before he took a boot to the face and his world went black.

CHAPTER 46

Cox had barely slept through the night, one eye open the whole time in case anything happened next door, while she waited for an update on the identity of the mystery moustached man. She had to be ready and prepared and hadn't even bothered to take her clothes off as she lay on top of the covers through the darkness.

She was just nodding off though after eight a.m. when the call came in from Tarkowski. She'd already spoken to Flannigan much earlier at four a.m. local time, when he'd turned up at the office in London. With Cox seriously tired by that point it had been a stilted conversation and one with little end product other than Flannigan agreeing he'd get back to her once he'd had time to digest developments. She'd tried getting in touch with Aydin since, but to no avail.

Hopefully Tarkowski had something more meaningful to say.

She answered the call and sat up in the bed as her tired head pounded away. She needed more caffeine.

'Good morning, Agent Cox.'

'Yeah, you too. So?'

A sigh. That wasn't a good start. 'I've no idea where your man Mohammed Akhbar is.'

'You're kidding me?'

'I'm sorry. I've had people over to his apartment. At the mosque too. No sign of him or his car.'

This was exactly what she'd feared.

'What about Namur and Dawood?'

'I haven't got clearance for a full-time tail—'

'Why the hell not!'

'Agent Cox, I think we've been through this before.' His tone was now snarky, but then hers had been too. 'I've been plenty involved in this for you, and I'll continue to assist, but so far you've given me nothing concrete in return. Just one man's word. A man whose whereabouts are currently unknown.'

'Doesn't that tell you the story?'

'Not really. If you think it would help, we can send someone to Namur's home to confirm if Nasir Al-Addad really is there. But what then? I thought you were playing the long game here. Just getting me to verify the guy is alive and in Dearborn isn't going to help much if we have to blow your position in doing so.'

He had a point there.

'But I do agree we need to keep a close eye on this.'

'We need more than that. And the man I sent you the picture of?'

'Nothing yet. I'll keep you updated, but in the meantime there's not much more we can do.'

Cox wanted to argue that one, but she wasn't really sure what to say.

She heard movement next door.

'I've got to go.'

She ended the call and jumped off the bed and moved across to the opposite wall. Listened for a few moments. There was definitely action in there. The next second she heard a door

327

opening in the corridor. She raced to the spyhole and looked out. She couldn't see anything, no one walking past, but could hear the men right outside her door somewhere. She heard another door opening, then closing, then more voices.

Were all four of them now in the room next door?

Cox peeled back from the door and put her ear to the wall again. The muffled voices of the men vibrated through the plasterboard but there was simply no way she could pick out the words. Whatever they were saying, she expected they would be leaving any moment. Perhaps just to get breakfast, but perhaps this was it. Their purpose in Venezuela was finally about to be revealed. Or were they done and ready to head back to the US already?

Cox quickly got herself ready and pulled on her shoes. She grabbed her purse with her IDs. She didn't have a weapon here as she hadn't had time to arrange for one and she felt naked and vulnerable unarmed now as she stood and waited.

A commotion outside the hotel grabbed her attention. At the same time the room next door went strangely quiet. Cox stepped to the window. She looked out to see a military Jeep speeding past the security checkpoint at the hotel's outer gates. The two security guards there were on the floor, moving but dazed.

'What the hell?'

Cox focused on the speeding Jeep. The few people outside in the early morning sunshine had sensed the danger and were running and shouting. Cox expected the Jeep to slow as it approached the hotel entrance. For the soldiers onboard to jump from the vehicle and rush into the hotel, though quite why she thought that, she had no idea.

But the Jeep didn't slow. In fact it was speeding up.

It was only when Cox caught a glimpse of the driver — plain-clothed, and alone — that she finally realised what was wrong. She quickly pulled her phone up and was scrolling for the number as the Jeep ploughed into the hotel entrance.

There was a booming crash below, and Cox braced herself a split second before the devastating explosion erupted.

CHAPTER 47

A bucket of cold water was enough to rouse Aydin from his semi-conscious state. His head jerked up. He rattled and bucked against his restraints for all of two seconds before he recalled where he was. He slumped again.

Hands shackled together and suspended above him, his body hung from a chain hooked to the warehouse roof that was clasped around the cuffs on his wrists. His body dangled uselessly, his bare feet, which were also cuffed together, scraped on the cold floor beneath him.

'There we go,' said Benny.

He was standing in front of Aydin, empty bucket in his hand. Beyond him was Namur, glaring defiantly at Aydin, arms folded.

With water dripping down his brow, Aydin shook his head like a dog would and looked about the place. The morning delivery had already been. There were now six large pallets in the warehouse.

Aydin's eyes caught Namur's and the big man smiled and moved forward.

'Benny, do the honours.'

Benny nodded and took a knife from the top of one of the pallets. Not just any knife. It was Aydin's. He looked down

330

at himself. Other than his lack of shoes and socks, he was still clothed, though he had lost his coat and jumper at some point.

Aydin tried not to flinch as Benny held the knife out. He grabbed Aydin's shirt and pulled it away from his skin and slowly moved the knife underneath. Aydin bucked again.

'You might want to rethink that,' Benny said, his face stern.

Aydin felt the tip of the knife nick his skin. He got the point. He kept still, though was seething with anger as Benny slashed through his remaining clothes, boxers and all. Not that Aydin was embarrassed or ashamed by his indignity.

'You're probably wondering how long I've known?' Namur said.

Aydin didn't look at him, and he made no attempt to answer the question, even though he did want to know the answer.

'But I won't tell you,' Namur said. 'I know it will only add to your torment to wonder. *Where did I go wrong? What was the mistake I made?* Those are questions only you can answer now.'

Namur took another step forward. With his head bowed Aydin could see Namur's feet now.

'I'll tell you this,' Namur said. 'I've known long enough. Long enough to make sure our plans were still viable, and long enough to find out who you really are . . . Aydin Torkal.'

Hearing his own name shocked him, though given the position he was in he guessed it was inevitable that Namur had found out, not just that Aydin was an imposter, but also his true identity.

'I could hardly believe it at first,' Namur said. 'Of course I knew all about you and your brothers. After all it was my cousins, men I grew up with, who had such a big hand in your development. To have one of you in our midst . . . I'm almost honoured. Other than the fact that we were sent the runt of that litter.'

331

Namur spat on the floor. The glob of mucus splatted right next to Aydin's toes.

'But I do still need to know *why* you came here. Who you're working with and what they know. Not because it will make a difference to your fate now, or to our plans, but because . . . '

He seemed to lose his trail of thought.

'You like to be in control,' Benny said. 'And because we'll gut anyone who was involved in this deceit.'

Namur said nothing to that but took another step forward. As did Benny. Aydin's head was wrenched up. He averted then closed his eyes.

'You don't have to look at me,' Namur said. 'If you think that makes you stronger then OK. But it doesn't.'

Aydin guessed he was right. He opened his eyes. Held Namur's stare for a moment.

'That's better,' Namur said. 'No need for rudeness among comrades. Aydin, have you heard of *lingchi*?'

Aydin had, but he gave no indication of that, even as his brain was processing the horrible thoughts that rumbled away.

'Death by a thousand cuts. A form of execution used in China for over a millennium. Although officially banned now, it's still used in certain circles. In China. Beyond.'

Benny lifted the knife to Aydin's gut. He pushed the tip of the blade into the flesh, not quite enough to nick it. Then he suddenly yanked across and a two-inch slash opened up. Not deep, but the pain was still enough to cause Aydin to wince and groan despite his best efforts to show nothing.

He realised Namur was smiling now.

'Did you know there are some reported cases where more than *three* thousand cuts were made. Sometimes performed over several days. The men would be kept awake and alert with opium, though in many other cases the procedure was actually surprisingly quick. Performed in public, in front of crowds, it could be over within half an hour. Hundreds of cuts. Fingers, toes, ears, noses, tongues all removed too. Flesh from arms and legs and backs sliced off. Limbs removed. Can you imagine the agony? Sometimes family members would attempt to bribe officials to ensure an early cut to the heart, but most weren't so lucky. You, Aydin, are not so lucky.'

Benny took the knife and moved it up towards Aydin's armpit now. He was only inches away, so close Aydin could smell his breath again, just like in Namur's house the day before.

Why hadn't Aydin taken the chance when he had it? Now he was helpless.

Benny pressed the tip of the blade into the skin just below Aydin's armpit and drew downward. Blood oozed and dribbled from the inch-long slice that opened up, past Aydin's waist.

'Two down,' Namur said. 'You might have guessed that we're starting slow. We've such a long way to go, you see. But you know there is one aspect I'm torn about?'

He paused as though he was waiting for Aydin to prompt him to carry on.

'Sometimes the first cuts made were to the eyes. Some executioners believed it made the ordeal even more horrific if the poor bastard couldn't see what was coming, if they didn't know what was next.'

Aydin tried to stay strong. Even as Benny's eyes met his. The bloodthirsty look on his snarling face was the most chilling thing Aydin had ever seen, even worse than anything he'd witnessed at the Farm. Benny grabbed an ear. Aydin winced but he could do nothing.

'But no such luck for you, Aydin,' Namur said. 'Whatever we do to you, and believe me, it will get worse, you're going to see it all. You'll see as we slice you into more pieces than you can count. There'll be nothing left of you in the afterlife. That's the price you pay for your life of treachery.'

Benny lifted the knife up. Initially there was a strange, almost warming sensation as the blade sliced through Aydin's flesh. Then the pain came. And Aydin couldn't hold it in now. He gritted his teeth as he roared. Much to Namur's continued amusement. Benny . . . he didn't look amused at all. He was too focused on his work.

After a couple of agonising seconds, Benny pulled back, holding the dripping appendage in his hand. Aydin shivered with revulsion at the sight, bowed his throbbing head again. Benny dropped the cleaved off ear and it fell to the floor by Aydin's feet with a pathetic squelch. A tear escaped Aydin's eye and landed right next to his ear.

Aydin's mind wandered. Not because he was delirious – not yet anyway – but because of a painful memory that suddenly surfaced. The day he'd been forced to cut the ear off a helpless man when he'd been just a teenager at the Farm. The first of many elements of his initiation into a world of violence.

Though had he really been forced, or simply coerced? He'd actually felt power and relief at achieving the feat back then. In many ways that day had been a defining moment of his time there.

Perhaps this was now the payback he'd long deserved.

'And believe me,' Namur said, ducking down so he was in Aydin's line of sight, 'you might think you can hold out on us, that even though we'll leave that tongue in your mouth, you'll be strong enough not to use it. But there are nine hundred and ninety-seven more cuts to you that say you can't. Sooner or later, you will tell me everything . . . and there's nothing you can do about that.'

Aydin closed his eyes and braced himself as Benny reached forward with the knife once more.

CHAPTER 48

Caracas, Venezuela

The whole building shook and the ground rumbled when the bomb exploded. Cox subconsciously grabbed hold of the windowsill as if doing so would somehow protect her if the floor beneath her collapsed. Thick black smoke and wisps of flames burst up from below and past her window, blocking out the light, the room turning dark in an instant.

After a few seconds of strangely subdued silence, the noise that took over was screams. People below in the mess, people outside running.

Cox snapped into focus when she heard a rallying call from next door. She rushed over to the spyhole. She heard the door in the next room opening, but the footsteps padded away from her room, rather than past and onward to the nearest lifts. Cox carefully pulled her door open and peeked out. She held back a gasp when she saw two black-clad figures casually walking away. Each had a utility belt crammed with combat gear and ammo, and an assault rifle in their hands. Cox understood the grim reality now. They were heading in the direction of the conference rooms down the corridor.

A bedroom door further along from the men shot open and a smartly dressed bald man darted out. He took one look at the two armed men striding towards him and froze. One of the men lifted his weapon and a flurry of gunfire blasted. Several holes were punched into the bald man's chest and he collapsed to the ground, wide-eyed.

Cox gasped in shock and there was a clunk as the door next to hers opened again. She whipped her head back inside and ever so gently pushed her door shut, being careful not to make any noise. She pressed her eye to the spyhole. Karim and Tamir were standing right there outside her room, dressed in black just like the other two. They were shouting down the corridor to their friends.

'Check every room,' Cox heard one of the men shout back. 'Don't let anyone get away.'

Karim and Tamir nodded then strode off in the opposite direction to their friends.

Cox spun round and sank down against the door, trying to get her breathing and her mind under control. With a jittery hand she took her phone from her pocket. No signal. No Wi-Fi. Had communications been jammed? She bolted up and rushed to the bedside table, picked up the telephone handset. No dial tone.

The rat-a-tat-tat of gunfire echoed along the corridor and into Cox's room. She heard heightened screaming. Dozens of people, their voices drowned out by the huge cascade of gunfire. When there was a momentary pause Cox realised she was shaking.

'Come on!' she shouted at herself.

She had to do something, but what? She was unarmed, she had no way of contacting the outside world, but she couldn't just sit there. She raced back to the door. Checked in the spyhole that there was no one there. There wasn't. She opened the door and stuck her head out again. She looked left. Several bodies lay strewn on the carpet. No sign of the gunmen in that direction but the cacophony of screams and gunfire somewhere in the distance continued.

She looked right. Saw Karim and Tamir further down the hall. Tamir lifted his knee and drove the heel of his boot into a bedroom door to smash it open, then stormed in. Karim followed somewhat sheepishly. Cox heard a woman screaming. Then laughing from Tamir? Then a single gunshot.

A second later Tamir strolled back out with a wide smile on his face. Karim behind him, had a far more uneasy look. Cox ducked back inside when Karim looked over. She held her breath. Tried to concentrate on the sounds of the two men.

'Next one's yours,' Tamir said.

Karim said nothing. Moments later another bang as the next bedroom door was crashed open. More screaming. Two gunshots this time.

Cox closed her eyes and put her hand to her mouth to mask her panicked breathing.

There was nothing she could do. She couldn't take on the attackers. And she couldn't get past them with them working from one end of the floor to the other.

Cox darted across to the window. Smoke was still billowing below but was far thinner now and Cox stared at the scene of devastation outside. Two ambulances had arrived. Scores of people were out there, most of them bloodied and dazed. A solitary police car. No sign of any real help yet for those remaining trapped inside.

Did the people outside even know what was now taking place on the top floor?

Cox pushed open the window, but it was designed to only give a few inches. There was no way she could get out that way, even if she could overcome the fact that she was on the fifth floor. With the window open the noise from outside grew louder. It was almost disorientating. She quickly pulled the glass shut again. As horrific as the screams and gunfire and the laughing of the shooters along the corridor was, Cox had to hear it. She had to know how close they were.

They were very close, she soon realised. In fact when the next gunshots came Cox was sure she could sense the vibrations through her bedroom wall.

They were right next door.

She only had seconds to act. Cox threw herself to the floor. Lifted the valence of the bed she'd barely slept on. She could easily crawl under and hide there, but wouldn't they check somewhere so obvious?

Cox felt around the underside of the bed. The mattress, sitting on top of wooden slats, had a dust cover enveloping it. Cox pulled herself out, lifted the end of the mattress up and pushed the whole thing up against the wall. She grabbed the thin fabric of the dust cover and tore at it with her fingernails, opening up a slash three feet long. She pushed the mattress back into place. Heard the voices right outside her door.

'Yours or mine?' Tamir said.

'Mine,' said Karim.

The thudding noise on the door caused Cox to jolt. The door didn't open, but Cox was nearly out of time. She dove under the bed. Contorted her body and slithered between the mattress and the wooden slats.

Another, louder bang at the door and she heard the lock splinter and the door crash inward and smack off the wall. Then came their heavy footsteps as they stormed in.

As quickly as she could Cox slid across and into the slit in the dust cover and pulled the ends together then froze.

Her breathing was too heavy for her to hold it in, but she tried her best to slow it and to make no sound at all as she listened for the men.

The footsteps stopped. Then a burst of gunfire. So loud and so close that it made Cox's ears ring. Another burst and the bullets thwacked into the mattress Cox was clustered under. The thick foam and spring construction did a good job of deadening the rounds but Cox still felt a sharp pain in her thigh. She grimaced and bit down on her tongue and squeezed her eyes tightly shut.

When she opened them moments later the space she was in was lighter than before.

One of the men was looking under the bed.

Then everything went dark once more as he replaced the valence.

'Unlucky. There's no one here,' Tamir said with a chuckle. Cox did now hold her breath, so she could more easily hear the footsteps of the men as they thudded out of the room.

Only when she was sure they were gone did she let out a desperate exhale.

CHAPTER 49

Cox didn't move for what felt like an age. She couldn't. She was too scared and too confused. Beyond her hiding place the bedroom door remained wide open. She knew it did because she could still hear the shooters' voices so clearly. They were back in their own room next door now. All four of them. Their rampage was over. For now. They were talking. Initially the mood when they'd congregated had been ghoulishly jubilant, but it was turning sour now.

'We needed hostages,' Cox thought she heard one of them say. 'It's too late now.'

They were arguing. What was going on?

Then there was an eruption of gunfire once more. It lasted several seconds, but it sounded different to Cox from earlier. Less echoey. When the shooting stopped and Cox heard shouting outside the hotel, down below, she realised why. The attackers were shooting out of the windows.

At civilians, or had a tactical team finally arrived?

The booming sound of high-calibre rounds a moment later gave Cox the answer. Not a tactical team as such, but the army? The bullets sent across in retaliation thunked and crashed into the hotel walls. When the barrage stopped there was more angry shouting next door.

Cox decided it was time to move. The foursome were done with their initial onslaught across the top floor, there was no sense in staying where she was. She pulled herself out of the crevice and her body thumped lightly onto the bedroom floor. She held her breath a moment but there was no indication the noise had alerted anyone next door. She dragged her body out from under the bed, but remained low, close to the carpet as she twisted around.

She looked down at her thigh. There was blood everywhere. She stuck her fingers through the hole in her trousers and flinched when her nails touched the hypersensitive edges of the wound. The bullet was right there, wedged in the outer layers of skin and flesh. Were it not for the mattress it would have been much worse.

Cox closed her eyes and bit down and her whole body tensed as she dug her nails around the side of the crumpled metal slug and prised it out of the wound with a suck of blood. She tossed the bullet away, as though angry with the inanimate object, then pulled herself up to peer out of the window, her head low, just above the sill. She didn't want anyone taking potshots at her.

She wasn't sure if she was relieved or horrified by what she saw.

Half a dozen army personnel carriers. Dozens of armed soldiers on foot. Two artillery weapons, and a full-on combat tank with gun. All clustered around the outer edges of the hotel's grounds.

She spotted a man with a loudspeaker towards the centre of the congregation. He pulled the speaker up to his mouth and she could hear his projected robot-like voice, but with her window shut could barely make out a word.

Something to do with surrender. Give up any hostages.

Is that why the army weren't advancing? They didn't realise the attackers had already killed everyone up here?

If Cox could somehow get word out . . .

She flinched when there was yet another rattle of gunfire from next door. Small plumes of dust rose up where the bullets sank into the dry ground right in front of the soldiers. The man with the loudspeaker hunkered down and scuttled backward. The soldiers returned with their own far superior firepower, and Cox threw herself down as the large rounds whizzed and clanked and thunked all around the wall and window right by her.

She couldn't stay here, so close to the firing line.

When the next momentary respite came, Cox sluggishly moved for her door. The corridor outside was all quiet now. Cox could hear the men talking next door, debating still, but they were all clustered somewhere inside the room. She had a chance to run . . .

Before she could talk herself out of it, Cox did just that.

She burst out into the corridor and half raced, half hobbled towards the lifts. She looked back every couple of steps but the attackers weren't there. They had bigger problems to deal with.

She reached the lifts. Slammed the buttons. They weren't working. Had the electricity been cut? She moved over to the mangled-looking stairwell door. Smoke from the fires below was creeping in through the gaps between door and frame, and as much as she tried, Cox couldn't prise the door open.

The attackers had barricaded themselves on the top floor. Cox had nowhere to go.

But she did have one more option.

She desperately limped away and in through the open door of the first bedroom on the corridor. She winced and averted her eyes as she stepped over the bloodied bodies of the dead man and woman in there. She moved to the window. Peered out. The stand-off was still in full swing.

Her idea was crude, and potentially ill thought out, but Cox didn't have many options right now. She gritted her teeth as she reached down and pushed her thumb into the open wound on her leg. She drew her shaky hand up and pressed her thumb on the glass and began to write.

The letters were a mess. The blood too thick in places and dripping all over, and too thin in others and barely legible.

Would the soldiers even understand English? Her brain was too frazzled to think of the Spanish words.

Eventually, mentally and physically drained, she stepped back to look at her handiwork.

Four terrorists. Room 514. NO HOSTAGES.

All it needed was for someone to look. Cox was tempted to bang on the window, but she couldn't afford to make the noise, even if she was now several rooms away. Instead she stepped right up to the glass and frantically waved her arms about. She'd already noticed there was more than one soldier with binoculars out there. Surely one of them would see her?

It only took a couple of minutes. Although the reaction was negligible – perhaps deliberately so? – she could see by the way the soldiers were moving and organising themselves that they'd taken notice of her.

Or was Cox just imagining it?

No. This was it.

The negotiator, if he could be called that, disappeared from sight altogether. The foot soldiers clustered together in different groups as though some were readying for an assault. The top hatch of the tank was closed tightly shut.

And then, without warning, came the boom.

The whole tank jolted and shifted back as fire and smoke blasted from the end of its huge gun. The impact of the massive shell caused the whole hotel to wobble and shake.

A blast of air and grit reached right down the corridor and past the room Cox was in.

She felt like smiling. Almost.

Seconds later there was another boom as a second shell was blasted from the tank. This time the dust from the explosion was even greater and it billowed into the room Cox was in and she pulled herself down and grabbed the edges of the bed sheet next to her to breathe through. After a few seconds she regained her sense of hearing to be greeted by a muted silence.

Then she heard shouting. Pained shouting. Coming from further along the corridor.

The attackers weren't all dead. Yet.

Cox battled through the pain in her leg and the fog in her mind. She got to her feet and dragged herself along to the door. Smoke and dust and grit filled the corridor still, but Cox was sure she could see movement ahead.

As the smoke settled, she made out Karim. Face covered in blood and grit, he was limping along towards her. Their eyes met . . .

Cox found an inner strength and she sprinted forward. Karim couldn't move quickly enough, he was too dazed. Cox barged into him and they thudded to the ground with her on top. She wrestled the rifle from his limp grip.

Then looked up to see Tamir stumble out of 514, just a few yards ahead. He was almost as out of it as Karim was. Almost, but not quite, because he was lifting his gun.

Cox jerked Karim's rifle up and pressed on the trigger and fought to control the recoil and adjust her aim as bullets flew out of the barrel. Her rushed shooting saw the first half dozen rounds miss the target and rake the wall next to Tamir, but after that . . .

Tamir went down in a gush of his own blood.

344

No chance for respite though. Cox didn't see the fist from Karim coming. He clattered her on the side of her head and with a roar of desperation and survival instinct he hauled her up and practically tossed her aside, sending her crashing into the corridor wall. The rifle clattered away as Cox lay dazed.

Snarling, Karim got to his knees.

Cox noticed a twitch on his face. Recognition?

'You?'

She wasn't sure what he meant by that.

His hand reached to his side to draw out his hunting knife. He paused, confused when he realised it wasn't there.

His eyes flicked down to Cox's hand as she launched herself for him. He moved his hands up to protect himself. Did a good job of holding her at bay, but he was too weakened and they fell back onto the carpet.

Cox shouted in anger as she plunged the knife down with a double-handed grip. The blade sank into Karim's neck and he gargled and spluttered blood as he choked. Cox remained there, straining and grimacing from effort as she pushed down as hard as she could.

Karim finally went still.

When she was absolutely sure he was dead, Cox rolled off him and stared up at the ceiling. As she tried her best to stave off unconsciousness, her ears caught the welcoming bangs and crashes further down the corridor as the soldiers furiously fought to break through the stairwell door.

CHAPTER 50

The needle to the thigh was enough to rouse Aydin from his comatose state, though whatever they'd injected him with – adrenaline, morphine, both? – wasn't enough to give him the strength even to properly lift his head.

'Good morning,' Namur said, though with his head bowed Aydin couldn't see him at all and the sound of his voice was echoey and distant.

The next second Aydin squirmed and flinched when a powerful blast of icy water smacked into his chest. The water from the jet hose continued for what felt like an age, and Aydin, eyes only half open, groggily watched as the clear liquid turned to red as it dripped from his skin and pooled on the floor.

When the water finally stopped, Aydin was left a gibbering, shivering mess. He spluttered to try to clear the water and blood from his mouth.

'That's better,' Namur said. 'Now you're all cleaned up Benny can see what he's working with.'

The mention of Benny caused Aydin to quiver. He wanted to beg. Wanted to plead with them not to carry on the torture they'd started . . . the day before? Aydin couldn't be sure when it was, though the natural light pouring into the warehouse through the translucent panels in the ceiling suggested it was now daytime.

'But before that,' Namur said, 'there's someone who'd like to meet you.'

Namur went quiet. Aydin drifted again.

'Talatashar,' came the croaky and unfamiliar voice. 'Talatashar, look at me when I'm talking to you.'

Talatashar. The number thirteen in Arabic. Aydin's name at the Farm. A word, a name he despised. The way it rolled off the tongue, the way the soft ending faded away. Everything about it, about what it represented, was grotesque.

And it enabled Aydin to somehow summon an inner strength. He lifted his head. First set his eyes on Namur.

'That's better,' he said.

Aydin's gaze flicked across to the man next to Namur. Nasir Al-Addad. His frail body was crumpled into a wheelchair. There was an oxygen mask around his neck, which he'd pulled down under his chin. A tube from the mask trailed behind him to the grey canister attached to the seat back. His pale skin was leathery. Everything about him looked withered and lifeless. Except for his eyes. His eyes burned bright with power and confidence and . . . hatred.

'I finally get to meet one of the chosen ones,' Al-Addad said. 'It's just a shame it's you, rather than one of your brothers.'

Aydin didn't have the strength to say anything in return to that, even if he'd wanted to.

'When I was given my last diagnosis, the doctor told me I had six months to live . . . that was over eighteen months ago,' Al-Addad said. 'I've been wondering what I've done for God to favour me, to give me this extra time. Now I think I know. It was so I could share this moment.'

Namur muttered a prayer, giving praise to Allah.

347

'I never met one of the graduates before,' Al-Addad said, 'but I see now what a mistake we made with *you*. We should have spotted the warning signs earlier.'

What warning signs? Was he talking about Aydin in Dearborn or at the Farm?

'I always told my brother this could be the downside. That if we created something so efficient, so powerful, that we could struggle to control it.'

No. He was talking about the Farm. And he was talking as though he knew everything about it. Which was only helping Aydin to garner further inner strength.

This was why he was here, in America. This man could well be the missing link he'd been searching for for years.

'My brother is a smart man,' Al-Addad said, 'and he was perfectly suited as the Teacher at that place. Wouldn't you agree?'

In a twisted way, Aydin did. The sociopathic Teacher did everything expected of him at the Farm and thereafter while his students were planning their attacks in Europe.

'But he wasn't a real tactician,' Al-Addad said. 'Sometimes he struggled to see the bigger picture. For that, he needed me.'

Aydin did now try to speak, much to Al-Addad's and Namur's surprise, but the two words he tried to say were garbled beyond comprehension even to him.

'Excuse me?' Al-Addad looked confused.

'Shadow . . . H-hand,' Aydin said.

Al-Addad looked almost amused now.

'Ah, yes, of course. You have done well in your search, haven't you? Of course I heard about your escapades last year. Your actions which resulted in the Farm being destroyed, with my brother being imprisoned. He is still imprisoned, isn't he? Or did MI6 simply execute him while they had the chance?'

The shake of Aydin's head didn't really answer the question, but Al-Addad moved on anyway.

'But Shadow Hand? That's what MI6 called their little pet project. Except it wasn't *their* project at all. It wasn't Edmund Grey's either. It wasn't my brother's, and it wasn't mine.'

Al-Addad let that one dangle as a crooked smile wormed across his face.

'Didn't you ever ask yourself how I came to be here in America?' Al-Addad said.

Aydin had asked the question plenty. The problem was he'd not found an answer.

'I'd say it's probably the same way you did. Whether you're Aydin Torkal or Jamaal Rashid, there's only one way you could get here so freely.'

Al-Addad paused. Aydin felt he knew the answer the old man was alluding to, but he wasn't going to give Al-Addad the satisfaction of finishing for him.

'Of course, back when I came here, Homeland Security wasn't even a thing, but you know what I'm getting at, don't you? I'm here because I'm protected. Homeland Security. CIA. Because whatever you might think about the Farm, whatever you might think about me, the simple fact remains that it wasn't my brother or anyone else you've trailed around the world to destroy who set that place up. It was the American government.'

The bombshell was left to hang. And it truly was a startling revelation to Aydin. Even Namur looked slightly taken aback, as though he hadn't known the whole truth until now. Al-Addad's smile grew wider and he let out a horrible laugh – more like a cackle.

'Yes, MI6 can do some nasty things, I'm sure you'll agree, but the CIA, the Pentagon, the White House? They really like to bring their A-game, to coin an American phrase. A level

349

of self-centredness unmatched across the world. The people in power here, generation after generation, they're happy to destroy anyone and anything to advance their own misguided and overinflated interests.'

Al-Addad paused again. Aydin could sense he was angry as he talked about the country who had given him a home, his hatred obvious.

'You probably saw as much with our shipments from South America?' Al-Addad said.

Aydin, a little confused, looked around the warehouse. He hadn't realised until now that the pallets were all gone. No trace at all.

'Weapons made for America, but sent by the government here to other countries not just to help win wars, but to help *start* wars. For what? For greed. It really is that simple. Always. Except this time, we're turning those weapons back on these disgusting excuses for human beings.'

Aydin closed his eyes as he tried to process it all. His muddled brain was flitting between the answers he craved about the Farm and what was unfolding about attacks which were surely soon to take place on American soil. The reality was it was the latter that was most pressing, even if it wasn't why Aydin had really come here.

'The same could be said of the Farm,' Al-Addad said. 'Not our idea, but that of an American. A man who happily retired to a luxurious ranch without a care in the world, despite the destruction and misery he'd caused during his life. In fact, he got medals to exemplify his heroism. You know the entire purpose of the Farm was only to stoke the flames. They knew Westerners would die. Europeans. Americans. They knew it but they didn't care. They *wanted* it because they needed the excuse. Collateral damage is worth it, always.'

'My . . . uncle,' Aydin said.

Al-Addad laughed again. 'Your uncle? He was nothing. Which is why no one cared one bit when his use was over and we made him disappear.'

There was a banging noise off to the side. Aydin grimaced as he twisted his head to see Benny walking into the warehouse. He headed over to Namur and whispered something into his ear. Aydin couldn't tell what they were saying but as he was straining to hear he noticed Al-Addad was staring at him intently, a satisfied look on his face.

Namur nodded and bent down to Al-Addad and said some hushed words to him as Benny moved out of sight somewhere behind Aydin.

'It's OK, Talatashar,' Al-Addad said. 'You don't mind if Namur heads out now, do you? He has more pressing matters to attend to. I, on other hand . . . ' Benny stepped back into view now, knife in hand, angry sneer on his face as always, ' . . . have been so looking forward to watching this.'

Aydin winced as Benny stepped towards him with the blade.

CHAPTER 51

Caribbean Sea

Cox understood how it looked. Most people would likely think it bizarre, almost insulting, that so soon after being a key party in the halting of a massacre which claimed fifty-four lives, she would be flying out of Venezuela, but she had no choice but to keep on the move, fearing that it was only a matter of time before the next wave of attacks.

Carlos Valencia had hastily arranged for a private charter jet to take Cox from a military airbase in Venezuela directly to a private airstrip several miles outside Detroit, the organisation of that final leg of the journey having been assisted by Tarkowski of Homeland Security. Cross-agency and cross-border teamwork really did exist at times.

Still, Cox felt horrendous at having to leave the scene of devastation at the Eden Hotel so soon, and immensely guilty for what had happened there. Bodies were still being dragged from the wreckage, panicked work colleagues and family members were searching for survivors, police and the army were trying to pull together the pieces of exactly what had happened and who was to blame, while Cox was swanning about in a private jet.

Yet her anger and disappointment at herself was nothing compared to the distress she was feeling, not just at having been caught up in the terrorist attack, not just at having been shot, and having killed two of the terrorists at close quarters, but at the fact that *she* could have prevented it all. If only she'd given Tarkowski the word to stop the men leaving the US . . .

Tearful emotion was welling somewhere deep inside Cox's mind, but she was doing her best to stop that well erupting, for now.

Whatever had happened in Venezuela, whatever was still happening there now, she needed to stay focused, however fragile she felt, both mentally and physically.

After a mere five minutes of sitting in silence and waiting, she bit the bullet and made another phone call. This had been the same for the first two hours of the flight, with an almost constant dialogue with one of either Valencia, Flannigan, Kaufman or Tarkowski.

This time it was Flannigan who Cox called.

'Anything?' she asked when he finally answered.

He sighed before he spoke. Exasperation at her non-stop badgering? Or simply a sign that nothing was moving as quickly as Cox was wanting it to.

'You tell me?' Flannigan said.

'They identified the man the terrorists met with.'

'Who did?'

'Valencia, my contact at SEBIN. The guy in the hotel is called Enrique Osorio. Former general of the Venezuelan army. I was literally just reading an online news report stating the attack was targeting Westerners . . . I don't buy it.'

'You're now telling me this wasn't the work of an Islamist terror cell? But—'

'No, it absolutely was, but think about it. The four attackers arrived in Venezuela with nothing but a cabin bag each. They didn't even leave the hotel at any point once they got there. Those weapons, all that gear, was there ready and waiting for them. Not to mention the driver of the car that exploded. Who the hell was he?'

'You're saying the army helped them set this up? The army who blasted the terrorists to pieces?'

'That's exactly what I'm saying. A splinter group from the Venezuelan army set this attack up. Perhaps Venezuela isn't our main concern, but I'm betting this was politics. Emilio Torres, a multi-billionaire exiled from his homeland, working in cahoots with an ex-general. I'd put money on some of their key rivals being among the dead.'

Another sigh from Flannigan. 'You were right. That's not our concern. Or not yours anyway.'

The rumbling thoughts in Cox's head made a little more sense. 'Coming back to my point, this all makes sense. Torres is a supplier of weapons—'

'He is?'

'Just hear me out. Say that's what the deal in California was. Weapons. Bombs, whatever. The means for our terrorist cell to wreak havoc on US soil. The reason Aydin saw no money change hands at that deal was because payment wasn't in cash. It was in actions. Whatever Torres sold in that deal, in return Namur agreed to supply his men for Torres's nefarious purposes on his home soil.'

Silence. Cox pulled the phone from her ear. The call was still rolling.

'Did you get that?' she said.

'You really think Namur would sacrifice his own men like that?'

That well rose up suddenly and Cox had to fight to keep it down. 'Who gives a shit whether they were sacrificed, whether they knew it was a suicide mission or whether I was just in the right place at the right time. They're all dead, and good bloody riddance. The problem we have now is figuring

354

out what's coming next. Before it's too late. We know some of the locations where Namur has contacts. We know those locations match up with the deliveries from Torres. We have to assume attacks are planned in each of those cities.'

'Agreed. And I'm working closely with the US on that now. But the worst case is that those locations were dummies. Remember what happened with Aydin and his brothers?'

Cox did. The cells had very deliberately set up in prime locations, largely European capitals, for the very purpose of drawing attention there, all the while planning attacks at much lesser protected locales.

'But you have nothing yet to report on any of those locations?'

'You'd already know if I did.'

Cox grumbled and ended the call, using anger and frustration to keep despair and distress and grief and worst of all guilt at bay. She took a couple of minutes to compose herself, then it was time for Tarkowski again.

'Cox, I've nothing new. I'm sorry.'

He sounded harried. Was that just because of her?

'You haven't located any of them?'

'No.'

'What measures are in place to stop them?'

'Measures? We're looking for them. We have APBs out across the whole of the country now, we've got heightened police presence and Feds checking out key public and government buildings in all of the locations we suspect might be involved, but that's as much as we can do for now.'

'As much as you can do?'

'As much as we can do based on the limited intel we still have. No one will sign off on the military on the streets, on martial law, on mass evacuations or whatever it is you're going to suggest I do next. It would cause chaos, and where

355

would we even start? We still don't know if these locations are targets or not.'

It was a fair point, not that the reality made the situation any more palatable to Cox. Tarkowski and Flannigan had no idea what she'd been through just hours before. She couldn't let another attack like that happen. She just couldn't. Something had to give.

The fact Namur and the others were off grid now spoke volumes. They were ready, and without a concerted effort from the police and the Feds and every other agency out there, there was a big chance the terrorists wouldn't be found in time. In fact, there was only one person who possibly could do that now.

Aydin.

But where the fuck was he?

CHAPTER 52

Dearborn, Detroit

Aydin's brain was so battered, so weary and drained, that he wasn't even sure if he was conscious or not. Was he actually still alive, or was the pain and suffering he was enduring because he was already in hell?

'Ok, I've seen enough of this,' Al-Addad said.

His voice was like a beacon, causing Aydin's brain to stir and dragging it back to reality. Kind of.

'I want to see him in pieces. Maybe then he'll talk. Give him another shot.'

Aydin didn't feel the needle this time, but he did feel the surge of cool liquid in his depleted veins. His heart picked up from its sluggish rhythm, his brain was suddenly more alert, if only a little.

'Start with the toes. Then the feet.'

Aydin only realised his eyes were open when Benny came into view, crouched down in front of him. He grabbed hold of Aydin's foot and tried to leverage it so he could grasp the toes, but with Aydin slumped forward and his ankles shackled, toes set back with the tops of his feet dragging on the floor, he couldn't get to them. So he went for the keychain on his side. Unclasped the cuffs around Aydin's ankles, and yanked one of his feet forward.

'Cuts,' Aydin said.

Benny paused and looked up. Aydin's delirious brain was sure the man's eyes were on fire, like he was staring into the eyes of the devil himself.

'Wait,' Al-Addad said. 'Give him the chance.'

'Cuts,' Aydin said again. At least that was what he was trying to say.

'Cuts?' Benny said, snarling. He looked back down to Aydin's feet to carry on his work. 'He's not talking. He's ranting.'

'Namur said . . . death . . . by cuts,' Aydin said.

Benny looked up again.

'Pliers. They . . . don't cut.'

'They don't? Cut. Chop. Sever. It doesn't matter. You'll soon be begging for me to stop.'

'You . . . failed.'

Benny straightened up now. His snarling face moved close to Aydin's.

'*I* failed? Let me remind you of that in a few minutes, *Talatashar*.'

That word again. That name. It brought so much emotion to the fore, so much anger and hatred.

Aydin's reaction was almost involuntary. He hadn't thought about it, and the sensation as his lips widened into a toothy smile felt surreal and alien and out of his control.

Benny's eyes pinched a little, as though he didn't know how to react to Aydin's unexpected taunt.

Aydin would never find out. Before Benny did anything, Aydin hauled his knees up and wrapped his legs around Benny's waist. He interlocked his feet and squeezed as tightly as he could. He plunged his head down and sank his teeth into Benny's jaw.

He'd aimed for the neck, but this would do. Aydin chewed down. Gnashed his teeth from side to side. Benny screamed and writhed but his arms were pinned tight to his sides and he couldn't get free.

Benny pulled back his torso, yanked back his head at just the moment Aydin whipped his head back too. A chunk of flesh ripped from Benny's face, leaving a gaping hole exposing his gums and teeth. Aydin spat the flesh out. Blood poured from his mouth.

Without thinking he went in again. Benny was shouting and fighting but Aydin had an animal strength, from where, even he didn't know. This time he did find Benny's neck. He sank his teeth in again and ground down and tore away another even larger chunk of flesh and skin and sinew.

Benny's eyes were rolling. Aydin relaxed his legs and his foe dropped to his knees as he clutched at his gaping wounds.

Aydin caught sight of Al-Addad across the room. Panic and disbelief covered his face as he fumbled for his phone. Aydin growled in anger and swung on the chains he was hanging from. It only took a few back-and-forths to get some momentum going, and then he used all of the muscles in his core to haul his legs upward and over his head. He latched them onto the metal beam above him. Covered in blood and running beyond empty, he wouldn't be able to hold the almost impossible position for long.

He jerked on his wrists and lifted them towards the hook further above him and the chain his wrists were tied to popped out of its hold.

Just in time, as Aydin's ankles slipped from their perch, and Aydin had just enough alertness to shift his body round and avoid a nasty fall on his back or his head.

He landed feet first and rolled into it – not entirely deliberately – clattering down in a heap, in a pool of his own blood, right next to the still-writhing Benny.

Aydin pulled himself upright. Looked down at the stricken man by his feet. Benny's panicked eyes caught Aydin's a split second before Aydin drove his heel down onto Benny's face. The contact was brutal. Benny's already vulnerable jaw shattered and teeth and bone spilled onto the floor. His body twitched. He was still breathing – more like gurgling on his own blood – but he certainly wasn't going anywhere in a hurry.

'Fuck!' Al-Addad shouted as he bashed his phone with his fingers.

No signal? He looked up at Aydin and stopped what he was doing. No one was coming to help him.

Aydin's chest was heaving. Sweat droplets mingled with the blood that covered his body, causing his skin to glisten and the look of panic and horror on Al-Addad's face said it all.

'Were you counting?' Aydin said through a mouthful of blood. How much was his and how much was Benny's he really didn't know. He spat out some, could do nothing but gulp back the rest.

'W-what?'

'Were you counting?' Aydin said through gritted teeth.

Al-Addad shook his head. He looked like he didn't have a clue what Aydin was talking about, but Aydin guessed it was more likely denial.

'Because I was,' Aydin said.

He crouched down to Benny's side and took hold of *his* knife.

'One hundred and twenty-six.'

Al-Addad was quivering now.

'One hundred and twenty-six cuts,' Aydin said, 'and I gave you nothing.'

Aydin was fighting to keep control of the animal inside him. His body was shaking with anticipation and rage. He twisted the knife in his hands. Pressed the tip with his finger. Oh yes, it was plenty sharp enough. The patchwork of open wounds on Aydin's body was testament to that.

He barely even heard Al-Addad's screams as he moved forward with the knife.

'Now let's see if you can do any better,' Aydin said.

CHAPTER 53

The pilot's voice came over on the tannoy to say they'd be landing in twenty minutes. Cox didn't know why he hadn't just stuck his head round the door. He was only sitting all of fifteen feet away.

She stared out of her window at the white scene below, the high-rises of central Detroit visible in the distance.

Her phone rang.

She looked at the screen. Not a withheld number, but one she didn't recognise. She begged for her gut instinct to be right as to who it was.

'Hello?'

Nothing on the other end. Cox looked at the screen. It was definitely connected.

'Hello?'

She heard breathing now. It was erratic. Laboured but intense.

'Hello? Aydin?'

Still nothing. A prank call? Surely not. Was it just a bad line? Cox was about to hang up and redial the number, but then . . .

'Rachel.'

It was Aydin. Cox's heart skipped several beats.

'Aydin. What's happening?'

'Rachel . . . Please . . . You need to listen . . . very carefully. We . . . don't have much time.'

CHAPTER 54

Aydin, out of breath from effort and in desperate need of respite, looked down at the two mounds of butchered flesh and bones in front of him. He wasn't proud of what he'd done. He hadn't enjoyed a single moment of it, nor did he now feel in any way satisfied or fulfilled.

Yet every action he'd taken, every cut and every slice, had been absolutely necessary and deserved.

He dropped the dripping knife and moved over to the corner of the room. Picked up the hose. He needed to be quick now. The cold water against his hacked-up skin was excruciating. He could only bear it for a few seconds until he had to stop. That was enough to get the worst off, and at least to get *their* blood off.

He didn't bother to tend to any of his wounds. There simply wasn't the time now. If he survived this ordeal, he'd just have to live with the scars.

He slipped into a combination of clothes and coats from Benny and Al-Addad. The garments smelled disgusting and were of little solace to Aydin's weary state. At least the scent would keep him fired up.

Aydin was soon driving away in Benny's Ford Explorer. Perhaps an apt vehicle given Aydin's next destination.

He again used Al-Addad's phone as he drove, but he couldn't reach Cox now. Where was she? He wondered about what the response would be to what he'd told her. On the phone it seemed like she'd believed every word he'd said, and she'd promised to take action, but would she? And even if she did, would the Americans believe her and be able to provide a useful response in time across the multiple cities about to be the targets of the planned deadly attacks?

Aydin was racing down Route 12 when the answers to those questions became more clear. Up ahead the looming green glass-fronted building housing Ford's world headquarters came into view. Known colloquially as the Glass House, the giant blue insignia of the company was visible on the concrete parapet at the top of the building for miles around, and Aydin could see on the glass of the building below the sign the reflections of dozens of flashing lights.

As he neared he saw the building was already surrounded and he realised he wasn't going to get much closer in his vehicle. He parked up on a verge and headed onward on foot, a blanket from the car wrapped around him to act as a hood and cloak against the cold, and to hide his still bleeding face.

It was clear the police hadn't been at the scene long, and the evacuation process was hectic and in full swing. There were tens of police cars, ambulances, fire engines. A police cordon was set well back from the building with a mass of jittery-looking office workers still rushing from the building and heading that way. Many of the early leavers, gathered by the cordon with nowhere else to go, were shivering fiercely in their shirts and suits, presumably having hastily left the building without their overcoats.

Aydin moved closer, being sure to keep his head down as much as he could and to sidestep away from anyone in uniform. He spotted two large black trucks belonging to the Michigan State Police with *Bomb Squad* emblazoned in big yellow letters. A couple of people in thick green bomb suits were racing away from it towards the building. Were more of their colleagues already inside? If not, they were likely running into a deathtrap. By the time on Al-Addad's phone there was only two minutes left now.

Further along the cordon Aydin noticed a couple of Middle Eastern men being hassled by two street cops. The men were angrily protesting their innocence, even had their office IDs around their necks, but the cops were still treating them with suspicion and disdain.

Then, as Aydin continued to scan the area, he saw them. They were standing away from the crowds. Two men. One Aydin didn't recognise, but the other, dressed in a Michigan State Police uniform, was Namur. Definitely Namur. Even with the cap over his head and the uniform, Aydin knew it was him.

He moved in that direction. Momentarily lost focus of his objective to be calm and cautious.

'Hey you,' a man said.

Aydin heard, but initially ignored him.

'Hey, stop there.'

Aydin glanced across now. Saw a police officer, hand on hip, with his eyes on him. The officer, determination and panic in equal measure on his face, took a step forward. The crowd between him and Aydin parted slightly, everyone on edge. Aydin turned back to where Namur and the other man were standing. They had no idea Aydin was there, but they were still thirty yards away and Aydin had a more immediate problem now.

He looked at the policeman who was edging forward still, muttering something into the radio clipped high on his chest.

Then there was a murmur in the crowd beyond. The policeman naturally turned to see. A wave of panic quickly spread outward from the building to the cordon.

People were running and screaming from the building now, among them several people in uniforms and bomb suits waving their arms frantically in the air. The crowd around Aydin began to swarm and to retreat, outright panic setting in within an instant.

Aydin's eye caught the policeman's again as people rushed all around. The guy just didn't know what to do.

In the end he did nothing.

Without any further warning there was an almighty boom, and the blast wave from the huge explosion knocked both Aydin and the policeman and everyone else around them to the ground.

CHAPTER 55

'We've done it,' Tarkowski said.

Cox squeezed the phone in her hand and closed her eyes, welcoming the relief as the car sped along I94. Up front Agent Collins of the FBI expertly weaved the Escalade in and out of traffic as they raced towards Dearborn.

'Five men in custody,' Tarkowski said. 'Eight men shot dead. Attacks in Chicago, Cleveland, Pittsburgh and Minneapolis stopped without any civilian casualties.'

'Don't be so sure just yet,' Cox said, a little annoyed that she couldn't just enjoy the moment. 'I've worked against groups like this before. You need to be alert for secondary attacks. Devices already planted.'

'I know that, and we're all working on it. I've had word that Ford HQ is being cleared as we speak. But . . . it's the only place where we haven't got hold of the culprits.'

'I'll be there in moments,' Cox said as she stared out of the window at Ford HQ in the near distance.

'I'm standing outside now,' Tarkowski said. 'I'll see you here.'

Tarkowski ended the call. Cox looked at her watch. Time was up . . .

There was a distant rumble then a raucous noise and before Cox had looked up a blast of air smacked into the Escalade and

Collins battled to keep the speeding SUV on four wheels. Cox was thrown left and right in the seat and her head smacked painfully off the window.

'Shit,' Collins said when he'd finally straightened the beast.

Shit indeed. Cox righted herself and stared at the huge ball of fire and smoke bursting into the sky where before there'd been Ford World Headquarters.

They were too late. Cox closed her eyes again. No relief this time. She was trying to hold back tears.

No. She wasn't going to cry now. Whatever emotion she had inside from the events of a hellishly traumatic few hours, she had to keep it in for now. This wasn't over yet.

They soon arrived at the scene of devastation. Grit and dust still filled the air so soon after the blast, and as Cox stepped from the car it was clear there was no semblance of order or response to the explosion yet. Police and paramedics and civilians — both injured and otherwise — jostled and rushed here, there and everywhere. It was chaos.

Mostly chaos, anyway.

Because about forty yards away Cox saw one man walking with purpose. Heading away from the confused and injured crowds, pushing past people, his focus and determination cut a stark contrast to those around him. With a large and thick blanket wrapped over his head and shoulders, he looked like a hobo from the back. But Cox knew he wasn't.

'Aydin!' she shouted.

CHAPTER 56

Despite his already battled state, while most people were wearily shaking their heads on the floor, Aydin was up and on his feet while the grit and fragments of brick and glass and metal and plastic were still falling to the ground.

He supposed he had his barbaric training at the Farm to thank for his ability to push his body beyond most people's comprehension, not to mention the inner rage and determination for vengeance that continued to spur him on.

He searched through the dust and smoke, managed to find his bearings, but as the clouds finally cleared, he realised the spot where Namur had been standing was now empty.

With a surge of panic, Aydin's eyes searched. No, Namur hadn't got away, not yet. But he was almost at his getaway car – a marked cruiser belonging to the Michigan State Police. Supposedly.

Aydin moved forward with more purpose again. Up ahead Namur opened the passenger door. The other guy – was he a genuine police officer? – sat into the driver's seat.

'Aydin!'

Her unexpected voice almost caused him to stumble.

He carried on.

'Aydin!'

370

She wasn't far away. He turned briefly. He had to. What if she was standing there with a line of FBI agents, all of them with their guns trained on his back?

But she wasn't. She was all alone. Unarmed and pushing her way through the crowds to follow him.

He couldn't stop now.

Back in front of him the police car was moving. He wouldn't let them get away. Aydin moved into a jog. Then a run.

People around him were taking notice once more. Because of how he looked, how he was moving? Or because of Cox's continued calls after him?

Whatever it was, it caused a police officer further ahead, standing next to his squad car, to look over.

He locked eyes with Aydin. Then looked beyond to Cox. Then back to Aydin.

Aydin had no choice. He pitched right and sprinted straight for the cop. He dove for the guy as his hand went down to his side to whip the gun from its holster. They crashed to the ground and Aydin leaned back and threw his head down onto the officer's nose. Blood spurted. Aydin grabbed the gun and jumped back up.

'Aydin, no!' Cox shouted.

He didn't heed her warnings. Didn't even look at her, though he could sense by now that everyone around had seen the melee. Police would be swarming on him in seconds. But they were the least of his worries. He couldn't let Namur get away. Not after what they'd done. Tried to do, at least. Namur deserved no better a death than Benny and Al-Addad, and he certainly didn't deserve to be allowed to live in a cushy jail.

Aydin glanced inside the open door of the police car. The keys were in the ignition. He jumped in, turned the key, released the parking brake, thumped the accelerator and the car shot forward.

Civilians screamed and darted out of the way. More than one person was brushed aside, lucky to get away with nothing more than a scrape, and only inches from something much nastier. Confused police officers drew their weapons but didn't know whether to shoot or not.

Two of them did. The bullets thunked into the squad car's metalwork. One hit the back passenger window and it shattered into hundreds of pieces.

But seconds later Aydin was away from them all and heading for the slip road for Route 12.

And he had Namur's car in his sights.

Aydin glanced down to the buttons on the dashboard. Pressed one after the other, flipped switches and eventually the siren blared and he saw the reflection of the flashing red and blue on the car's bonnet.

Would Namur assume it was a genuine officer giving chase, or did he know?

Either way, it was soon clear that the driver of Namur's car had figured Aydin was after them, as having entered Route 12 at a relaxed speed, the needle was now edging past ninety as Aydin battled to close the distance.

And he wasn't the only one. A hundred yards in the distance behind him, he had his own pursuers. At least three police cars. Two motorbikes. Was Cox there somewhere?

Aydin tried not to take notice. Perhaps this time he was in a fight that he wouldn't walk away from. That time comes for everyone. One thing was damn sure; Namur wouldn't walk away either.

The state police car headed right, and hurtled up the exit slipway. Aydin followed. Up ahead the brake lights of Namur's car flicked on as it slowed for the junction. Aydin kept on going, in two minds as to whether to brake at all. If he didn't would he be on them in time and able to smash into them?

No. They were already turning.

Aydin slammed on his brakes. The car skidded left and right and Aydin was inches away from crashing through the barrier and plummeting back down onto the road below. Somehow he kept all four tyres on the icy tarmac and tugged sharply on the steering wheel and skidded round the corner to the right. Cars on the road honked and swerved to avoid him, but Aydin came out unscathed.

In fact, his lunatic manoeuvre had gained him several yards on Namur, and his continued reckless driving meant he was able to further gain as they raced south and east.

Towards the river.

Was that deliberate? Did Namur have an escape route planned already? A boat to take him across the water to Canada?

Aydin wouldn't let that happen.

Sure enough, the water was soon in sight. Namur's car crashed over a kerb and into a narrow alley. Aydin followed, flinching as he lost a wing mirror in the process. At the end of the alley Namur's car banked left and they were both soon hurtling along a connector road, the water on their right, a huge steel mill up ahead in the distance.

Is that where they were heading?

No. At the last second, before the car smashed through the chain-link fence at what looked like a little-used side entrance for the mill, it suddenly swung a hard left. This time Aydin didn't follow. He was so close he didn't need to.

He pushed his foot further down. The car lurched forward and smashed into the side of Namur's vehicle.

Aydin had braced himself for the impact, but it was still brutal. His head, his whole body, shot forward. The airbag deployed and smacked into his face, sending him crashing back again.

His car carried on for two or three seconds before there was a final sudden impact and everything went still.

Aydin was seriously dazed. On the brink of unconsciousness once again. But he wouldn't let this moment pass.

He growled with determination as he forced open his door and half clambered, half fell out of the car.

The front end of his vehicle was crumpled beyond recognition, looking like it had already been through a crusher, and was wedged a couple of feet into the side of Namur's car.

The driver, whoever the hell he was, had no chance. His bloodied head dangled out of what used to be a window, what remained of his torso contorted horrifically.

He was dead.

Namur, though . . .

He was busy trying to pull himself out. He was bleeding too, from a gash on his head. He heaved open his door and collapsed to the ground the other side. Aydin edged round, gun held out. He was aware of the cascade of sirens quickly closing in behind him. That wouldn't stop him now.

Namur was soon on his feet, clutching at his side. He glanced over. Aydin expected something. For him to try to attack. If not physically then at least verbally. But the parasite of a man simply turned and hobbled away like the pathetic coward that he was.

Aydin followed.

'One hundred exactly,' Aydin said. Namur didn't react at all. 'One hundred. That's how many cuts it took on those two. Though, I have to admit, I didn't have much patience with Benny.'

Namur shook his head but said nothing. He carried on limping and dragging himself away, heading for the water just a few yards in front

'Stop, police!' came a shout from off to Aydin's right. He turned to see the line of cops, about fifteen yards away, hunkered behind their open car doors, guns drawn.

'Stop, or we'll shoot.'

Namur glanced over in that direction but he wasn't stopping. And neither was Aydin.

'No!'

Cox this time.

'Don't shoot him!'

Aydin glanced and saw Cox racing beyond the police line towards him.

Was she there to stop Aydin? Or to stop the police from shooting him?

Did he even care now?

All he knew was he couldn't let Namur walk away from this.

He looked back at his nemesis.

'It's only a shame I didn't get to show you, what I showed them,' he said.

Aydin lifted the gun and fired.

CHAPTER 57

A single shot. The bullet smacked into the back of Namur's head and a pulse of blood sprayed out from his skull as his body jolted forward and thudded down onto the ground.

Cox knew what was coming next.

'No, don't shoot!' she shouted as she spun round to look back to the police line a few yards behind her.

No use. One shot. Two. The first hit tarmac, the second hit Aydin in his arm. He turned and Cox ducked as he pulled his gun round and fired several times before he darted away, towards the water.

'Get out of the goddamn way!' came a shout from behind Cox.

Screw that. Cox chased after Aydin. Her being in between him and the police might be the only thing to save him.

Aydin was soon only yards away from the barrier, the icy water beyond.

'Miss, get down!' came another shout.

She could hear the boots of the policemen right behind her, but still didn't heed their warnings. Ultimately it made no difference to the officers.

Another four shots echoed, each made Cox flinch. Three near misses, one leg shot that caused Aydin to stumble and crash down and the gun he'd been holding flew from his grasp.

Cox stopped and spun round, 'Another shot and I swear your lives are over,' she spat at the group of onrushing policemen. Much to their surprise and annoyance, she'd at least given them pause for thought and reluctantly they all came to a stop.

Aydin pulled himself back up. Kept on hobbling to the barrier.

'Aydin, you don't need to run,' Cox said, trying to sound as calm and as amenable and sincere as she could. 'You're not the bad guy here. We can clear things up.'

Aydin kept moving.

'We did it,' Cox said. '*You* did it. Again. Come back with me.'

He stopped now and turned round.

She held back a gasp when she saw the state he was in. Every bit of skin she could see was covered in cuts and scrapes, slices and gashes, and the clothes he was wearing had large wet patches where blood had soaked through the layers.

'Aydin, you're a hero.'

Her words caused him to pause. He locked eyes with her. What was he thinking?

'Hands in the air! Get down on the ground!'

The angry shout of the policeman cut right through whatever thought had been in his mind. Aydin's face screwed into anger.

Yet he did slowly lift his hands above his head.

'Sorry, Rachel. Not this time.'

'No!'

Did he fall? Or was it a jump? Either way, the next second his body tumbled backward over the railings and he plummeted head first out of sight. There was a splash as Cox raced forward.

But by the time she reached the barrier and looked down, the only evidence of Aydin at all was the rippling of the water, and the thin trail of blood heading down into the darkness below.

CHAPTER 58

London, England

Back in frozen Michigan Cox had strangely longed to be in England on a bland, grey winter's day. Yet since she'd returned home, she just found it miserable and depressing.

Perhaps that was more down to her recent mental state though.

She huddled into her coat as she sat on the bench looking out over the murky water of the Thames, the London Eye spinning slowly on the other side of the water. People roamed about all over, oblivious to the dangers that lurked in hidden corners.

Sometimes Cox wished she could be just like them.

She sensed Flannigan approaching, but didn't look up to him or greet him at all as he took a seat next to her.

'We could have met in a bar or a coffee shop you know?' he said.

Cox would rather be outside, as grey as it was.

'I'd like to say you're looking better but . . . I know you're struggling.'

Cox said nothing to that.

'It's only been a couple of weeks, but it will get better,' he said, as though he were an expert. 'I'm not going to put any pressure on you, but your job is waiting for you. Miles wants you back, *I* want you back. You just need to say when.'

'I will.'

'Did you speak to the—'

'I don't need a shrink.'

'Says who? You don't have to pretend to be tough for my benefit. The things you've seen . . . it takes strength to admit you need help.'

'The things I've seen?'

Cox wasn't sure why she'd repeated his words, but her mind took her back. First to Venezuela where she'd so nearly become just another statistic, and where she still felt responsible for every last death in that damn hotel despite everyone else's conclusion that actually she was a hero. Then to Dearborn. To that warehouse where she'd found the remains of Nasir Al-Addad and Benyamin Dawood. Yes, she'd seen some horrors, she'd been stuck right in the middle of many horrors, but the gore in that warehouse, the smell and the sights . . . she couldn't wipe that from her mind, however hard she tried.

Yet it wasn't just the ghastly sight of those mutilated bodies that troubled her . . . it was the fact it was Aydin who'd done that. A man she'd known for years. A man who'd helped her, in his own way, multiple times. A man she'd tried to convince others, again and again, was good.

But what was the reality of a man who was capable of *that*?

Yet at least Aydin's barbarism had saved lives. Did that make it ok?

Back in Dearborn Aydin had talked to her about him wanting to have a real life, but being unsure if he'd ever manage it. In the past, Cox had always felt he wasn't damaged beyond repair, that he was young enough, and moral enough, to turn things round. But maybe he'd always been an animal. Maybe it was good for everyone that he was dead.

'Why did you come here today?' Cox asked.

'To see you.'

'Tell me what's happening.'

Flannigan sighed, as if that wasn't the purpose of them meeting, but he must have known she'd ask.

'We're still battling with the US on what comes out publicly about the Farm,' Flannigan said. 'But believe me, because of what Aydin found, there'll be heads rolling over there.'

Cox winced at those words.

'I'm sorry,' Flannigan said, clearly picking up on his careless speak. 'You know what I mean. One thing we can perhaps be grateful for is that the man responsible for the entire mess is already dead.'

Cox's intrigue perked up now.

'He is?'

'Albert Ponty. Former CIA. He died of natural causes aged eighty-one, three years ago.'

'You think that's good? He was the man who helped to set up the Farm, apparently purely to stir waters in the Middle East. He's responsible for the deaths of hundreds of people killed because of that place, not to mention the countless other lives that have been ruined. You think it's good that he died a hero in his country's eyes, and now never has to answer for what he did?'

'That's not what I said.' He sounded irritated at Cox's off tone, but she couldn't care less. 'But you have to see that it's good that there's a quick closure to this. No more running around the world trying to find the truth of that place. We're done. We can finally move on.'

Except Cox really wasn't sure she could.

'Emilio Torres was killed trying to escape the FBI,' Flannigan said. 'His comrade-in-arms in Venezuela was taken out by the army he used to serve. This time we got them all, Cox.'

'Venezuela?' Cox said. 'Which you told me wasn't our problem? Where three days ago there was a violent military

coup? Most likely prompted in part by the attack at the hotel.'
Cox had to fight once more to keep her emotion in check at
the mention of the attack. Would this feeling ever go away?
'I'm not so sure things are over this time. Not here, not in the
US, not in Venezuela. That's the problem. It doesn't matter
what we do, these things are never truly over. However many
bad guys we kill or capture, there are always more. People
are people. It's inherent in our nature.'

'Which is exactly the reason why there'll always be a position open for you at SIS.'

Cox sighed. She didn't have anything to say to that.
Flannigan looked at his watch as they sat through a few
moments of silence. Clearly he still had something left to say.

'I've not told anyone else this,' Flannigan said. 'But I thought
you'd want to know. And seriously, Rachel, I'm a good listener
if you want to talk. But please go and see that doctor. You've
got so much more to give still.'

He took a piece of paper from his coat pocket, unfolded
it and placed it down onto Cox's lap. Then he got up and
walked away.

She looked down at the article. It was printed from an internet
news site. A pretty poor excuse for an internet news site,
anyway. The type of website that loved a wacky conspiracy
theory, and ran headline stories along the lines of *My husband
was butt-probed by aliens and now he might be pregnant*.

The title of this article was almost as outlandish.

Freddy Kruger stole my bike.

It was the story of a fifteen-year-old boy in a small town in
Ontario, who in the middle of the night had heard a commotion in his back yard. He'd peered out of his bedroom window
to see a cloaked man stealing his bike. A man with a Freddy
Kruger mask on, according to the reporter, although the boy's
actual words were 'his face was all cut up like Freddy Kruger.'

Cox, heart thumping, grabbed her phone. Typed in the name of the town. It was a tiny place on the outskirts of LaSalle, in Essex County, Ontario.

A couple of miles from the Detroit River.

Cox looked again at the article. The date.

She closed her eyes. Partly in relief, mostly in despair.

These things are never truly over.

She crumpled up the piece of paper and pushed it into the bin next to the bench, then looked back at her phone.

She scrolled through her text messages from Flannigan. Found the number and details for the psychiatrist he'd recommended.

She sighed, pushed the burgeoning thoughts in her mind aside, then hit dial.

Credits

Rob Sinclair and Orion Fiction would like to thank everyone at Orion who worked on the publication of Imposter 13 *in the UK.*

Editorial
Emad Akhtar
Tom Witcomb
Lucy Frederick

Copy editor
Francine Brody

Proof reader
Linda Joyce

Audio
Paul Stark
Amber Bates

Contracts
Anne Goddard
Paul Bulos
Jake Alderson

Design
Debbie Holmes
Joanna Ridley
Nick May

Editorial Management
Charlie Panayiotou
Jane Hughes
Alice Davis

Marketing
Tanjiah Islam

Publicity
Alex Layt
Finance
Jasdip Nandra
Afeera Ahmed

**FIND OUT HOW IT ALL BEGAN IN THE FIRST
BOOK IN THE SLEEPER 13 TRILOGY**

Smuggled to the Middle East as a child.
Trained as one of the most elite insurgents of his
generation.
Forced to do things no one should, for a cause he couldn't
believe in.
But as his brothers were preparing to kill, he was looking
for a way out.
Now, on the eve of the deadliest coordinated attacks the
world has ever seen, he'll finally get his chance.
He will break free and hunt down those who made him a
monster.
He must draw on all his training to survive.
He is **SLEEPER 13**.

THEN FOLLOW AYDIN'S STORY IN:

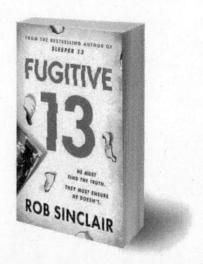

Aydin Torkal — aka Sleeper 13 — is on the run, hunted by both the world's intelligence agencies and the elite brotherhood of insurgents he betrayed. Until now.

MI6 agent Rachel Cox knows Aydin better than anyone — the only person who believes he's an ally, not the enemy.

So when a coded message arrives warning not to trust her own colleagues, Rachel must choose between her career and the truth.

As Aydin seeks those who destroyed his life, the trail leads closer to home than he ever expected.

But he will not stop until the job is done.

He will be relentless in his pursuit of revenge.

He is FUGITIVE 13.